Frank Coates was born in Melbourne and, after graduating as a professional engineer, worked for many years as a telecommunications specialist in Australia and overseas. As a UN technical specialist in Nairobi, Kenya, he travelled extensively throughout the eastern and southern parts of Africa. During his time there Frank developed a passion for the history and culture of East Africa, which inspired his first novel, *Tears of the Maasai*, published in 2004, after which he became a full-time writer. *Echoes from a Distant Land* is his seventh novel.

Visit Frank's website at
www.footloose.com.au

Also by Frank Coates

Tears of the Maasai

Beyond Mombasa

In Search of Africa

Roar of the Lion

The Last Maasai Warrior

Softly Calls the Serengeti

His father looked from Sister Rosalba to Sam and back again.

'Mr Wangira,' she said. 'For the love of-a God, if you won't do it for Sam, do it for your people.'

*   *   *

The silence around the fire that night, where Sam, his father and grandfather sat after the meal, was electric with undeclared sentiments. Sam could see his father had been greatly embarrassed by Sister Rosalba's outburst. It was bad enough that Sam's actions had attracted the attention of a white person, but because it was from a woman, and one with such strange notions about customs and beliefs, matters were quite a lot worse. Sam could feel the heat of his father's resentment as keenly as the heat from the flames.

His grandfather had come to discuss Sam's future, not knowing about Sister Rosalba's outburst until advised by one of his daughters-in-law. His presence added further gravitas to the occasion. Sitting on his short stool across the fire from Sam, he pinched closed a nostril with his finger and thumb and took a sharp intake of breath. The instant rush from the snuff caused an involuntary cough.

Sam felt reassured by his grandfather's presence, but he also had no doubt the old man didn't approve of the changes the whites had brought to their village: especially the changes to the way some Kikuyu were being educated. He thought his *guuka* couldn't understand the white people's version of education and, even if he could, he would think it a waste of time. Which, of course, it would be — for anyone who planned to be a farmer, living the same life his forefathers had.

His grandfather was the first to speak on the matter, as was appropriate. With eyes still watering from the snuff, he asked Sam's father, 'What do you make of this *mzungu* woman?'

'*Kali sana*,' his father answered.

Except for a few particularly expressive words, Swahili was seldom spoken by Sam's family. *Kali sana* — very fiery — was one Swahili phrase his father found useful.

The old man sighed. 'I have heard that she is telling the *askaris* that the Kikuyu must stop circumcising the girls,' he said, and took another snort of snuff. 'And there is talk of them increasing the hut tax so that we will have to send more of our young men to work in white farms to bring home the rupees. *Ai-ai-ai*. So many changes.'

'Too many,' his father agreed.

'In my day it was the younger men who fought for our Kikuyu ways. Men who had the fire in the belly to make them fight.'

It was unclear to Sam if the admonishment was intended for his generation or his father's. He glanced at his father, but read nothing in his expression to suggest he took it personally.

The old man nodded and sniffed. 'But she admires the boy.'

Sam understood that in his grandfather's eyes, he would always remain a boy. No matter he had been a warrior and a man for seven seasons of the long rains; no matter that he had survived a lion attack. He bore him no ill will because of it. He was his *guuka*, and all could be forgiven.

Sam's father gave a noncommittal grunt.

'And she says she has taught him the *wazungu* ways for ten years,' the old man added, shaking his head in disbelief.

This time his father merely nodded thoughtfully.

A long silence gave Sam time to ponder what his grandfather was leading up to, for there was no doubt that his meanderings were not merely the idle thoughts of the aged.

'Yes, in the old days the warriors would defend our Kikuyu traditions. But now, ah? Now it is impossible to fight the British. They are even more powerful than the Maasai were. And by them we were often defeated.' He sniffed loudly. 'So what are we to do? We can sit idly by and watch the *mzungu* stop the circumciser's blade. We could let him increase our taxes until we all must wear trousers to carry the money in our pockets.' He paused. 'Or we might send some of our best young men to learn their ways. We did that with the Maasai and, by so doing, we learned how to defeat them.'

The abrupt turn of the argument took Sam by surprise; he looked at his father, expecting to see shock and disagreement, but there was neither. His father must have known where the discussion was leading, and would not argue against the advice of one so old and wise.

Suddenly, it was agreed. Sam would attend preparatory school in Nairobi. After that, he would go to university in New York.

CHAPTER 9

1917

Kinangop Academy — the impressive stone building with its high clock tower on Protectorate Road hill — was originally an orphanage for white children, but since the turn of the century had been developed into a secondary school for white children from poor families and gifted Indians and native Africans.

Sam found that life at the academy was nothing like he'd imagined it. He expected the pursuit of academic excellence would be paramount, which was the situation he sorely needed if he were to meet the minimum academic requirements for entry into New York University. In fact it was excellence in sport that appeared to be Kinangop's most important objective.

The academy had long suffered the stigma associated with its charitable past. It was a situation every member of the teaching staff appeared determined to eradicate by setting high academic standards, but more importantly, by demonstrating Kinangop's superiority on the playing fields. They were therefore highly motivated to find among their students those with good sporting abilities, and to encourage them to try out for team selection.

It proved to be both a benefit and a disadvantage for

Sam. He was at least a year older than his classmates and this, coupled with his fine physique, brought him to the attention of the sporting staff.

While he was walking home to his dormitory one afternoon, the sports master imposed upon him to make up the numbers in a practice match. Sam tried to excuse himself by saying he knew nothing about rugby.

'Well, there's nothing much to know,' the sports master said. 'And you're big enough. Look, if someone gives you the ball, all you have to do is put it under your arm and run down the field with it.'

Sam did as he was told and scored a try with two boys hanging from his shirt-tails over the last ten yards. The master convinced Sam to sign up with the squad for the upcoming game against Goodswood Old Boys.

Kinangop Academy had not beaten their arch rivals since foundation, but thanks to Sam's dashing play on a flank, they won the very next game against Goodswood.

After his rugby success, he was drafted into several other sports teams, making his mark on the athletics field, where he won medals in high jump, the hundred-yard dash, the mile and field hockey. However, it was his expertise at rugby — which he soon loved with a passion — that made him the most popular boy in school and a favourite among the masters.

Of course, this all meant that Sam had less time to spend studying. His immediate task was to quickly catch up to the other students in almost every subject, but Ira told him he would have to do better than that. He had to finish in the top three to have a good chance to win selection for a place at NYU.

* * *

Although Sam had a gift for languages and was fluent in Kiswahili, Kikamba and English, and had a smattering of several other tribal languages, he struggled with Latin.

'If Latin is a dead language, why do we have to learn it?' he asked his tutor, Mr Maxwell.

'Because it is the root of many other European languages,' he said.

'Will I need to know any of these foreign languages if I win my place at New York University?'

'Not really. I imagine they only teach in English.'

Sam suggested Latin was therefore a waste of time, and not worth worrying about.

'Hmm,' Maxwell said. 'You know, Sam, in education we sometimes find gifted students in particular fields of study. We may find an excellent mathematician, a poet. But a true scholar is one who can master the complete field. You're quite an athlete, Sam. An all-rounder. You're good in many track and field events and you do very well in the decathlon. Are there any of the decathlon events that you don't enjoy?'

'Yes, sir. I don't like the high jump.'

'Why?'

Sam shrugged. 'I can see that running and throwing things can be useful, but jumping over a bar … I don't know if that's ever going to be needed.'

'I see. Do you know who won the decathlon at the Stockholm Olympics in 1912?'

'Yes, sir. It was Jim Thorpe.'

'Correct. He was an American Red Indian. Quite an outsider, even in his own country. Yet the King of Sweden called him the world's greatest athlete when he handed him the gold medal for the decathlon. Now, Sam, imagine you're in the decathlon and Latin is the high bar. Are you going to lose the gold medal — your chance to win a place at New York University — because you can't see a need for the high jump?'

* * *

Weeks after the end of the school year, when most of the students and staff had gone home, Sam remained in his dormitory awaiting word from New York University regarding his application for entry.

He reclined on his bed, arms folded behind his head, staring at the chipped paint on the ceiling, recalling the excitement of graduation night. The Nairobi evening had been warm for that time of year and the small assembly hall had been filled to overflowing with students and a large number of parents and friends. The graduating class of 1919, in caps and robes, had been seated in the front rows. Sam had come top of his class in all subjects except Latin, where he came second, and had been made dux of the academy. The applause had been overwhelming and Sam had been pleased, but the prize he wanted more than anything was his NYU invitation. Mr Maxwell, who was the coordinator for such matters, had said he'd heard nothing.

'How long will it take, Mr Maxwell?' Sam had asked.
'It could be weeks.'

'I'm not being invited because I missed top mark in Latin, isn't it, sir?'

'Not necessarily, Sam. Patience. These things take time.'

But the days had stretched into weeks. Sam had grown increasingly concerned.

There was a knock at the dormitory door and a moment later Mr Maxwell was standing there in the doorway.

Sam was immediately on his feet, studying Maxwell's face. He somehow knew he'd received news from New York.

'The academy's received this letter from NYU,' Maxwell said, pulling an envelope, already opened, from his jacket pocket.

His teacher's expression gave nothing away. Sam was afraid to speak. He stood there with his fists clenched by his sides and his eyes on Maxwell as he solemnly unfolded the letter and made a show of studying the contents.

'This time, a second in the high jump was good enough,' his teacher said as his face creased in a broad smile. 'Sam Wangira … you're going to America.'

*　*　*

A few days after receiving his invitation to enrol at NYU, Sam caught the train to Nyeri to visit his village. He told his family he would be leaving Igobu, and British East Africa, for a long time.

Sam explained he would study in America, at a university in one of the world's largest cities. His father nodded but remained silent. Sam could see he was unable to comprehend the news, but was too proud to ask the questions that must have filled his mind.

Word spread through Igobu. It was received with shock and consternation by the older generation in the village. Soon the whole community heard the news and large delegations came to Igobu to commiserate with his family. They spoke to his father in soft voices and glanced at Sam as if he were already dead. The old people came with sad eyes and blessed him for luck.

When it was time to leave, Sam's father embraced his son in a bear hug. He then held him by the shoulders at arm's length, and stared into Sam's eyes for a long time. Sam feared he'd find disappointment behind those stern eyes. He'd hoped for approval. In the end he found neither. It was impossible to know what was in his father's mind. Finally, Kungu dropped his arms and went to his hut.

Sam completed his farewells without seeing his father again.

* * *

Sam stood at the door of his rail carriage. Below him on the Nairobi Station platform were scores of his classmates, there to wish him bon voyage.

It wasn't Sam's first train journey. During his two years at Kinangop Academy, he'd made rail journeys home to Igobu for term holidays, but this time was different. He was about to travel over three hundred miles to the Indian Ocean, and Mombasa, where he would board a ship to take him to the other side of the world.

He was surprised at the turnout and wondered why so many had come to see him off. His journey to New York had obviously captured everyone's imagination. Most of the white boys' mothers had been sent 'home' to the British Isles for their births and regularly returned there for leave. Since the outbreak of the Great War, however, they'd been confined in British East Africa. Sam was the first of them to escape; perhaps this was the reason he had become a celebrity. He wouldn't admit even to himself that his teachers and classmates admired and genuinely liked him; nor that this was the real reason they'd come to see him off.

The students and teaching staff all agreed that Sam's scholarship to New York University was a triumph for the Kinangop Academy, and his sendoff was therefore a cause for great celebration. The tearful farewell at Igobu was forgotten in the jubilation of his school friends; and Sam was even more excited when a loud blast on the steam whistle signalled the train's imminent departure and Sister Rosalba appeared.

The students cleared a path for her and she stood before him with pride and sadness in her eyes.

'Sister Rosalba,' he said. 'Why … you're here!'

'Yes. I'm sorry I missed you at Igobu. The bishop called me away. But now I am here.'

'You didn't have to come all this way …'

'Maybe I just-a want to make sure you go,' she said with a smile.

'Thank you,' he said.

'Oh, it's-a nothing. I took the donkey wagon to Thika.'

'No … I mean, thank you for giving me this chance. I could never have passed the entrance test to Kinangop without you. And university would have been impossible.'

'If you owe anybody thanks, it is God for giving you that wonderful brain.' Tears brimmed in her eyes.

The whistle screeched again, and the train jerked forwards.

'Now go,' she said. 'And don't forget to write to me.'

Sam stood on the carriage step, waving to all as the train gathered speed. Soon Sister Rosalba and his school friends were lost from sight.

Sam had never felt more alone.

* * *

Sam had seen the lake at Naivasha, but the blue vastness that ran from the ring of white stone buildings of Mombasa town to rendezvous with the sky was terrifying in its immensity.

As the train snaked down from the hills above the island, Sam watched the Indian Ocean's intricate colours blend from pale green near the shore to deep blue beyond the broken white line along the reef. Every feature of the land and the town seemed to invoke the sea. Nearest to the wharf, where a flotilla of boats and huge ships sat among a swarm of bustling watercraft, the buildings were clustered around the shore like bees in attendance on the queen. From there, the paths and roads fanned out through lesser buildings set in clusters of greenery until, at the place where the long ribbon of the causeway anchored the island to the land, there was nothing but jungle and a thick mat of mangroves that swallowed whole sections of the silvered iron rails.

Later, after he'd gathered his various woven bags together and collected his ticket from the agent's office on Vasco da Gama Street, he stood on the dock with the black steel shell of the SS *Madura* looming above him. He felt so insignificant: he was a child again, holding his mother's hand as they stood below Kirinyaga, the mountain where God dwelled and which dominated the sky above him. People with eager faces lined the railing overhead. They seemed completely at ease, even pleased to be there.

He followed others up the gangway, which swayed, and something odd fluttered in his stomach. He clutched the handrail, but the feeling persisted. Even while standing on the deck, high above the water, which had now turned into a monolithic sheet of silver-blue, the world beneath his feet had become unnervingly indeterminate.

A food hawker moved along the deck offering passengers a selection of hot snacks from a box hung from a strap around his neck. Sam was staring into the water thirty feet below him when the whiff of curry pies brought a rush of bile to his throat. He vomited copiously over the railing.

*   *   *

As the *Madura* steamed north, Sam became increasingly unwell. His seasickness hardly ever left him. He lost weight and his sallow eyes retreated into their dark-ringed sockets. The brief ports of call — Mogadishu, Port Said, Naples — were mere respites between debilitating purges. At Marseille, Sam was almost incapable of walking. He left the ship and staggered into a waterfront hotel.

A bearded man sat at the bar with a glass half filled with a milky liquid. Sam watched as he lifted the glass to his lips and drained it. Sam's stomach heaved, but only the bitter taste of the bile reached his mouth.

He leaned against the doorframe; the room, the bearded man and the woman behind the bar became blurred.

'*Merde!*' the woman muttered when she noticed him in the doorway. Wiping her hands on a cloth, she came around the end of the bar towards him. '*S'il vous plaît venez à, monsieur.*'

Sam took a step forwards and his knees buckled. The woman caught him under the arm.

'*Êtes-vous malade?*' she said, helping him to a table.

'I'm sorry,' Sam said in English as he slumped into the chair. 'I don't speak French.'

'Are you ill?' she repeated with only a trace of an accent.

'I ... don't know. I just feel ... very weak.'

'*Un moment*,' she said and taking the bottle from in front of the bearded man she poured a measure into a glass and added water. The mixture turned milky. 'Drink,' she commanded.

The aromatic fumes irritated his eyes, but the woman stood over him, arms crossed, so he took a mouthful. A surge of blood rushed to his brain and his throat constricted. An involuntary gasp escaped his burning lips.

The man at the bar mumbled a disparaging grunt.

'More,' the woman said. Her voice was threatening, but she had a pleasant face and when he glanced up at her, she smiled. He finished the drink, and warmth spread from his belly through his whole body.

'You are off the *Madura*,' she stated.

'Yes.'

'Looking for a room?'

His eyes roamed around the hotel, from the stained timber glasses cabinet above the black marble bar to the half-dozen circular tables to the carpeted staircase. It hadn't occurred to him until that moment, but here was a perfect haven from his torture on the ship. Here he could find his feet. Here he could perhaps finally get some sleep.

'A room?' he said.

'*Oui*. I have a nice room for you. Two francs.'

The *Madura* could sail without him. He had long ago lost his enthusiasm for New York. In fact, he detested the name. New York and his dreams of adventure and education had been the cause of his interminable suffering.

'Yes,' he said. 'A room.'

'Come, I show you,' she said, and led the way to the stairs.

She glanced back and found Sam still fixed to his seat.

'Come. You can get your things later.'

Sam's legs were leaden and he leaned on the table while he got to his feet. His heart thumped and his face burned as he followed the woman's shapely bottom up the stairs.

On the landing, the threadbare carpet under his feet began to rise and fall in great waves like someone had hold of the end and was shaking loose the dust.

He heard the woman say, '*Quelle?*' just before his head hit the floor.

* * *

Sam awoke in a small but pleasant room lit by the yellow light of a paraffin lantern on the bedside table. His head ached and the cramps that had pinched his gut for many days were worse, but he had none of the last weeks' debilitating nausea. As the fogginess of sleep cleared, he realised his bunk was steady; and with a sigh of relief he remembered that he was no longer on board ship.

The door to his room opened and the woman from the bar peeped in.

'Ah,' she said, entering. 'You wake up.'

Sam noticed the woman had an armful of clothes, and at the same time realised he was naked under the sheet and light blanket. The clothes she carried were his. She noticed his expression and smiled.

'All clean now,' she said and then made a face. 'Pooh! How you stink. Do you think I would let you sleep in one of my beds when you stink like a donkey? No. Now you are all clean. How do the English say it? From top to toe.'

A number of questions flew into Sam's head, most of which he thought it best not to ask, but one of them was important. 'What happened to me?'

'Maybe I should have given you the bouillabaisse before the absinthe, yes?'

'I fell …?'

'Boof!' she said, making a gesture with her arm. 'Like a tree. You are very heavy. Joel, he helped me, but he is useless after four absinthes.' She shrugged. 'Don't worry, he didn't see your pee-pee.'

She laughed at his expression, then disappeared with a promise to return with the bouillabaisse.

Her name was Paulette, and Sam guessed she was about forty, though as she was white it was hard to tell. She told him that she and her absent husband, Aubin, owned the bar, but that she managed it because he was at sea for ten months of the year and in any case, she was the one with the bar-keeping experience.

She was a full-figured woman, with short hair, wide hips and a dimple in each cheek when she smiled, which was often. She could chat for an hour about the characters who came through the hotel door; and she was not the least embarrassed to reveal some of the amorous exploits of her years working in London's pubs when a young woman, fresh from school with only a smattering of English.

Within days Sam was feeling much better, thanks to the bouillabaisse and the pleasure he found between Paulette's ample white thighs. She was full of vigour and laughter in bed, not to mention endlessly fascinated by Sam's body, which she insisted he place close to the lamp so that she could study his veins and the tight springs of his pubic hair. She would lick him and tease him until he was ready to explode, but on the occasion when his lust drove him to a quick climax she patiently tutored him on the ways that a woman preferred to be bedded.

She was exuberantly vocal each time she neared her climax, especially while sitting astride him, her hands grasping his knees behind her for better purchase and her heavy breasts swinging. Sam wondered if the men in the bar below, or indeed the passers-by in the street, could hear her. She said the English were far better at bedroom words than the squeamish French. She used the word *fuck* with gusto.

He stayed in Marseille for four weeks, sending Ira three letters to defer his arrival another week, but finally he had to move on: Paulette's husband had sent word that he was homeward bound.

She gave him detailed instructions on how to find his way across France to Calais, and where to go in London to book his passage to New York. She told him that her husband said the best way to avoid the seasickness was to drink plain water with dry crackers whenever he could stand them. He should stay in the centre of the ship and, at all costs, avoid the bow or stern while crossing the Atlantic as it was well known among sailors that the rollers coming over the bow from the west would give any landlubber the worst seasickness imaginable.

Paulette held him in her arms for a long moment when he came to say goodbye. She made a joke about how his body had filled out thanks to her mothering and gave him a slap on the buttocks to send him off.

At the doorway he thanked her and she gave him a wink that sent a small tear rolling down her round, pink cheek.

CHAPTER 10

Paulette's plain water and crackers had not proven to be the complete success he'd hoped, but Sam was well enough to stand at the railing as his ship sailed through the early-morning mists of New York's harbour.

The bleak face of enormous buildings arose through the gloom like the Rift Valley's eastern escarpment clothed in haze.

The deep booming call of the ship's foghorn cast a pall over his excitement. The harbour, the buildings, the weather — everything suddenly felt threatening. Sam wondered how he could survive in this alien world.

Looking down at the upturned faces on the New York dock, Sam realised he had no chance of finding Ira in that seething mass. But his friend, beaming as always, was at the bottom of the gangway as Sam came down, carrying his single small suitcase. They embraced. Ira held Sam tight and appeared genuinely moved as he stood back to admire him.

'Look at you,' he said. 'So healthy. After such a terrible journey to Marseille — you look wonderful.'

Sam shrugged. 'Maybe I am becoming a sailor after all.'

Ira laughed, but tears welled in his eyes as he stared at Sam for a long moment.

'OK, let's go,' he said finally, clapping his palms on Sam's upper arms. 'I have a driver waiting for us out the back.'

The car was a black Cadillac Brougham with white-walled tyres. The driver opened the rear door for them; Sam sat and ran his hand over the fine seat covers of dark blue as the driver steered the car effortlessly through a press of vehicles. It seemed amazing that he avoided collisions at intersections where cars lined up like platoons of well-trained members of the King's African Rifles marching in procession.

Ira commented on the various points of interest they passed on their journey through the teeming city. He interspersed this with details of the plans he'd made for Sam.

'I've set up someone to help you with your language skills. Your English is fine, but it'll do no harm to get some help with your elocution and vocabulary. With some of his tips, you'll be drawling like a Yankee in no time.'

Sam heard only part of Ira's monologue as he swung his head from side to side, craning his neck at the window to peer into the soaring heights of passing buildings. In department store windows were lifelike male and female mannequins wearing fine clothes. A large picture of something called a hamburger dominated an awning over one store; and street vendors stood over smoking braziers selling a variety of food items to the passers-by.

'Where are we?' Sam asked when they alighted beside a set of stairs leading to a two-storey stone building.

'This is the place I've been telling you about,' Ira replied.

Sam looked puzzled.

'You haven't heard a thing I've been saying, have you?' his benefactor said, smiling. 'I fancy it's all a bit much for you. Come, I'll show you to your room.'

At the top of the stone steps Ira took a key from his pocket and opened the door. A short corridor led to a flight of stairs.

'My bedroom is up there,' he said, nodding to the stairs. 'But this is your room until you get established at NYU.' He swung the door open. 'I hope you like it.'

The room had a desk under a curtained window that looked over a small courtyard to a similar courtyard and window of the building at the rear. A narrow bed sat against the far wall and beside it was a low table with a lampshade made of something like parchment. It had a beaded fringe and a ship painted faintly on it. The other wall held a painting of red and yellow flowers bending their black-centred heads over the rim of a blue vase.

Ira was smiling apprehensively when Sam completed his inspection.

'Sam, I am so happy you agreed to come.'

'I'm happy I came too, Ira.'

'You … you are very dear to me, Sam. If there is anything you need, if you have any problems at all, you will let me know. Agreed?'

Sam nodded.

Ira waited for him to comment, but Sam didn't know what more to add.

'Oh,' Ira said, 'that's a letter for you.' He pointed at the envelope on the desk. 'It came a few days ago. I guess it's from home.' He laughed. 'Where else?' he said, and shrugged. 'I had a bathroom installed on the other side of the corridor for you. There's another upstairs … for me.' Ira's eyes roamed the room too. He went to the wall and made a slight adjustment to the flower painting. 'I have a larger house out of town, but I thought this one would be better while you get settled.'

Sam looked around the room again.

'If you don't like it, we can go to my place on Staten Island, you know. It's just that, well ... we need to do some shopping for you, and I thought ...'

Sam smiled an acknowledgement; nodded yet again.

'So ...' Ira said. 'What do you think?'

'About the room?'

'Yes, the room, Sam.'

'Ira, I think this is the most beautiful room I have ever seen.'

* * *

The letter, from Sister Rosalba, was written in formal English. He had never received a letter from her nor, now that he came to think of it, had he read anything she had written other than the cryptic comments she scrawled illegibly on the bottom of his lessons. He read the letter again, trying to see her face in the words, trying to recall the way she sounded in real life. But the words were sterile, making Sam feel even more remote from home.

Dear Sam,

I hope that this finds you well as we are here as it leaves us.

I am sorry for my delay in writing. I had to write to the Norfolk for Mr Ketterman's address.

Here we have much to do. The harvest is upon us. We go from school to the food garden and then back to school. The millet goes well, but the sorghum is not so good. There is much discussion about sorghum in the village. It has not done well for two seasons already.

So you can see that we are busy.

By now I expect that you are comfortable in your new home. I hope that your studies are going well.

I am writing this in the hope you are remaining in grace within the warm enfolding arms of your faith.

Go with God, my child.

Sincerely,
Sister Rosalba

Sam went to the window and stared across the adjoining courtyards to the other window. It was only lightly curtained, but he could see nothing beyond its reflective surface. Both courtyards were paved: nothing useful grew in either although he estimated that, properly planted, they could support a good number of maize plants — enough to feed the occupants of both houses.

He returned to the bed and sat beside his suitcase, Sister Rosalba's letter still in his hands. He ran his eyes around the interior of his room before settling on the picture of the vase of flowers. He briefly wondered if Ira had painted it, but discarded the thought. Then he wondered why anyone would bother painting a picture of a bowl of flowers when having the actual flowers would have been so much more appealing. It added to his confusion about everything American — from the towering statue of a woman holding a light in the harbour to images of giant hamburgers.

He flicked the switch of the bedside lamp. The ship sprang from obscurity into colourful life and the fringe of beads trembled in the light.

He studied Sister Rosalba's neat cursive script. It reflected her personality — the personality of a white woman who had foregone a life with family and friends in Italy to work with impoverished blacks in an obscure corner of a backward country. Until that moment, it had never occurred to him to ponder such a sacrifice.

Now, Sister Rosalba, Igobu, his parents and his life in Kenya had become distant and receding beacons of certainty in a world brimful of confusion.

* * *

Ira lay staring at the ceiling. He imagined he could smell the faint male odour that arose from Sam's warm body in the bedroom below; feel the smooth musculature of his firm flesh lying between the sheets; sense the vibrancy of his maleness.

He'd waited so long for him to arrive, but as always, his resolve to tell him how he felt had vanished as soon as he'd attempted to put it into words.

You are very dear to me, was the best he could do while in his heart he wanted to say so much more. *Sam, I love you.*

How many times had he dreamed of this night? Now it had arrived, he knew damn well his cowardice would prevail: he wouldn't say any of the things he'd rehearsed almost every day while awaiting Sam's arrival.

He had tormented himself with the fantasy that Sam would one day feel the same urge that drove Ira into a lather of lust. No, not lust. It could never be lust when it came to Sam.

Ira had kept his desires hidden while married to his wife and only on a few brief occasions since their divorce had he allowed them to find expression. And when he had, it was with such self-disgust and mortification that he retreated again into his emotional cave. With Sam, such an embrace would be so much more, but in his heart he knew it would never happen. He was a coward and now he was running out of time. Sam would but briefly sleep under the same roof before taking up residence in the college dorm.

And time was running out for Ira in another way too. He had learned that asbestos fibres had taken root in his lungs and woven a deadly web. The mines and the money they brought could be forgotten, but the result of that poisonous place could not.

*　　*　　*

It took Sam a long time to find his feet in New York and his place in university life. There were times during the first year when he almost gave up. It was only his indebtedness to Ira's generosity that kept him going; and only Ira who tried to boost his confidence in the face of an increasingly difficult workload and poor grades.

It might be something specific in his course that confounded him to the point of rage. 'Commercial law is crap,' he said at one stage, although he knew Ira disapproved of his use of the American vernacular. Sam said it was Ira's fault that he cursed because the elocution teacher he chose was from the Bronx and the bad language came packaged with the pronunciations.

Ira would speak calmly and offer to help him with his assignment. Together they would pore over the texts in Ira's large Staten Island house until the problem was resolved and Sam's desperate urge to abandon his studies and slink home to Africa was overcome.

As Sam's grades slowly improved, his confidence grew. In time he found the rigours of study much to his liking.

He would arise each day from his bed in the male dormitory and take a dozen circuits of the athletics field or swim a mile in the pool, before joining his colleagues for breakfast. Then he would study until his first class. At the end of the day he would usually go to the library where he would consume reference material and write notes in preparation for the following day.

On weekends he continued to visit Ira on Staten Island, but as he became more involved with the student body and its activities, these trips became less frequent.

He found it easy to apply his rugby skills to the running game of American football. He made the senior team on his first tryout and quickly became a key position player.

To the young white women on campus, he was an exotic — and forbidden — flower and therefore all the more interesting to the nonconformist element among them. Sam couldn't resist and bedded several, but these affairs were short-lived. Most of the young women were only interested in having Sam as a trophy and, after a brief dalliance, would manufacture an excuse to ease themselves out of the liaison.

It was an arrangement that perfectly suited Sam's needs: since he appeared to be the aggrieved party, none of the women felt offended. He had no desire for intimacy, and no intentions of building a long-term relationship. He'd never forgotten Mothoni, his first great love, who had chosen his arch rival, Johnstone Kamau, to be her first official lover.

In the eyes of a few of his female admirers he sensed more than mere lust or the avarice of a trophy hunter. In these situations, he was careful to keep his distance.

Those close to him were aware of his popularity. His closest confidant was his coach, Jake Freemore, who became concerned that Sam was not only breaking one of the college's rather moralistic house rules about fraternisation, but was also in danger of attracting the attention of others with more malicious intentions than those of his female fans.

Freemore was a former running back for the Jacksonville Colts, and one of the first black men to coach a gridiron team in the USA. He realised his prize recruit needed a lesson in living as a black man in white America, so during the term break he invited Sam to his family home in Georgetown, South Carolina.

* * *

In Georgetown, a town with an overwhelming majority of black Americans, most of them quite poor, Sam felt immediately at ease. Freemore's parents still lived in the little house where he was born, and the Freemore family — mother, father and grandmother — made Sam feel very welcome.

Sam loved the easy pace of the south. He enjoyed the music, the spicy food, and a feeling very similar to being among his tribe.

A few days after arriving in Georgetown, Freemore told Sam he'd like to take him out for a hamburger to a small diner in the better part of the city.

A moment after they were seated, the white manager appeared at their table.

'Ain't you Jake Freemore?'

'That's me,' said Freemore.

'Then hell, man, you should know better. You know I gotta kick your ass out of here.'

Freemore nodded. 'You're right, sir. I should've

remembered where I am.' He stood, indicating to Sam he should do likewise. 'We won't be bothering you no more.'

'See that you don't.'

Outside, Sam wanted to know what had happened.

'You been living a sheltered life on campus, Sam,' he said. 'You can find situations like that in New York,' he jerked his thumb over his shoulder to indicate the diner, 'but they ain't usually that polite. I brought you here because I know the owner was a fan from my days with the Colts. Anywhere else, we might have been beaten up. Bad.' Freemore explained the basic rules of segregation to Sam, who had heard of segregation, but it hadn't occurred to him that it applied to Africans. In many ways, it hadn't.

'You needed to know that outside NYU you're just another nigger,' Freemore said.

Over the following days, as he moved around town, Sam discovered just how much he was not able to do. Even in a city with a large majority of blacks, his skin colour prevented him from drinking from certain water fountains, entering some stores, boarding a bus by a particular door, or using a *whites only* public toilet. It came as a shock. In NYU he was known to be a foreigner but didn't realise he had been treated differently from black Americans.

The night before they were to leave for New York, the whole Freemore family joined Sam and Jake at the movies. Coming home, they passed a group surrounding a young black man who was no more than Sam's age. Sam could almost taste the hatred in the air and in the eyes of the young man he saw utter terror.

The group began to shove the black man back and forth inside their circle. Then one of the white men removed his belt and began to whip him.

Sam took a pace towards the group, but Jake grabbed him on the arm and drew him back.

'Sam, no,' he hissed into his ear. 'I know what you're thinkin', but we ain't gonna interfere. You hear me?'

Sam tried to shrug him loose, but Freemore, forty pounds heavier and still in good shape, held fast.

'Listen to me,' he continued. 'You and I might be able to bang some heads in there, but the kid's done somethin' to upset 'em, and he's gonna get a beatin' one way or another, then they'll let him go. Any other time and I might be stupid enough to do what you're thinkin', but my folks are here. These white boys got no respect for age or sex when they get in this mood.'

Sam looked at the older Freemores. They had backed away from the scene, and were as terrified as the man in the middle of the mob.

That night Sam stewed with pent-up rage and frustration. He had experienced an ugly side of America, one that he found difficult to reconcile with the America he had observed in the university — a place of unlimited opportunity and bountiful positive energy.

He became more inquisitive about this ugly, stunted side of the country when he returned to NYU, and searched for its meaning, its origins.

He knew a little of the history of slavery in East Africa. The Consolata nuns had related stories of the slavers, who had only in recent times been thwarted in their periodic plundering of the local tribes. The unfortunate ones, stolen from their families, would serve as household servants in sumptuous Arabian palaces in distant lands. He suspected that the nuns' version of history had been influenced by the tender age of their audience, but the history of America's slaves, whose unfortunate recruits were drawn from the other side of his home continent, was far more inhumane and often brutal. Sam read the history in horror.

His interests spread beyond America to the colonial powers' scramble for Africa. American historians took a high-minded stance against Britain's relatively recent incursions into East Africa, as their government was not directly involved. They portrayed Britain as the invader.

Sam had seen many of the benefits of the white administration's efforts to keep the peace among the tribes and to provide health services and a limited form of education, but the *pax Britannica* came at a huge price. The growing numbers of white settlers demanded more and more land. And they weren't content with just any land: they demanded the best and most fertile tracts. Even the Maasai, possibly the most militarily proficient tribe in East Africa, were incapable of resisting the whites' wholesale plunder. Sam discovered that in 1904 they had reluctantly signed an agreement to move from their traditional land in the Great Rift Valley to the Laikipia plateau. But then the white settlers realised that the plateau was far more fertile than previously thought, so seven years later the British broke their own treaty and again forced the Maasai to move, this time to the desolate southern end of their range.

Sam was offended by the wrongs perpetrated upon the Maasai. He knew that his own Kikuyu people were as culturally and emotionally connected to their land as the Maasai, and wondered how long it would be before the settlers began to covet Kikuyu land.

A sense of great injustice took root in his soul. Over the ensuing years it would slowly grow to affect his views of the British, their place in Africa, and his people's rights to their land.

* * *

When graduation day arrived, and Sam lined up with his fellow undergraduates, the auditorium was filled with family and friends from the front rows to where the overflow stood against the rear wall. All smiles.

Somewhere in the crowd was Ira. Sam could hear his occasional coughing and at one point he picked him out; he was beaming as proudly as any parent.

Sam didn't find the absence of his family upsetting. His father, with his several wives and many children, had always been a distant figure. His mother was a person he could now only recall through the eyes of a child.

It had been many months since he'd thought about Sister Rosalba, but she came to mind again while he waited in line to shake the hand of the assembled academics and receive his degree. She had written on the first Sunday of every month; the letters arriving like clockwork a month and a half later. They provided Sam with a tenuous lifeline to his family and Igobu, though he hardly ever found the time to respond. When they'd stopped arriving during his third year at college, his former existence had so receded in his mind that it took him six months to note their absence. He realised how irrelevant they had become and didn't trouble himself to write and check on Rosalba and the village. It was as if Igobu had never been part of his life. He felt like an American now. And it would be in America that he would build a new life and fulfil his ambitions.

CHAPTER 11

Ira sank into the armchair in his Staten Island sitting room and almost disappeared. He had lost more weight, but again refused to discuss his health with Sam other than to say that he'd found a new tonic and his general fitness was improving.

He'd no sooner settled into the seat than he sat forwards, resting his elbows on his bony knees and wringing his hands. Sam knew the gesture well. It meant that Ira was unhappy with him; and he knew why. Sam had decided to give up on his futile search for a job in New York. He'd been looking for months. Each time he won a place on the interview list, he made it no further. He had no illusions about why. He had qualified top in each of his last three years, but when the personnel managers laid eyes on him, the notebooks closed. Most had the courtesy to go through the formalities. Some even congratulated him on his CV. Many wrote polite rejection letters that talked about a very strong field of applicants and said that an extremely well-credentialed candidate had emerged from the recruitment process. But Sam knew otherwise. After a time, he'd become cynical to the point where he knew, if he didn't get away from New York and all its frustration, he would lose his mind. The west was unknown, but couldn't be more discouraging.

'Sam, I know I'm repeating myself, but I'm worried about your decision to go out there ...' Ira waved his hand vaguely — a small pale bird fluttering about the room. 'To ... you know ... the west. Why don't you come over to General Motors? I know some important people in the Cadillac division. They need good fellows with all the growth that's going on.'

'Ira, GM needs production managers, not accountants.'

'Then get a job as an accountant. You passed with flying colours, so there must be plenty of opportunities —'

'Ira —'

'I know the head of the finance department in Dayton Electric Laboratories. An old friend of mine from our days working on the self-starter, I could —'

'Ira —'

Ira stopped yabbering. He sighed and sank back into his armchair with a defeated look.

'Ira, don't think I don't appreciate what you're trying to do — what you've already done for me — but I have to make my own way now. I know this isn't your idea of a business, nor mine. But I can't continue to live off your charity. After a year or so I'll work something out.'

'So you've said. What I don't understand is what you'll do out there. You don't have the faintest idea what you'll find.'

Ira began to cough; Sam brought him a glass of water.

'Ira, when are you going to do something about that cough?'

Ira tried to speak and almost choked on the water. 'And when are you going to get some sense?' he spluttered angrily, struggling to find his breath. 'If you get into trouble out there with all those ... those red-neck cowboys, you'll be on your own. You've seen how difficult it can be for a black man in New York. Well, being an educated black man out west will be the death of you.' He struggled to his feet. 'And worrying about it will be the death of me.'

* * *

That Ira was right was Sam's recurring thought for the next four months. As he made his way west by rail, through whistle-stop towns in Pennsylvania and into the farmlands of the mid-west, Sam could find no one prepared to offer him work of more than a day or so. And everywhere was the barely concealed animosity of people wary of strangers — especially, Sam thought, black strangers. Whereas in New York he'd begun to feel part of the amazing American experiment in which thousands of the people displaced by the Great War had found acceptance and the opportunity to flourish, here in the insular mid-western states there was only rejection.

Sam's saving grace throughout those four months tramping from town to town was his ability to absorb all the new experiences and learn from them. In Detroit he learned how Henry Ford could make almost a million T-model vehicles each year and so cheaply that many of his workers could actually afford to buy what they made. Like *siafu* ants forging a track through the jungle, Ford's production line reduced the single very complex process of building a car to a thousand simple steps using men to build it a small piece at a time.

In St Louis, where the great migration of black Americans had seen thousands move from the south to the industrial cities of the north, he learned to enjoy blues, ragtime and jazz — music he'd never heard before.

Finally, in Texas he learned how a man and his horse could control a herd of cantankerous cattle with unimaginable beauty and grace. Although he'd seen horses at home in Africa, it wasn't until he became closely associated with them as a roustabout on a cattle ranch that he really appreciated their beauty. His instinct around any large animal was to treat it with respect; and it took many days before he summoned the courage to approach one of the cowboy's horses. It was a large black stallion, full of spirit and prone to curling its lips to show its teeth to passers-by. Sam chose it because it was by far the most beautiful animal he'd ever seen.

As he stood before the animal, whose sleek black head rose above Sam's, he whispered to it in Swahili. He wasn't sure why he chose Swahili rather than Kikuyu, or even English. Later he thought it might have been because Swahili was a musical language. Maybe he chose it because it was understood by all the many tribes of East Africa and somehow this capacity would extend to horses.

The horse snorted and lowered its head for Sam to scratch it between the ears. He was soon running his hands over the sleek neck and shoulders while the stallion blew soft warm breaths on Sam's neck and arms.

When the stallion's owner returned, he was at first annoyed by Sam's interaction with his animal, then surprised.

'Hey, man,' he said. 'How'd you do that?'

'Do what?'

'Make that mean son-of-a-bitch treat you so nice. He don't usually take kindly to attention. Whatcha been givin' him? Sugar?'

Sam shrugged. 'I gave him nothing. Just been stroking him. And talking. He just seemed so … friendly.'

'Friendly? That big sucker wouldn't know the meanin' of the word. Not even for me, and I've had him since a colt.' The cowboy studied Sam. 'You been working around here as a wrangler, right?'

'That's right.'

'So if you're so good with horseflesh, why aren't you out there on horseback with the rest of us?'

Sam smiled. 'I can't ride.'

'You can't ride? And look at you. Got that stallion purrin' like a kitten.'

Sam shrugged and continued to stroke the horse's flanks. They began discussing horses. Sam was again keen to seize any opportunity to learn. The discussion ended with the cowboy offering to teach Sam how to ride. 'Though I wouldn't get my heart too set on it if'n I were you,' he warned. 'Not everybody cottons on to it.'

* * *

Sam swung into the saddle of the old mare and walked her towards the high, burlap-covered enclosure. Inside it was the meanest wild prairie stallion anyone had seen in Montana, and a dozen cowboys were sitting on the fence to see the newly arrived horse-breaker meet his match.

Sam was accustomed to the overtly racist sentiments he encountered in his role as horse-breaker. Twelve months earlier, when he'd first discovered his innate ability to read a horse's mood and to gently condition it to accept a rider, there were jokes about mumbo jumbo and black magic. Those who knew he'd only just learned horse riding were amazed as he used his new method to firstly pacify the horse and then teach it to bend to a rider's wishes. Since then he'd been on the road, working his magic from one state to another.

Inside the enclosure he let the stallion become accustomed to the mare and rider, but when Sam slipped the lasso over its neck, it snorted and fought.

Sam patiently whispered to the stallion but this made no change in its mood. The watching cowboys grinned at Sam's Swahili and nudged their companions, making snide remarks.

After a few minutes, Sam did the unthinkable. He dismounted and let his mare out of the enclosure, leaving him alone with the snorting, belligerent stallion at the end of thirty feet of rope. An expectant silence fell over the crowd. The horse trotted around the perimeter and he let it settle before giving a sharp tug on the rope. The stallion's head jolted towards Sam, who immediately loosened the rope as he whispered reassuringly to it. The stallion was momentarily stunned into immobility, before resuming its pacing.

It took him longer than usual, but Sam continued to apply his technique until the snorting, stamping stallion allowed him close enough to touch. A murmur of disbelief rippled among the spectators.

After a further ten minutes in which Sam introduced the horse to the blanket, the reins, and finally the saddle, he mounted it; the cowboys sitting around the fence broke into spontaneous applause.

The men surrounded him when he came out of the enclosure, slapping him on the back and firing questions at him. He spent some time in conversation before the ranch's owner interrupted and handed him a telegram.

'It's from New York,' he said.

Sam walked a few paces away to open and read it.

He turned back to the owner and the circle of men, his face now a mask of shock and disbelief.

'I have to go,' he said.

*   *   *

The telegram had taken six weeks to track Sam across Texas, into Nebraska and finally to Montana. It had come from Esmeralda, Ira's housekeeper of seventeen years. In recent times, she had been taking care of Ira as well as the Staten Island house, although the old man would have strongly refuted any suggestion of it.

The telegram was brief: *Mr K poorly. Come soon.*

As the train rocked and rolled across the mid-western prairie, Sam castigated himself for leaving it so long between visits. He'd not seen Ira, now in his seventies, in nearly a year. He'd been ailing for some time, and Sam tried to keep in touch, but his constant travelling made it difficult to maintain contact.

The day lengthened to night and Sam dozed. In his half-asleep state he felt his usual discomfort rise at the thought of returning to the city. It wasn't a place he wanted to be now that he'd found the west's wide open spaces, its big sky and red sunsets, all of which he missed while in New York.

The vision of the west changed until it became the memory of his home on the edge of the great African savannah. He'd not previously associated America's plain states with Kenya; the overlap came as a surprise.

Also surprising was the realisation that his absence from New York now had little to do with his need to earn his living so far away from Ira, and more to do with his changing view of himself. Just as he'd forgotten about his life, his family and friends in Africa, he was saddened to recognise he'd moved on from Ira, his dear friend and generous benefactor.

*   *   *

Esmeralda opened the door and her broad white smile spread across her coal-black face.

'Oh, Mr Sam!' she said, tears welling in her eyes. 'So good to see you again.' She gave him a brief hug, but as she drew back she dropped her eyes to her hands, which she studied as she told him that the doctor said Ira didn't have a whole lot of time left.

'It's the fibres, you know,' she said. 'From the mines.'

'When did the doctor last come?' Sam asked as he headed along the hall towards the stairs.

'Yesterday. He comes 'bout this time 'most every day.'

Sam thanked her then climbed the stairs two at a time. At Ira's door he halted, his hand on the door knob. After a moment he knocked, but when he heard no reply he opened the door and peered in.

The bedroom was dim: the autumn afternoon's light glowed around the edges of the drawn curtains.

He went quietly to the window, opened the curtains a little and stared out into the garden. A breeze chased the golden litter of the birch trees around the curving concrete driveway.

Ira's cough caused him to turn to the bed, where he saw the old man squinting into the light.

'Is that too bright for you, Ira?'

'Sam? Is that you?' He got his arm free of the covers and shielded his eyes.

Sam came around to the other side of the room and dragged a chair to the bedside. Ira was pale and his cheeks had sunken beneath dark-rimmed eyes, but they lit up when he could see his protégé.

'Sam! How long have you been here? It's so good to see you,' he said between strained breaths.

Sam patted Ira's shoulder. It felt as narrow as a bird's under the thick cotton pyjama top.

'Me too,' Sam said. 'I came as soon as ... as soon as I heard you were ill.'

'Thank you, Sam. I'll be fine. Just a little congestion on my chest.'

He coughed again.

'I was out west in Montana. I always leave a forwarding address, but sometimes letters get delayed, and —'

'Sam,' Ira interrupted, 'it's OK. I know how difficult it is to keep in touch. You're here ... that's the main thing.'

'Esmeralda told me what the doctor says.'

'He's as bad as she is. Worries too much.'

'I should have come earlier,' Sam said, moving to sit on the side of the bed.

Ira put his cool, thin fingers on Sam's hand. 'I'm so glad you could come, Sam,' he said.

'I'm not going anywhere for quite a while.'

'Good,' he said, and gave Sam's hand a squeeze. 'I love you, Sam,' he said, softly.

Sam brought his other hand over and patted Ira's. 'I love you too, Ira,' he said.

Ira smiled his wan smile again, and nodded. 'But I mean, I really love you, Sam. Always have.' He gasped for breath. 'From the very first day I set eyes on you out there in the forest.'

Sam felt a lump rise in his throat. 'Ira …'

'Dear Sam. There's no need to speak. I just needed to tell you, before … before it's too late.' His words trailed off with a laboured breath.

Sam nodded. 'I'm glad you did.'

Ira's hand tightened on his.

There was a brief knock on the door and a middle-aged man carrying a black briefcase entered the bedroom.

'You must be the doctor,' Sam said.

'I am,' the man said, extending his hand. 'Dr James Hawthorne.'

Sam tried to retrieve his right hand from Ira's grip, but couldn't. Ira held it with surprising strength.

'Ira?' he said, but there was no answer. Ira's eyes were closed and his thin face was calm and at peace.

CHAPTER 12

In the days following Ira's death, Sam barely moved from the parlour in the Staten Island house. Esmeralda brought him trays of food, which he picked at, leaving most of it for her to clear away. At night she nagged him to get some sleep before retiring herself, but he awoke most mornings stiff and cold in his chair, where he would sit for hours, watching the birch leaves flutter to the ground. He studied his feelings, almost dispassionately, and pondered Ira and his strange, unhappy life.

Ira had once told him of the revolving door theory of life. It seemed particularly apt in his case. If Sam had been away from the village when Bill Hungerford came on his recruitment visit, he would not have been drafted onto porter duties and he would never have met Ira, which had been the turning point — the revolving door — to the rest of his life. It was hard to imagine himself as that innocent village boy, agape at the sophistication of the white man.

When Ira had, at the last possible moment of his life, declared his true feelings for him, Sam had been stunned. He now reflected upon those early years in an attempt to find any hint of Ira's deeper love for him. He couldn't. Certainly there had been times when Ira's celebration of Sam's successes would overflow into an enthusiastic embrace or even an impulsive kiss on the cheek, but those were rare and, in any case, the affection seemed more like a father's than a lover's. Only now did Sam realise how painful it was for Ira to have been so physically close but so emotionally remote from where he wanted to be.

In Sam's whole life he'd had only one occasion when his feelings for another had been similarly painful. It was when Johnstone Kamau had stolen Mothoni from him on the night they should have tied the grass together. He had been able to put the memories behind him, but the sting of rejection lingered whenever he let his mind stray back to that time.

He could barely imagine how badly Ira must have suffered when every day of his life with Sam was filled with unrequited love.

James Hawthorne, Ira's long-time friend and physician, arranged the funeral. It was a depressing day, rainy and cold. Sam stood beside Esmeralda, who sobbed while a rabbi muttered and chanted indecipherably.

Sam stayed on in Ira's Staten Island house after the funeral, wondering what to do next.

After a few days, he realised that not only had Ira anticipated his death, he had carefully planned what should happen thereafter.

Sam was sitting on the rear porch when Esmeralda announced he had a visitor.

'For me?' he asked her.

'Yessir, Mr Sam. He done ask for you by name. "Mr Samson Wangira," he said. He gave me this here card to show you.'

The business card read: *Joshua Samuels — Attorney at Law*.

Sam went to the door and invited the man into the parlour, but didn't ask him to sit. He suspected he was trying to sell his services.

'Are you Mr Samson Wangira?' he asked.

'Yes,' Sam said, becoming annoyed at Samuels's officious tone. 'What's this about?'

'I am the executor of Mr Ira Ketterman's estate,' he said. 'And I am here to inform you that you are a major beneficiary.'

When he revealed the extent of the inheritance, Sam had to sit down. He was stunned. Under Kikuyu custom, the eldest son inherits his father's only possession, the family land, and perhaps a few livestock. Sam had no way of understanding how he had any right to Ira's wealth and he told Samuels so.

'How can I accept this?' he asked. 'Surely Ira has family.'

'He has none. Apart from the housekeeper, Miss Esmeralda Smith, who Mr Ketterman has generously provided for, you are the sole beneficiary.'

'This is ridiculous,' Sam protested.

'Mr Ketterman anticipated that you would have some difficulty accepting your inheritance. He asked me to give you this.'

He handed Sam an envelope. It had a red wax seal across the opening.

'I'll leave you to read your letter in private,' Samuels said, and walked out into the hall.

Sam broke the seal and pulled out a neatly typed page.

My dear Sam,

You are reading this because I am no longer with you, and you are finding it difficult to accept my bequest.

It is considerable, but is only a small part of what I believe I owe you.

It was only a few years before we met that I found out I had only a limited time. I suppose to have lived this long has been a bonus. You have such a passion for life that I gained strength from merely being a witness to it. Perhaps I managed to steal some of that fervour, and that is why I've lasted so long.

The strength of our friendship has given me more years than I deserved; more years than anyone expected. Take your inheritance as my way of repaying you for those extra years. The thought of dying alone was abhorrent and without you I might well have ended it early rather than bear that loneliness.

Asbestos dust does awful things to a man's chest, but even had I known all those years ago that working in the mine might have this effect, I'm not sure I could have done anything about it. Poverty strips us of options, and I had few choices back then. I hope that this money enables you to avoid those stultifying effects and enables you to use your wonderful attributes and zest for life to carry you high.

I hope you accept my gift as a small gesture of my eternal love and gratitude. However, should you feel uneasy with it, you might consider doing something to relieve poverty somewhere in Africa, where there is so much suffering.

Love
Ira

PS The shares are in Ketterman Industries, a company I formed after I developed the electric starter motor. They give you one hundred per cent ownership. You may do with the company as you will. Naturally, I would hope that Ketterman Industries may continue in some form, but that too is your decision.

* * *

Sam's inheritance did nothing to end his unease. In fact, it worsened it by removing his need to return to the west and his work as a horse-breaker.

He went on a drinking spree, rendering himself almost stupefied in one binge after another. He awoke one morning, naked, in a garish hotel room. The prostitute he vaguely remembered picking up the night before was gone, as was his wallet.

After a month of such profligate behaviour, he realised he was simply avoiding a decision about his future. In the midst of his unsuccessful search for work in the mid-west, when he barely had enough to survive, the choices were simple: he had to find something, anything, to do to earn the next meal. Now his choices were limitless. He put his mind to the task of finding something to absorb his energy.

He considered taking control of Ketterman Industries, and spent some time in the plant, studying the theory and practice of electrical engineering as applied to electric motors, but he had no aptitude for engineering tasks, and the existing management were handling the company quite competently.

He rented a quiet cabin deep in the Vermont forest to contemplate his situation. On one long walk in the mist of morning, he felt a surge of nostalgia. The trees that climbed the hills to the sky were very different, but the solitude and the grandeur of the landscape reminded him of home.

He missed his African way of life, where the only really important decisions concerned what crop needed to be planted and at what time.

He remembered too Sister Rosalba's plea to his father when she was trying to convince him to let Sam go to university. 'Mr Wangira,' she'd said. 'For the love of-a God, if you won't do it for Sam, do it for your people.'

He asked himself how he could contribute to the welfare of his people if he remained in America. Of course, he couldn't: so he decided to return home at least to assess his future.

Over the following days he strengthened his resolve to break out of his lethargy and return to Kenya, but he felt he wasn't quite ready for that next step. He applied for an extension on his lease on the Vermont cabin, but the owner refused. Sam made him an offer that changed his mind and settled in to enjoy the peace and solitude for another month or so.

A year later he locked it up, and headed to New York, and home.

PART 2
DANA

CHAPTER 13

1929

Dana, Lady Seddon, stood on the veranda admiring the surrounding colour in the rampant red bougainvillea, blue morning glory and violet passionfruit flowers. In the upper reaches of the highlands, at seven thousand feet, the sun had an intensity that could draw out every available ounce of colour. At certain times, as just now, the limpid air seemed to magnify the hills and draw them tightly around the Kipipiri valley, enfolding it in silence.

She was feeling unsettled and was not sure why. Her husband, Edward, was in a good mood, as he tended to be when the farm was running well. The wheat crop was looking promising this year with just the right balance of rain and warm dry weather to ripen it. No: it was not Edward. While Dana could find cause to complain about his drinking and gambling, there was nothing troubling in their relationship.

They were reasonably compatible, and had been so since their meeting a little over ten years earlier at the Chelsea Tennis Club, where she was drawn to partner him in the mixed doubles. Dana was just nineteen and Edward Northcote was dashing and rich. And married. He was introduced to her as the 10th Earl of Seddon. The title added to his attraction and he seemed quite taken with her. Over drinks after the game, he invited her to a dinner party, with her mother as chaperone. She accepted.

She later learned that Edward had had a number of love affairs during his fifteen-year marriage, alleviating her guilt over its end. He swore that his feelings for her were different — and, of course, his divorce and proposal to her were proof of that.

They went on a month's honeymoon to Italy and with the removal of the need for hurried and clandestine meetings in hotels or friends' bedrooms, she found she had both an aptitude and a great liking for sex. In fact, she found it impossible to resist any opportunity to indulge.

Her own affairs began before their first anniversary. It wasn't entirely due to her discovery that Edward had not given up his interest in other women, but that was enough excuse to take a series of lovers of her own.

Edward was furious when he eventually found out, but Dana said she could see no harm in it. It was the twenties, she told him, and the new decade had different rules. Many of her friends had what were being called *open marriages*, because people had the time and the money to enjoy themselves. In the end, Edward could hardly expect his modern young wife to abide by rules he himself could not follow.

Among their London friends was a group of free spirits who had a similar philosophy. Soon Edward and Dana were at parties whose attendees had the primary objective of swapping partners for the night.

When she and Edward moved to Kenya — mainly to avoid her husband's creditors — they soon found a similar group of compatible friends.

In the so-called White Highlands, where friends might be five or six hours' hard ride away — and even neighbours an hour or so over bad roads — the isolation made dinner parties a popular form of entertainment. Because of the distances involved, the guests would be invited to stay overnight. Dana and Edward frequently entertained in this manner, but about once a month they invited around a dozen of their most intimate friends for a special weekend of eating, drinking and dancing. They called themselves the Zephyrs, after the name of the Northcote farm.

The Zephyrs comprised people with two specific qualities: firstly, they must be the *right type*, which meant they were generally from British, or more particularly London, society, having transferred their lives to Kenya for one reason or another — usually with the financial support of family trusts or endowments. Although they chose farming against a life in the city, to call them farmers was stretching the definition. They were aptly called *veranda farmers* because they managed their farm from the comfort of their verandas rather than out in the pastures and fields with the workers. In most cases, their agricultural and pastoral interests, although vast, were seldom more than hobbies or a means to raise extra cash to further indulge themselves in the few luxuries available to them in that far-flung corner of the Empire.

The second requirement was that they be an adherent of the hedonistic school of philosophy. Not that any of the group had studied the philosophical reasoning behind hedonism, although the topic had come up around the dinner table on occasion, but they had at least to be in agreement with the spirit of hedonism: that pleasure was the only intrinsic good.

The second requirement would normally constrain membership to those conforming with the first. Hedonism was not a practice of the poor, and certainly not of the vast majority of Kenyan farmers, who could only survive by long and arduous hours trying to coax a living out of the soil.

Although there was no stipulation on the age of members of the group, they tended to be around the thirties and forties. Dana's sister, Averil, was typical. She was thirty-five, slim and attractive, and had shared Dana's interest in a free-spirited life when they both lived in London. At fifty-two, Edward was the oldest, and Polly and Dana, at twenty-nine, the youngest.

All Zephyrs were married or at least in partnerships except for Ann, who was invited and agreed to remain a part of the group after her husband returned to Britain following their divorce. The odd woman caused no problems, as none of the women objected to an extra woman in any activities involving couples, and many of the men preferred it.

Dana and Edward would greet their guests with a cocktail, accompanied by an army of servants who would whisk suitcases away and carry buckets of hot water to fill baths in the *en suites* to the bedrooms. As they prepared for dinner, Dana would circulate between the rooms refreshing drinks and stopping for a chat as her guests bathed or dressed.

Although a few dabbled in cocaine, or *bhang*, as marihuana was locally called, alcohol was the social lubricant for the evening and Dana liked to use the first cocktail to set the theme for the games that would follow dinner. It might be a Lime Daiquiri, a Blue Velvet or a White Lady. The clue for the game of charades would therefore be lime, blue or white.

Dana loved to entertain. She and Mary, the Kikuyu cook, spent hours discussing recipes. The plain fare that usually comprised most people's meals in Kenya would never do. It was four courses of French cuisine at its finest, miraculously prepared in Zephyr's Spartan kitchen annex.

By sundown all the guests had bathed and were assembled on the veranda for more cocktails. They were dressed in their pyjamas, which had become *de rigueur* for their gatherings.

Many of the group grew experimental crops and the conversation often centred on what plant had worked and what hadn't. Even many crops that had been initially successful ultimately succumbed to some blight or pest — another casualty of the unusual combination of tropical sun by day and sub-alpine air at night.

On the weekend just past, Dana thought she'd excelled herself.

After ablutions, the evening progressed as many had. The drinks flowed, and everyone shared their news and gossip. Polly — who prided herself on always having the latest gramophone recordings — had taken charge of the music.

Dana soon declared it was time for dinner. She took them into the dining room where a large polished table was set with silver platters, crisp linen napkins and crystal glasses. An urn of soup was ceremoniously placed on the table and the feasting began.

Wine was scarce in Kenya, but whisky was not. At seven thousand feet, the alcohol combined with the altitude led to lively discussions. There was much talk about upcoming social events in Nairobi. Race Week — the biggest social event on the calendar — was discussed in detail although it was still some months away. The group planned to go to Torr's Hotel, which was renowned for its dance band.

After dinner, and more drinks, the staff were sent to their quarters and the party retired to the large sitting room where Polly put a new Fats Waller recording called 'Ain't Misbehavin'' on the wind-up gramophone player. Everyone danced in the glow of the open fire and the flickering light from several tall candelabra.

After more alcohol and more dancing it was time for games. They commenced with charades. Dana had chosen some risqué themes that encouraged participants into suggestive poses. Soon, everyone had joined the spirit of the game and the excitement built.

Dana had then announced she had a new game and produced a large sheet, which the men strung up across the room.

Dana had explained the purpose of the game was to identify the person on the other side, but only by feeling through the sheet. A successful guess won a key to one of the bedrooms, to which the couple retired for the remainder of the night.

The men had gathered on one side and the women on the other. The female team chose one among them to stand at the sheet while one man after another groped through the sheet to try to guess the identity of that person.

The roles had then been reversed, but the women had insisted that the men undress before they made their play. The game, and the night that followed, had been hugely successful.

Dana's Zephyr dinner parties brought a touch of excitement to what might otherwise be long periods of inactivity and boredom. One of the few rules was that the affairs must never be allowed to become serious. Sexual contact outside the dinner parties was forbidden.

Edward also insisted that Dana not become pregnant. He said there must be no doubt over the paternity of the heir to the earldom. When the time came to plan a family, they agreed they would reconsider these arrangements. It was a plan that had suited Dana perfectly well until lately, when she started to wonder about having a family.

She remembered family outings with Edward's daughters from his first marriage. Dana approached them with dread: she felt the girls resented her for causing their parents' divorce. Even though she knew this was untrue, she felt helpless to deny it. She also felt threatened because she and Edward had no children of their own. It was the reason she had pressed him to start a family early in their marriage, but after several months and visits to the specialists, nothing happened.

Childlessness was a void in Dana's life, but she knew that her unfulfilled longing for a family was not the only reason for her melancholic mood: she couldn't decide if she would now sacrifice her way of life for the sake of a child.

On an impulse, she decided that the best medicine was to take one of the horses for a ride.

* * *

Inside the stable, the sun shot a bolt through the golden drift of dust suspended in the fusty air, which was heavy with the cloying, sweet odour of horses and fresh dung.

Her best Race Week chance, Toby, the gelding, had his muzzle deep in the feed trough, which her stableman had recently filled. He flicked his tail in recognition as Dana came near to scratch the white poll between his twitching brown ears. He was a simple creature, a good runner when it suited him, but feckless when he was not in the mood. What put Toby in the mood was a secret Dana had yet to discover. He could win a race on a whim, then just as easily drop his head and run like a dog in a mud bath. If Toby was to win during Race Week, Dana had to spoil him with attention and enough rich fodder to put him in the right frame of mind to compete. Even then, it would be a matter of luck.

She saddled up and led him outside.

Dana set Toby off in a canter and they were soon on the high, dry plateau, with the air warm in her hair.

Above the eighty-acre fenced wheat crop, Dana drew the horse to a halt. They were both panting. Dana patted Toby's smooth neck, whispering to him. She often came here among the foothills of the Aberdare Ranges to think. There was something about these high ridges, touching the clouds, and the ravines that cut deeply into their flowing green flanks that commanded respect. It was a perfect place to unravel her thoughts.

The wheat was surrounded on three sides by the brooding forest that had been subjugated by men for the purpose of farming — but never completely defeated. Small tree shoots sprang up among the grass clumps in the hundred-yard clearing before the wheat fence. Vines threw curled tendrils into the air above it, finding nothing.

The last breath of the day's breeze sent a shiver through the wheat stalks and then they were still. The silence was profound.

Dana always felt that the plateau was pensive when the sun was dying and the air still. She now revisited the thoughts she'd had below on the veranda and tried to explore her unease. Was it unease or just impatience? Impatience with Edward, who always wanted things his way. He had promised her she could have a child when they returned to England, but there was no knowing when that might be. She knew he had a plan to rejuvenate his finances while in Kenya, or at least to pay his creditors from an inheritance from one of his many well-heeled relatives, but time was not on her side. She was approaching thirty; but it was not only her age. What worried her was doubt over whether she could conceive at all. The doctor told her after the abortion she'd had at age seventeen that she might not be able to become pregnant again. The uncertainty made her fret; she wanted to know one way or the other.

With the breeze gone, a mist came sneaking from the dank forest, drifting in coils, low to the ground and across the grassy spread before the wheat.

A bird's call came from the forest. And another. It was the time of day when they gave one final song to celebrate the sun before it sank behind the horizon. There was the guttural, three-note call of a francolin; the coy snicker of a laughing dove.

A long-tailed sunbird darted from the forest — a flash of metallic gold and olive green. It was being pursued by its mate.

The unmistakeable call of a hadada ibis came from the trees behind her. *Haw, haw, haw*, it screeched — a terrible sound, like the voice of a disgruntled god. Dana felt a shiver run down her spine. As if to confirm her ill feeling, the forest fell silent.

Toby snorted nervously and shifted his weight from side to side.

'Ssh, fella,' Dana said, a soothing hand on his neck.

She ran an eye along the line of forest. Nothing moved except the topmost branches of the tall podocarpus trees and that wisp of mist at ground level. Then she felt, rather than heard, a heavy thud and a soft, rumbling sound.

Deep among the undergrowth the foliage moved; there was a loud snap, like a dry branch broken underfoot.

The rumblings grew louder and Toby took a number of steps backwards. Dana tightened the reins. 'Steady, boy.'

The leading elephant's enormous head, probing trunk and sweeping tusks parted the foliage as the massive beast stepped from the tight growth of the forest and into the wide cleared space before the wheat fence. She came on without hesitation although Dana, holding her breath, was sitting astride Toby not forty yards away. The old matriarch, with tattered ears and a tusk missing the last foot of ivory, led the herd — elephants of many sizes — in a slow and very deliberate procession. They came abreast of Dana and it was too much for Toby, who snickered his fear.

Dana was afraid to make a sound. She considered letting Toby have his head so they could be off, galloping down the hill to safety, but there was something mesmerising about the procession passing her: the mass of bodies; the single-minded, trancelike, step-by-step tread. Even the calves were able to keep a dignified pace beside their mothers or aunts.

Dana felt there was something strange happening. It was not the normal movement of a herd of elephants — and she'd seen plenty. It was more like a religious procession: the priest carrying the swinging incense burner, followed by altar boys, the choir and the congregation.

The ground shook with the elephants' footsteps. The belly-rumbling sounds were quite plain now, although she still couldn't say whether she heard them or felt them.

The herd's path took them towards the setting sun and the wheat fence, where the suspended dust and rising mist threw a golden halo around them.

The matriarch barely paused at the stout wire fence. It was laid flat in a stride and she and the following herd carved a deep furrow into the wheat field as they ploughed into the misty gloom in single file.

It had only taken minutes for the herd to appear and then, just as swiftly, to disappear through the wheat and over the hump in the land. They didn't even pause to feast on the grain, but continued on towards Lake Naivasha, following some ancient imperative.

Dana relaxed the firm hold she had on the reins and let Toby head for home, but the spectacle of the old matriarch elephant, doggedly following her instincts to ensure the survival of her herd, had touched Dana.

She decided that some things could not be stopped or ignored. All animals were born with certain instincts, and were driven by them. Otherwise they disappeared from the earth. Perhaps it was time for her to free her own instincts too.

CHAPTER 14

Sam was confined to his cabin for most of the journey from New York. His old enemy — seasickness — laid him low again.

He rented a hotel room in Southampton to recuperate before continuing his journey, and met an old merchant seaman in the bar who commiserated with him.

'Green tea,' he said, when the topic of seasickness came up. 'Take it three days before sailin' and ye'll be right. I couldn'a spent thirty-six years at sea without me green tea.'

Sam promised to give it a try, but he was already on board, bound for Mombasa, before remembering to take it.

It tasted dreadful, but he persevered.

Three days out of Southampton, Sam could confidently leave his cabin and take the air on deck. After a further day he was able to join his fellow passengers in the dining room at dinner.

An African fellow — possibly a Kenyan by his accent — sat at a neighbouring table. He was outspoken and confident and had an opinion on every subject raised, which Sam was able to follow in detail as the conversation on his own table had died soon after pleasantries were exchanged.

The man was charming and all the women at his table appeared to hang on his every word.

There was something familiar about him, and Sam watched him as he rose from his table. Although he met Sam's gaze as he passed, there was no hint of recognition. On the other hand, Sam was now quite sure who the other Kenyan was.

It had been a lifetime's experiences since they'd met, but the mannerisms were the same and the voice, now even more resonant, had the same inflections and compelling qualities as before. He spoke like a man who expected his listeners to believe that his every utterance was important. The piercing eyes had intensified and seemed to be lit from deep inside his head, which, even as a boy, had been big and shaggy like a lion's.

Sam excused himself from his dining companions and followed the man out onto the deck. He found him standing at the railing, smoking a cigarette and gazing out across the Atlantic. The light of an almost full moon threw a broad silver shaft across the ocean and the glow of the man's cigarette illuminated his chiselled features.

'Excuse me,' Sam said. 'I believe we know each other.'

The man was immediately on guard, like an attack dog waiting for the signal to lunge. 'I think not,' he said, and the softness of his tone belied the tension in his shoulders and the set of his jaw.

'It was many years ago,' Sam said, this time in Kikuyu. 'It's Kamau, isn't it?'

He was a head shorter than Sam and, as he looked up at him, his eyes narrowed in thought. He peered at Sam for some moments before suddenly exclaiming, 'My God! It's Wangira. Samson Wangira.'

Sam nodded. 'Johnstone Kamau.'

He continued to stare at Sam.

'Samson Wangira,' Kamau repeated, nodding slowly as the silence built.

'Returning from abroad, as you are,' Sam said.

'Yes, I've been in England for a year. What about you?'

'In America. For quite a lot longer.'

Sam didn't intend it to sound like a boast, but as Kamau turned to face the ocean it was obvious that he had taken it that way. Kamau took a long draw on his cigarette, then threw it into the water.

'Well,' he said, squaring his shoulders. 'I imagine we'll have plenty of time to talk about the good old days.'

The sarcasm was obvious.

Sam didn't respond.

Kamau said a frosty good night, and Sam watched him walk towards the door. Before he'd gone far, he turned back to Sam.

'By the way, Wangira, I have changed my name.'

'Again?' Sam said, recalling a tense conversation they'd had when little more than children. 'How many names does one man need in his lifetime?'

He shrugged. 'Names can change to suit the circumstances.'

'You seem to find many of those circumstances,' Sam said. 'So, what am I to call you these days?' He refused to let Kamau play his little game of secrets.

'My name is now Kenyatta. Jomo Kenyatta.'

* * *

Sam avoided Kenyatta whenever possible for the remainder of the journey, but there was no avoiding his pontificating at dinner, even from the other tables.

Earlier that first night he heard Kenyatta tell those at his table that he'd been to England on a study tour sponsored by the Kikuyu Central Association. His considered opinion, from which all present could now benefit, was that the bourgeois clique running the country were imperialists of the worst order.

And he wasn't finished with the luckless British settlers at his table; they were about to make their start in the colony.

'Are you people aware of the latest atrocity inflicted upon us Africans?' he said. 'Every native man and woman must wear on their person, every hour of every day, a little identity badge called a *kipande* — a pass which contains their personal and financial details and a record of any work they have done for the whites. Can you imagine that occurring in your home country? I think not. Can you also imagine how easy it is for a disgruntled employer to destroy the good record of some unfortunate worker who he might have taken a personal dislike to, by recording something damaging on his card? He could put *indolent* or *petty thief* or *insolent*. The African has no opportunity to contest it, and can be given a stiff punishment if he attempts to alter his *kipande* himself. This is what you are going to in Kenya, my friends. A country whose original owners are not allowed a vote. They are governed by foreigners and forced to wear labels like common farm animals.'

Kenyatta's story of the *kipande* surprised and concerned Sam. He hoped it was just another case of Kenyatta sounding off for the sake of it, but if true, it meant that the country's administration had their foot on the throat of the local population.

He tried to imagine his proud father being told to conform to such a degrading situation. He was quite sure he would fight it, and would be in gaol as a result of it.

He was glad to be going home to see for himself how much his country had changed.

* * *

The rusted wreck of a small steamer reared from the fringing coral reef as the SS *Medina* entered Mombasa's turquoise-hued harbour.

Sam stood at the railing of the upper deck and breathed in the scent of spices and the inimitable odour of tropical decay. It was hot: hotter than he recalled it.

Ahead, the white coral-stone houses' red-tiled roofs stood out among coconut palms and mango trees, bright red hibiscus and bougainvillea, and the succulent deep-green leaves of the frangipani.

It took him back to the time when, years earlier, he had boarded a similar ship to take him to America via England. He could remember his excitement as they'd set sail. Until that morning he'd never seen the sea, and the prospect of being surrounded by the boundless expanse of the Indian Ocean had sent shivers of apprehension down his spine. Now it was just another journey, albeit one about which he had mixed feelings.

With the shores of Kenya in sight, he allowed himself to think about home. He recalled his childhood and a game played in the dust with small smooth stones. He couldn't now remember its name but he and his friends could play for hours or until a fight erupted to end it. The animosity was forgotten the moment the next game began. There were his trips to the market where his father would, on occasions, magnanimously buy a hand-span of cane sugar for each of his many children. Sam smiled when he remembered the joy such a small treat could yield. Even the work in the maize field with his mother and siblings could become a game of hide and seek when the smaller children disappeared among the tall stalks.

He was returning jaded by his year of solitary confinement in the forests of Vermont and in need of revitalisation, but he wasn't sure if he was prepared for a return to his friends and family. He had lost touch with them when Sister Rosalba suddenly stopped writing. If it hadn't been for the loss of Ira he might have remained in America to continue his great adventure with the country.

The *Medina*'s steam pistons clunked rhythmically as the ship angled towards the new concrete wharf. Sam could hear the longshoremen chatting and joking in the cadenced tones of the Swahili tongue. It had been a long time since he'd heard it and, although he had been fluent before departing, he now struggled to understand some of the connotations. He imagined it was the nuances of the coastal people's Swahili that eluded him.

He joined the queue of first-class passengers at the head of the gangway, and felt a tug on his suitcase. A smiling porter introduced himself in Swahili.

Sam answered in English, which had become heavily seasoned by his elocution lessons in the Bronx and his time in the west.

'America?' the porter asked.

Sam found it easier to lie than to admit his failings in Swahili.

'Sure am, buddy,' he said with as broad an American accent as he could manage.

Sam turned and found Jomo Kenyatta wearing a derisive smile.

* * *

Sam realised his assumed American-ness was useful. At least some of the prejudice he might otherwise receive as a native in his own land was avoided: when people thought he was an American, even a black American, they were at least courteous.

That is not to say that the whites immediately accepted him on equal footing, but when he appeared sufficiently wealthy to afford fine accommodation and expensive clothes, they begrudgingly treated him with respect. Even the usually patrician landed white settlers paid him small courtesies, treating him almost as one of their own. Since his travel papers were not yet finalised, and no one quite knew where to place him, he hadn't yet been compelled to carry one of the hated *kipande* passes.

It amused Sam to let the deception continue and, as a result, he made no attempt to speak in Swahili or to lose his American accent.

In Nairobi he booked into the Norfolk, the best hotel in town, where his fine London linen and New York suits soon won him a nomination for membership of the Muthaiga Club — the gathering place of local business leaders and the upcountry gentry. Once installed at the club, he was introduced to many well-connected people eager to help him find a business opportunity in Kenya.

It was a week later when, leaving the Bank of India building on his way to a company agent's office, he saw a familiar face on Government Road. It was an old man from his village — a friend of his father's — driving a cow towards the market. He was wearing the traditional long brown cloak, leather sandals and beaded necklaces, with a large cylindrical tobacco tin fitted as an ornament in his stretched earlobe.

A rush of memories swept him to thoughts of his family and village. He could see his mother in her food garden, his father tending the cattle and children running everywhere. He stood at the kerb watching the old man until he disappeared into the crowd on Government Road.

CHAPTER 15

Sam sat back in the carriage, unsure if his impulsive decision to visit his home had been wise. He had changed; he worried that his family and friends in the village would feel awkward in his presence. Perhaps he would appear to them more of a *mzungu* than a Kikuyu. Would he be able to talk to them at all? So much had happened to him that would mean nothing in Igobu.

The process of change had happened slowly — too slowly for him to notice while in America — but now that he was heading home, his early years in the village came from what seemed like a different life.

The train line now extended past Thika to Nyeri, then all the way to Nanyuki. Progress.

From Nyeri he hired a car to take him to Igobu, but had to abandon the journey five miles from the village when the pitted road reverted to a footpath.

He carried his jacket over his shoulder and wound up his sleeves, but still arrived at his home village hot and sweaty.

When he walked through the village outskirts, the dogs barked and the children ran screaming to their mothers. A small and inquisitive crowd gathered at the outlying huts. Finally, someone recognised him and a howl of ululations arose from the women. The crowd approached; many hands patted him tentatively, and once his identity was confirmed he was seized and almost carried to his family home.

Igobu had changed very little. There was a handful of new family compounds, here and there a hut sported a corrugated-iron roof instead of the traditional thatch, and of course a batch of new children swarmed about the common space. Otherwise he had landed in exactly the stamping ground of his own childhood. His head swam with disorientation.

His father came out of his tent, puzzled by the commotion at his door. He remained a big man and perhaps even still the strongest in Nyeri Province, but to Sam's eyes he had shrunk. They embraced, but their conversation was hesitant, like that of two good friends separated by the years sometimes is. His father's mannerisms had changed. No longer did he thrust out his barrel chest and look over his nose as he talked: he was more reserved, even a little unsure.

Sam's mother came from her hut, at first not recognising him perhaps because of his Western clothes, but she soon dissolved into grateful tears, wailing and slapping a hand into his chest as she rested her head against it. She told him she'd never forgiven him for leaving the village, but thanked Mogai for his return.

When the crowd had dispersed and Sam sat with his family, feeling quite uncomfortable in his suit, his grandfather arrived, frail and querulous.

'They say this is how my name is written,' the old man said, pointing to a piece of card he removed from a canister hanging around his neck. 'And this is the mark of my finger. They say I must carry this everywhere I go!'

He turned the card to Sam then looked at it again, studying it as if it were something he'd not seen before.

He made a face and added in an incredulous whisper: 'And I must show it to any *askari* who asks to see it.'

'*Guuka* hates the *kipande*,' his father explained. 'The rest of us are used to it now. What can you do?' He shrugged. In the old days Kungu would have been incensed, storming around the village and demanding the chief take action.

'And now we are Kee-nya,' his grandfather continued. '*Kee-nya!*'

'So I heard, *guuka*,' Sam said. 'A new name. Just another change, ah?'

His grandfather gave him a disbelieving look. '*Pah!*' he said, and spat into the dust before walking away.

'He is in poor health,' Sam said to his father, preferring to comment on the more obvious physical changes than to the more worrying change in his grandfather's character and disposition.

* * *

Sam walked alone to the mission school. It had been one of the first to be established in the region and Sam was there when it was built. The roof of fronds was steep and much higher than the squat traditional huts that the Kikuyu built, but the men of Igobu built it as requested by the missionaries.

After the first wet season, when the chill rain swept in on the wind from the mountain, many parishioners stayed away and the men were again co-opted into supplying labour and materials, this time to add frond-panel walls. But in the next dry season it was too hot, so they cut large window openings into the new walls to allow the light and cool breezes to enter. Sister Rosalba had planted white roses around three sides of the church.

Father O'Dwyer made monthly visits from Nanyuki, thirty miles away. He came in his little donkey trap to say mass in the *makuti* church. Sam had been mightily impressed by the priest's vestments, which could be red, purple or green satin, depending upon the liturgical calendar. The ochre-painted, feather-clad medicine man, so feared and respected by the Kikuyu, was colourless in comparison. The vestments alone had won many converts.

During Sam's time away, the church had been enlarged by the addition of two thatched annexes, one each side under the original high thatched roof. It was no longer the elegant, soaring structure he remembered. Now it appeared to be just a bigger, fatter version of the squat Kikuyu huts that surrounded it.

The school had gained an additional thatched classroom. He stood in the playground as the children trooped past him with round and curious eyes.

The teacher, obviously a nun, but wearing a lighter form of the Consolata Sisters' habit, came towards him.

She smiled and said, 'I'm Sister Sirena.' There was a question in her eyes, but she resisted voicing it.

'Hello, Sister. I am … I was a student here. Many years ago, obviously. But I am wondering if I might see Sister Rosalba.'

'No, I'm sorry. Sister Rosalba passed away years ago.'

'Oh …'

'I was sent out from Rome as her replacement.'

'I see. How did she … Had she been ill?'

'No. It was an accident. I understand she was very proud of her roses. White roses. A little innocent vanity about her name, perhaps.'

'Her name?'

'Rosalba — white rose.'

'I see.'

'I'm told she was having trouble keeping her roses safe. An old female elephant would come some nights to pluck and eat every last one of them. Sister Rosalba would rush outside and chase her away. One night, she went out, thinking it was the same elephant, but it was a young bull.' She wrung her thin white fingers together. 'It must have been awful for the sisters. She had been thrown to the ground and ... crushed.'

Sam thanked her and headed back to his parents' compound, but he wasn't ready to meet more friends and relatives. He took a side path that he recalled led to the stream that supplied the village. It was at this stream he'd once seen a leopard, thinking it was an *irimu* — a spirit. He remembered he almost wept at the power and the beauty of it; even now there were tears in his eyes recollecting it.

But it wasn't the memory of a leopard that brought on his melancholy. It was Sister Rosalba's face that came back from beyond his years of absence. How could he have so cruelly ignored her letters? She had given him a hunger for knowledge, even when that knowledge was difficult to accept. *If God didn't dwell on Kirinyaga, where else could he live?* It was she who had planted a seed in his mind that sprouted as soon as the light of an opportunity appeared. It would have taken so little effort to respond to her letters, and to have her pass on his love to his family.

He could see her bustling among the children, her veil flying behind, while in pursuit of some urgent matter, probably a child in distress. Sam recalled her as always busy, always hurrying, but what had she achieved? Within the context of his experiences in America he now knew more about the life Sister Rosalba had left behind in Rome, or whatever other city had been her home. How could she leave that sophistication and find satisfaction in teaching dirt-ignorant kids in a little place like Igobu? And then to die here, suddenly and ignominiously, under the large flat pad of an elephant. It was too bizarre and too wasteful of a life that might have achieved something useful elsewhere. He tried to imagine his own life continuing on the path he was taking until Ira lifted him from it. He shuddered.

He returned to his father's hut, his eyes still hot with tears, but he had lost the ability to socialise. His family pressed him to stay overnight, but he couldn't. He realised the village where he had spent his childhood could never again be home. He left, promising to return another day.

As he headed back to his car, he realised he would find it difficult to keep his promise to return. He had changed too much. It brought to mind another conversation with Sister Rosalba.

He'd been to see the *mondo mogo* for a love potion to use on Mothoni. The nuns didn't approve of the tribe's witch doctor, and Sister Rosalba challenged him about his beliefs.

'Samson, Samson,' she'd said, shaking her head. 'I know it must be hard for you. On one hand you want to have a good education, one that will see you enter the white man's world. The Lord knows you have the ability. But on the other hand you are first a Kikuyu; and you are now about to become a warrior.'

'Yes, Sister,' he'd said.

'Do you remember what we have taught you about the Kikuyu ways?'

'Yes, Sister.'

'And you remember what we've said about the games you boys play with the girls at this time of your life?'

'Yes, Sister.'

'Hmm, then what is it to be?'

Sam didn't understand the question.

'What do you want to be, Samson? A Kikuyu warrior or an educated man?'

Remembering his reply now, he was wryly amused by his younger self's naivety.

'Why can't I be both?'

Impossible. He couldn't be both. Not then; not now. His time in America had irretrievably changed him. There was now no choice. The country was racing towards a European culture. He was no longer a warrior. He wasn't sure if he were even a Kikuyu any more.

CHAPTER 16

Dana awoke with Edward's freckled arm flung across her body and the sheets in a tangle. His chest rose and fell with the rhythmic breathing of sleep and he was softly snoring. She had always found it slightly distasteful to awake beside the man she had been intimate with during the night. It was one of the reasons they didn't share a bedroom.

She knew Edward preferred to sleep where he fell at the end of love-making, and last night Dana had been prepared to be accommodating.

In fact, the whole evening had been composed to please Edward. Dana had unashamedly set out to seduce her husband so he would be in a favourable frame of mind for the matter she intended to raise with him. She knew he would be difficult to convince, but equally, she knew she had to try.

The night had begun as it usually did. They dressed for dinner, although there was just the two of them. She wore a clinging silk gown that swept the floor. It was a little old-fashioned and she seldom wore it, but it was Edward's favourite.

They made small talk while Faizal, their Somali servant, served the soup. During the appetiser — a very tender guinea fowl — Dana began to act a little flirtatiously. After Faizal had served the impala and coconut main course, Dana told Edward she was wearing the pink suspender belt that he particularly admired under her gown. This sparked his interest, but then during dessert she added that she was wearing no underwear. The night's progression was then almost assured.

There was a soft knock on the bedroom door. She slipped out from under Edward's arm and, at the door, took the tea tray from Faizal.

'Edward,' she said, as she placed the tray on the table beside her bed. 'Edward, darling. I have your tea.'

Stirring, he snuffled a form of reply.

'Come, darling. Take your tea. It'll pick you up.'

He opened an eye then closed it again. 'Thank you, darling,' he mumbled.

'Come on,' she coaxed. 'You were a lot more energetic last night, my dear.'

He smiled and lifted his head. 'Thanks to your shenanigans,' he said.

Dana chuckled. 'I didn't hear you complaining.'

She had to admit, it had been a successful seduction, culminating in her sitting astride him, suspender belt intact, and riding him to his climax.

He sat up and fondled her bottom through her silk dressing gown as she poured his tea.

'Now stop that,' she chided, and moved out of his reach to add the milk and sugar.

She sat in the armchair and watched as Edward took a tentative sip of his tea.

'Ahh ...!' he said, predictably. Dana could place a bet on which of the many vocal rituals he could use in any one of a range of situations. They included his little homily — God ...! Save ...! The King! — as he climaxed.

She let the tea revive him before beginning the conversation she'd spent days planning.

'Edward, darling?' she began.

'Hmm ...?'

'You know that we've discussed the matter of having a family of our own.'

There was a pause before he acknowledged her. 'Yes ...'

'Well, I've been thinking about it quite a bit lately.'

She waited for a response. When it didn't come, she went on. 'And I think that now would be a good time to start trying.'

He replaced his cup on the saucer. 'Now?'

'Yes,' she said, keeping her gaze on the bedspread rather than let him see the uncertainty in her eyes.

'Have you considered our lives here?' he asked. 'We would be most circumscribed by any attempt at a pregnancy. I presume I don't have to remind you that it was your extramarital affairs that put us here in the first place.'

You mean your debts, she thought, but kept her retort to herself.

'Your, ah, *needs*, Dana, gave rise to our decision to delay that sort of thing. Neither of us is suited to a monogamous relationship. We both know that.'

Dana knew it was silly to want a child under their present circumstances, but logic had taken flight at dusk on the hill as she watched the matriarch elephant lead her family from the forest to the distant lake.

'Couldn't we just try, and not change anything else?'

'That's preposterous! And have you get pregnant to god-knows-who? No, it will never do. We will stay with what we agreed; and when we go back to England, well ... we'll review the matter. Until then, I shan't hear another word on the subject.'

The African sky was ink black behind the stars. Across the heavens, the diamante band of the Milky Way was scattered like an unloved trinket. A shooting star appeared like an arrow piercing a black velvet curtain and was quickly gone.

Cool air spilled from the high ridges of the Aberdare Ranges. It rolled onto the farm's high eastern pastures, gathering the earthy scent of mist-moistened grass, then ambled through the vegetable *shamba* with its rows of beans, leeks and tomatoes. It played with the petunias around the veranda, where Dana reclined in a cane swing chair gazing at the silver sliver of the moon suspended in the sky like a lantern.

Midnight air, she called it.

The farmhouse, named Zephyr by her overly imaginative husband, creaked and sighed when the cool breeze arrived after twelve hours of hot equatorial sun. Edward had built Zephyr in the style familiar to any Englishman: two storeys, a short veranda skirting the main entrance, bedrooms each side of a central hall, whitewashed brick walls with protruding casement windows and cedar shingles that ran to the steeply pitched, corrugated-iron roof.

Midnight air. Dana enjoyed the symmetry of it: the warm gentle breeze by day, and the cool breath of night — the bold interloper — sneaking like a lover through the bedroom window when all is quiet.

But it was already five in the morning. Dana had been unable to sleep and had lain awake on her bed for hours in anticipation of the excitement of the coming morning. When she finally conceded that sleep was impossible, she pulled on her khaki slacks, her pale green shirt with the many pockets and her leather vest to ward off the morning chill. Walking quietly down the hall, she passed Edward's bedroom and the snuffling snores that always followed a night on the whisky, and entered the study, where she took her .350 Rigby Mauser and a double-barrelled shotgun from the gun rack.

She loved the Rigby, but hated the shotgun. The Rigby was slender and potent. Its twenty-six-inch blue-grey barrel could deliver death at great distance and it had a satisfying recoil that knocked Dana's slender frame backwards if she were not properly braced.

The shotgun was ugly and heavy and, with the Rigby, too heavy for one gun bearer. She included it because Bill Judd had told her it was good insurance at close range, but it meant she would have to take Benard, the new boy, to help Jonathan, her regular gun bearer.

The fourth member of their safari would be Ndorobo, who would lead her to her quarry. On dainty feet, the little hunter would scamper into the hills above the farm where he would use his magic to find the hiding place of her lion. 'The night I was born, a lion was also born,' he'd once said in answer to her question about his hunting skills. 'He my brother. I know what he know.' It was the longest conversation he'd ever had with Dana, preferring at other times to use signs and grunts to make himself understood.

In the east, the hulking, shadowed shoulders of the Aberdares appeared against a faintly lighter sky. In silhouette they were enormous, and seemed more savage with their many folds and valleys concealed in the darkness. Among those secluded undulations, in the dappled grassy clearings before the hills merged into the bamboo forest, Dana's lion would be waiting. She wondered if it would know it was she who had already, if unsuccessfully, stalked it. Would it know that when it wandered into her domain it had set in motion the process of its own destruction? Would it know at the moment of its death that it was not a great white hunter who had bagged it, but a mere woman, part wanderer herself?

It was the anticipation that thrilled her. Knowing that the wilderness she was about to enter might prove deadly made her skin tingle. It was like the interval — the heart-stopping moments — between the meeting of eyes between man and woman, and the confirmation that the desire was mutual.

She let her mind wander languidly back to the previous weekend's dinner party. It was a great success. Her present favourite was Archie who, like his wife, Polly, was a great dancer and the life of the party. But it wasn't a matter of choice in these matters, it was luck — that's what made it so exciting — so she had to wait and see what the cards would bring.

'I see you, *bibi*,' said a voice from the gloom.

She'd not heard him approach. She seldom did. 'I see you, Ndorobo,' she said, although he was still concealed in darkness.

'And *bwana*?'

'Sleeping.'

Ndorobo always asked, but Edward never joined them on safari. In these matters he chose to let his young wife do as she pleased.

She stood, pushed her fringe back, and captured it under the rim of her hat.

'Bring Jonathan and Benard,' she said. 'We go.'

*   *   *

In the Kenyan highlands, dawn never comes languidly from sleep. It leaps upon the landscape like a ravenous beast, devouring morning mists, tossing golden dawn colours into sleeping valleys.

Jonathan had arrived at the house owl-eyed, but as soon as Dana handed him the Rigby, he slung it over his shoulder and was immediately alert. Not so the young Benard, who shuffled his feet and let the snout of the shotgun dip dangerously close to the dirt until Jonathan gave him a poke.

Ten minutes from the house, Ndorobo spotted the lion's spoor in the damp soil and pointed it out to Dana. The huge pug mark, missing a claw on the front left paw, proved that the lion that had been stalking Edward's cattle for weeks was still around. Ndorobo had told her it was an old male with a limp, the likely result of a battle lost while trying to retain leadership of the pride. 'He old. Very angry,' the little man had said sagely, making a pantomime of the old male skulking away, leaving his harem to the younger, stronger victor. He shook his head sadly, and added, 'Very angry, that old one.'

Without the pride to assist in the hunting, the old lion had grown hungry and in desperation had found easier game on the Northcotes' farm. He had taken two calves and a heifer in the last month.

Ndorobo scuttled among the grassy tussocks in a widening circle, head down, his skinny rump bobbing, until he found what he was seeking. A second set of pug marks told him the remainder of the story, which he shared with Dana without speaking a word. He swept his hand from the hills to the valley and pastureland. The big male had come out of the Aberdares, used the rocky outcrop on the property's northern boundary for reconnaissance, and passed the point they were now standing before heading to the home pasture where the herdsmen had confined the cattle for safety. Another gesture indicated the uproar from the dogs — the barking that had awoken Dana around midnight — at which time the wily predator had retreated back into the hills to await a more favourable opportunity to seize one of Edward's cattle. Ndorobo pointed the way.

Since arriving in the White Highlands nearly five years before, they had always been *Edward's cattle* because, as he seldom neglected to remind her, his was a landed family. Her antecedents were tinkers and fortune-tellers, as was obvious from her olive skin and emerald eyes. In any case, her motivation was not to save Edward's precious cattle: the lion had broken into the enclosure where she kept her thoroughbred mares and killed one before the staff chased it away.

It was the third time she'd made the journey into the hills in search of the old killer, and she was determined to avenge her loss by making it her last.

Ndorobo headed towards the hills, with Jonathan and the Rigby a pace ahead of Dana. He carried the rifle as all good gun bearers should — over the shoulder pointing forwards, with the butt towards Dana. It meant that the Rigby was in arm's reach and in a position ready to be immediately fired. Benard took up the rear with the back-up heavy-calibre shotgun.

They climbed towards the east where the sun was still mercifully concealed behind the high timbered slopes. Even the previous farm owners, in their enthusiasm to supply the colony's insatiable demand for good timber, had made no attempt to clear this rough and broken land, smothered in meandering vines. It remained an outpost of the forest: a reminder of the wilderness that lay beyond the next valley. Occasionally a mist, or the remnants of a cloud, floated past them down the slope, tangling itself in the lianas and wrapping the roots of the soaring podocarpus trees in diaphanous silks.

They approached the crest of the first ridge and sunlight began to spear through the thinning trees. Dana shielded her eyes, but she did so reluctantly, not wishing to miss the first moment when the glorious panorama was revealed.

Suddenly the ground gave way in a downward tilt. The trees parted and the morning breeze, Edward's zephyr, was chasing the mist away, revealing the verdant pasture with only the occasional giant podocarpus or cedar thrusting into view. This was where Edward had been fattening his cattle and where the old lion had found them easy pickings, before the herd was moved closer to the homestead.

The valley swept past their vantage point through an arc from Mt Kipipiri, carrying a tributary of the Malewa River northwards before it made its long sweeping bend to the west to join Lake Naivasha. On the far side of the valley rose the Aberdare foothills, the first part of which was the formidable and almost impenetrable bamboo forest. It was in this valley that Dana would have to take the lion. To hunt it in the forest was madness.

Dana and the gun bearers rested while Ndorobo inspected the trail ahead. He soon returned, his head bobbing with excitement.

'*Hapa chini!*' he said, pointing into the valley. '*Simba!*'

Dana needed no Swahili to understand he'd found the lion. She and the others hurried after him to the rim of the valley, where Ndorobo stopped and pointed downwards. Straining her eyes for many moments, Dana saw what appeared to be a grass clump move. She took her field glasses from Benard, and focused them on the movement. It was her lion, but it was in a clearing and would be impossible to approach without being discovered.

Ndorobo had the answer. He pointed out a game path that swept away to the north and would keep them behind a small ridge until reaching the valley floor. On the north side of the lion there were at least a few small shrubs and trees that would offer some cover. The wind was favourable. Dana nodded and they hurried on behind Ndorobo, who moved across the slope as if floating a few inches above it. The others struggled to keep up.

Dana was perspiring when they reached the broad flat plain. There was a succession of scrubby bushes ahead, but the lion, if it were there at all, was lost in the grass, which stood three feet high in parts.

Ndorobo seemed to know exactly where it was concealed and led her on without hesitation. After a few moments he stopped and held up his hand, listening. After the exertion of the stalk, where she was almost doubled over to remain below the grass height, Dana could hear nothing but the blood pulsating in her ears.

Satisfied, Ndorobo continued, this time signalling to her that the lion was close and that they should be very silent.

He took a brief glance over the grass tops and nodded. Dana raised her eyes slowly. The old male lion was still in the clear, but only fifty yards from it was the beginning of the bamboo that ran up the side of the hill parallel to the lion's path. It appeared to have spotted them.

Jonathan silently handed her the Rigby. Keeping her eye on the lion, she took aim, waiting for it to show more of its flank, but it held its position, staring at them.

Dana knew the best range to attempt a lion kill was no more than sixty yards. She estimated the lion was just under a hundred yards away — the absolute limit recommended for a free-standing shot with the Rigby.

The lion opened its jaws, yawned, and ran its tongue around its lips. It then turned towards the bamboo.

Bill Judd swore that a lion always gave one last look before disappearing into cover.

Dana smiled over the gun sights as the lion paused before the bamboo, turning for one last glance at its pursuers. It was the target she needed and she slowly squeezed off a shot.

The lion grunted in pain and surprise. It staggered, but didn't fall, then took two large bounds, disappearing into the wall of bamboo.

'Damn!' Dana muttered.

She now had no choice but to follow it into the bamboo forest, where only one of them could emerge alive.

* * *

Dana faced the wall of bamboo. The culms were the thickness of a man's leg. It seemed impossible that a full-grown male lion could have penetrated it, but upon closer inspection she could see slender pathways meandering among the golden poles.

Ndorobo was studying the pool of blood on the grass. Head down, he followed invisible signs to a small gap in the bamboo screen. He pointed at a bloody smudge on the bamboo and slowly shook his head.

'Yes ... I see it,' Dana said, nodding in acknowledgement. 'And it's not going to be easy to find him, is it?'

Ndorobo shrugged to indicate it would be wise not to try.

'I have to go in after him,' she said to herself, though by their expressions she could see that Jonathan and Benard had heard her.

'You don't have to come,' she said, and took the Rigby from Jonathan. 'Wait here until I get back.'

She pressed through the bamboo poles without further thought. It didn't pay to think about the wounded lion, lying invisible somewhere in the almost impenetrable green forest.

For her first fifty tentative paces she could see no more than five yards ahead, but then the bamboo thinned and there were patches where the old stalks had been flattened, probably by an elephant, and she could see twenty, even thirty yards ahead. Provided she spotted the animal in time, she had enough room to fire off a shot before it was upon her.

She stepped carefully. The bamboo was like a cocoon, trapping the heat and blanketing all sound. The short panting breaths were surely too loud to be hers. Sweat trickled from her forehead and down the back of her neck, saturating her shirt.

A sharp *crack* stopped her. She couldn't say from what direction it came, but it was close. She waited for another, but nothing more came. She moved on, cautiously stepping over the fallen poles, but at the same time trying not to take her eyes off the space ahead.

Another sound, this time from behind her.

She swung about to find Ndorobo there, his finger to his lips. A few paces behind him was Jonathan, shouldering the double-barrelled shotgun.

Her relief gave way to a moment of anger. She might have shot them, but when Jonathan gave a small shrug she forgave him, and nodded. Their support gave her courage and she moved ahead again with a little more determination.

After a hundred yards, Ndorobo gave one of the little tongue-clicks he used to attract her attention. Dana could see no sign of trouble ahead and turned back to him. Ndorobo's eyes were fixed on a thicket of young shoots, and he slowly raised his pointed finger to it.

Dana could see nothing.

She blinked away a bead of sweat, and suddenly the lion was full in her vision, bounding towards her.

She swung the Rigby to her shoulder, fixed the front bead on the lion's charging body and, without consciously aiming, fired first one barrel and then the second.

The lion careened on, carried forwards by its massive bulk, but its legs had gone and it tumbled to a halt not more than ten feet from her. Dead.

Ndorobo danced around the body, making high-pitched keening sounds, then he slid his knife from its scabbard and, lifting the lion's massive head, held the knife under its throat. He cocked his head to ask the question.

'No,' Dana said. 'I don't want his head. Or his mane.'

The lion's mouth hung open, revealing his enormous fangs. One of his large incisors was missing. She found the fang beside a small pointed stone that the lion must have struck with its jaw as it crashed to the dirt at her feet.

She picked it up and studied it. It was a clean break at the gum line. It might have been the incisor that ended her life if her shot had gone astray.

She slipped it into a pocket on her vest.

CHAPTER 17

Sam returned to Kenya just when the world developed a taste for coffee. Prices were on the rise and the growing prosperity in Europe and America assured continuing expansion of the market. The Kenyan highlands had the perfect climate for it and many white settlers, including some of Sam's new business associates, had planted coffee there.

Growing coffee didn't interest Sam greatly, but the highlands' refining facilities, consisting of a number of small and inefficient sites, did. He could see an opportunity to form a coffee cooperative where the growers agreed to send their beans to a single efficient refinery and share the savings.

He drew up a partnership deed with a number of big growers, who agreed to send their coffee to Sam for refining. Others promised financial support. In the meantime, Sam bought a coffee farm with good prospects to realise a sizeable capital gain when the refinery arrived and made it more profitable.

Sam made an appointment with George Caruthers, the manager of the Nairobi branch of the Bank of South Africa, and a member of the Muthaiga Club, to formalise the bridging finance.

Caruthers showed Sam the contract, the details of

which had already been informally agreed in the convivial atmosphere of the club.

'It all seems to be in order,' Sam said. 'We plan to start without delay.'

'I can assure you, Sam, the bank is behind you all the way. And if I may say so, I've seldom seen a better business case than yours. Well done.'

'Thank you.'

'Now, if I could have your signature here, and here,' the banker added, pointing to the contract.

'I just need to correct the name. Williams,' Sam said.

'Oh, is it not Samson Williams?'

'I was using the name Williams in America. But since this is a legal document, I'd better use my real name, Wangira.'

Caruthers straightened in his chair. 'Wangira? But that's a ... a *native's* name.'

'Kikuyu, to be exact.'

Caruthers's smile faded and his usually florid face paled. 'But ... then ... um, it's not possible ... I mean, I'll have to change the contract papers.'

He scooped the documents together.

'You'll have to leave them with me,' he said, obviously annoyed. 'You should have told me.'

'I didn't think about it until now. But what's the problem? Isn't it just a matter of correcting what we have here?'

'Oh, no,' Caruthers said. 'We have to have them retyped.'

He told Sam it would take another couple of days to renew the papers.

Sam was annoyed about the delay, but when he returned to the bank later that week, a teller told him that the bank's offer had been withdrawn.

Sam insisted on seeing the manager, but when he did, Caruthers simply said the bank had reconsidered its exposure to the coffee market and had decided not to proceed further. The matter was beyond his control.

*   *   *

Three days later, Sam went to the Muthaiga Club for the usual Friday evening gathering of his associates. Only John Drew was there; he had been Sam's strongest supporter and the driving force behind the syndicate. Sam was relieved to see him, and was confident Drew would have a suggestion on how to handle the setback.

'You should have told us, old man,' Drew said.

'What difference does it make if I'm an American or not? It's still a good idea, and I'm prepared to put up nearly half of the money.'

'Ah, but well … You see, we thought it was American money. And we assumed there was other American money backing you.'

The discussion went nowhere.

Early the following week, Sam bumped into Kenyatta on River Road.

'You know, Wangira,' he said after a brief greeting. 'You are so stupid … Did you actually believe these white fellows would do business with a Kikuyu?'

Sam was taken aback that Kenyatta could even know about his business arrangements. He struggled to make a reply to the effect that he had no idea what Kenyatta was talking about.

Kenyatta smiled. 'It's really quite a small town, you know. And there are Kikuyu ears everywhere.'

'You can't always believe what you hear,' Sam said dismissively, hoping to close the matter, and curtly said goodbye.

'It's an unwritten rule. Whites don't lend to blacks,' Kenyatta said, not yet ready to let the matter drop. 'I know. I've seen the Bank of South Africa's books. Not a single African name on them. A few Indians. But not a Luo, a Kamba, or a Kikuyu anywhere.'

'You seem to know a lot about the country's business world, Kenyatta. And with that Savile Row suit, you look like a proper English businessman yourself. What line are you in?'

'The only business that matters a damn,' he said. 'Politics.'

Now it was Sam's turn to smile. He knew of Kenyatta's political activities. 'A Kikuyu in politics. What a waste of time. I understand there's actually a written law against that.'

'Presently. But that will change. In time. Eventually there will have to be a lot of change. You know that.'

Sam shrugged. He was still smarting from Kenyatta's taunts and didn't want to continue the conversation. He started to move away.

'You're a bright fellow, Wangira. There may be a place for you in the Kikuyu Central Association.'

Sam knew of the KCA and Kenyatta's role as general secretary; he'd recently been promoted from editor of the association's newspaper. Sam had read a few issues. They were quite mild. The administration seemed happy to ignore them.

'I don't think so,' he replied.

'Think about it,' Kenyatta insisted.

Sam might have been interested, especially after his treatment by the bank and his former business partners, but not with Kenyatta in charge.

'Thanks, but no thanks.' Sam continued down River Road.

'One day you'll see the need for us,' Kenyatta called after him, determined, as usual, to have the last word.

* * *

Sam was shocked by the treatment of people who were prepared to go into business with him when they thought he was a black American, but not when they found out he was a countryman. He'd seen the ugly side of racism in America, and hated it, but until that time he'd believed the whites in Kenya to be guilty of the lesser crime of paternalism. Now he could see it for what it was: racism pure and simple.

It disheartened and disillusioned him, but it was the institutionalised discrimination by the bank that got him angry.

He felt quite sure he was not the first or only black Kenyan to have failed to raise finance for a business venture. He wondered what others did when faced with similarly prejudicial treatment.

He made enquiries in the villages around Nairobi and found dozens of situations where a small loan would make an enormous difference to people's lives. A farmer might need cash for seeds or farm implements; a pastoralist a loan to buy a good blood-stock ram or bull to improve the quality of his stock. None of the banks were interested, even though the risk could be secured against assets and was covered by the better returns in crops or produce. Even an Indian immigrant who wanted to start a small *duka* by the roadside could get a loan, but an African villager wanting to do the same could not.

This brought to mind Ira's words encouraging him to use his inheritance to improve the life of his fellow Africans. He began to see his failure to secure finance as a sign that he should follow Ira's advice. But it wouldn't be a charity. It would be a business based on growth through participation at the village level.

He began a trial operation in a handful of villages where he knew the chiefs were honest and able to keep accurate records. For those who were not adept at record-keeping, he insisted they employ someone from the village, usually a young man educated at a mission school, to do the job for them.

It was the beginning of Sam's bank — a bank with no name, no buildings or offices, no office bearers, and no commission agents except the local chiefs who put forward clients they knew and trusted and who collected the repayments. Word spread. Within a year Sam had hundreds of small loans placed with dozens of villages all over Kikuyuland.

Occasionally there were defaulters who couldn't meet the cash repayments and he sometimes found himself the owner of a cow or a dozen goats. This sideline grew into a profitable stock and produce business that he spun off into a subsidiary while he remained focused on the bank.

When a storm or fire destroyed a crop or other livelihood, the chief would send word to Sam who would visit to arrange a loan. He soon became every small farmer's hero.

His reputation spread, and he was soon a successful businessman, unknown in the white business community, but one much admired and loved by his fellow Africans.

* * *

Sam bought a run-down farm in Kiambaa, about ten miles out of Nairobi, surrounded by twenty acres of good pasture and forty acres of forest. He enjoyed the solitude, but was seldom there, spending his time travelling to the various villages that constituted the branches of his bank, now called the Rural Bank of Kenya for legal reasons imposed upon him by the government.

He retained his small flat in the grounds of the Muthaiga Club although he let his membership lapse. He now found it unpleasant to deal with members of Nairobi's business world. He had lost money on the coffee scheme, but it was the manner in which he had been treated by the bank and the shallowness of people he had liked and respected that created the lingering distaste. He now preferred to deal with simple African farmers and had no need for the social life and the type of company on offer at the Muthaiga Country Club.

However, he found the Muthaiga flat convenient when he was in town on business, and kept up the rent. It was also useful on the occasions when he found a woman whose company he could enjoy for a day or so. He managed to avoid any longer term commitments, no matter how charming these women were in his bed, because his busy upcountry schedule kept them at a safe distance.

The expansion of the bank was restricted as Sam was its only source of capital, but it grew slowly, enabling him to extend his network into other tribal areas. Soon he had at least a small presence in most parts of the country.

*   *   *

Jomo Kenyatta came out of the New Stanley Hotel as Sam was entering it. Kenyatta had gained a few pounds and now sported a beaded rimless hat and a colobus monkey-fur fly whisk. As far as Sam was concerned, the outfit was all part of Kenyatta's self-promotion.

The two men seldom met, but when they did, it usually resulted in a mental joust or a barely restrained slanging match.

Kenyatta was also sporting an attractive woman on his arm. He'd heard that Kenyatta had married a white woman during his stay in England, but had left her there, choosing instead to find a Kikuyu wife more appropriate to his political aspirations.

'Ah, Wangira,' Kenyatta said, beaming. 'You are looking extremely fine this morning.'

There was no doubt he had the attributes of a successful politician. His smile could be quite disarming.

'Thank you, Jomo,' Sam replied. 'Good morning. And good morning to you, ma'am,' he added, nodding to the woman on Kenyatta's arm.

'You see, my dear. That's what an American education can do for you. Good manners, like a true southern gentleman.'

But Kenyatta didn't bother to introduce his wife, preferring to go on the attack.

'I hear you are becoming something of a capitalist in the reserve,' he said.

'You mean the Rural Bank of Kenya? It fills a need, don't you think?'

'You're missing the point, my friend. You can't buy the Kikuyu's allegiance with shillings.'

'What makes you think I need allegiances? I'm a businessman, meeting people's requirements.'

Kenyatta studied Sam in silence for a moment. He had the most compelling eyes. Sam had seen him demolish opponents in a debate before he opened his mouth by the sheer power of his presence. Sam was aware of Kenyatta's tactics and didn't flinch under his gaze.

'If you'd come along to our meetings, as I've suggested on so many occasions,' Kenyatta said, 'you'd find out that the most important thing on every Kenyan's mind — in fact, every African's mind — is his land.'

'You may be right. But I know he also needs the capital to develop it. Kenya can't build a nation on subsistence farming. That's the fate of a colony; and we must make whatever changes needed to make the break.'

'*Pah!* While you were being indoctrinated into capitalism in America, I was studying agrarian reform in Russia. They know about the importance of land. Every communist is a Kikuyu at heart.'

'But is every Kikuyu a communist at heart?' Sam countered. 'I don't think so.'

'I'm an African first, a Kenyan and a Kikuyu. Where do you stand?'

'What makes you think I'm not all of those things?'

'Because you are too close to the imperialists. You and your fancy American accent and your British banker's ways. Be careful, my friend. Be very careful.'

'Why?'

'Because there will come a time when you will be asked to state your allegiance. And your very life may depend upon your answer.'

* * *

As Sam was visiting one of his bank's representatives in the Embu District, four hundred miles away in Abyssinia, a dense cloud darkened the sparse grasslands. It floated over Abyssinia's southern border with Kenya where the candelabra euphorbia stood like sentinels and the spiky sansevieria blades poked holes in the breeze. Turkana herdsmen tending their goats and camels looked up in awe at the cloud, and Turkana children ran to find hiding places.

Locusts had not been sighted in East Africa for more than thirty years; and what had now caused this plague of biblical proportions was unknown, but they came from faraway Egypt in such numbers they turned day into night.

Millions of them died in the wide waters of Lake Rudolph, but countless billions more continued south, into the wooded hills of the Pokots' land, and onwards to the Mau escarpment where they tumbled into the Great Rift Valley like a black avalanche. There they devoured maize and millet, leaving the fields festooned with broken and bare stems. Beans, barley, lucerne and other forage crops disappeared under their onslaught and, when all the more nutritious vegetation was taken, they consumed even the thin covering of valley grasses — the last vestige of fodder for the herds and flocks.

The swarm climbed the Kikuyu escarpment and, for a day or so, Sam and the farmers of the fertile hills outside Nairobi held their breath, hoping the prevailing northerly winds would sweep the plague southwards down the Great Rift Valley. But the northerly dropped and the locusts invaded the lush food gardens of Kikuyuland.

When the plague descended on Kiambaa, Sam watched the sky darken, then dashed outside to rally his staff to pen his small herd of cattle while he lassoed his horse and took it to the stable.

For the remainder of the day, all he could do was to stand at the window of his Kiambaa farmhouse and watch his twenty acres of pasture disappear. Meanwhile, in Nairobi, no garden, bush or vegetable was spared.

Within three months, it was obvious to Sam that many of his farming clients would be forced to default on their loans.

He thought the bank might survive the disaster, but another, even greater calamity was looming much further away. It had nothing to do with drought or pestilence, famine or flood, but it was to prove more devastating than any to Sam's finances.

Many thought the Wall Street crash of 1929 would remain a localised phenomenon, but it grew tentacles that eventually reached to all corners of the world.

* * *

From the blistering heat of the Amboseli Plains came a Maasai herder carrying his load of cattle hides to the trading post at Namanga. He dumped the fifty-pound load on the weighing machine at the *duka*, and waited while the Indian trader weighed them.

He had no use for cash other than to pay his poll tax; and he made this, his annual pilgrimage, in preparation for the tax collector's visit.

The herder couldn't read or write, nor could he tally the various brass weights being loaded on the other side of the balance, but he knew to within half a pound that his load was the same as the one he'd carried forty miles to Namanga last season.

The trader scribbled figures on a pad, counted out a few notes and a handful of coins and slid them across the counter to the herder.

The Maasai's face fell before he erupted into a tirade in Maa, jabbering about the price offered and accusing the Indian of thievery.

The Indian understood not a word, but the Maasai wasn't the first in his store to complain. He returned fire in Parsi, telling the Maasai that it was not his fault that the Mombasa merchants had dropped the price from thirty shillings per frasila to six.

The Indian trader couldn't explain the price fall. He knew nothing of the chain of events following the collapse of the New York stock market. He didn't know that unemployment in Europe had soared and people could no longer afford new shoes. Shoe stores cancelled standing orders. Footwear factories slashed their leather orders and the tanners cut back their demand for hides. Dramatic falls across all the industries were occurring all over Europe.

The Maasai herder had never heard of Europe and most of Sam's clients never suspected events on the other side of the world could affect them. They did, and the Rural Bank of Kenya went into bankruptcy.

*   *   *

Sam paid off the few staff he had, and let them take any of the farmhouse furniture or fittings they wanted. Then he sold the Kiambaa farm for a pittance, and prepared to move his personal effects to the Muthaiga flat.

The new owner would take the cattle and other livestock. Sam wanted to keep his horse, but couldn't find a way and regretfully left it too.

He took the little mare for one last ride over the dirt tracks surrounding Kiambaa. He enjoyed riding and it reminded him of his time as a horse-breaker in the American west. Riding always made it easier for him to think; and he again wrestled with the question of his future. He had very little money. His only asset was Ira's electrical business and patents, which were virtually worthless in the present financial situation.

As he unsaddled the mare he knew that if he could somehow find work with horses it might overcome the bitter taste left from the collapse of his business, and the financial ruin of his many clients.

CHAPTER 18

1930

Edward was reading a month-old *Times* from the latest bundle of newspapers to arrive from London.

'Do we really think this Labour chap, Ramsay MacDonald, can do anything about this wretched Depression?' He gave the page an irritated flick. 'The market's still floundering, for goodness' sake!'

Dana picked up the *Sunday Express* and casually flipped through the articles as she nibbled on a piece of toast. She fingered the lion-fang pendant sitting at her throat on a short silver chain. Faizal's friend had done an excellent job, setting the base of the fang in a silver clasp with a tiny lion motif engraved on it.

She knew enough to let her husband have his rant, which he didn't confine to politics. He fumed about the state of the roads, the weather and anyone who displeased him. In the latter case he could carry a grudge for years; the 10th Earl of Seddon was not a man to forgive and forget.

After ten years of marriage, they'd arrived at something of an accommodation. Edward would allow her the occasional extravagance, such as her taste for fashionable clothing, and she would not remind him that he had lost most of his family's inheritance by gambling too heavily on the stock market. The crash of the year before was still recent enough for her to draw down on the reserves of Edward's guilt in cash for her occasional extra needs. He had, however, recently drawn the line at adding to her small thoroughbred herd, and no prompting of implicit guilt, sexual persuasion, or sulking could alter his decision.

Jonathan appeared at the end of the veranda. He shuffled his feet to indicate he had something to say.

'Yes, Jonathan?' she asked.

'There is a man to see you, *memsahib*.'

'What man, Jonathan?'

The servant mumbled his reply.

Edward, scowling over his newspaper, demanded he speak up.

'It is the matter I told *memsahib* about many days ago,' he said, this time louder than necessary.

'Blasted impertinence!' Edward snorted. 'Keep a respectful tongue in your head, boy, or I'll have it knocked out of you.'

'It's all right, dear. I'll go see to it.'

Dana followed Jonathan outside, through the flower garden enclosure, to the stable. It was one of her casual farm labourers, an itinerant, who a month ago had asked Jonathan to pass on the information that he knew someone who had a small horse. Curious, Dana had pressed him for details. The horse was for sale, he'd said, but when Dana questioned him further, he became coy and defensive, as if he had inadvertently admitted to a crime, which Dana thought could quite possibly be the case.

She dismissed the fellow, not wanting to become involved. If this someone knew someone who had stolen a horse, then it was not a matter for her. She was not about to assume the position of policeman.

It was not uncommon that a native came to her with a story fabricated to grab her attention. Invariably there was no substance in them. She assumed they liked her to think they knew someone important — important enough to own something like a horse. Or perhaps it was just to gain the kudos for holding the *memsahib*'s attention for the few moments it took to spin a story.

She asked the man what he wanted this time and he again repeated his story about his friend and the small horse, but that the small horse was now sick.

'What do you want me to do about it?' she asked the man sternly. The thought of a sick horse disturbed her, but she was not yet convinced the story was genuine.

'My friend would like to know if the *memsahib* who also owns a horse would like to buy this beautiful small horse, which is also now very sick, and also maybe will soon die.'

The man's candour seemed to suggest he was telling the truth. Perhaps there was indeed a horse for sale, but what convinced her to investigate further was that this horse, small though it may be, might soon die unless someone did something about it.

She sent a small boy who had been idling near the stable to tell Edward she was on an errand and followed the man to a clearing in the forest about a mile away. It was surrounded by a thorn *boma* sufficient to keep the predators at bay, but too small for the horse, which, apart from being a runt, was on the brink of starvation. Dana could immediately see why. The enclosure had not a blade of grass. Whatever it might have had at the outset had long ago been consumed, leaving the packed, dry earth devoid of growth. Strewn around the enclosure were tufts of the near indigestible fibrous stalks of forest grass, of such poor quality as to be impossible to sustain the creature for any length of time. The little filly was not sick, it was starving. It was such a sweet thing, she was prepared to pay the man his price, but she didn't want to be accused of theft, so she asked how he came to have the horse.

He said another Kikuyu had given him the horse.

'I have not heard of any Kikuyu who keep horses,' she said.

He agreed and said that even he didn't believe the man was a Kikuyu because he wore *mzungu* clothes, but spoke Kikuyu fluently.

Dana had limited knowledge of such matters, but thought the little horse was an Abyssinian, meaning it was probably already at its full height, but the breed was famed for stamina and endurance. It was doubtful the filly had a pedigree unless generations of wild horses, bred within the confines of the towering canyons of Abyssinia, could be considered a case of line breeding.

She hadn't thought beyond getting the filly back to health, but as she led her to the farm, she formed an idea — an idea that might require some persuasion before Edward would agree. It was, however, an idea that excited her, and could help overcome the boredom of her isolation out there on the edge of the Aberdare Ranges.

* * *

Dana was emerging into the bright light of morning when she saw Jonathan returning to the yard at the head of his half-dozen men.

'Did you find him, Jonathan?'

'No, *memsahib*.'

She'd sent the men to scour the thickets around the farmhouse for her new yearling colt — the young thoroughbred she'd bought just after she rescued the filly from the forest.

She glanced at the filly in the enclosure beside the stable. In the months following her rescue, she had quickly regained her condition with the help of the nutritious Kipipiri grasses. She was a beautiful little mottled grey, with a snow-white mane and tail and a heart bigger than herself, and Dana had named her Dancer for her spirited high-stepping gait. It was her purchase of Dancer that had given her the idea of starting a breeding program.

The filly stood a good two hands shorter than Toby. Her elegant pasterns and fine cannon bones reflected her Abyssinian ancestry, which was an excellent start, but she needed to cover her with a good stallion. Toby was gelded, so was useless for the purpose. She couldn't afford to buy a tested stallion and hoped the colt would eventually prove his racing capabilities. That, however, was a couple of years away. She had no money for the alternative, which was to pay stud fees for a stallion to service Dancer, and Edward could not be persuaded to help.

Having failed to find the yearling near the house, she thought he must be in the high pastures. She would have to find him before the day was done. It was not beyond the bounds of possibility that another lion had invaded the farm's territory, but even a leopard or a hyena could be equally destructive if the colt remained outside the home pen overnight.

Dana went to the shed adjoining the stable, where Jonathan helped her fold back her roadster's canvas top. She pressed the starter button and thrilled to the sound of the motor as she warmed it with a few revs. She then drove across the grasslands towards the four hundred acres they held in the high ground.

Dana had purchased the Willys-Knight roadster from the president of the Muthaiga Club the previous year. She was immensely proud of its silver-grey livery, red spoked wheels and black guards and running boards. She loved to collapse the white canvas top for a breezy spin around Nairobi, scandalising those matrons who still thought it unseemly for a woman to drive. The car was a pure indulgence — a luxury she'd permitted herself before her interest in horses exhausted Edward's limited tolerance for such extravagances.

Not far from the house she scattered a herd of Thomson's gazelle, the stag's propeller tail flicking as he shook his tiny antlers in annoyance.

She checked the quality of the pasture as she drove. They'd been spared the worst of last year's locust plague but it had been unusually dry for the time of year and the grass was thinning quickly. She expected she would need to buy fodder for the horses before the rains came. Another expense.

A dozen zebras trotted off to a safe distance. Dana stopped the car and stood up behind the wheel to check the herd with her field glasses. It was possible the colt might have found comfort in the company of the zebras, but he was nowhere in sight. Upon reflection, she thought it more likely that the zebra stallion would have seen the colt as a threat and chased him off.

She drove almost to the edge of their cleared land, beyond which the forest held sway. She stood on the running board and scanned the edge of the savannah. A movement caught her eye. Almost hidden in the thin lines of trees, a couple of giraffes ambled through the cedar and podocarpus. A moment later they had melted into the forest.

The sun was high and Dana was about to turn the car for home when she saw a cloud of dust rising against the eastern sky. She squinted into the glare as she drove towards it.

A herd of about a dozen horses cut across the sloping grasslands towards the north, with a single horseman at the rear, keeping the stragglers and outliers under control. She was annoyed. There was hardly enough pasture for their own animals without sharing it with itinerants.

She stopped the car. Even from a distance, Dana could make out the quick dainty steps of animals born to be fleet of foot. The high-stepping hooves and perky angle of their tails showed spirit and strength. She thought there was a resemblance between these horses and little Dancer, her Abyssinian, but that was most unlikely. The Emperor of Abyssinia had declared it a crime punishable by death to remove any of the country's bloodstock from his mountainous domain.

The herd was now only a quarter of a mile from her but in another minute they would be into the steep valley and out of her reach. She tooted the roadster's horn. The herdsman turned towards her. Dana waved to him: she must know more about these magnificent animals. But after a moment's hesitation, the distant figure wheeled his herd over the rise and away — to where, Dana could not imagine. Certainly, she knew of no one in that vicinity who kept such animals, and the rider didn't look at all familiar.

It might have been just the shade from his broad-brimmed hat, but otherwise Dana would have said the rider was, most improbably, a black man.

CHAPTER 19

Dana bent beneath Dancer's neck and ran her hand down her foreleg. The filly's muscles twitched as if they were suspended on springs and she put her wet muzzle at the back of Dana's neck and snorted hot breath into her shirt.

'I know, girl,' Dana said. 'It's tender there.'

With the filly's continued improvement and her good showing on the training track, Dana had decided to enter her for the upcoming Race Week's events in Nairobi. Toby had not shown much in his training runs and Dancer had proved Dana's best chance of picking up a first and the much-needed cash prize.

Dana knew Dancer was well below her best the moment she checked her time on her early-morning workout. She also knew why.

'Don't worry, my precious. We'll get it right for you before Race Week,' she added, straightening up and putting her hands on her hips.

As she said it, she wondered how she could make it so. The little filly had developed soreness in her tendons and it had reached the stage where the pressure bandages couldn't alleviate it. Dana had alternatively tried massage, then rest, then light exercise. Nothing seemed to ease the situation. She sighed, her rising costs looming large in her mind. Edward was losing patience as fast as Dana was losing her capital. If she didn't score a win during Race Week, she would have to pass up her dream of becoming a thoroughbred breeder, and put her three horses out to grass.

She had foolishly given Edward an opening to vent his displeasure by raising the matter of a new dress that morning at breakfast.

'A new dress? Whatever for?' he'd said.

'Race Week is coming up. Actually, two new dresses.'

'You have a wardrobe full of beautiful dresses.'

It was true, but she knew Lady Gladys Cartwright would be there, leading her usual coven of Nairobi's moral guardians. She didn't want to disillusion her by wearing something respectable.

'Edward, don't be so plebeian. You know very well I can't wear any of those old rags. I'm an owner. What if Toby or Dancer wins?'

'My dear lady, racehorse owners are, by definition, never winners. It's always money. A new set of silks here, race entries and stabling charges there. Countless bits and pieces of leather. And God knows how the vet can charge so much for damn horse pills.'

'This lady horse needs *dawa*,' Jonathan intoned solemnly, interrupting her thoughts. 'Strong *dawa*,' he added.

Jonathan had a great belief in the power of Kikuyu medicine. It seemed they had a *dawa* for everything. There was *dawa* for making babies, *dawa* for ripening the maize, and *dawa* for making a man attractive to a woman.

'If this little sweetheart is going to win the Jeevanjee Cup,' Dana said, 'she'll need *juju* rather than *dawa*.'

Jonathan spat on the straw. The mere mention of magic made him nervous. According to Jonathan, it was a known fact that talking about *juju* was enough to give a malicious medicine man — should he have the mind — the excuse to use black magic against innocent people. Spitting helped to alleviate the risk.

'No, *memsahib*,' he insisted. 'Kikuyu *dawa*. We call it *mugaita*.'

Dana was absorbed in her thoughts. There was a vet in Nakuru who claimed to be successful with bad legs, but it was doubtful he'd agree to come so far when he was sure to be busy helping more influential owners prepare their horses for the upcoming season.

'This *dawa*, it is very good *dawa*,' Jonathan went on.

'Very well,' Dana said in resignation. 'Bring this very good *dawa*, and we'll give it a try.'

* * *

In the stable a week later, Jonathan lifted a gourd and poured a dollop of gunk into his hand.

Dana leaned over it. 'Yuk!' she said. 'It smells horrible.'

Jonathan beamed. '*Ndiyo*, *memsahib*. This a very fine *dawa*. Very, very strong.'

'What *is* it?' she asked, peering more closely at the substance. It was a green vegetable mash with small purple globules in it — perhaps berries of some kind.

'It called *mugaita*, *memsahib*.'

'You told me that, but what is it?'

Jonathan shrugged. 'It is … *mugaita*.'

Dana sighed. 'I don't suppose it can do any harm if we just make a poultice of it. Pour some in that bucket and smear it on Dancer's leg after her exercise walk.'

* * *

Dana watched as Jonathan trotted Toby out onto the farm's training track — a flat, cleared oval behind the staff huts. He was an able horseman, a skill that Dana had fostered, much to the surprise of her friends and neighbours. It was considered a poor investment to teach an African new skills because labour was so cheap. Why put an African on a horse when you could send a dozen on foot? But Dana needed someone to take the horses for rudimentary circuit training before paying a professional jockey to do the fine-tuning in advance of race days.

At the end of the training gallop, Dana clicked her thumb to stop the timer, but she already knew that something very strange had occurred that bright, crisp morning. A glance at the stopwatch confirmed it. Toby had lopped twenty seconds off his regular three circuits of the farm's training track. Toby, the lethargic, the fluky performer, Toby the indolent, the slacker, had just run his best time. Ever.

Jonathan brought him in, his smile indicating he'd also felt Toby had performed well.

'What did you do to him?' Dana asked.

'This Toby horse feeling very good this morning, *memsahib*.'

'But, I don't understand.' She looked at the watch again. 'He's run a mile rate of ... under two minutes.'

Jonathan couldn't contain his grin. 'Very, very fast,' he said, nodding vigorously.

'Well ... my ...' Dana was speechless. She was thrilled with the result, but perturbed that she couldn't explain it. Had it been his recent training regime? Dana's closer attention to his feed? Her insistence that Jonathan give him an extra rub down after his runs? None of it could explain his turnaround in form because even before

Dancer developed leg soreness, her times had not improved under the same regime.

Like many aspects of horse training, Dana found it a mystery, or as Jonathan might express it — *juju*. Magic!

* * *

There was none of the usual feeling of tedium in the Albion lorry as Dana, Jonathan and Benard made the journey down to Nakuru the next day. They'd been making the trip once a week since the training program for Toby and Dancer began in earnest. It gave the jockeys Dana had signed up for Nairobi the chance to get acquainted with their mounts, and the opportunity to give the horses their heads in a real race situation. The added excitement that day, which had touched all of them, was to test Toby on a proper racetrack and get a better measure of his apparently better times. It would also allow an assessment of Dancer's recovery — and her ability to compete with horses of Toby's newly improved ability.

After a couple of warm-up gallops, the jockeys trotted the horses to the fourteen furlongs starting point. Dana set the stopwatch, and a moment later the trial race began.

Dancer leaped to the front, as she usually did, but Toby's longer stride slowly gathered her in. As the horses passed Dana for the first time, Toby drew level with Dancer. Gradually but indisputably he continued to make up ground. At the end of the race he'd won by three or four lengths.

Dan Tucker, Toby's rider, walked the gelding back to the saddling area where Dana waited with a broad smile.

'He did well, didn't he?' she asked, as Tucker swung down from his mount.

'He did indeed. What time did he make?'

Dana checked the watch again to be sure. 'Twenty seconds better than his previous best,' she said proudly.

'My God! What have you been doing for him?'

'Why, I …' She didn't want to admit she had no idea. 'I suppose it's just the new workout schedule I have him on up at Kipipiri.'

The jockey didn't appear convinced.

'And better grazing,' she added. 'That little bit of rain has come at a good time.'

'I see, well, I'd say Toby has made a real improvement,' Tucker said with more conviction than she'd heard from him since hiring him. 'But why hasn't little Dancer seen the same improvement? On her previous form, she should be finishing ahead of Toby by the same three lengths.'

Dana turned her palms up and shook her head. 'I have no idea,' she admitted glumly.

'Maybe you need to think about starting Toby in the Jeevanjee Cup instead of Dancer.'

The prospect of swapping Toby for Dancer in the feature event of Race Week didn't appeal at all. She knew it was unprofessional, but Dancer was her sentimental favourite and nothing would please her more than leading the pretty filly into the presentation ring under the noses of Nairobi's society. She could see the look on Gladys Cartwright's face. It would be sweet revenge for all the scurrilous remarks she'd made behind her back.

Oh, she would do anything to wipe that supercilious smile from her face.

* * *

Dana strode down towards the Zephyr stable, Ndorobo trotting behind. Having complied with Edward's wish that she go to Nairobi before him, she was now keen to be on her way. It had only taken a mention of shopping to have Edward agree she should go a few days early.

She felt the first touch of warmth on her bare legs and glanced up at the sun. It was now well clear of the Aberdares, and she chided herself for her tardiness. She wanted the horses stabled in Nairobi by mid-afternoon, and her first gin and tonic in her hand by dusk.

She was pleased to find Jonathan already at the stable with the Albion lorry backed up to the loading ramp. Benard was slouching against the railings at the stable door. He straightened as Dana swept into view.

'Jonathan,' she said without breaking stride, 'have you loaded enough feed for the trip?'

'I am doing it just now, *memsahib*.' He hurried towards the hay bales, hissing at Benard to follow.

In the stable, Dana entered Dancer's stall. The filly snuffled a greeting. Running her hand down the neck to the flank and foreleg, Dana could feel the ripple of taut muscles under her fingertips.

Dancer accepted her probing fingers on the sore tendon. To Dana's inexpert touch, all seemed well.

'So girl, what are we going to do with you?' she whispered to the horse. 'Are you up to the St Leger? Will I put Toby in the Jeevanjee instead of you?'

Dancer dipped her muzzle into the feed trough.

'I feel you're the better horse for the distance, but Toby is doing so well in training.'

The filly continued to feed.

'I can't let Gladys Cartwright beat us, Dancer. I'll just have to go with the best I've got, and at the moment I'm afraid that's Toby.'

*   *   *

The Albion rolled out of the farm with Dana following in her roadster. She would stay with the horses until they had successfully negotiated the fifty treacherous miles from Kipipiri.

The first part of the journey entailed a steep descent from the foothills of the Aberdare Ranges into the Great Rift Valley near Naivasha. The next section — the climb up the Kikuyu escarpment — was the most difficult. Here Dana would take the wheel of the Albion, entrusting her Willys-Knight to Jonathan until they reached Kijabe at the top of the escarpment. She valued her horses even more than the roadster.

The remaining twenty miles into Nairobi were relatively safe, so Jonathan would again take over while Dana drove on to ensure the stalls at the racecourse were ready for her two mounts. Dana had taught the sharp-eyed Ndorobo to keep watch for potholes and to thump the dashboard when he spotted one so that Jonathan could take evasive action. It was a task she had no doubt Ndorobo enjoyed as much as Jonathan resented it.

Dana had eased back half a mile to stay out of the Albion's dust cloud. As she reached the Malewa River crossing, she came upon a small herd driven by the same lone horseman she'd seen a couple of weeks previously. This time he had no escape, trapped between the river and the road. She drew the roadster to a halt beside him. She was surprised to find he was someone's black employee.

'*Habari*,' she said, greeting him in Swahili.

'Good morning, ma'am,' he replied, touching the brim of his hat.

The accent confused her. 'Oh ... I'm sorry. Good morning.'

His smile was broad and, considering she had mistaken him for a native, quite generous. She dragged her eyes from his and studied his herd. They were as she'd at first suspected — Abyssinians.

'You have some very fine horseflesh here,' she said.

'Thank you. They're starting to put on a little condition.'

'Thanks to my husband's Kipipiri grass.'

'The Willys-Knight,' he said, running his eyes over the roadster. 'I remember you.'

'Well?' she said with a raised eyebrow.

'Well ... thank you for the short agistment. I appreciate it.'

'I should think an apology would be more appropriate.' A smile played on her lips as she said it. 'People up here don't take kindly to trespassers, but if you'd knocked on our door we would have been happy to help you out.'

'Well ... I wondered about that. But I thought that if a black stranger knocked on your door, driving a herd like this, maybe I'd be welcomed with a shotgun and a whole lot of questions, rather than a smile.'

'They are beautiful,' she said, again looking over the animals. They were mostly mares with a few yearlings or younger, and a couple of fine stallions. 'But, how ... Where did you get them?'

'As I said, a whole lot of questions,' he replied with a grin.

'Point taken,' she acknowledged. 'Let me put it to you another way. If a person was looking to purchase one of these animals, no questions asked, where would she look?'

He studied her for a few moments.

'Ma'am,' he said, 'if this wasn't the White Highlands I might make an exception and answer you. But since that's a leading question, and I'm still trespassing on your land, I'll just bid you good day and thank you again for the hospitality.'

He rounded his horse and gave a flick of his whip. '*Hah!*' he said, sending the herd trotting off.

Dana watched him go. She liked his style — the way he looked directly at her as if he knew what she was thinking. If he did, she thought, he might be very surprised.

CHAPTER 20

Pomeroy's on Sixth Avenue, just down from Torr's Hotel, was not only the most stylish clothing store in Nairobi, the tea salon he operated from kerbside tables was a favourite meeting place for women with modern tastes.

Meet me at Pomeroy's, Dana said in a message sent to her sister, but Averil was not yet at the tables when Dana arrived so she strolled into the fashion store, a thin line of cigarette smoke trailing from her long, ivory-tipped holder. She ran her fingers over the dress on the mannequin at the entrance, admiring the soft material on the bodice, and the felt of the fitted cloche hat. Flapper fashion was still in vogue among the affluent Kenyan settlers, and Dana adored it. She loved the short hems and straight lines. They suited her shape, and were perfect for dancing. The bobbed hairstyle, popularised by Coco Chanel, also pleased her. She couldn't imagine the task of maintaining her earlier bouffant coiffures out on the farm at Kipipiri without professional help.

She greeted the sales assistant, and ordered a pot of tea.

As she was waiting, Averil arrived with a flurry of kisses and greetings, before sitting beside her at the table.

'Oh, I do love that divine hat,' Averil said. 'It's the bee's knees.'

Dana touched a hand to it. 'Thank you. I barely had time to get into the Norfolk and freshen up before dashing here to meet you.'

Averil and her husband, Bill, had followed Dana and Edward to Kenya. Bill was one of the few among their group of friends who had been on the land back home in England. He was interested in cross-breeding the indigenous Boran cattle with good beef cattle. He'd bought a Devon bull from the line originally imported from England by Denys Finch Hatton who, like Edward, was a younger son of an earl. Bill was supportive of Dana's new thoroughbred scheme and gave her the benefit of his experience in cattle breeding.

'Is that a new dress?' Dana asked her sister.

'Hardly, but I'm about to shop for one. Will you help me choose?'

'Love to, but let me finish my tea; and while I do, you must tell me all you know about this new fellow, Whiteman. I hear he has a large stable and has entered several horses over the week.'

'Whiteman? Actually, it's Major Roger Whiteman. Formerly of the Coldstream Guards, apparently. He's married to a countess.'

'A countess with money, apparently.'

Averil leaned forwards, conspiratorially. 'Something of a dark horse himself, I understand.'

'How so?'

'Well, nobody knows anything about him.'

'That hardly qualifies for notoriety. I don't know a thing about ninety-nine per cent of Kenya's European population.'

'But they're nonentities, my dear. I'm talking about

society people. Speaking of which, Bill and I quite enjoyed your last dinner party. When's the next?'

'Thank you,' Dana said. 'I'm so glad you had fun.'

'Those saucy little parlour games you invented are very ... stimulating.'

'Everyone seemed to think so,' Dana said. 'Who was your partner for the night? Oh, yes, it was Archie — Polly's Archie. Oh, there's Gladys Cartwright across the road. Don't look. Ghastly woman. Did you read her letter to the editor the other day?'

'Wasn't it a scream? *Let us hope that the ladies in the member's stand use a little decorum in their dress standards this year.* But let's not bother about Gladys Cartwright; tell me, sister dear, what have you been up to lately? Any gossip?'

'Gossip?' Dana said, her finger tapping her bottom lip. 'I'm not sure it's gossip, but I've had a mystery man come calling.'

'Really?' Averil's eyes lit with interest. 'Do tell.'

'Well, he's tall, dark and handsome. A black American, I suspect, but absolutely smashing.'

'Sounds delicious.'

Dana told her about the herdsman and his horses and the brief conversation they'd had.

Averil began to chuckle.

'What is it?' Dana asked.

Her sister smiled. 'I was just thinking about how we've been discussing widening our dinner guest list with some more, well, interesting people.'

'Are you thinking about my dashing mystery man?'

'Exactly. And to make up the numbers, we could invite Lady Cartwright for the men.'

They burst out laughing.

* * *

Dana and Polly climbed into the rickshaw outside the Norfolk Hotel, deep in conversation. The two rickshaw boys needed no directions: it was obvious from the ladies' outfits that they were bound for the opening day of the Nairobi races.

The rickshaw gathered speed, with one boy pushing and one out front pulling on the pole. They left the green western rises of Nairobi behind, travelling past the line of Indian stores built on the swampy land along River Road that sold everything from a pound of nails to a bolt of finest Persian silk, to the racecourse, sitting on the hard black-cotton soil just short of the railway line.

The first day of Race Week had a party atmosphere; and it was the only time Dana could enjoy the fun. Her horses would not race until late in the week, but they would require all her attention in the days beforehand.

Although he was a keen racegoer, Edward, along with the other husbands, tended to skip the track on the first race day. They thought it more of a fashion parade than a day for serious racing, and were content to sit instead on the Norfolk's veranda, sipping gin and watching the world go by.

Dana dropped a coin in the leading rickshaw boy's hand and the two women joined the throng milling about the entrance.

The women's dresses reflected the current fashion of straight skirts, high hems and two-tone colour schemes. Being Race Week, the hats were an eclectic collection.

Polly wore a straight, pale blue dress, cut to just below the knee. It had a boyish look, with a high loose neck that she wore buttoned to the top. A dark blue floppy bow tie with trailing tails matched the long narrow waistcoat that had pale blue embroidered roses low on each side. Her hat was tall — Polly could use a little extra height — with a narrow curved brim that completely covered her short, dark hair.

Dana's dress had a neckline that plunged in a deep V and was made of a light, soft, cotton material in pale grey with cerise floral motifs. It was a similar length to Polly's, and seemed to float in the light breeze. A fabric belt was tied loosely below her hips. Her cerise hat had a wide downturned brim.

The sun was vertical and too hot. They decided to go to their seats and have a drink while awaiting Averil and their other friend, Georgina.

Climbing the steps into the grandstand, they passed Lady Cartwright in her reserved front-row seat. She gave Dana and Polly a nod and a chilly smile as she ran her eyes over the young women's outfits.

When they took their seats, six rows back, Dana said, 'That should fill out another letter to the editor.'

Polly giggled.

Averil and Georgina arrived just before the first race and the women retired for lunch in the large marquee on the grass behind the stand.

They returned to the betting ring to some excitement. A rhino had wandered from the *bundu* and held up the start of the third race. It gazed myopically at the mounted course marshal who tried to send it on its way, but then lowered its head and charged him.

It wasn't unusual to have a disruption of this kind on the first day of Race Week, though these were more typically caused by Thomson's gazelle or bushbucks. The racecourse generally lay fallow throughout the off-season and herbivores of one variety or another regularly took advantage of the tall grass. The previous year a herd of impala had taken up residence on the course and was soon evicted, but the rhino would not budge.

The course steward called for reinforcements and the bandmaster of the King's African Rifles' band rode to the infield with his rifle. The ill-tempered rhino gave him a baleful look, then lowered his head for another charge. The army man hit his target between the eyes and the rhino collapsed in a puff of dust where it had stood. The crowd roared their approval and the band struck up an impromptu 'For He's a Jolly Good Fellow'. A contingent of African workers hurried across the field and, with ropes and pulleys, they hauled the rhino onto a cart and trundled it away.

Race three commenced fifty minutes late, but the rest of the festivities unfolded as planned.

Dana decided to have a bet on the last race and wandered among the bookies, looking for good odds on her selection. A tall black man in a black homburg hat and grey suit caught her eye. He followed the American fashion of a short jacket with padded shoulders, which on his physique was quite eye-catching. He had his head in a race book and didn't notice her until she stood beside him.

'I thought it was you,' she said.

He studied her for a moment. 'Ahh ... the lady with the beautiful roadster,' he said.

'And the free pasture, apparently,' she said.

'Will I never win forgiveness for my sins?'

'You haven't asked it.' She gave it some further thought. Here was an opportunity. 'You might if you can tell me where you get your horses.'

'Why do you ask?'

'Because I need a stallion for my three-year-old.'

'The little Abyssinian grey.'

'Yes,' she said, wondering how he knew about Dancer. But he went on; distracting her thoughts.

'I'll keep that in mind if I find someone with an Abyssinian standing at stud.'

It wasn't the answer she wanted to hear. She suspected he could somehow arrange a horse himself, but was being coy because of Abyssinia's restrictions on their export and the Kenyan penalties should he be caught.

'You'll have to excuse me,' he said. 'I have to place a bet on the last.'

'Do you have a winner?'

'I think so,' he said. 'Archer's Post. It's worth a flutter.' He turned towards the bookies' ring. 'Until next time.'

Dana watched him go. She couldn't place his accent although she was quite sure it was from some part of America. He was unusual in many ways, and quite interesting, not the least because he was a black man with what appeared to be complete acceptance within Kenya's white society.

The starter's bugle signalled the call to the barriers.

Fifteen minutes later, Dana stood with her friends, cheering as the field thundered down the straight. Dana held a five-pound ticket on the horse the stranger had tipped her.

Archer's Post came in at twenty to one.

CHAPTER 21

Dana was pleased to see Jonathan and Benard giving the horses a rub down when she arrived at the track before dawn on Tuesday morning. Toby's great track times had given the men renewed motivation. As well as the bragging they could enjoy over the opposition stable hands and strappers, they knew a win would mean a big tip from Dana.

Her early-morning start was to discuss tactics with the jockeys and to give the two horses a good workout under race conditions.

Dancer had recovered from her leg soreness, but her times, although quite good, had not come up to Toby's standard and it appeared that Dana's earlier decision to run the gelding in the Jeevanjee Cup had been the correct one.

When the jockeys arrived they discussed how to arrange the training run and agreed that Toby should carry a light weight while Dancer would carry her real race weight to test her legs. The horses would gallop over the same fourteen furlongs set for the cup. Dancer would be entered into a shorter event, but Dana decided to race her against Toby to give the gelding a realistic race experience and to gain familiarity with the track.

The two horses cantered off to the starting point on the far side of the racecourse. Soon they were barely visible through the ground mist. Dana trained her field glasses on them as they jumped from the starting line together.

After a furlong, one of the horses had opened up a handy lead, which, by the turn, had become three lengths.

As they galloped towards her down the straight, Dana could more clearly see them, but there was something wrong. The horse that now had a commanding lead of about five lengths was not Toby the big gelding, as she had expected, but little Dancer!

* * *

After the training gallop, Jonathan and Benard led the horses around the walking enclosure to cool them before returning them to the stables for a vigorous rub down.

Dana had been sitting on a bench watching them for ten minutes, trying to fathom the situation. Dancer's time had improved slightly, but Toby had reverted to his previous plodding mediocrity. The form reversal was even more startling since Dancer had carried a heavier weight than her bigger stablemate. It just didn't make any sense.

Dana remained seated on her bench, thinking, as the boys walked the horses back to the stables. Her confidence plummeted. She had made a great deal of Toby's improvement to Edward. Now he'd want to know why it had changed so dramatically. Toby had improved his performance without her knowing the reason, and now had reverted to his old form, again without her knowing why. She couldn't admit to him that she didn't know.

'You don't look very pleased.'

Turning, she saw the mystery horseman — she still didn't know his name — had approached without her noticing.

'Oh … Hello.' She touched a hand to her hair. She must look a fright. 'You get around.'

He shrugged and smiled. 'A little. I'm Sam. Sam Williams,' he said, extending his hand.

'Dana Northcote.'

His clasp was firm, but his skin was surprisingly soft. He wore smart grey slacks, a grey homburg and a navy jacket. He looked like a horse owner or trainer, which made sense considering his presence in the stabling area. It was an odd combination: illegal smuggler and thoroughbred owner. He became more interesting by the moment.

'Do you have a horse entered this week?' she asked.

'No.'

'I see.' It put a dampener on her theory. She wondered how long she could persist with her quest to discover who he was and what he did without appearing rude. 'Then why come to the stables if you don't have a horse?'

'Why must I be looking for a horse? Maybe I'm looking for you.'

'Me? Whatever for?'

'To see if you backed Archer's Post,' he said.

'Oh! Yes, I did.'

'Then am I forgiven?'

'For your unforgiveable trespassing?' she said, smiling. 'You most certainly are. I won a hundred on him.'

'Wonderful! Then we're both winners.'

He was silent for a moment and it appeared he was weighing his next comment carefully.

'You have a wonderful smile,' he said at last.

Dana coloured. She couldn't believe she could be embarrassed by a compliment on her smile, but there was something compelling about him.

His smile wavered, giving her a glimpse of a previously unexpected vulnerability. 'May I buy you breakfast to celebrate?'

She hesitated a moment, before nodding. 'That would be nice.'

She wasn't quite sure what she had in mind by accepting his invitation. Maybe she simply wanted to know more about this man. Whatever it was, she decided to follow her instincts.

He took her to the member's reserve for a breakfast of toast and tea for her, and eggs for him, during which they had a lively conversation about horses and the racing industry.

The waiter refreshed their cups, and they sipped their drinks in silence.

'I feel you are unhappy about something,' he said.

She was taken by surprise, but in that brief silence she'd been reflecting on Toby's inexplicable reversal of form.

'Why do you think that?' she said to cover her confusion. How could he know?

'Black magic,' he said with a disarming smile that held such warmth and genuine concern that she briefly felt compelled to unburden herself on this charming stranger.

'I can read minds,' he added to encourage her to speak.

She was almost persuaded.

'Really?' she said, stalling. 'Yes … I suppose I am a little unhappy. I'm worried about my horse, Toby.'

'Oh?'

'Yes. You see, he's always had patchy form, but until this morning he'd been running some excellent times on the training track, but now … it's gone.' She sighed and shook her head. 'And I have no idea why.'

'I'm no expert,' he said, 'but I've bought and sold plenty of horses over the last few years. Maybe I could look at him for you.' His smile returned.

Why not? she thought. 'Well … thank you. That's kind of you to offer.'

The boys were again rubbing down the horses when they arrived at the stables.

'This is Toby,' she said, pointing to the first stall.

He ran an eye over the gelding, then nodded.

'And this is my little darling, Dancer.'

'She's very pretty,' he said, stroking Dancer's sleek neck, before giving it a firm pat. 'What's that he's rubbing on her leg?'

'Oh, that's Jonathan's special *dawa*. She had sore legs and we've been rubbing that into them over the last week or so. I don't know if it was the *dawa* or just nature taking its course, but her legs seem to be better now. We're still using it, just in case.'

'Can I see the *dawa*, please?'

Jonathan handed him the bucket of evil-smelling mixture.

Sam sniffed it, then looked at Toby.

'Are you using this on Toby?'

'No; he may not be the fastest, but he's not had any injuries to blame.'

Sam was silent for a moment.

'Back at Kipipiri, do you have separate stalls for the horses, like here?' he asked.

She thought it a strange question. 'No, they share a large stall.'

He took the bucket to Toby and offered the offensive goo to the gelding.

Toby dipped his nose into the bucket and nickered in appreciation.

Sam let the horse take a few licks before removing it.

'You say Toby's times have improved recently. Have you noticed any other changes?'

'Yes, I suppose he's been a little more sprightly.'

'Sprightly?'

'You know, active. He's never been a horse that likes to train, but recently he's been snorting and keen to get going. I imagined it was all part of his new fitness.'

Sam sniffed the bucket again, then turned to speak to Jonathan who appeared as surprised as Dana as she realised that Sam was speaking Kikuyu.

'It's *seketet*,' he said, turning back to Dana. 'The Kikuyu call it *mugaita*. Your man here, Jonathan, lets Toby take a few licks while he applies the poultice to the grey's legs.'

It still made no sense to her. 'What's that got to do with his times?'

'*Seketet* is a stimulant. It comes from the bark of a tree — I can't remember the name of it — and can be pulverised into a powder. The Maasai have traditionally added it to their tea before a battle. The Nandi use it as a painkiller and take it for weeks before circumcision.'

'A stimulant.'

'Yes. It explains Toby's recent form. His times improved while he had daily doses up at Kipipiri, but now he's in a separate stall, he can't steal it from the bucket.'

'Amazing. Did you know about this, Jonathan?'

'No, *memsahib*. All I know is it is very good *dawa*. Good for everything.'

'It's a side-effect not generally known to the Kikuyu. From the little chemistry I can remember, I think it's like an anabolic steroid — a stimulant and muscle developer. It's a good thing he's stopped taking it. It's dangerous.'

Dana's thoughts began to spin off in many directions.

'But no harm done,' Sam said. 'It seems he's getting back to normal — whatever that might be.'

Dana was deep in thought.

'So ... I'll be going then. Things to do before the races today.'

'Yes. Thank you for the information. Very interesting.'

He took her hand, holding it before saying goodbye.

She watched him go, knowing she'd see him again.

* * *

Sam had nothing in particular to do before the races started. He simply thought it prudent to take leave from Dana Northcote.

She was an attractive woman, with green eyes and bobbed, light brown hair tinted a honey colour that accentuated her olive complexion. She had a petite but well-rounded body. All in all, she was a real beauty — though if Sam were to name the characteristic that most appealed to him, it would be her boldness. He thought most white women were insipid creatures, deferring to their menfolk in almost every situation. Sam liked women with spunk. And Dana had it.

He smiled at the nonsense that had crept into his brain. It was the very impossibility of seducing a white woman, particularly one as attractive as Dana Northcote, that made thinking about it such a waste of time. There was no chance she would be interested in him. He'd done some research and discovered she was married to an earl, one with considerable influence in government circles. He didn't want a serious involvement with any woman, certainly not a woman with a rich and powerful husband.

When it came to women, he knew he should keep to the relative safety of casual affairs. There were plenty of beautiful black women available whenever he needed one. He therefore resolved to stay far away from the potential trouble that was Lady Dana Northcote.

As he headed towards the grandstand he decided he'd keep his distance from her, but at the back of his mind he wondered if he'd remain so decisive if she showed the slightest interest in him.

CHAPTER 22

The dance at Torr's Hotel was a fixture of Race Week that everybody anticipated with excitement — especially the women from upcountry. They had few opportunities during the year to dress up let alone dance to a nine-piece band. The music flowed as did the alcohol, which was consumed in no small measure.

Everyone from the racing fraternity was present, which meant the most affluent and therefore influential members of Kenyan society. The Governor was there with his wife, as were all the members of the Legislative Council. The Japanese ambassador and a middle-eastern prince added an international flavour.

Dana and Edward had exchanged partners — he was now dancing with Georgina and she with Georgina's husband, Phillip.

'Congratulations on a simply splendid dinner party last month,' Phillip said.

'Pleased you could come.'

'I'm the one who was pleased — to have had you as my partner for the night.'

'Now, now, Phillip. You know the rules. We are not supposed to discuss things that happen at Zephyr.'

'You think that everyone else isn't? Look at Edward and Georgina, giggling like school children.'

'We can't assume why, and you know the rules as well

as I do, Phillip. I too enjoyed our evening, but we must leave it at that. Otherwise I will have to stop this conversation.'

Phillip shrugged. 'If you insist,' he said.

As the band commenced the next bracket, she was surprised to be invited to the floor by Major Whiteman.

'Dana Northcote,' he said. 'So pleased to meet you at last.'

She was somewhat flattered. She had no idea he knew of her. 'Major Whiteman,' she said.

'Roger, please. May I call you Dana?'

'Of course.'

As they danced, the conversation went inevitably to horse racing. Neither would give an inch regarding the superior merits of their respective champions.

'I heard your Toby ran some good times at training,' he said. 'But it sounds like you favour your little mare.'

'I do. She's a darling with a heart as big as herself.'

'I've heard that about the Abyssinians, but some of the stock from up there has a weakness in the canons. I'm not sure I'd be running her in anything over a mile if I were you.'

'Why, Major Whiteman, I do believe you are afraid to race against my Dancer.'

'Don't be silly.'

'Well, it certainly appears that way. Why else would you spread such rumours?'

'I tell you what, Dana. If either of your horses beats any of mine, I'll double the prize money for you.'

'I see … and what is your prize if one of yours wins?'

'I've been looking for a nice little mare for my daughter. Something safe and steady. Like your Dancer. The mare will be my prize.'

Dana bristled. The implied sneer at her darling Dancer infuriated her. In a rush of pique and without giving the matter any thought, she accepted the bet.

It was only back at the Norfolk, now sober and in bed, did her rash decision strike home. The thought of her beautiful Abyssinian trotting around a show pen as a child's pet sent a shudder of horror through her body. She was determined to avoid that occurrence at all costs.

* * *

Dana lowered her field glasses and shook her head. 'Back to his old times,' she said to Polly, standing beside her at the rail.

'And he was doing so well in the trials,' Polly commiserated.

Dana made no reply, but it confirmed Sam Williams's explanation of his form reversal. 'And now I have to face Roger Whiteman and his taunts,' she said with a sigh. She hadn't had the heart to admit to anyone about her foolish wager with Whiteman.

'Speak of the devil …' Polly said.

Whiteman swept up to them, beaming. 'Good afternoon, ladies,' he said. 'Wonderful race, don't you think?'

Dana said nothing.

Polly made a valiant effort to defend the indefensible Toby.

Whiteman laughed it off. 'Let's hope for your sake that your Abyssinian does better on Saturday,' he said before excusing himself.

'What is he talking about?' Polly asked.

Dana, despondent and guilt-ridden, admitted her impulsive wager.

'Oh, Dana!' Polly said. 'How could you risk losing her?'

'I know. I'd had too many drinks, and I was just angry. And so stupid,' Dana said, shaking her head. 'I don't know what I can do.'

But a desperate plan had already started to take shape in her mind.

* * *

The St Leger was Race Week's premier event and attracted the best horses. It was a race of fourteen furlongs for three-year-old fillies and colts. The bookies placed Major Whiteman's horse, Longonot, as favourite. Dancer was ten to one.

Dana was in the grandstand with Edward as the field gathered at the starting stalls on the far end of the straight. She watched Dancer prancing and skittering as the starter called them to the barrier.

'She seems very excited,' Edward said, watching through his field glasses. 'That's a bit unusual, isn't it?'

Dana bit her lip. She'd had no idea how much *seketet* she should add to Dancer's feed and was now beginning to doubt the wisdom of it. If the filly didn't settle down she'd be too excitable to make a good start.

The horses were at the barrier. A few moments later, the crowd roared.

'They're racing!' Edward shouted.

Dancer had reared in the starting stalls and missed the jump from the barrier. She was four lengths behind the tail of the field as they came down the straight.

Dana groaned, but as they thundered past the grandstand for the first time, the filly was making up ground at an astonishing rate.

'He can't hold her,' Edward said as the jockey hauled on the reins. 'She can't keep going at that pace, surely.'

But Dana understood: Dancer had taken the bit or ignored it as it cut into her mouth.

'What's that fool of a jockey doing?' Edward said as Dancer took the next turn five horses wide, meaning she covered a great deal more ground than the leaders tucked in on the rails.

The field had spread out along the back straight with Dancer behind the leading pack of horses but still within touch if she had the stamina to last the remaining six furlongs. Roger Whiteman's champion, Longonot, was ideally placed — on the rails and a length behind the leader.

Into the home turn, and the crowd went wild: Dancer had overtaken the rear pack and was gaining on Longonot, who had taken the lead. A momentous battle was developing between the big colt and the plucky Abyssinian.

Through her field glasses Dana could see the lather foaming on Dancer's flanks. She was spent, but wouldn't give up. Never having needed to touch her with the whip, the jockey put it away, riding her hands and heels into the straight.

Head to head they fought out the last furlong or so. No other horse was in contention now. It was Longonot or Dancer.

The crowd roared encouragement, but Dana vainly screamed, 'No! Pull her up!' and dashed from the grandstand, forcing her way through the crowd towards the rail — but before she reached it, Dancer flashed across the finishing line, a length ahead of Longonot.

Dana watched in horror, tears streaming down her face, as her beautiful horse staggered to a stop and dropped her head, blood dripping from her muzzle, and sweat pouring down her quivering flanks.

* * *

Instead of a triumphant entry to the saddling yard, with the mounted jockey riding high to acknowledge the accolades of the crowd, he had dismounted and led the broken horse into the enclosure where Dana was waiting. When she took Dancer's reins she knew she would be doing so for the last time — the filly would never race again.

The crowd knew none of this, enthusiastically applauding the most courageous performance anyone had ever seen.

The Governor presented Dana with the St Leger trophy and the winner's cheque. She tried to make a speech, but her throat closed over. The crowd applauded again, this time for the winning owner's touching humility.

Major Whiteman stepped up and congratulated Dana too, then handed her a stuffed envelope. She looked at it, her mind a blank. By the time she realised it was her winnings — her thirty pieces of silver — he'd left the podium. The envelope weighed heavily in her hand.

The Governor returned to the microphone and concluded the ceremonies, but before she stepped down from the podium, Dana caught sight of Sam Williams among the crowd. She could see in his eyes that he understood what she had done, and that he could see the guilt she had managed to conceal from everyone else.

She could have lived with the consequences of her stupidity if no one knew of it. When the news went out that the brave little filly that had won the St Leger would be retired from the track, she and Dancer would still be champions in everyone's memories. She wasn't worried that Sam would reveal her secret to anyone: he didn't appear to be that kind of person. But the fact that he knew she was not the hero everyone believed her to be rankled.

In that moment Dana wanted to hate him for what he knew, but she could also see that he, among all of them, understood her grief.

CHAPTER 23

Soon after Race Week, Sam had a reason to stay the night in Gilgil. He made an early start for Nairobi the next morning, but decided to ride out to the nearby Northcote farm to check on the little Abyssinian mare.

When he reached the farm he had second thoughts. He knew it was Dana he wanted to see, rather than the mare, and instead of going to the farmhouse he rode to the back of the property where he'd found an old abandoned *banda* when he passed through on one of his visits to Abyssinia.

He boiled water and took his cup of tea outside the *banda* to enjoy the sweeping view. He liked the tranquillity of the place; and he sat sipping his tea and pondering the foolishness that prompted him to take such a long detour for no reason.

He shook off the mistake and rode down the hill. From the first rise above the homestead he spotted the mare as one of the syces led her from the stable into the home enclosure. Her gait had improved, but she still favoured her left foreleg. It confirmed his original suspicion that she had split her canon bone — a situation not uncommon among wild Abyssinian horses, but one that could be cross-bred out of their progeny.

It was then he recalled Dana's earlier enquiries about getting an Abyssinian stallion from him.

The memory cheered him. Next time he passed through he would have an excuse to call in and discuss business.

*   *   *

In the early weeks of February, through the persistent drizzle of what some of the old-timers called the grass rains, Dana found it difficult to get back into her usual routine. She couldn't bear to be with the horses, delegating their feeding and exercise to Jonathan and Benard. There was nothing she could find to fill the empty space left when her love of her horses was shadowed in shame. If she chanced to see Dancer in the paddock, she'd quickly turn away.

Edward was totally unsympathetic. It wasn't his fault, of course. He was unaware she'd given Dancer the drug that had caused her gallant little filly to break down, but she resented his attempts to chivvy her out of her mood.

That morning broke without a sign of rain. For the first time in weeks, she took care in choosing her clothing and went for a long walk. She was feeling much better as a result, but when she returned to find Edward at breakfast in one of his surly early-morning dispositions, it dampened her mood.

'Good morning,' she said, as she sat and poured herself a cup of tea.

'It's about time,' he replied as he replaced his cup and carefully smoothed first one side of his ginger moustache, and then the other. It was a habit, almost a ritual, he adopted whenever he was annoyed with something or somebody. It was his way of keeping calm. And it always irritated her.

'What do you mean by that?' she asked.

'I'm saying it's good to see you back to your early rises.'

'I'm always an early riser.'

'Since we no longer share a bed, it's hard to know when you arise. Or retire for that matter.'

'Edward, we decided long ago that we'd not share a bed. Don't you recall? And since you won't give me a child, what would be the point?'

'Anyway, it's about time you stopped moping.'

'So you've reminded me on several occasions.'

'Oh, for God's sake, Dana! It's only a fucking horse.'

'You don't understand, do you? You've never understood anything about me.'

'I understand this much — you've spent the last six months fussing around with those stupid nags, pouring money into them, and for what? A complete waste. Fifty guineas for the St Leger. It won't even cover the fodder.'

'What else have I to do around here?'

'I should think that now that you've won your precious race, you can help to manage the bloody farm. God knows we need some profitability.'

She was on the verge of reminding him that she had been against the idea of coming to Kenya in the first place. Neither of them had any experience in farming. In fact, she'd pleaded with him not to leave London. But thanks to his gambling debts and disastrous business decisions they'd been forced to flee his creditors. Instead, she pushed back her chair and left the table.

She strode out the gate into the warming air of the highland morning. She immediately felt better and on an impulse — or simply by force of habit — went to the stable.

Dancer was standing, head lowered, in her stall. Toby whinnied a greeting. She gave him a pat and scratched his ear, then went to Dancer's stall. The filly shook her head as Dana opened the gate and ran her hands along her flanks. Then she cradled the filly's head in her arms and gave her a kiss on the cheek.

'My poor baby,' she said, stroking the horses's neck as she continued to hold her head in her arms. After a moment or two she stepped back and looked into Dancer's eyes. 'Why don't we go for a little walk? Would you like that? Maybe it'll cheer us up.'

She slipped a light saddle over her, and a few minutes later they were heading down the track towards the gate. Dana intended her outing to end there, but the sun lifted her spirits. She even imagined Dancer's step had picked up as they followed the road to the gate then veered left to climb the ridge towards the treeline that demarcated the edge of their property and the beginning of the Aberdare forest.

At the highest point of their land she dismounted and walked to the shepherd's hut under a large tree a hundred yards from the encroaching forest. It was a single room with a fireplace in the centre and a small bed. She had christened it the shepherd's hut when they'd first moved to Zephyr and she didn't yet understand enough Swahili to call it a *banda*. The Africans who used it when the ranch had carried a great deal more stock than she and Edward owned probably took shelter there from the rain. Nowadays, they were able to keep the stock within close proximity of the farmhouse, so the *banda* was no longer needed, but Dana liked it. It reminded her of the cubby house she'd had as a child and always gave her a feeling of security when she stepped inside it.

She slipped past the tanned hide covering the door and sat on the cot. It had a number of skins on it, including a zebra skin that she stroked, enjoying the coarse hairs against her palm.

She came outside again and, after the dimness, the bright light assaulted her eyes as she followed the smoky blue line of the mountains down the slope where, a mile or so further on, past a couple of low ridges, sat the house. The breadth of the vista always bestowed on her a feeling of peace and contentment. Now she let her eyes drop to the course of the river as it dodged among the thick green patches of scrub to the west.

She noticed a lone rider heading towards her. She felt some alarm: the intruder was on private property, and she was a long way from the security of her house.

She walked quickly towards Dancer and swung into the saddle to watch his approach before making a retreat. His high seat in the saddle indicated he was a horseman; as he drew closer, she was relieved to recognise Sam Williams.

She was thankful she'd at least put on a nice pink blouse that morning. She dismounted and patted the blouse's collar to make it flat. Then she shook her head to get her hair to sit right.

'Morning,' he said, looking down on her from his saddle.

'Good morning.' She was at a loss for small talk.

'Should I join you, or have you come up here to be on your own?'

She had left the house with the intention of being alone, but now that he was there with that slightly shy smile, she felt the need for company, a need she'd not felt since the races.

'Please do.'

He dismounted and she led him to the shade beside the hut where a large branch had broken from the tree during the last big blow. They tethered their horses and sat on the log.

'That's a very unusual pendant,' he said. 'It's a lion's fang, isn't it?'

She touched a finger to her throat. 'It is,' she said. 'My first and only trophy.'

He nodded. 'It fits with your character.'

She waited for an explanation, but he changed the subject. 'I came by a few weeks ago. Just after Race Week,' he said.

'You did? I was at home, surely.'

'I didn't go to the house. I sat up here for a while. I love this place. Every time I pass here, I come to this very spot. It helps me think, and you can see everything.' He paused for a moment. 'I didn't see you out. I reckoned if you were feeling up to having visitors you'd be out riding.'

She smiled. 'That was very kind of you.' She was touched by his thoughtfulness. 'You know about Dancer ... About what happened to her. I could see it in your eyes.'

He nodded.

She glanced towards the filly, nosing a clump of grass. Dana plucked a grass stalk and slowly began to shred it. 'I'm grateful you didn't report me to the stewards. I deserved it for my selfishness and stupidity.'

'I'm the last one who could run to the authorities. I imagine you've already realised I'm not so perfect myself.'

'A horse smuggler is nothing.'

'Sometimes with a little gold in the saddlebags too. But I'm not sure Emperor Ras Tafari would agree that taking his precious Abyssinians from his country is nothing.'

She smiled in spite of her sadness. 'How did you get into that business?'

'Probably because I failed at everything else.' He was smiling too.

'No, seriously. How is it that an educated American gentleman comes to Africa and gets involved in a business that takes him to the wildest parts of the continent?'

She thought she must have offended him because he remained silent for a long time before saying, 'My name is Wangira. Samson Wangira. I have an American elocutionist and six years in the States to thank for this accent. The fact is, I'm a Kikuyu, born and raised at the foot of Mt Kenya.'

He told her how he saved the life of a wealthy American businessman who later sponsored him to enter New York University; after that he learned about horses in the mid-west.

'You accuse yourself of being selfish and stupid,' he said. 'You're not the only one. I was too selfish to keep in touch with people — family and friends — who loved me in spite of my years of separation from them. Too selfish to keep in touch. And too stupid to appreciate the love of a good friend.'

He told her about his family and the nun who had helped him in his early education. He spoke with feeling about the Jewish man who had loved him but had never taken advantage of a young man's gratitude. She became absorbed in his story and was surprised at how he was able to relate the facts with such honesty.

'And now I'm in the horse business, in a manner of speaking.'

'And I'm out of it,' she said. 'The horse business, I mean.'

'Why? Because you've had some bad luck with your little mare here?'

'Bad luck? She'll never race again, and she was my best prospect.'

'You once asked me about a stallion to put to Dancer for breeding purposes. Why not continue with those plans? You know she has the qualities to be a champion. She could still give you some champion foals.'

In her remorse she'd forgotten about that other side of her plans for Dancer.

'Can you get an Abyssinian stallion for me?'

'I can. It may take time to find the right one, but I can keep it in mind as I travel around. If you are prepared to wait. Let me put a business proposition to you. In return for the stud services of a stallion — to be provided — I would like to use your property to rest and agist my horses before driving them on to Nairobi.'

'Isn't that what you've been doing?'

'Well, yes ... but now it'll be on the level.'

'I'll need to talk to Edward, but I don't think there'll be a problem with that.'

'Good. As they say in America: we have a deal.'

He reached out his hand.

She hesitated before taking it. 'On one condition.'

'Yes?'

'You allow me to give you dinner tonight.'

A smile slowly spread across his face, and he nodded. 'I think I can agree to those terms.'

She accepted his handshake, feeling the hard strength in it.

* * *

Mary had done wonders. The roast lamb was succulent and her golden pudding and custard was a marvel on such short notice. Sam seemed to enjoy it.

'There's more,' Dana said, nodding at Sam's empty plate beside her.

'Oh, please … I've already had two helpings.'

'Will you join me in a port, then?' Edward asked.

'Thank you, but no. I don't drink these days.'

Edward had been introduced to Sam during Race Week as Sam Williams — an American. When he corrected that error, Edward, to his credit, and despite the whisky, remained a good host and seemed to be enjoying Sam's conversation.

He warmed even further to Sam upon learning of Dana's proposal to put one of Sam's Abyssinian stallions to her eligible mare. In time he could see Zephyr becoming a stud for Abyssinian racehorses.

As Sam described the finer points of the Abyssinian breed to Edward, Dana took the opportunity to study her visitor more thoroughly. She watched his mouth as he spoke. It was very expressive. And his skin seemed so smooth she had the urge to stroke his arm. Yet he had the build of a man hardened by years in the saddle. She remembered the firmness of his handshake earlier that afternoon.

She interrupted them. 'Before you go too much further, Edward … Faizal is about to retire, and I believe we should invite Sam to stay in our guest room tonight.'

'No, please,' Sam said. 'Don't go to any trouble. There's a guest house in Naivasha.'

'It's obviously too late to ride anywhere,' she said.

'She's right you know, old man,' Edward agreed. 'Leopards. The high country's crawling with them at the moment. Must have been the dry that brought them all out.'

'It's settled then,' she said. 'I'll get the bedroom set up for you.'

As she left the dining room she heard Edward say, 'Never mind Dana. She loves to fuss. Let her sort things out while you and I chat. Will you join me in a port?'

Dana bristled at his condescending manner. Edward made a habit of it after a few drinks. She had become accustomed to it, but in the presence of guests it was particularly annoying. She nevertheless held her tongue and went to organise Faizal.

* * *

Edward was monopolising the conversation when Sam noticed Dana re-enter the room. He sensed she was annoyed by her husband's manner, which didn't surprise him. Edward had been quite rude.

'Ah, there she is,' Edward said. 'I was just telling Sam about your little folly, dear. Did I say folly?' He snorted. 'I do beg your pardon, I meant *filly*, of course.'

Dana coloured.

Sam glanced at her, then turned to Edward. 'Edward, I don't think that's —'

'Sam's far more sensible,' Edward went on, ignoring his interjection. 'His plan to turn your little hobby into a stud makes a lot of sense. Buying and selling horses rather than feeding them for no good reason. Now that your Dancer is only good for the glue factory, it's a good thing he came up with the idea.'

Sam waited for Dana to respond, but although he noticed her lip tighten and tears well up in her eyes, she said nothing.

Edward's bullying behaviour was not unusual among some backward African men, who treated their women as common chattels, but he'd not seen or heard of it among the whites. Somehow he'd concluded that although there was often an inequality existing between white couples, the women were at least treated with respect.

Edward continued his sarcasm until Sam had had enough. He abruptly stood. 'Edward, thank you for the evening, but I think I'll call it a night.' He slid his chair under the table.

'What? Already? What about a coffee? Mary! Coffee for Mr Wangira. *Pesi pesi!*'

Sam turned to Dana.

'Thank you for a wonderful dinner, Dana. You've been most kind. And I look forward to working with you … and Edward, in the future. But now, if you'll excuse me, I'll take myself off to bed.'

Faizal was in the guest room, turning down the bed and placing a hot-water bottle under the covers. Sam thanked him as he left and then sat on the bed to remove his boots.

He wondered if Dana had been aware of the proximity of his leg to hers during dinner. He certainly was, and could almost feel the warmth of her thigh next to his.

He slipped out of his clothes and slid naked between the sheets.

Sleep eluded him.

*   *   *

A loose floorboard squeaked as she padded, barefoot, past Edward's bedroom to the far end of the hall. The nightlight at the top of the stairs threw her shadow ahead of her, coming to rest on the door to Sam's bedroom. She hesitated a moment, her hand on the handle. The fine hairs on her arms and the back of her neck tingled as they did before a storm when the air was hot and alive with static, and the clouds gathered and rumbled. Every fibre in her body seemed acutely tuned to her surroundings. She had never before noticed the fine panelling on the bedroom door nor the ornamental moulding surrounding the door handle.

She turned the knob and, as she stepped into the room, she could faintly sense his maleness — a smell like dry straw and leather.

A memory came starkly to mind from her childhood. She was no more than ten when she came into the stable as a stallion mounted a mare. Her father shooed her away, but not before the raw sexuality of it had been etched into her mind. The placid acquiescence of the mare, the power of the stallion, and the wild look in his normally docile eyes strengthened her interest in matters of sex.

Sam's male scent had thrilled her when she sat next to him at dinner, her thigh inches from his, occasionally touching it as if by accident. The parlour games that she and her friends and their husbands played during their parties were mere child's play compared to what she was now contemplating. The games Dana invented to tease and titillate were an exciting prelude to the grand finale when partners moved off to bed for the night or, should the mood take them, only part of it, before swapping yet again.

On those nights there were few rules except for the firm agreement among all couples that there would be no fraternisation outside the dinner parties. The very temerity of her bold action now heightened her excitement, and she could no more stop than she could cease breathing. It was like the situation with the stallion: she was driven by a mindless, undeniable passion that drove her on to complete what she'd started.

'Who is it?' His voice came softly from the bed, which she could see in the moonlight through the open window.

But surely he must know it was her. It caused her to pause as she fleetingly lost her confidence. Perhaps she had misread the events of the evening as he held her gaze, and casually let their fingers touch while reaching across the table.

'It's me,' she said. 'I … I just wanted to apologise for Edward.'

He lifted himself onto an elbow.

The room thrummed with tension. There was a moment's hesitation that seemed like an age before he spoke.

'Come,' he said, and she went quickly to the bed, but held back. This was a step too far, even for Dana.

He reached out and caught her hand, pulling her off balance. She fell on him and his mouth was on hers, smothering her with the force of his lips.

They clung together for breathless moments before he lifted her from him and swept the covering aside. She caught a glimpse of his rampant erection and a moment later, as he pulled her to him, felt it through her thin cotton nightdress.

'I prayed you'd come,' he said.

'Don't speak. Kiss me.'

His lips were full and firm as he explored her tongue with his, drawing back only to help her out of her shift.

She moaned and clutched his shoulders, feeling his muscles ripple and leap as he rolled her from him and threw his leg across her, pinning her to the bed.

'I've wanted you from the first moment I saw you,' she said. 'I want you now. More than I've ever wanted anybody.'

His hands were moving over her breasts and he bent to take one nipple gently into his mouth, sucking and licking it. He let his hands slide over her body, into the ripples of her ribs and the valleys of her groin, then gently playing across her moistening labia.

His firm cock filled her hand and she stroked it lovingly. 'Oh, I want this, Sam. I want you. Now.'

He swung his body over her with his knees between hers. She arched her back, lifting her hips towards him.

In the light from the window she saw his eyes fill with passion. Then he lowered himself down and into her.

She stifled a cry of pleasure.

CHAPTER 24

The dawn air was sweet. A fragrant, earthy mist drifted across the high savannah as Sam and his horse melted into it. The last Dana saw of him was his hand raised in farewell. The vapour cloud of her breath hung in the air and Dana stood for a long time, her cashmere wrap clutched to her body, hoping the mist would clear so she could return his wave, but by the time it stirred in response to the sun's kiss, he'd gone.

It was a liquid morning — her favourite — the kind of morning that promised a fine day, full of sunshine and warmth. She willed it on, though she loved savouring those moments too, as the sun climbed, setting fire to the land east of the Aberdares. Then slowly, slowly it made its imminent presence known in the golden shafts it sent spearing through the chinks in the mountains. She stood enfolded in her wrap until the first peep caught her eyes, momentarily blinding her.

She turned away and walked slowly towards the house and its weathered façade now gilt-leafed in the morning light.

She didn't want the dawn to end, but she had not wanted the night to end either. When she awoke, snuggled into Sam's broad back, she wanted to remain so forever, watching his shoulders move with the heavy breathing of sleep. His dark brown skin demanded she touch it and when she did she was surprised at how smooth it was; how firm and smooth. He'd stirred then and turned to her, lifting his arm to draw her to him and soon they were making love again, this time slowly, as in a dream.

'Fancied a bit of black cock, did you, dear?'

Edward's voice startled her.

She continued up the steps to the veranda. 'Good morning, Edward,' she said.

'I shouldn't be surprised if you've been rutting with the field workers as well.'

'Edward, please. Don't be disgusting.'

'Well, why not? All dogs are the same colour in the dark, eh what?'

She walked past him to the breakfast room where she shoved a few kindling sticks into the cast-iron stove and placed the kettle over the opening in the top.

After a few minutes, he joined her. 'How long has this been going on?'

'It wasn't planned, Edward. It was just one of those things. It happened.'

'I understand that, but we have an arrangement, and this appears to be outside of that, don't you think?'

'I'm sorry,' she said. 'I should have told you, but I had no intention of … Anyway, it just … happened.'

'Will it happen again?'

She had already considered that question and had no answer. She and Sam hadn't spoken about it so she had no idea of his intentions. 'I'm staying at the Muthaiga Club,' Sam had said, in the only hint that he may want to see her again.

'I don't know,' she said.

'Let me make this clear, Dana. While I may have my reservations about the suitability of your bedroom partner, I don't have any objections to you fucking him provided you abide by our agreed arrangements.'

'You mean stay within the Zephyr group?'

'Precisely.'

She couldn't argue. Edward was quite correct, and she'd agreed to the rules of the game before they started it.

Her first thought was that although she wanted Sam, she wanted him all to herself. She didn't want to share him with her girlfriends, although she felt quite sure that many of them would be excited about the addition of exotic and ordinarily forbidden fruit to their games. But even if Sam agreed to be a part of their party nights, he would never fit in, and Edward very well knew it.

So why would he make it so difficult for her to be with Sam? She knew Edward well enough to believe he wasn't threatened by her sexual relationship with the new man. He'd shown no sign of it in any of her exploits with the men in their group, or those she'd shared her bed with in England when she and Edward began their open marriage. In fact, she suspected that it excited him. More than once he'd hinted that he'd like to be present while she was making love to one of the others. He didn't want to participate, he said, just to watch. He went so far as to ask the opinion of a couple of the men, who told him they wouldn't mind. Dana did though, so it never happened.

But Dana quickly realised what was on Edward's mind. It was not a racial concern. Although he had a paternalistic attitude to black Kenyans, he had none of the extreme views of many of the settlers of his class. The issue was that Edward was a snob. It wouldn't matter what colour a man might be: unless he was of the right type, which to Edward meant of the landed if not titled gentry, they were socially unsuited.

She knew Edward would be watching her: if she went to see Sam again, he would find out and most likely, and justifiably, cut her off without a penny. On the other hand, if she invited Sam into their group she faced even more risks. If, as she suspected, Sam was shocked by her and her group's outrageous behaviour, she might not only lose him, but suffer his disgust. On the other hand, if he agreed to join and was not accepted by the others, he would hate her for exposing him to such humiliation. Equally unsettling: if he was accepted by them, Sam would no longer be special to her.

'No,' she said. 'Inviting him into the group is quite impossible.'

'I absolutely forbid it any other way.'

'Then it's settled,' she said softly. 'It's over.'

*   *   *

The densely wooded slopes of Mt Marsabit rose above the dry, blood-red earth. Being due west of the extinct volcano meant Sam was now about four or five days from the border. On his return in about a month, he would employ local Boran and, when they'd travelled too far from their tribal lands, Rendile tribesmen to help with the muster until he was close to home. But for now he was alone, and had plenty of time to think.

He'd delayed his departure for a couple of weeks, hoping to hear from Dana, but from her silence concluded she'd realised her error, and changed her mind about seeing him again.

He knew Dana Northcote would be dangerous, but he had always thought it would be because of the stigma attached to sexual relations across the racial divide.

Although there were many white men who, far from home and other European women, had taken comfort with an African woman, it was a far different matter between a black man and a white woman. Such a relationship could fire strong feelings in the European community — particularly among the men. But from the moment that Sam first felt attracted to Dana he had been prepared for that risk. The danger that he now confronted was that Dana had become more than a merely desirable woman: she'd penetrated the barrier he'd erected against a serious relationship.

She was strong yet vulnerable. He wanted to share her strength so that together they could defy convention. At the same time he wanted to shield her from the storm that a relationship such as theirs was bound to whip up.

He was thirty-three, and knew enough about the world to know he should respect her wishes to let their affair end. But he also knew himself well enough to know, given the chance, he wouldn't allow her to.

* * *

The Abyssinian tribesmen were anxious to make their sale and be gone. A death sentence awaited them should the Emperor's men discover their felony. The high-country horses were corralled for Sam's inspection, and he'd already selected a few. What he wanted now was the high-spirited stallion pacing the rails: he would be perfect for Dana's mare, Dancer.

Somehow the leader of the horse smugglers had perceived Sam's interest in the stallion and was making it difficult for him to purchase it at a reasonable price. He decided to bluff it out, walking away from the dealer to call his men together ready for the muster. But the stallion was exactly the horse Sam needed to have reason to visit Dana again. He would bargain and haggle, but at the end of it, the stallion would be his.

'And what about the stallion?' the Abyssinian asked.

'What stallion?' Sam said. 'This old bag of bones? It is not worth my grandmother's broken teeth.'

'It is the best stallion I have captured in all my years,' the Abyssinian insisted. 'Look at those eyes. There is the fire of hell in them, yet he is as sweet as an angel in heaven. Nobody could find a better animal for the stud.'

'*Pah!* The stud, you say? More likely he'd fit the farm plough rather than a mare, but I don't think he has the stamina even for that. Take him away. I already have enough for the journey home.'

'But look at those legs. A village could be built on such strong posts. A city.'

It was clear the dealer didn't want to remain in the outpost any longer and was keen to do business. There was a rumour that a contingent of soldiers was making a routine patrol along the border and he wanted to be able to make a fast retreat to his mountain homeland if they came his way. The stallion was too expensive to release to the wilds again, but too much trouble to conceal until the next customer happened by.

* * *

It was May, and the long rains of 1931 were overdue. Everyone feared another drought. In Dana's circle of friends the concern was that unless the rains came soon, the new season's racing events due to begin in Nakuru in

June would be washed out. The timing of the year's social calendar was at stake.

The doldrums — the stifling windless time before the trade winds brought the rain — were always difficult for Dana. The humid air seemed to smother her like a hot, wet sheet, and her hair was perpetually limp. Wearing anything more than a loose-fitting cotton shift, including underwear, was unbearable. And she felt she looked a fright in a shift.

She'd not organised the usual Zephyr dinner party in April, nor would she do so in May while the climate remained unchanged. She was in no mood for such frivolity. Let Averil or Polly organise one, she thought.

At these times she really missed England's seasons: the bite of an autumn wind, even the chill of winter, were the stuff of her dreams.

Edward was immune. He went about his daily routine — he seemed to have become more involved in the farm of late — without seeming to notice Dana's smouldering irritation.

'Why don't you go for a spin into Nairobi?' he asked after Dana lost her temper trying to fix her hair into something resembling neat.

'I can't be bothered,' she whined.

'Pick up Polly on the way and stay a few days.'

'No. But I will take a drive down to Gilgil. I need a few items. Do you care to join me?'

'No, my dear. I have to collect a scarifier from the Banfields'.'

The Banfields were the nearest of their Zephyr friends and John Banfield and Edward often shared farm equipment.

Edward took the Albion, and drove out the gate with a wave.

Dana climbed into the Willys-Knight roadster, and drove down to the *dukas* at Gilgil. Immediately she had escaped the claustrophobic confines of the ranch she felt better.

She idled away an hour, chatting to a neighbour about the weather and other trivial matters, bought some soap and a handful of hair clasps, and headed home again.

Her heart leaped when she saw a herd of Abyssinian horses in the holding pens outside the stable; when she drove up to the house, Sam was standing there, hands in his pockets, wearing an uncertain smile.

She hadn't seen him in more than two months. Although she knew she should have contacted him in some way, she hadn't been able to bring herself to do so. On her infrequent visits to Nairobi she had avoided the Muthaiga Club in case he was there. She'd imagined her emotions would hold sway if she saw him; now she knew that was true. The memory of his body on hers, of his mouth and his strong presence came flooding back with such intensity that it took her breath away.

She sat for a moment behind the wheel, trying to regain her composure, but when she climbed out of the car she was immediately aware she was naked under her thin cotton dress. She fluffed out the folds and tried to pat her hair into some form of shape.

'Hello, Dana,' he said as she approached the veranda.

'Sam! It's so nice to see you.'

When she'd reached the top of the steps and stood before him, he searched her eyes, but she avoided them by giving him a brief hug.

'You've been back to Abyssinia,' she said, dragging her eyes from him. The herd of about a dozen horses was barely able to fit into the stable enclosure.

'Yes ... I haven't heard from you, but I presumed you're still looking for a stallion for stud.'

'Of course. Yes, I am. And I've been so busy I've hardly been out. But look at me — where are my manners? Come inside, I'll get you a cold drink.'

'Thanks, but I've already had one.' He nodded to the table and the empty glass.

'Oh, then Edward's here?'

She knew he wasn't because the farm truck was not in its place behind the house.

'No, Mary brought it for me.'

'Wonderful.'

Dana clasped and unclasped her hands in front of her, desperately trying to find something to relieve the tension between them. Sam didn't help by studying her in silence.

She was racked with guilt for not contacting him and explaining that she couldn't sleep with him again. Now she realised it appeared that she had simply shrugged the whole affair off as unimportant.

'Well ...' he said at last, 'I'll take the herd up to the top enclosure ... I mean, to let them graze for —'

'Yes! Of course. The agistment. As we agreed.'

'It'll only be for a day or so before ... before I move on to Nairobi.' He smiled self-consciously, and started towards the veranda steps. 'Oh, before I go —'

'Yes?'

'You'll want to see your stallion.'

'What? Yes, I do.'

'I've put him in a spare stall.'

They walked in silence to the stable. Dana was aware of his discomfort, but she felt powerless. Her life was so complicated. How could she explain Edward's offer to let him join their group and her refusal to share him? How could she begin to explain her extramarital life to him?

The stallion was black with a splash of grey on his withers. He lifted his head as they entered the stable. He was big for an Abyssinian, maybe fifteen hands, and wasn't afraid to show his temperament, snorting loudly when Dana came closer.

'He's beautiful,' she said, reaching out to stroke his neck. The stallion stepped back and shook his head.

'He'll take time to settle down, but he's the best I've found up in Abyssinia for months. Mating him with Dancer, who has the speed, should throw foals with good staying ability.'

'Thank you, Sam. I'll take good care of him.'

'I know,' he said, and took her hand in his. 'Dana, I wondered if I should be here at all. When I didn't hear from you, I thought you might have had regrets about what happened. I mean, you're married and —'

'It's not that, Sam.'

He reached out to her, placing his hand lightly on her shoulder. It sent a shiver through her.

'We were very indiscreet,' he said. 'I presume your husband has found out about us and you've had second thoughts.'

'It's not that. Edward and I don't have a conventional marriage.'

She didn't know how to continue and knew he was confused by her reserve. She so desperately wanted to explain. But how? 'Sam ...' she began. 'Sam —'

The rattle of the old Albion coming through the home gate interrupted her. Edward had returned. She led Sam from the stable and sighed with relief. Until that moment she'd never regretted the decision she and Edward had made to live an unconventional life together, but the prospect of explaining that decision to Sam made it seem at once mad and shameful.

* * *

The Abyssinians were at that stage of their journey where they had become accustomed to the routine. Sam found that if he kept the numbers down to around a dozen horses they were easier to drive when he was working them on his own during the final leg of the journey. Now, as he headed them up towards the Northcotes' high pastures, they were very willing. They seemed to know they would find good grass and cool air there, reminiscent of the highlands of their home.

Sam needed the easy ride. He'd hoped Dana would have explained why she hadn't been in touch, but she'd said nothing. He regretted coming. He would stay the night and perhaps another to rest the horses, then leave her. He'd obviously made a big mistake.

How ironic, he thought to himself. I let down my defences just once and again the woman I have chosen has not chosen me.

CHAPTER 25

After Sam left for the high pastures with his horses, Edward had been unusually kind and solicitous. He brought Dana a gin and tonic at sundown, and sat with her on the veranda watching the sun go from gold to blood-red.

'You came back early,' Dana said, referring to his visit to the Banfields'.

'Yes. John's in Tanganyika and Eliza's gone to Nairobi for the day.'

'Did you collect the scarifier?'

'The scarifier? No.'

'But you had arranged to pick it up. Surely John wouldn't have minded.'

'No. I'll go another day.'

Dana dabbed at her throat with her lace handkerchief, and sighed. 'I'm so listless in this heat,' she said.

'It's ghastly, especially for you, apparently.' He added more ice to her gin and tonic. 'Do you miss England, my dear? The cool days; the cold nights?'

'I do, sometimes.'

'I must admit, I'm finding it difficult myself this year. And it's not just the weather. I've been giving this a great deal of thought ... maybe it's time we went home.'

'Home? You mean, to England?'

'Yes. Prices are falling. Blasted socialists. Farm produce is worth nothing these days, and by the time you include the freight to market or the docks, you're lucky to break even. I'm fed up. To be honest, I've started putting things into perspective. I'm having second thoughts about what we're doing here in Kenya. I mean it's not home, is it?'

'Edward, what on earth ...? This is quite a revelation.'

'I know you didn't want to come in the first place, and I should have listened to you. We have so much more in England. So that's what I've been thinking. Maybe it's time to go home.'

'Can we? What about your creditors?'

'The family have come into a little extra money and they've offered to sign it over to me. They're calling it an advance on my inheritance. I think it's a damn decent show of them. I'd like to accept. Will you come with me?'

'Edward ... this is so sudden.'

'I know. I'm sorry.'

He reached a hand across the gap between their chairs to take hers.

'I'm very fond of you, Dana. You know that. And I know I am a little abrupt at times. I've learned something about myself since being here — and it's not just that I'm not a farmer. This is a very strange place. We amuse ourselves, I suppose, but we had a good life in England too. I think we could make a new start there. What do you say?'

'Edward, I ... I'm not sure. Can I have a few days to think about it?'

* * *

It had been an odd night. Edward had been charming and amusing, as he could when he left the whisky in the bottle. His regrets about his behaviour seemed sincere; and now, after many years of her persistently asking that they abandon their pointless quest to make a success of farming in that most unusual of climates, he was now suggesting they should leave. She didn't instantly agree and that was also rather strange. As she lay in bed later that night she wondered why.

Although life in Kenya was comfortable, it was not home. There was nothing about it that reminded her of England unless it was the rare occasion where a glimpse across a misty hillside, with the green grass tinged golden by the dawn, and when the air was still and fresh, brought to mind the moors of the south-west. But five minutes later, when the sun burst from behind the hills with its characteristic and unseemly haste and laid its hot hand on the skin, the illusion would be lost. Or else what might have been a Dartmoor pony turned out to be a zebra, and spoiled the illusion.

And the sun. It was inescapable. Although she made every attempt to hide from its rays, her skin was as brown as a washer-woman's. It would take months in England for her colour to become suitable for an evening frock. The saving grace was that in the White Highlands it was at least cool on most evenings. She felt quite sure no Englishman could survive at sea level.

Kenya was certainly not home, and quite unsuitable for a normal life. But there was a part of her that would miss that stark landscape with its endless skies and exotic species.

Dana didn't think of herself as a particularly adventurous person, but when she thought of her previous life in England, it seemed quite insipid compared to the frequent clashes with the wildlife that even a colonial life as ordinary as hers involved. There was nothing in England to compare with the thrill of tracking a wounded lion in a thicket. An evening ride on one's own property here might reveal a stalking leopard or an angry young bull elephant or buffalo. A rifle was a more useful component of her accoutrements than a parasol.

She thought of her friends and wondered if she'd miss them, or they her. The fun-loving Polly was closest to her, but Polly had a demon within her that drove her to lengths that might ultimately bring disaster. Her taste for cocaine had tempted her to experiment with heroin. She now went nowhere without her little silver syringe.

Averil was family, but without the wider context of aunts, cousins and other older members, the relationship had no depth. Averil was like a playmate at a birthday party with no adult supervision. The life her group of friends had, sharing each other's partners, was superficially exciting, but she sometimes wondered if they were doing it for the sensual experience or as some form of sexual competition where the winner was the one best able to convince the others that he or she was having the most fun.

From the darkness she heard a soft knock, then her door opened.

'Dana? Darling? Are you awake?'

'Yes, Edward. I'm awake.'

'Sorry … it's just that … I was wondering, if I might, you know …'

'Come to bed, Edward,' she said, and lifted the sheet on the other side.

He slid in beside her and kissed her gently on the cheek then moved to her lips as he rubbed her midriff and slipped his hand under her nightdress.

Dana tried to put her troublesome thoughts from her mind, but she hadn't been able to resolve all the issues — they threatened to intrude upon the moment.

Edward was becoming excited. He smothered her with kisses and his fingers played gently in her wetness. She reached down to return his caresses.

He was above her and she opened herself to him.

Suddenly, she was suspended high over the Aberdares, but able to see all the details of her bedroom. It was as if she and Edward were characters on stage or in a silent moving picture.

A moment later, Edward rolled from her, breathing heavily, and Dana regained her equilibrium.

Long after Edward had kissed her tenderly and gone to his own bedroom, Dana lay awake, trying to understand what had happened in the moments after Edward had begun to make love to her. The answer had some connection with unresolved thoughts about leaving Kenya. It dangled in the darkness just beyond reach.

She tossed and turned. Distressed and overtired, she used an old trick to bring sleep. She imagined a life in England with Edward, concentrating on feelings of acceptance and support, security and comfort. It didn't work perfectly this time, though; and she finally allowed herself to admit that her distraction — and her indecision about the return home — came from her unresolved feelings for Sam.

*　*　*

Dana awoke thinking of Sam. She had been a coward not to tell him about her open marriage. Now she felt she had no way forward with him; by letting him go without some explanation, he probably felt hurt and believed she had no further interest in him.

She had allowed her remorse to fuel other emotions, like loneliness, so that when Edward had arrived at her bedroom door the previous night she was grateful, and welcomed him into her bed. Making love had always been her escape from feelings of vulnerability, and she knew that Edward understood it, and probably preyed on it. Now she was angry that she had succumbed.

She couldn't blame Edward for her cowardice with Sam. He had stuck to their agreement about avoiding relationships outside the group and believed a new life together back in England was what she wanted. But as the day wore on, Edward became increasingly troublesome. Having broached the subject of going home, he couldn't let it rest. Throughout the day he pestered Dana with a recitation of all the attractions of England and insisting she make her decision.

'Edward, this is all new to me. You might have been planning it for some time, but you didn't take me into your confidence. As I said last night, I have to think about it.'

'What's to think about? You're my wife.'

She glared at him. 'There's the farm. And the horses.'

She hadn't meant to mention the horses. She knew he'd have no sympathy for her desire to overcome the disaster with Dancer by putting her to stud.

'The horses? The horses!' he raved. 'What is there to think about? You get rid of them, of course. I don't doubt there are plenty of fools out there dreaming of fame and fortune on the track. That new chap Whiteman, for one.'

'Edward, for God's sake! Leave me be. I've told you, I need time.'

He stormed off, returning minutes later to announce he had work to do and that he'd be gone for a couple of hours.

Dana was pleased to see him go.

Mary was spending her day off on a visit to family in Naivasha, and the isolation played on Dana's mind. To take her thoughts off it, she decided to organise her wardrobe, which was untidy and had been annoying her for some time. She found a few garments she thought needed to be discarded, but after half an hour she lost her enthusiasm.

She wandered down the hall and opened the door to what had been Sam's bedroom that night. The darkness suited her mood. She lay on the bed and imagined she was again in his arms, recalling his hands and mouth as he made love to her.

He was only a few miles away. She peeped out the window. A strong wind had arisen, blowing dust and leaves through the barren garden. It was a lonely, dismal sight, but she had to do something with this restlessness — something that kept her from Sam.

She went downstairs and stood at the door. The sky was dark and heavy with cloud. It wasn't the first time the weather had teased her with promises of a break in the doldrums, and was typical of the fickleness of nature at that time of year. The clouds would promise much but deliver nothing for weeks, until one day the heavens would open and the first torrential downpour would bring blessed relief to human and animal alike.

She put aside her misgivings and hurried across the compound — her skirt wrapping around her legs in the wind — to the stable, where she quickly saddled Dancer. She had no intention of travelling far, and Dancer had

had little exercise over recent days. She thought the walk would be beneficial to both of them.

When Dana led her from the security of the stable the mare whinnied and shied at the swirling dust devils scampering across the yard.

'Ssh … easy girl. Settle, my darling,' she cooed to her.

Dana headed the filly to the west, not daring to take the northern road that would lead past the track to the *banda*. Within a few minutes, with Dancer's steady gait taking her mind away from her temptation to be with Sam, she found herself trying to recall the details of her life in England after she had married Edward. It was now so far away in time and space that she had difficulty doing so.

She had lost track of the time and realised she'd come much further than she'd planned. Looking into the sky, she found the clouds had begun to swirl and billow, black and threatening, high into the heavens.

She was more than halfway to the Banfields' and, recalling that Eliza was home alone, decided to call in for a visit and to take shelter in case the storm actually eventuated.

Immediately she came over the rise on the track leading to Eliza and John's ranch she saw the old Albion parked at the front door of the farm house. She at first thought that Edward had changed his mind and decided to collect the scarifier although John was not at home. Then she saw Eliza's house servant and cook sitting under a tree some distance from the house; as she approached they stood and walked away rather than greet her as they usually would.

Dana's surprise turned to suspicion. She dismounted and walked through the home garden and into the parlour unannounced. The sounds from the bedroom were unmistakeable.

Dana stormed into the room to find Eliza on the bed and her husband between her legs with Eliza's fingers grasping his thinning red hair.

'Dana!' she spluttered.

Edward turned and simply stared at her.

Dana spun on her heel and left the bedroom without a word.

In the garden she found a pitchfork planted into the soft soil of a flower bed. She took it to the Albion truck and, with all her might, sunk the tines into the front tyre, which gave a very satisfying pop. She then went to the remaining three tyres and within a minute the Albion was sitting on its wheel rims.

* * *

Dana eased the filly into a fast walk, afraid to strain her stamina too much, but she felt an urgency to climb to the high pastures as quickly as possible. The wind got under the brim of her hat and flung it away. She let it go.

The sky was now the colour of ink, but a thin brilliant stripe along the western horizon gave the tossing grasses an eerie glow. The wind swirled and tugged at horse and rider. A worrying thought entered her mind. Maybe Sam had become angry with her for her off-handed reception and he'd decided to take the horses onwards to Nairobi without waiting to rest them. She would be stuck alone in the hut until morning. It was a frightening prospect, and she briefly considered turning back, but the hope that he would be there spurred her on.

The sun dropped and in the darkness she had no idea if Dancer was still on the narrow track leading to the hut. There were many stumps and antbear holes across the hills, and she had to trust the horse to find her footing. In spite of her urgency to find the safety of the hut she slowed Dancer's gait to little more than a walk, but the filly was very unsettled, tossing her head and wanting to veer away to the left. Now Dana wished she'd fitted the bit instead of using just the simple noseband.

From up ahead and to the right, Dana heard the cough of a leopard and realised the reason for Dancer's nervousness. The predator was obviously taking advantage of the early darkness to search for prey. Dana let Dancer ease off to the left and hoped she could resume the correct course when they'd distanced themselves from the leopard.

A loud snarl came from the darkness. Dancer reared and plunged then took a great leap forwards, throwing Dana from the saddle. She hit the ground with a sickening thud and at the same moment there came the crack of thunder.

She took a moment to regain her senses, then she shouted for Dancer, but her voice was ripped from her mouth by the wind.

Dana scrambled to her feet, fighting her panic. She knew the leopard was close and would now be emboldened without the intimidating presence of the horse. She listened, but could hear nothing above the howling wind. The silence could mean that the leopard had gone on its way, or was now stalking her in earnest.

Walk, don't run, she told herself, as she continued up the slope, but with the last of the daylight now gone, she had no way of knowing whether she was heading in the right direction.

A shadow loomed at her from the darkness.

Her heart caught in her throat and she surrendered to her panic and took flight.

Something snared her arm.

She screamed.

'Dana! It's me. It's all right. It's me.'

'Oh, Sam!' she sobbed, and fell into his arms.

CHAPTER 26

Dana glanced around the *banda* while Sam was outside putting Dancer into the *boma* he'd built to protect the horses. She marvelled at how easily a little warmth and light could dispel a bad experience.

He returned with a handful of sticks to stoke the fire in the middle of the hut and, as soon as he'd straightened from his task, she wrapped her arms around him again, feeling the long strong muscles of his back and his warmth. She didn't want to ever let him go.

He stroked her hair and kissed the top of her head.

'I've been watching all day,' he whispered. 'Hoping you'd come.'

'I wanted to, but I've been afraid.'

'Afraid?'

'Yes. What I feel about you frightens me.'

'Don't be frightened.'

She stroked his back from his shoulders to his waist then ran her hands down to feel the muscles of his buttocks.

'I'm better now,' she said. 'Being with you makes me feel alive. Wonderful.' She looked up at him. 'I want you, Sam. I'll always want you.'

He kissed her softly and his lips lingered on hers as his tenderness slowly turned to passion.

She pulled at his buttons and when she'd stripped the shirt from him she helped him loosen the clasps on her new-fangled brassiere. When their last items of clothing fell to the floor, he lifted her and laid her on the cot. She felt the coarse hair of the zebra hide against her back and Sam's smooth skin as he lowered himself onto her.

*　*　*

They lay naked in the flickering light of the fire with one of Sam's woollen blankets pulled over them. Dana's head rested on Sam's shoulder and as his breathing returned to normal he enjoyed the feel of her fingers idly caressing his abdomen. The wind had abated; it was no longer howling through the forest above them, but occasionally gusting enough to part the door covering and make the flames briefly dance in the fireplace.

Dana asked how he knew she was approaching the *banda*.

'I heard the leopard before the wind came up,' he said, 'and I went out with my rifle to watch over the horses. I saw you coming up the hill, but then I lost you in the gloom until just before the leopard pounced. I must have got lucky with my old Rigby.'

'It was your rifle!' she exclaimed. 'I thought it was thunder.'

After he'd released the shot his heart almost stopped when he thought he'd missed the leopard and hit Dana. If he'd had time to think, he might not have taken the shot because of the risk, but then the leopard would have torn her apart. Thinking back on the possible consequences, the cold hand of dread touched him, and he felt such a strong sense of loss at the thought of going through life without her that a hot wave of nausea threatened to overwhelm him.

He forced the notion from his head and played with her hair. It was so much finer than an African woman's. It slipped like silk through his fingers.

'Have you always been in the horse smuggling business?' she asked.

'No. I'm quite new at it. A few years ago I almost became a respectable settler — a coffee man, in fact.'

'When was that?'

He felt her snuggle close to him. He loved the feel of her compact body pressing against his, and her warmth.

'It's quite a long story. Are you sure you want to hear this?'

'There's nowhere else I'd rather be,' she said. 'No one I'd rather be with.'

'It must have been five or six years ago … yes, it was 1926, and I had just come home from the States. I had a big idea, and plenty of money, but not quite enough to get it all started.'

'What happened?'

He explained the scheme and how all the coffee growers would share the benefits of the refinery.

'But when the bank realised they were dealing with a *native*, they went into a spin. Apparently the banks have an unwritten policy not to lend to Africans. There was nothing said officially. The bank simply backed away from the agreement to extend the remaining twenty per cent I needed.' He shrugged. 'So nobody won.'

'And that was how you lost your money?'

'No. I didn't lose a lot of money on that. I only lost some people I thought were friends. I lost my money, quite a deal of money in fact, through anger.'

'Anger? What do you mean?'

'When my business associates and friends abandoned me simply because I was a black African instead of a black American, I was stunned. But it was the institutionalised discrimination by the banks that got me angry. I was determined to strike back, to do something for the ordinary Kenyans who the banks refused to help.

'My anger drove me into a business I had no idea how to run. When it failed, I failed a lot of people who had come to rely on me.'

She reached up and kissed him on the cheek. 'So now it's Abyssinian horses.'

'Yes. For now, I'm sticking to something I know.'

Sam slipped his arm from around her shoulder and added some fuel to the fire. When he returned to the cot, Dana lifted herself onto an elbow. She placed her warm hand against his cheek, ran a fingertip down his nose, and tickled his lips with a long fingernail.

'What will we do, Sam?'

He knew what she meant. This was more than a brief fling that could be enjoyed then forgotten.

'I don't know,' he said. 'All I know is that I don't want it to end.'

CHAPTER 27

Dana drove past the Muthaiga Club's main building and on through the car park to an area of bush beside the golf course. It was then only a short walk to the flat Sam used while in Nairobi. Both agreed it was most important to avoid raising any suspicions around the town, and a rendezvous in a Nairobi hotel was sure to be noticed. It had been a month ago that they had their first meeting at Muthaiga; and on each of the four occasions since, she'd safely made her way to his door without seeing anybody she knew.

Edward knew she was with Sam on the night of the storm when she didn't come home until the following afternoon. On that occasion he could say nothing considering she had caught him in bed with Eliza Banfield, but Edward didn't know they had continued to meet. Nairobi was a small town with an even smaller white community. Dana and Sam didn't want their affair to be the topic at every dinner table from Mombasa to the lake, so discretion was essential.

She and Edward had resumed a cordial but cool relationship. He continued to talk about leaving Kenya as soon as possible, but now made it clear he would do so with or without her. With no assets or means of support, Dana had no option but to go with him. This made her uneasy about continuing her relationship with

Sam. She liked him very much. He was kind and attentive and the sex was more exciting than any she'd had, but neither of them had used the word love, and they made no plans together beyond agreeing the next time they would meet. With Edward pressing her for a decision, she decided to raise the matter of their future to find out if Sam wanted more than what they had.

This was not the first time she had planned to do so. Two weeks before, when Sam came through Kipipiri with more horses from Abyssinia, they met again in the *banda*. It was the perfect occasion to raise the matter as, unlike in Nairobi, she didn't have to hurry home until late afternoon. On that occasion they dozed after making love and then made love again as the sun sent pins of light through the *banda* walls to move like fireflies over their naked, sweating bodies.

She preferred making love there in the *banda*, because at the Muthaiga Club she arrived late morning, but needed to leave by mid-afternoon, otherwise she'd be caught on the treacherous road down the escarpment after dark. However, as she picked her way through the bush towards Sam's flat, she had to admit it had an extra degree of excitement. The secrecy of their meetings added a touch of danger, and her body tingled in anticipation.

She knocked gently on the door and he opened it with that broad smile that said he was happy she was there. He drew her to him as he closed the door and they kissed. His lips pressed warmly against hers and he wrapped his arms around her and slid his hands to her bottom.

'You have no underwear on,' he said with a grin.

'Exactly. Isn't that how you like me dressed?'

'It is,' he said and took her in his arms again, fondling her as he slid the shoulder strap from her dress.

'No,' she said. 'Don't undress me. I want you now. Take me here, standing at the door.'

He lifted her dress and felt her wet warmth with his fingers, and rubbed her little nub until she moaned for him.

He opened the front of his pants and, gripping her under her buttocks, used his weight to pin her against the wall then pressed into her.

As she clung to him, teeth biting into his shoulder, she couldn't think about love, but she knew she never wanted this to end.

* * *

'Sam?' she said from beside him on the bed.

'Hmm ...?'

He sounded as if he'd come from a light sleep.

'Sam, can I ask you something?'

'Anything, my darling,' he muttered.

'Seriously. But you don't have to answer if you feel you can't.'

'Mmm ... must be something important. I'd better listen.' He raised himself on an elbow and rested his head on his hand, looking at her.

She felt self-conscious under his gaze and lost her nerve.

'Edward wants to leave Kenya,' she said bluntly, then bit her lip. It wasn't at all how she'd planned to tell him.

He stared at her for a long moment without a word. She tried to read his expression, but failed.

'I see,' he said. 'And you will leave with him, I presume.'

'I … well … Yes, I suppose I will.'

He nodded.

'Unless …' she began, then paused. 'What are you thinking, Sam?'

'I'm not thinking anything.'

'Yes, you are.'

'What could I be thinking?' He swung his legs over the side of the bed. 'Could I think that a Kikuyu man — a horse smuggler — and a white lady could live together in Kenya? The same Kikuyu man who had been laughed out of the Muthaiga Club when he dared suggest he could build a coffee refinery with white partners? Surely not.'

He smiled to take the edge off his words, but she could see the bitterness remained.

'It depends on how we feel about one another,' she said, reaching a hand towards him. He ignored it.

'Dana, don't you see? It doesn't make any difference what we feel about each other. It's what others feel about us that matters.'

She slid from under the covers and sat beside him. 'We don't need to think about anyone else. The rest of the world can do and think what it likes, can't it?'

Sam remained tight-lipped.

'Sam?' She tried to catch his eye but he stared straight ahead.

'What do you feel, Sam? Is what you feel strong enough to overcome the ugliness out there?'

He went to the window and stood there, glaring down the track and across the garden to the Muthaiga Club's steep tiled roof.

'Sam?'

'You don't understand, Dana. You can't understand. That's the problem you have. You can't imagine what it's like to feel animosity aimed at you simply because of the colour of your skin. But I can tell you this much: if we allowed ourselves to do as you suggest, to … to just ignore the whole world, you would soon enough feel something similar. Oh, yes. And then we'd really have questions to ask: How strongly do we feel? Is all this worth it?'

* * *

Dana came in from the garden lugging a basket brimming with tomatoes and potatoes. She swung it upwards to the dining table, but caught the edge, sending the vegetables bouncing across the floor.

'*Damn it!*' she said, and sank into a chair.

Edward came in from the study.

'Dana … Are you all right?'

She held the back of her hand to her forehead. 'Yes, I suppose so.'

'Darling, you look exhausted. And hot. Do you have a fever? Let me see.'

He placed his hand on her forehead. 'Hmm, you are a bit feverish. Are you keeping up your quinine?'

'I started taking extra when I began to feel ill, but it doesn't seem to help.'

'Then it's off to Dr Whitmore with you. Can't have you coming down with malaria just as we're planning to leave.'

* * *

Surely he was wrong. It was not possible. Dana stared at him as her mind raced through dates and people and places. Three months. It could only be Sam ... or Edward.

'Are you sure? I mean, about the timing,' she asked.

'It's not an exact science,' he said. 'But I would guess you are still in your first trimester. Somewhere between eleven and fourteen weeks. Don't you know when you had your last period?'

She shook her head. 'I'm not regular. I don't understand this. I take precautions, and I ... I didn't conceive early in my marriage. I was told I might not be able to at all.'

'Obviously your advisers were wrong,' the doctor said. 'Mind you, we can't be too critical of them. We didn't know a lot about infertility back then. I take it you're not pleased with the news.'

Was she pleased? She was ... *overawed*. On the one hand, she was delighted. On the other, Edward would be furious. He'd warned her not to get pregnant. But accidents can happen with contraception. Surely he'd understand that. She couldn't think about what might happen next.

'No!' she said. 'I'm pleased. Very pleased. Just surprised.'

On her journey home she tried to think of a way to handle the situation with Edward. She knew his first response would be to insist upon a termination. She had agreed to it in principle. When Polly had become pregnant under similar circumstances, Archie insisted on a termination, arguing quite correctly that there was no way of knowing if he or one of the other members of the Zephyr club was the father. She could explain to Edward that the timing of the pregnancy meant the father could be none of their dinner party friends. But Edward knew about her first night with Sam and, even if she could convince him that it was his and to allow her to have the baby, the child might be black. That would be the end of her life with Edward.

* * *

Edward was calm. Very calm. When Dana told him she was pregnant he was sitting in the parlour with a pile of English newspapers. His face reddened, but he said and did nothing for a few moments. Eventually he arose from his chair and walked out to the veranda, his hands clasped behind his back. He stood there studying the hills surrounding the farm and when he returned his expression was composed.

'This is totally unexpected,' he said.

'Yes. I'm sorry. I was taking precautions, but —'

'Wasn't this supposed to be impossible?'

'Well, no … not impossible, but *unlikely*, according to the doctors.'

'But you've had it confirmed by Dr Whitmore?'

'Yes.'

He nodded. 'At least he can be relied upon to be discreet.' He stroked his jowls. 'I will make arrangements to have it terminated.'

'Edward, I'm sure it's yours —'

He held up a finger, halting her protest. A flicker of anger crossed his face. 'There is no way you can be sure of that. It will never do. You will have it terminated. I will arrange it.'

She knew it was pointless trying to convince him otherwise. In her mind she had already been through every argument she could imagine and lost them all comprehensively.

Edward returned to his armchair, gave his newspaper a noisy rattle, and resumed his reading.

A week later — a week during which nothing changed in their normal routine — Edward handed her a railway ticket.

'You leave for Mombasa in five days,' he said. 'Dr Alessandro himself will collect you at the station. He thinks you will need a few days to recuperate. Your return ticket is open-dated.'

That night she lay in bed with the cool mountain breeze ruffling the curtains. She stared at the shadows dancing on the ceiling, thinking of Sam, who was somewhere in Abyssinia and not due back for a fortnight.

What had been in his mind when they last met? He wouldn't open his heart to her. He was angry, perhaps not at her, but at the world.

She ached to see him, but what would he say about the baby?

* * *

Dana had written and destroyed several notes to send to the Muthaiga Club for Sam. In all likelihood, she would be back from Mombasa before he came through Kipipiri again. In any case, what could she say? He was so sure they couldn't survive as a couple in Kenya. How much worse would it be if she had a white child? Even a black child? There was just nowhere in Kenya where they could live in peace.

The temptation to share her secret with one of her friends — Polly or Averil — was almost irresistible, but if she told them about Edward's objection to the baby, she'd have to tell them why and she didn't want to reveal Sam to them. This troubled her: perhaps Sam was right. The stigma attached to being a white woman with a black lover might be greater than she could bear. She was alone.

She tried to be appreciative of Edward's consideration as the day of her departure drew nearer. He helped her arrange a delivery of dry feed for the horses so they avoided colic from the thick new pasture that followed the start of the rains. He was sweet on the several occasions when she was on the point of tears, but when she looked into his eyes, hoping to see compassion and a reprieve for her baby, she found only determination.

* * *

Edward acted like a conspirator in a crime story, keeping Dana secreted in the first-class waiting room at Nairobi as the train filled with passengers. He had considered using Gilgil station, a mere ten miles away from home, but the news that Dana Northcote had caught the train to Mombasa alone would be all over the highlands within a day.

He hurried her on board at the last moment. Placing her suitcase on the rack, he kissed her on the cheek with the conductor's whistle screeching in her ears.

Dana was alone in the small carriage, watching tents and huts flash by her window as the train climbed from the swampy flats surrounding Nairobi, over the Embakasi rise, dotted with Maasai villages, and onto the Athi Plains. Herds of zebra and wildebeest bolted in fright at the sound of the train's whistle. It was an amazing transformation. Within less than a hundred miles, the land had changed from high, rolling green hills and forests to a sea of yellowed grass undulating to a distant pale blue horizon.

At the Athi River bridge a herd of elephants bathed and trumpeted. Dana watched them as she passed, reflecting upon the speed of events over the previous days.

The gently rocking carriage enticed her into sleep. She dozed through the heat of the day, but awoke in fright, unable to get her bearings. Weird baobab trees, whose naked, spindly arms reached pleadingly to the heavens, stood sentinel in endless grassland.

They stopped at a *dak* bungalow at dusk to eat a hurried meal as the staff made the beds in the first- and second-class carriages. She ate little and slept badly through a night punctuated by whistles, jolting carriages and strange dreams.

The sun rose over the Taru Desert with menace, but there was not a living thing there to fall prey to its deadly rays. The earth, thorn bushes and stones had been bleached the same pitiless grey. The world was a barren place.

Dana felt a terrible foreboding. What if this pregnancy would be her last? It was a miracle that she'd conceived at all. What if she, like the landscape, could never again light the spark of life?

After an hour of stultifying sameness within which Dana fretted about the impending abortion, a sprig of green appeared on a bush and was gone in a flash. A moment later, another. And another. By the time the train reached Rabai at the crest of the headland that swept down to the Indian Ocean, the landscape had been reborn. A verdant forest had replaced the desert. It was as if the earth had arisen from its own ashes and given birth to a brave new garden.

Dana had also gone through a form of rebirth. As the train huffed and puffed into Mombasa station she was now in no doubt about what she had to do. She could not forego this chance — perhaps her last — to have a child.

She alighted from the train, ignored the top-hatted figure who politely asked if she were Mrs Northcote, and found a small Indian hotel in a back street of the old quarter where she again considered her decision and her ability to carry it through. She had the doctor's sizeable fee in her purse, and another small amount she could access from her bank account. It was enough to survive for the term of the pregnancy.

At the post office she sent a telegram to Edward: *Have changed my mind about new delivery. Will await its safe arrival and advise.*

CHAPTER 28

As Sam made the long ride back from Abyssinia with his latest herd of ponies, he had plenty of time to reflect upon his last meeting with Dana. He knew he could have handled the situation better, had not his injured pride interfered.

When Dana told him she would be leaving Kenya with Edward, she seemed to accept the situation with equanimity. He'd thought they'd shared something beyond the obvious enjoyment of each other's bodies, and her attitude came as a shock. His response had been harsh and ill-considered.

She left him there then, nursing his damaged pride, saying she was already late to make her journey back to Kipipiri. She was right, it was late, but he later felt it was his thoughtless words that had sent her hurrying home.

He'd remained on the bed, thinking with the taste and the smell of her lingering, until the last of the sun fell from the drapes, and the darkness took its place. There was a world of visible difference between them, which of course was what white Kenya would see. But with such obvious differences, it was easy to bring their similarities into sharper focus. They needed time to explore them more fully, and if he let her go, they would never know what they might have lost.

By morning, he'd made up his mind to go to her before returning to Nairobi. He'd tell her she was too important to him to let her go; they had too much in common to let superficial differences part them. He'd say that of all the challenges they might face together, it was more important to test their feelings than to miss their chance at happiness. He'd ask her to leave her husband and make a new life, somewhere, with him.

The silver Willys-Knight roadster was sitting under the vine-covered lattice as he rode towards the farmhouse. He still had the excuse of their agistment agreement to explain his presence there.

'You're too late, old man,' Edward, pleased to enlighten him, said. 'Dana left for England a few days ago.'

'Already? I thought you were still thinking about it.'

'Change of plans. I'll be following her pretty soon, of course. When I've settled our affairs here. I'm afraid you'll have to find another place to rest your horses.'

Sam was numb as he rode on to Nairobi. The animals were exhausted, and he was too, but there was something wrong. Something very wrong. Dana would not have made that decision without at least informing him. He knew she had at least that much affection for him. He arrived in Nairobi in time to stable the herd before boarding the night train to the coast.

*　　*　　*

Dana stood on the sea wall beneath Fort Jesus, watching a fishing *dhow* make its way across the old harbour. The helmsman's mate gathered the lateen sail to the yard and swivelled it around the mast to make the tack. The crab-claw sail filled with the wind, and the spritely craft lifted its nose and ploughed through the light chop towards the mouth of the harbour.

She had come to the waterfront to think. Having declared her intentions to Edward, she knew he would be on the next train to Mombasa. Indeed he may already be en route. The old Arab trading port of Mombasa was bigger than the young upstart, Nairobi, but not big enough to conceal a lone white woman. She had told Edward of her intentions without knowing how to implement them.

A gust of wind came up and tried to snatch Dana's hat but she caught it in time.

'Ah, the *kusi*,' a voice from behind her declared. 'It wants the *memsahib*'s fine hat.'

She turned to find an old man with a face like chiselled leather standing a few paces away. Apart from his dark brown face, he was otherwise completely white: a white beard and hair; a long white *kanzu* and white *kofia* cap.

'The *kusi*?' Dana asked.

'The sou'easter, you would call it, *memsahib*. It is very strong today.'

'Oh, I see. The south-east trade wind.'

'And it carries the *dhows* northwards to Arabia with trade goods. Spices and sisal, coffee and maybe a little gold. I myself would be sailing, *inshallah*, if I were twenty years younger.'

'You were a sailor?'

'I once owned the finest *dhow* in all of the Coast Province. One hundred tons she was.' His eyes, buried in a host of wrinkles, twinkled. 'With the *kusi* we would sail to faraway Arabia. We were like the wind itself.' His eyes misted and his smile wavered. 'Ah, but now, what can I do? I can show my grandchildren the *dhows*. And I can remember the beautiful places. I can remember how things were.'

'Where else did you sail?' she asked.

'Many places. Lamu, Kismayu, Mogadishu. Many, many places. All the way to the Red Sea.'

'This place you mention, Lamu. It's on the north coast of Kenya, isn't it?'

'It is, *memsahib*. My third wife, Jamina, she is from Lamu.'

'How far is it?'

'To sail there — one day when the *kusi* is with you.'

'And what about by road?'

He smiled. 'No roads, *memsahib*. Only by sea. These new captains, they like to do business in Lamu. They don't like to sail the *dhow* to Arabia these days. They can make money with cargo to Lamu and they are home in a week or two. Not like me. Six months I wait until the *kazkusi* comes from the north-east. Then I come back home from Arabia.'

Dana looked again at the *dhows* on the harbour. There were those that appeared to be the size of fishing boats, but larger ones too.

'Did you say there are no roads to Lamu?' she asked, interrupting him.

'To Kilifi, yes, *memsahib*. To Malindi, not good. But to Lamu? No. To Lamu you must take to the sea; the *dhow*.'

'Then I would ask a favour of you, *mzee*.' She used the polite title for an elderly gentleman. 'I would like you to help me arrange a *dhow* to take me to Lamu.'

If he was surprised, he didn't show it. 'To Lamu ...' The old man stroked his chin. 'Yes, it is possible. I have many friends with *dhows*. When would the *memsahib* like to go?'

'Now.'

* * *

In spite of her rush to leave Mombasa, she realised that to board a *dhow* dressed as a European would invite attention — the kind of attention that might tip off a European man looking for his missing wife. She went to the market and bought a number of *kangas* and a head scarf. She arrived late at the sea front where she found the old man wringing his hands.

'Hurry, *memsahib*,' he said. 'The tide is turning.'

He took her bag and led her down the steps of the old stone wharf to a small skiff. A boy of no more than ten sat at the tiller.

'My grandson will take you to Captain Masood.'

He pointed to a large *dhow* bobbing at anchor in the harbour. An unfamiliar flag fluttered at the masthead and men dressed in *dhotis* and headscarves hurriedly loaded sacks from a lighter drawn alongside. In her haste to get away, she hadn't contemplated the journey in any detail. Now she realised she would be at sea on a strange craft with men she'd never met, going to an island she'd only heard associated with slave traders. She turned her eyes from the *dhow* to the old man.

He was smiling at her. 'The captain is a friend of mine,' he said. 'He will keep you safe.'

Although she'd only known him a few hours, there was something about the old man that elicited trust. Maybe it was his old-world manners, or the way he held her eyes when he spoke.

'Thank you, *mzee*,' she said. 'You have been very kind.'

She extended her hand to him and he took it in both of his. His hands were very soft and his fingers waxy and cool.

'I hope you find the peace you seek in Lamu,' he said, looking into her eyes. 'And whatever fortune comes your way, may Allah grant you the strength to accept it.'

He held her hands for a long moment and she felt he had more to say, but couldn't because time was against them. She had the odd feeling that the old man somehow knew the reason she was going to Lamu. He seemed to have such wisdom and she felt that if she could tap into it she would find the answers she needed. Why was she having this baby? What would happen when she did? How would she survive if Edward disowned her? The old man would know these things. If only there was time for him to tell her. She realised too that he was the only one who knew of her journey. Her only connection to her real life. If she never arrived in Lamu nobody would know where to look.

He pressed her hands. 'It is time. May Allah go with you, *memsahib*.'

She stepped into the skiff and the boy cast off. The little craft moved swiftly towards the *dhow* where two men were wrestling with the sail. The *dhow* was larger than it appeared from the wharf.

She turned to wave farewell, but the old man had gone.

*   *   *

Dana had had a few days' head start so, immediately the train pulled into Mombasa, Sam went to a shipping agent. He learned that a ship had left for England the day before, but the agent eyed Sam with suspicion when he asked if Countess Dana Northcote was on the passenger manifest.

'And what does that have to do with you, *kafir*?'

Sam contained his anger. 'She's a friend.'

'Is she now? Well, friend or not, the manifest is confidential. Now, if I were you, I'd bugger off before I call the native policemen.'

Still hoping that Dana might have taken passage on a later ship, Sam searched the streets and alleys for hotels, enquiring about her.

'I'm looking for a European lady who might have checked in over the last few days. Light brown hair. Green eyes. About so tall.'

Most of the managers refused to give him any information. Many threatened him with the police. It confirmed the problems they'd have living together, but it didn't deter him.

He read the shipping schedule in the newspaper and noted that vessels of the British India Steam Navigation Company and Deutsche Ost-Afrika, sailing from Tanganyika, were due out over the next few days. He was on the wharf an hour before boarding times to search for Dana among the hubbub of embarking passengers.

Amid the festivities, kisses and friendly farewells, the *oompah*ing of the Mombasa brass band and the draping garlands of paper streamers, he searched for her. When the ship's horn sounded its departure, he felt its deep reverberations collide with his heart.

His last chance was among the few passengers taking passage on a cargo ship, the MV *Mogadishu*, bound for England via a series of piddling ports. After it despatched its passengers and cargo, she was made ready to sail again to Britain. All day he waited, sitting on a stack of cargo pallets or strolling up and down the wharf to kill time. Passengers embarked singly, usually untidy men with a rucksack over their shoulder, or occasionally a small family group with cloth-covered bundles and suitcases bound with twine. There was no bustle or haste and very few people came to see them off.

Sam waited into the evening and, at around eleven that night, long after the last of the passengers boarded, the crew cranked up the gangway, and she sailed. He continued to watch the ship as it made its manoeuvres preparatory to leaving the harbour. He waited because he could think of nothing further he could do. Against all his instincts, he'd let Dana into his heart and this was his punishment: she'd abandoned him without so much as a kiss goodbye.

He'd been searching for two weeks and only one person had recalled seeing someone like her. An old man he met wandering along the harbour wall nodded and smiled when he described Dana, but the man was doddering and confused. He claimed — clearly mistakenly — that she had sailed a few days earlier to an obscure island up the Kenyan coast: Lamu.

CHAPTER 29

The voyage had taken less than twenty-four hours, but with a following sea, it had been an uncomfortable one for Dana. The nausea that had prompted her to see her doctor in Nairobi returned full force; it was with shaking knees that she staggered ashore at Lamu.

With the solid stone wharf beneath her feet, she allowed herself some time to revive, watching the bustle of activity until the young deckhand Captain Masood had assigned to her returned to take her to a guest house.

He led her from the brilliant light of the sea front into a warren of deeply shaded alleys, some no more than a yard or so wide between rough coral-stone walls. The houses had huge, elaborately carved wooden doors and shuttered windows. People streamed through this labyrinth. Most of the women wore the purdah and veil. Some, like Dana, were dressed in brightly coloured *kangas*. The men were in spotless cream or white *kanzus* or *dhotis*. Dana had difficulty keeping up with her guide as everyone had to give way to the many donkeys carrying the commerce of the town on short, tottering legs. In some places they passed through tunnels formed by buildings connecting houses on each side of the alley. Occasionally Dana could catch a glimpse of a rooftop garden trailing bougainvillea and other creepers into the alleys below.

As Dana became completely disoriented, and certain she would never find her way out of the maze, the deckhand stopped at a double set of wooden doors. He leaned against one side and, when it swung open, gestured Dana to follow. After a moment's hesitation she did so. When he closed the door behind her the clamour of the alley, the donkeys, the crush of people, the noise and the bustle, were immediately gone.

Dana gasped. She was in a courtyard with a narrow path that meandered through a jungle of ferns, palms and flowering shrubs. A tinkling fountain rained on goldfish glinting in a lily-covered pond and an enormous bougainvillea climbed the wall to a second storey, which had rounded stone archways and stained timber balconies. A canary warbled in a cage hanging from a bower covered in orchids.

The young man had disappeared inside the house, leaving Dana to marvel at her surroundings. She found a small table tucked away in a corner, and two chairs, one of which was occupied by a ginger cat, which began purring even as she approached.

She sat with the cat, feeling so contented in this blissful place that she thought she might also begin to purr.

She had started out on her journey with trepidation, having no plan other than to find the freedom to make her own choice about her pregnancy. Now that she had found this refuge she knew what she would do. This was a place of tranquillity. A place to give birth and to prepare for whatever life might then offer. Whether it was to be destitution or acceptance, if she were ever to find the strength to face that future it would be here in this garden of Eden.

* * *

Dana spent many long hours in the garden, reflecting upon her decision. Initially, the peace and beauty of the guest house garden gave her strength. Then, like a thief in the night, loneliness crept from the corner of her mind where all her insecurities lay, and teased them into life.

During the day it was Polly and her friends who she longed to see — and Averil, who was more of a dear friend than an older sister. She missed their company, their mindless chatter about fashion and the latest dance music. Gossip about the neighbours and whispered conversations about their last dinner party. She missed their outings — a cup of tea at Pomeroy's, a gin and tonic at the Norfolk or Muthaiga Club. A day at the races.

At night she thought of Sam. She yearned to be in his embrace, to run her hands along his strong arms and body as he propped himself above her, kissing her, and for the delicious pleasure he gave her as he lowered himself onto and into her.

She had no idea what information Sam had received about her disappearance. Presumably, he would learn she was not at Kipipiri. Most likely Edward would have invented an explanation about her departure that would satisfy their friends: an ailing relative in England and a dash to be at the bedside; a mysterious illness needing specialist treatment. Whatever the reason stated for her sudden flight, Sam had every right to expect a message from her. But she couldn't risk it. The postmark on her letter would reveal her hideout. When he knew she wasn't in England he would become suspicious about the reason for her disappearance. He would perhaps try to find her and so would discover her pregnancy.

They'd shared a deep passion, but they had not explored beyond that. There had been no talk of love or a commitment to the future. If the baby turned out to be his, she didn't want him to feel obliged to support a family he hadn't deliberately created. She felt entirely responsible for her predicament.

If the baby was Edward's, then she had other options, but she could not look beyond the birth. Her life would hang suspended until then; though once she'd settled, she took stock of her situation.

The baby was due in February. By then all her funds would have been exhausted paying the guest house costs and meals. She'd made no provision for the unexpected and would need money to pay for a midwife and items for the baby.

She thought she would be able to use her modest bank savings to bolster her cash, and although the Lamu post office acted as an agent for her bank, she worried that Edward would be keeping an eye on those funds and, if they were withdrawn, use his influence with the bank to discover where the money was transferred. She decided to leave it untouched until after the birth.

She'd left most of her important jewellery items in the box on her dressing table at Zephyr, but had thrown a small beaded bag of other pieces into her suitcase before she left. There was her lion's fang trophy that she'd been carrying back and forth to Nairobi for weeks. Her intention had been to have it fitted with a silver chain in place of the plain leather thong, but she'd repeatedly forgotten to do so. There were also two pairs of inexpensive earrings, and a spare watch. None of them would amount to much.

Now she looked at her rings. She had a plain gold wedding ring, which had belonged to her beloved grandmother. There was also the sizeable diamond that Edward had bought her after they were married. He called it their post-marriage engagement ring. Dana had been twenty at the time, and would have dearly loved an engagement party as was the custom among all her friends, but Edward refused. He thought it inappropriate that the 10th Earl of Seddon be formally engaged after divorcing his wife of fifteen years.

The gold dealer near the spice market made her a reasonable offer and Dana sold it with not a touch of remorse.

With her short-term financial position secured, she decided to write a note to Edward, which she sent by *dhow* to Mombasa for posting.

Dearest Edward,

This is to let you know I am safe and well.

I have decided to have our baby in the hope that when you see it you will find it in your heart to love and accept him or her. If you do not, then I will raise the child on my own.

I will contact you again when the baby is born at which time we can discuss our future and the future of our child.

Love
Dana

PS Please don't trouble yourself by trying to trace me through this letter. Although it is postmarked Mombasa, I am far from there.

CHAPTER 30

In the four months since her arrival, Dana had seldom seen the Swahili owner of the Kidege Guest House, which quite suited her. He was a middle-aged man with bad teeth and a worse disposition, always complaining about the costs of running his business. Dana was almost always his only paying guest and she thought she, of all people, could have been spared his ill temper.

In the owner's absence, Kidege, or Little Bird, Guest House was effectively run by Amina, a big-bosomed black woman from Uganda. She could not be persuaded to explain how she travelled from Jinja, where the Victoria Nile embarks upon its long journey to the sea, to work in Lamu, but Dana suspected it had something to do with a man, because Amina remained unmarried in a place where women were in great demand as second, third or even fourth wives.

Amina was pleasant company, which was fortunate. As October approached and the *kusi* died, the heat became too distressing for Dana, now five months pregnant, to move comfortably around the island during the day.

It was time to find a midwife, and she asked Amina for help. Uncharacteristically, her new friend was reticent.

'*Memsahib* should be in Mombasa for this baby,' she said, as she plucked the dry laundry from the upstairs railing.

'No, I can't go to Mombasa. I came to Lamu to have my baby.'

'No doctors here for a white lady, *memsahib*.'

'Then a midwife will do. Surely there's someone here in Lamu who delivers babies. Won't you take me to her, please?'

Amina fussed with the sheet she was folding, straightening the corners and smoothing every last wrinkle.

'Amina,' Dana implored. 'Please?'

Two days later, Amina led Dana through the serpentine alleys to a small stone house in a part of the town she'd not seen before.

The midwife was old with crooked teeth and fingers gnarled with arthritis, but she had a kind smile in her rheumy eyes. Amina had barely completed the usual salutations before she started feeling Dana's belly. Then she stared into her eyes and ran her hands up her arms and down her body to her legs.

Dana felt like a yearling in an auctioneer's yard, being examined for flaws and infirmities.

Amina continued to translate Dana's explanation of her pregnancy, but the midwife seemed uninterested. Instead, she went to a large chest where she withdrew some carved wooden images and items of bone and ivory. She waved each of them over Dana, making a humming sound and occasional muttered remarks. Dana asked what she was saying, but Amina shrugged, saying it wasn't in any language that she could decipher. Finally, the midwife smiled her crooked smile and announced to Amina that she would be able to deliver the *memsahib*'s baby.

Amina thanked her and, as Dana made the tortuous walk back to the cool escape of Kidege Guest House's garden, she wondered what Dr Whitmore might think of the midwife's diagnostic methods.

* * *

Even Kidege's beautiful garden became too constrictive after a while, so Dana occasionally went for a walk in the evenings.

Strolling through the market on one such occasion, she saw a white man. His was the first European face she'd seen since arriving in Lamu. She was excited at the prospect that she was not the only foreigner on the island. Perhaps he had a wife — someone from a similar background to hers — with whom she could share news and ideas. Maybe she was a mother and would able to reassure Dana that her concerns about her pregnancy were unfounded. But she lost him in the crowd.

Upon returning to the guest house she sank into the padded sofa and shared her disappointment with Amina.

'I actually thought he saw me, and then ran away,' she said.

'This man,' Amina said, as she chopped the sweet potato, 'he has fat belly, red face and a *kitenge* of many colours?'

'Yes, that's him. He looked about sixty. Do you know him?'

'Hmmph,' she said. 'My friend be his housekeeper for so-o-o many years.' She tossed the sweet potato pieces in the pot, making a splash. 'And still he will not marry her.'

'What does he do here? And why would he run away?'

Amina shrugged. 'Why would he not marry beautiful lady like my friend Mimi? He a strange one, that Dr Cahill.'

'A doctor? Then I should meet him. Where is his office?'

'He have no office, this one. No more a doctor. Now he is … how you call it? A drunkard.'

'Still … it might be good to have someone else in case the midwife …'

Amina put down her cutting knife, and sitting beside Dana, took her hand.

'No. For you, everything be coming good. You no need this crazy doctor man.'

'But look at me, Amina.' She put a hand on her abdomen. 'Look at the size of me. Something must be wrong, or I got the dates wrong.'

'Big belly, big baby. That is it. You no should worry.'

Dana felt childish. She seemed to be constantly fretting about her baby. Amina, who'd had no children, seemed to know more about pregnancies than she did. If she could find at least one other voice of reassurance, drunkard or not, she felt sure it would give her the confidence she needed.

'Do you think you could ask your friend Mimi to ask Dr Cahill to come and see me some time?'

Amina sighed. 'I try. But he a strange man, that Dr Cahill.'

* * *

It was November, and the blessed *kazkusi* had arrived from the north-east, bringing modest relief to the stifling heat. However, it did nothing to remove Dana's concerns about the progress of her pregnancy, which increased with her size. And her panic was not relieved at all by her midwife.

She decided to take matters into her own hands. If Dr Cahill wouldn't see her, she would go and see him. After all, he was a doctor, and a white man. He had responsibilities.

Amina consulted with Mimi and when she returned gave Dana the details of the arrangements. Her visit should conform with a time most likely to find the doctor both sober and awake — a difficult assignment.

As Amina led her to the doctor's house, she recited a litany of accusations against the hapless Dr Cahill, principal among which was his shameful dereliction of his duty to marry Mimi, who had stood by him for years in spite of the fact that he was a drunk and had little money to spend on her.

Amina stopped at a heavily weathered gate set in a high coral-stone wall, little different from others in the laneway. She pulled on a cord and a bell rang faintly on the other side.

The gate opened and Mimi greeted them warmly. She was a tall and elegant Somali woman in her mid-forties with a hint of an Italian accent to her excellent English.

'Oh, you poor thing,' she said to Dana. 'You look so hot. Come, we can sit in the garden. It is still cool at this time of morning.'

She led them through a garden almost the rival of Kidege's, with creepers and shrubs filling every corner except for a small vegetable garden of tomatoes, beans and some kind of leafy green vegetable.

She had arranged three chairs in the deep shade of a wisteria vine. As they chatted, lilac flowers dropped around them.

'I suggested you come at this time,' Mimi said, 'as it is too early for David to be drunk, but early enough to be here before he returns from the fish market. I'm afraid he can be quite rude to visitors.'

'I understand Dr Cahill's not practising these days,' Dana said.

'No. Not for years. Certainly not since he bought this place.'

'And when was that?'

'Thirteen years ago. In 1919.'

Mimi explained that she was then governess to a wealthy Italian family's children. Cahill had been in Lamu for about a year and bought the house from the Italians when they sold out after the war.

'He was quite a handsome man back then,' she said, a little wistfully.

'Do you think he will see me?' Dana asked.

Mimi looked sad. 'I pray he will, but … well, he knows your situation already, but he told me to tell you he's not a doctor any more.

'How can he turn away from a life of helping people?'

'He is a good man, but something happened that made him give the work up. He won't tell me what it was, but I'm sure if he started again, and was able to keep away from … well … to avoid —'

Just then, the gate bell rang.

Mimi stood. 'I won't tell him you're here. It's best to use surprise to say what you want to say.'

She watched Mimi hurry to the gate. She swung it open and Cahill entered, kissed her tenderly on the cheek, and made his way up the path. He stopped for a moment to examine the tomatoes, before arriving under the wisteria.

Dana stood and smiled. 'Good morning, Dr Cahill.'

He was startled, and stared at Dana for a long moment, before turning his gaze to Amina and finally to Mimi, who kept her head up although it was clear she felt uncomfortable under his scrutiny.

'It's my fault for invading your privacy,' Dana said. 'For which I apologise. I imposed upon Mimi because, as you can see, I'm about to have a baby, and I'm afraid I may need your help.'

'You've come to the wrong place, Mrs ...?'

'Northcote. Dana Northcote.'

'... Mrs Northcote. I no longer practise. Now, if you'll excuse me —'

'Dr Cahill. This is my first child. I'm worried, because when I was seventeen I had an abortion, which unfortunately went wrong.'

The information caused him to pause, before saying, 'There are many good doctors in Kenya, Mrs Northcote. I suggest you take yourself to Mombasa, and place yourself in the hands of one of them.'

'No. I can't go to Mombasa. Or anywhere else for that matter. My husband doesn't want me to have this child, and I know he will make it very difficult for me if he finds me before I have the baby.'

'That is a matter between you and your husband, surely.'

He stepped around her towards the door.

Dana caught a strong scent of spices on him. She thought he must have spent the morning in the spice market.

'I don't think it's his child,' she said hurriedly, putting her hand on his arm.

'As Shakespeare said: *It is a wise father who knows his own child*,' he said. 'Perhaps you worry unnecessarily.'

'No. I think it may be a … a black man's child.'

She thought she saw a flicker of understanding in him. She hurried on. 'I'm thirty-one, Dr Cahill. I don't have to tell you the complications that can arise. I want this baby and I don't care if it's white or black. I'm sure this is my last chance for a child and I have given up everything for it, but that's not important. What is important is …' She put a hand to her midriff. 'I'm afraid … I'm terrified that I might lose it if I don't have you to help me.'

Mimi came forwards to stand beside her in support. She looked pleadingly at Cahill.

Cahill dropped his gaze to Dana's hand resting on his shirt sleeve.

'I'm sorry, Mrs Northcote,' he said, gently removing her hand. 'But I can't help you.'

He walked past her into the house.

* * *

In the three weeks following her unsuccessful visit to consult Dr Cahill, Dana had confined herself to the cloistered environment of the guest house. She told Amina it was because it was too hot to be moving around Lamu, but the truth was she had fallen into a depression caused by the very thing that brought her to Lamu — the isolation.

She longed for the company of her friends, especially Polly. Polly would have so many convincing anecdotes to reassure Dana that her pregnancy was progressing completely normally; Dana would cease worrying and for once enjoy a dreamless sleep. They would laugh about her concerns and all would be well. But Polly was not there.

A number of times she had written to Sam telling him how much she missed him, but tore each letter up. It would be an act of cowardice to involve him at this late stage. She had made her choice and now had to see it through, alone.

Her only tentative contact with her previous life, and therefore her sanity, was the newspapers that arrived irregularly in Lamu on passing *dhows*. There would occasionally be a reference in the society pages to someone she knew; even one of her friends. She once saw a photo of her sister, Averil, at the opening of the Nairobi horticultural show. There was a photograph of a group of her friends — members of the Zephyr dinner club — at a ball at Torr's. They all looked so slim and happy. She put her hands on her enormous girth and sighed.

Amina brought the newspapers when she could find one in the markets, but it had been over a week and now, of all times, Dana needed to know that the world she knew was happily progressing in her absence.

She waited until late afternoon, when the sun had relinquished its savagery, and ventured forth with her parasol to the market. The Indian haberdasher, who took delivery of the few newspapers brought to Lamu, greeted her warmly, asked how she was feeling, and handed her a copy of the *East African*.

After a brief conversation with the stall-owner, Dana tucked the newspaper under her arm and started back to the guest house. At the edge of the market she felt a little unsteady, due to the effects of the heat, and sat on a bench seat to rest under a mango tree.

She unfolded the paper to note the edition was only a week old. It must have arrived in Lamu that day. Her eye was drawn to a familiar picture on the front page. It was Polly. The caption read: *Medical mishap*. She quickly scanned the article: *Dead on arrival at Nairobi General … medical mishap … self-administered medication … a silver syringe found beside the body …*

Dana was on her feet, the newspaper heavy in her hands. A wave of vertigo swept over her. She staggered and tried to regain her seat, but her legs would not hold her. She slumped to the ground.

* * *

Dana awoke with Amina's worried face hovering over her.

'*Mungu angu!*' Amina said. 'My God. She's awake.'

Dana looked around the room — her room in the guest house — and found Dr Cahill standing behind Amina.

He came forwards and took her pulse. Then he placed a hand on her forehead.

'Hmm,' he said.

'Am I all right? I mean … the baby?'

'You have a certain determination about you, Mrs Northcote. You are not to be denied, you could say.'

'What do you mean?'

'I mean, you not only chose to draw attention to yourself in the busiest part of Lamu, you did so just as I was coming to the market to buy my newspaper.'

'But what about my baby?' she said, becoming fretful and annoyed at the same time.

'Babies,' he corrected.

'What? What did you say?'

'I said "babies". You should have said, "What about my babies?" Plural.'

Dana stared at him.

'Hmm … I can see you're a little surprised. I'm not. Spotted it the moment I saw you in my garden. Still carrying them quite high, so you've got some time yet. But not much more I should think. You're quite big already. Took two strong fellows to carry you here on a trestle top.'

'Are you saying I'm having twins?'

'I am.'

'Twins …?' she repeated, with a mixture of pleasure, surprise and panic. At least Dr Cahill was there: it was an immense relief. She smiled. 'Thank you for bringing me home.'

He pretended not to hear.

'Stay in bed,' he said, and started to leave. 'I'll see you in a couple of days.'

'Doctor?'

He stopped at the door and turned back to her.

'It's not that I'm ungrateful, but what made you change your mind?'

He reflected upon it, and appeared about to speak … instead he turned again to the door.

'As I said, I'll see you in a couple of days.'

Dr Cahill's visits became more like chats between friends than routine medical appointments. He would bring the newspaper and they would discuss current affairs. At other times they talked about their respective homes in England, the London theatre, the books they'd read, and horse racing, which had been a pastime of his while running a practice in the Midlands. Dana explained how news of Polly's death had led to her collapse and he was quietly comforting.

One day, close to Christmas, they sat in the garden and avoided talk of home and what Christmas might entail. Instead, Dana was curious about Cahill's decision to settle in Lamu. It was the next best thing to knowing why he'd abandoned his practice; he'd firmly changed the subject whenever she tried to ask.

'Why did I choose Lamu?' he said, repeating her question. 'Why, my dear, look around you.' He indicated the Kidege Guest House's beautiful garden. 'Tranquillity. Lamu has it in abundance. And peace. The Muslims are a very peaceful people. Not like we warlike Christians, dashing around the world, shooting off our cannons and the like.'

'Surely you could have your peace and tranquillity, and still practise your profession? It would make such a difference to these people to have a doctor trained in Western medicine.'

'Ha ha,' he said, rising from his garden chair. 'The medicine men around here would probably hold a different view. But I must be getting back. I'll see you tomorrow, Diana ... I mean, Dana, of course.'

'I remind you of her, don't I?' Dana said, acting on a hunch.

Cahill paused. 'Actually, an amazing resemblance. Spotted it first time I saw you. She was younger of course, but otherwise ...'

'Your daughter?'

He nodded. 'Yes. Diana Maree.'

'What happened?'

He tightened his lip in the expression he usually wore when an uncomfortable subject came up — and Dana had discovered a few during their talks — but this time it slipped away, and his face sagged. He stared at the ground. Dana watched him wrestle with his thoughts. Finally, he slumped into his chair and rested his elbows on his knees. His face was drawn and he looked all of his sixty-six years.

'She was sixteen. A beautiful girl. Outgoing. Full of life, and eager to explore it. Nothing like the retiring violet her mother was when we met.'

He told Dana how he'd always been open with his daughter, answering her questions frankly. The previous year they'd discussed the changes her body was undergoing as she went through puberty.

'Therefore you can imagine how horrified I was, when she came to me to say she was pregnant.'

He said he was furious at first.

'How could she be so foolish? I mean, against every accepted convention of the day, I'd given her sensible and accurate information about sex and the need for her to take care so she could avoid exactly this situation. How then could this happen?' He shook his head. 'When I calmed down, I realised it was no good bemoaning the unfairness of the situation. I had to deal with the facts. Our daughter's future was at stake. My wife and I wanted to keep the whole affair quiet.'

He looked across the table at Dana. She could see that the wall holding back his pent-up emotions was crumbling, and large tears misted his eyes.

'Can a father be blamed for wanting the best for his only child? I decided she should remain at home once the pregnancy started to become obvious, and I would deliver the baby myself. Instead of following the sensible course and putting Diana under the care of a gynaecologist, I worried about her future. How would she find a decent husband if it became known that she'd gotten into trouble?'

He dropped his eyes to his hands, which he opened and closed, examining them as if he'd not seen them before. His fingers were long and elegant; surgeon's hands.

'The delivery went terribly wrong. In my panic I made some fundamental mistakes. Diana began to haemorrhage. The blood ... I ... I lost her there on the operating table.'

At this point he started to sob. His shoulders shook as he lost the fight to control the outpouring of grief.

Dana struggled from her seat and stood at his side. She placed a hand on his shoulder.

She refilled their cups. The doctor blew his nose on a large handkerchief he pulled from his pocket before he took a sip of tea. It seemed to give him strength.

'I started to drink heavily. My marriage ended and I decided to give up medicine.' He shrugged. 'I came here to start again.'

Recalling Amina's assessment that he was a drunkard, she asked, 'And has alcohol remained a problem for you?'

'No. Not alcohol. It's too hard to get it in a Muslim place like Lamu.' He paused again; it was a morning for painful admissions.

'When I was a young man, I travelled to Poland and, together with friends, experimented with the Polish habit of drinking ether, flavoured with spices. As a doctor I had access to ether and after Diana died, well ... Now I get it from a Pole in Watamu. Taken with cloves and cinnamon, it's quite pleasant. And the coast has plenty of spices.'

Dana recalled the faint scent of the spices as he paused beside her on the first day she spoke to him in his garden.

'And now? Are you keeping sober?'

'Mostly.'

'Will you be able to manage when my time comes?

He hesitated a moment too long to give Dana the confidence she needed.

'I will.'

＊　＊　＊

Dana was at the end of her patience. Her pregnancy seemed to have lasted years. The babies kicked — and seemingly fought — all night, keeping her awake even more than the heat. Her feet were like melons and her back constantly ached.

She had lost all fear of the births and now simply wanted to be delivered of the twins and have her body, and her life, back under her own control.

The garden, which had been her refuge, was now her prison. She often spent her time in its solitary shaded corners to replay the events that led to her present situation. Her existence had shrunk so much that she could scarcely believe she'd had a life in Kipipiri. She doubted that her grotesque body could have ever been locked in a passionate embrace. Her friends faded into obscurity and although she'd left him only months before, Sam was no more than a distant dream. There was no one in her life who she could call on for support; and now the imminent birth of her babies had condemned her to remain in Lamu until it was over. She felt trapped and afraid.

Her self-confidence was shattered and she had come into the garden with pen and paper to write to Edward. She needed reassurance that everything would be all right after she gave birth. She wanted to tell Edward that she would leave for England with him as soon as she was able, if he was still of that view.

Before she reached her chair, Dana gasped, and dropped the pen and paper. The pain was short, sharp and very intense. After a moment it eased, but it had frightened her, and she made her way from the fountain at the bottom of the garden back to the house.

The pain came again. Worse. She bit her lip, thinking that it couldn't be the time. It was only January and full term was not until next month.

She paused to take a breath and it came again.

A cry escaped her. She tried to be calm. What if it was the babies? It was too soon. What if it wasn't? Something could be terribly wrong!

'Amina!' she called, holding the weight of her belly in her two hands.

She felt water trickle down her legs. Or was it blood?
'*Amina!*'

* * *

Dana reluctantly returned to consciousness. She was in the airless heat of her small bedroom with the walls again threatening to close around her.

She recalled Amina helping her to her bedroom. After what seemed like hours, Dr Cahill had arrived, looking more frightened than she felt. Then the smell of cinnamon and cloves filled her nose as he poured a quantity of ether onto a piece of gauze. It carried her away in a blessed release from pain.

A voice came through, demanding she push.

Dreamless sleep followed periods of intense pain.

Push!

She heard someone scream. It sounded like her voice. The gauze again. She drifted into a twilight place interspersed with visions or dreams. At no time was she sure what was real and what was not.

Push!

The pain returned, jolting her rudely awake.

Push!

Cloves and cinnamon filled her head.

Dimly she saw Dr Cahill lift a white baby smeared with blood. She tried to hold onto the sight but she slipped quietly away — only to return to semi-consciousness moments or hours later to see another baby in his arms. A dark baby. A black baby.

Now, fully conscious, she tried to resurrect the images. Some had been real while others, she thought, had to be the ether.

Amina was at the bedside, nodding and smiling, and fanning herself with a large feathered fan. She waved it towards Dana, fluttering some air in her direction. It cleared her head.

Also beside the bed was a crib, with two bundles loosely wrapped in cotton.

Dana stared at her babies — the term strangely foreign to her mind. Two babies; two colours. A black baby and a white baby, just as in her dreams.

She turned to Amina, who was still smiling, as if there was nothing odd about it. Had she even seen the babies? She wasn't sure her eyes weren't playing tricks on her. Perhaps she was still asleep.

At that moment, Dr Cahill came into the room, his eyes on a book open in his hands and his spectacles at risk of falling off the end of his large red nose.

'Ah! You're back with us,' he said. 'Just in time.'

He looked to the ceiling, thinking. 'That is, *you* are just in time. No, that's not right. I should have said *I* am just in time ... to see you awake. Conscious, that is.'

'Doctor ...?' she said in a quavering voice. She was unable to form the question she needed so desperately answered.

'What? Oh, yes. As I say, just in time.' He dropped his eyes to the book again and began to read from it. 'Superfecundity: from the Latin; *fecundus*: fertile, and *supra*: better than average.'

He lifted the book up to show her the cover. 'Look at this — *Ogilvie's Dictionary of Medical Conditions*. I knew I kept these old books for something. Had them since medical school.'

Dana gave him a pleading look.

'Yes ... well. Superfecundity. The fertilisation of two

eggs by separate acts of sexual intercourse.' He looked over his glasses at Dana. 'Quite rare, as you can imagine, but more to the point: how would we ever ordinarily know that we were looking at a case of superfecundity? I mean, these little ones might simply be dizygotic twins — non-identical twins. In which case we could only deduce if it was a case of superfecundity by discerning a marked difference in size, that is, one twin conceived in one ovulatory cycle and the other in the next.

'Dr Cahill ... please!'

'Sorry, sorry. Where was I? So your twins are clearly a case of two ova released in the one ovulatory cycle, or *superfecundation*, or more correctly, *heteropaternal superfecundation*, meaning they are from different eggs *and* different fathers. Rather obviously, I should think.'

'But ...' Dana said. 'How is that possible?'

'Quite simple, really. The white twin is a girl baby, conceived from the sperm of a white man, and the, um, mixed-race child is a boy, conceived from a black man.'

Dana recalled that she had made love with Sam and her husband on successive days. Removed from the emotion of that time, the memory now brought with it a flush of embarrassment.

She reached for the crib.

Amina lifted the white baby girl to her. Dana took her and held her close to her face, inhaling what reminded her of the aroma from a baker's shop when the loaves have been just taken from the oven. The little one squirmed and screwed up her watery blue eyes.

Dana tucked her into the crook of her arm and asked for the other baby.

He was slightly heavier but he had the same warm smell as the girl. His head was covered with a dusting of dark hair, where the girl had none. His skin was the colour of milky coffee, with only the palms of his hands to match his twin sister's. He opened his mouth, puckered and made a squeak.

Amina smiled. 'He wants milk,' she said.

'Oh,' Dana said, and Amina helped her loosen her blouse. She placed the darker face to one nipple and the pink one to the other. It took some balancing, but soon they were comfortably placed.

It was only as she watched her babies contentedly suckling that she realised that her future had suddenly become a great deal more complicated, and she would very soon be forced to face the changed circumstances of her life.

PART 3
JELANI

CHAPTER 32

1945

Sam sat back in the impressive new cart he'd been allocated and let the horse find its own pace. It was hot. Around him the country was tinder-dry and suffering the worst drought in living memory. It made his task that day even more difficult.

He understood why the Governor had given it to him. He was the right man, perhaps the only man, who could do the job without causing widespread trouble.

He hadn't expected to be doing this kind of thing when he accepted the appointment to the Legislative Council. Governor Mitchell had made it clear he wanted him to be more than a figurehead. He gave Sam every reason to believe he could make changes in the country.

'I want you to get out and about, Mr Wangira,' Mitchell had said at their meeting. 'You have great support among the Kikuyu because of your small loans business. And I am told it extends to other tribes as well. I want you to use that goodwill to advance the government's programs.'

Sam said he would; and for some time did so enthusiastically. It took longer for him to comprehend the reality of British politics and how it trickled down to this far-flung section of the Empire.

There were people in Britain who were pressing their government to dismantle the remaining colonial systems throughout the Empire, and when the Labour party under Clement Attlee was elected in July of that year, the movement gathered further momentum.

In Kenya, the Governor allocated seats in the Legislative Council where the white settlers and Arab and Asian residents could vote for their candidate of choice. This was not the case for the African seats. The British were keen to support democracy, but only to a degree. Trusting their African subjects to make their own choice was apparently a step too far. The two African representatives were directly appointed by the Governor.

While Sam was initially honoured by the appointment, he soon felt like a fraud. The appointment gave him no power in the Legislative Council and only earned him the disdain of his constituents as his promises repeatedly failed to materialise.

He had come a long way from banker, to horse smuggler, to politician, but he had a deal more to travel before he would be allowed an effective voice to speak for his people in the governing of their country. He remained in his position because he believed that the necessary changes would eventually come.

In the meantime, he often found himself in this role — the bearer of bad news. His message to the people of Kobogi in the hills above Embu was that the government wanted to move them from their traditional land.

The Governor told Sam that before any decision was made he wanted to hear his first-hand assessment of the mood of the people in this first village chosen for resettlement. But Sam knew it didn't matter what the villagers said, the resettlement would go ahead because the land was too valuable to leave in the hands of sustenance farmers.

It made him sick to the stomach to be part of the charade, but he had sworn to act as a faithful servant of His Majesty when he assumed his office.

However, he'd made no promise not to try to change those policies.

*   *   *

When Sam entered the village, nobody realised he was a representative of the government. He wasn't surprised. He had no staff — not even an *askari* — and nobody had been sent in advance to Kobogi to announce his imminent arrival. He just walked his horse into the village; and when the children flocked around him — they always became excited when a stranger arrived — he met them with equanimity, holding the hand of the boldest among them as he made his way to the chief's hut. He knew that most white officials, even when they bothered to visit the villages, were reluctant to touch anything, let alone the children, whom they tended to avoid at all costs. And although not all representatives of the government wore a uniform, most did if they had the opportunity to do so. Sam wore a suit.

A group of young warriors watched him walk past, trying not to appear too interested. It was for children to make a fuss, but he knew they were curious, especially when he greeted them in Kikuyu.

Sam found the chief's hut and introduced himself formally and properly. The chief, like everyone else, was taken aback by the stranger's visit.

Sam explained that the Governor had sent him to Kobogi to discuss various matters.

The chief said they had never had a visit from someone in the government.

'Before I give you the Governor's message, I would like to hear from you, your elders, and perhaps your warriors, if that is your wish.'

The chief arranged a chair for Sam and, with the elders sitting with him and the entire population of Kobogi in a circle around them, they began to talk.

'We need food,' the chief said. 'Our food gardens have failed for three seasons. Our storages are empty, and we are eating next season's seed stock. We have petitioned the DC, but he has done nothing for us.'

Sam had prepared for this situation. The whole country was in a similar position, but he still found it difficult to answer in a way they could accept. After all, the British had taken possession of the country promising to bring peace and prosperity.

He said he would speak to the District Commissioner and do what he could, but everywhere there was hunger. He told them that in the north, where the land was drier, matters were even worse. Many starving people had walked off their land, leaving their cattle, sheep and goats to fend for themselves, and were begging in the streets of Nanyuki, Thompson's Falls and Nakuru.

The chief and elders nodded. They'd obviously heard similar stories from the administration in Embu. He didn't want to promise what he couldn't deliver, but he knew the Embu DC had a stockpile of grain for needy cases. He promised the chief he'd raise their situation as a special request. It was the least he could do.

One old man asked how it was that a Kikuyu was in the government.

'I am an appointed member of the Legislative Council,' he said. 'Appointed by the Governor to represent the Africans.'

'Then if you are a friend of the Governor, surely he will listen to you when you ask him to send food. Look at us,' the chief said, indicating his gaunt colleagues. 'We are all but finished.'

'I can't tell the district commissioners what they must do. And I can't speak directly to the Governor; I can only make my thoughts known through the messages that pass between the Legislative Council and him. The Governor then decides what he should tell the district commissioners.'

'Then why are you here?' someone else asked.

'I'm here because the Governor has asked me to —'

He paused. What was the point in asking these people if they would move from their land? As a fellow Kikuyu, he knew the question was ridiculous; the answer totally predictable. Land wasn't simply a matter of assets or even of livelihood. Land, traditional land, was an integral part of the Kikuyu psyche, handed down, father to son, through the generations. It would be an insult to ask the question, especially during such trying times.

'I'm here because the Governor has asked me to send you his best wishes. He asks that you remain strong during these troubling times.'

If the chief was perplexed by the banality of the message he didn't show it, and asked Sam to thank the Governor for his good wishes.

As Sam was returning to his cart, a group of young men stood in his path. The one who stood at their head was tall and broad of chest. At first Sam thought he and the others were warriors — they were about that age — but then he noticed they wore none of the traditional insignia of the warrior class.

The young man said his name was Jelani Karura. He was quite fair-skinned, and Sam thought he might have been of mixed blood.

Jelani told Sam he and his friends needed help.

'We are not permitted to speak at village meetings,' he said, 'because we are uncircumcised. But as you can plainly see, we are of an age when we should already be warriors. Instead we are treated as children.'

'Why is this so?' Sam asked. 'Isn't it a matter for the chief and elders to set the date for your ceremony?'

'It is,' he said. 'But the AIM have forbidden it.'

The African Inland Mission had been in Kenya for more than fifty years with the stated objective *to bring the Glory of God to the peoples of Africa*. They'd done particularly well in Kikuyuland. Three-quarters of the Kikuyu people had been *saved* from paganism. They were called *kirores* — reformed Kikuyu. They believed in the word of Christ as taught by the African Inland Mission.

The remainder followed the customs and traditions of their ancestors, which they considered to be moral and proper. This was completely at odds with the missionaries' view, for they refused to forgo their belief in Mogai, the creator, and to otherwise change their ways to those of the Europeans. This group, about a quarter of the village, were called the *aregi*. They were a tribe within the tribe.

'Those with me,' Jelani said, indicating his group of friends, 'are *aregi*. And we want to be initiated.'

Sam looked around the group. Here at last was an issue where he may be able to help.

'I'll speak to the chief,' he said, but he knew that convincing the old man was only part of the problem. The real issue was overcoming the influence of the African Inland Mission — a powerful group with strong connections to the colony's administration.

* * *

Sam climbed into the cart and trotted the horse out of the village. The track to the Embu road was deeply rutted and signs of the drought were everywhere. He could see the desolation in the food gardens and, although he was hopeful of getting some assistance from the DC, he left the village feeling inadequate and frustrated. He had some of the titles of office, but none of the power.

If the DC was a polite person, he would listen and nod and say he would do what he could. If he were not, Sam would be shown the door soon after entering his office. Most of the old-timers had no sympathy for the recent trend towards localisation.

After riding for three hours, Sam made a decision. He didn't want to arrive at the DC's office appearing dusty and hot. Instead he looked for somewhere to stay in Kutus, just sixteen miles short of Embu, and found a small hotel — the Settler's Retreat. It carried a sign endorsing it as a government rest house, which meant he merely had to show his Legco credentials and sign an accommodation warrant to be given a room.

He entered the hotel brushing the dust from his coat sleeves.

The white woman who was standing behind the desk looked up. 'No Africans,' she said.

Sam smiled in spite of his annoyance. It was a common reaction.

'I'm a member of the Legislative Council,' he said, producing his papers with the Governor's signature and seal.

She examined his letter at some length. 'So you are,' she said, giving him an appraising look. 'I imagine you'll be wanting a room, then.'

'Thank you. With a bath if possible.'

'This is the Settler's Retreat,' she said with a wry smile, 'not the Norfolk. But you're in room number six.' She handed him the key. 'There's a bathroom down the hall and a wash basin in your room.'

He thanked her and carried his bag to his room.

After bathing, he took a fresh white shirt from his bag, and retied his tie. He was tempted to remain in shirt sleeves, but decorum, and the slightly crumpled appearance of his shirt, swayed him. He donned his double-breasted jacket, and headed towards the dining room.

The manageress was standing behind the small bar in the corner of the dining room.

'Would you care for a pre-dinner drink?' she asked.

Sam raised his eyebrows. Africans were forbidden to buy alcohol, although there wasn't an Indian *dukawallah* that didn't flaunt the law, and illegal distilleries existed in almost every village.

'I recognise you,' she said. 'Remembered your name too when I saw it on your papers.'

She was smiling at him, amused by his baffled expression.

'I'm Georgina. Dana's friend.'

She had appeared vaguely familiar when they'd met earlier, but he'd often had trouble remembering white peoples' faces — they all looked the same.

'Oh, of course. Georgina.' He extended his hand this time. 'Nice to see you again.'

She nodded, still smiling.

'Gin and tonic?'

'Thank you.'

She poured him his gin, and herself a double. They spent a few minutes trying to recall when and where they'd met.

'I know,' she said at last. 'It was at the races. You were with Dana.'

He could recall her now. She was seldom with her husband, and usually had a drink in her hand. The years had not been kind to her. He remembered her as a pert and attractive young woman. She was now carrying at least an extra forty pounds. Under heavy make-up, her furrowed face showed the ravages of the years, and her eyes were already bleary with drink.

They chatted about Dana's horses and the day Dancer won the Nairobi St Leger. He couldn't ask the questions that had been on his mind throughout their conversation, but Georgina volunteered the answers and the information stunned him.

'I haven't seen nor heard anything about her for so long. Of course, I heard she'd divorced Edward and remarried a few years after she left us.'

Remarried. Dana had given him the impression she would never leave Edward, not for anything or anyone.

She took a mouthful of drink and studied him over the rim of her glass.

'But you probably knew all about that,' she said.

Sam knew she was testing his reaction and tried to keep a neutral expression. 'Can't say that I did,' he said, and waited for her to continue.

'Yes. She kept it quiet, but her sister, Averil, went back a few years ago, and we got all the news.'

Georgina continued to talk, but Sam paid little attention. In the dozen or so years since Dana left him, he'd had plenty of women. He stayed with none of them for more than a week. No one could be compared to Dana, and none commanded the powerful emotions she was able to raise in him.

Something in Georgina's rambling monologue grabbed his attention.

'What was that?'

'I said, Averil had never seen her sister's baby.'

'Dana had a baby?'

'Yes. Must have been ... oh, 1931 or early 1932. Shortly after she left Nairobi.'

He remembered the passion of their last meeting in his flat at Muthaiga.

Again, Georgina was studying him, and Sam held his breath.

'A gorgeous little girl,' she said. 'Spitting image. Fair hair. Green eyes.'

* * *

Sam had an early breakfast in the dining room. He was served by a middle-aged Embu woman who gave his white shirt and tie sideways glances, but said little more than was necessary. When he passed the desk to return his key, Georgina was there, looking owl-eyed in the morning light.

'You're off then,' she said cheerily.

'Thank you for your hospitality.'

'My pleasure. Any time.'

He nodded. A thought crossed his mind to enquire about Averil, and maybe obtain her address, but he let it go. No use disturbing old memories unnecessarily.

'Goodbye,' he said, and headed for the door.

'Oh, Sam,' she said from behind him at the desk.

Sam turned.

She eyed him up and down.

'I mean it. Come back any time.'

'Thanks, Georgina. I will.'

There was a warm breeze stirring the dust on the ride to Embu. By the time he tied the horse to the pole outside the District Commissioner's office, he was hot, thirsty, and dusty. He pushed through the door marked *His Majesty's Government. Mr William Hudson, District Commissioner, Embu District.*

The DC's secretary appeared surprised when Sam introduced himself as a member of the Legislative Council, but went into the inner office, returning moments later to say that the DC was busy and that Sam should wait.

After an hour, during which time five people were shown in to the see the District Commissioner ahead of him, Sam was becoming increasingly annoyed. From experience he knew he must be patient, reminding himself he was there to represent the people of Kobogi: it would do no good to allow his personal feelings to intervene.

When another half-hour had passed, the DC came out and appeared surprised to find Sam in his outer office.

'Good morning, Mr Hudson,' Sam said, rising to his feet as he spoke.

'Oh, you're ... you're ...?'

'Wangira. Sam Wangira.'

'Yes, look, Mr Wangira, I'm a bit busy right now. Would you mind making an appointment with Collins here, and I'll speak to you some other time.'

Sam's jaw tightened. 'Actually, I've been waiting for the best part of two hours, sir. And I'm returning to Nairobi this afternoon.'

Hudson frowned.

'It shouldn't take too much of your time,' Sam added.

'Very well,' the DC said, doing nothing to conceal his annoyance. Turning to his secretary, he said, 'Ring the club will you, Collins? Tell them I'll be a few minutes late for lunch.' He turned on his heel and re-entered his office.

Sam followed. Hudson sat behind his desk, which was festooned with papers.

'Now, what can I do for you, Mr Wangira?'

'I was out at Kobogi yesterday. That area's been very badly hit by the drought. There's no food in the gardens, and it could be weeks before the rains come. They're surviving on roots and berries.'

'I know all that. Their leaders are in here every other month. But what do you want me to do about it?'

'Many of the settlers on the eastern slopes got the first of the rains and have been able to reap an early harvest. A lot of their maize is sitting in the government granary down near the Siakago road. I saw it on my way in this morning. Why can't you send a load out to Kobogi? The village can repay you when they harvest their crop.'

'Send them a load on credit? What do you think I'm running here, a bloody produce co-op?'

'It's just a book entry, for God's sake, Hudson. You could even charge them interest if you're that way inclined, but if you don't do something, some of the old people out there aren't going to see another harvest. If it's a matter of money, I'll pay for it myself.'

Hudson's face coloured. 'Listen to me, Wangira,' he said through clenched teeth. 'Just because you can make a knot in a necktie doesn't qualify you to sit here in judgement. I've been in the service of His Majesty's government for thirty years, and I'll be damned if I'll take cheek from a jumped-up nigger. If you want to spend some of your money you don't have to waste my time. Take off your fancy Savile Row suit coat, get your black arse down to the store, and load the fucking maize yourself.'

CHAPTER 33

All of Jelani's family were traditional Kikuyus — the *aregi*. When the African Inland Mission and their converts — the *kirore* — attempted to interfere with, and in some cases ban, traditional Kikuyu customs, it created a great schism in the village, leading to trenchant animosity between the two sides. But this didn't keep Beth Wambui — a *kirore* — and Jelani Karura — an *aregi* — from falling in love.

The teachers from the African Inland Mission would have disapproved of the relationship had they known, but Jelani and Beth kept it a secret. Beth's family knew, and thoroughly disapproved of the match.

To call their love a relationship was probably overstating the matter. They were unable to spend much time together and, to Jelani's dismay, Beth was determined to stay a virgin.

'I've been thinking about it,' she said. She paused and her tongue lightly touched her top lip. It was a habit she had whenever dealing with a difficult thought. 'And I don't believe we should do anything. That is, anything more than we've already been doing.'

'But why?' he pleaded.

'It's the right thing to do,' she said. 'We must keep ourselves pure until we can be properly married in the Christian church.'

Jelani had previously experimented with sex, so his purity was already compromised, but he didn't have it in his heart to tell Beth. He rationalised his omission because at that time he had followed traditional beliefs regarding sex and felt no shame or obligation to adhere to the Christians' rules about love games among the young. At the time, such games were considered by his family and the community to be normal behaviour provided there was no risk of pregnancy. And every *aregi* girl knew where to stop to avoid that situation.

Jelani had no doubt that he was in love. Every time he saw Beth he felt his heart jump and then beat like the wings of a sunbird. When he touched her, even those careful touches that Beth permitted, Jelani's blood raced and he wanted her more than anything he'd wanted in his life. If it was necessary to become a Christian to have his Beth, Jelani decided he would do so. The challenge of telling his parents and, even more difficult, his grandfather, could wait for another day. The details would be arranged. Everything that could be done would be done when the time came. And for Jelani, whether for love or for lust, the time couldn't come soon enough.

*　*　*

Jelani sometimes wished he wasn't an *aregi*. It placed him at odds with Beth's family. It also placed him among the minority of Kikuyu. All his life he'd felt out of place. Being *aregi* didn't help.

As a child he'd been taunted about his light skin. The older boys called him *dukawallah*, saying his skin was more the colour of the Indian man who owned the store on the Nairobi road than of a real Kikuyu.

They also ridiculed him because of his eyes, which were brown with flecks of green. His mother called them lion's eyes, but the older boys said they were like those of the wildebeest — the buffoon of the grasslands.

When he was much younger, it was such taunts that led him to ask his mother why he was so light while she and his father had normal skin. She evaded the question.

One day he overheard a group of elders discussing the Ugandan woman who had brought Mama Karura's child to the village. They called that child *Zesiro*, but Jelani knew he was his mother's only child, and ran home fighting back the tears welling in his eyes.

In a breathless torrent he told his mother what he'd heard. She calmed him and admitted he was not a child born of her body, but the child given to her by a Ugandan woman, a distant in-law of a man in the village. The woman had come to Kobogi because she knew there was a woman here who could have no children of her own and who desperately wanted one. It was, she said, how she and his father had come to have Jelani, or Zesiro, as he was then called, for their son — a child chosen ahead of all the other children in the world without parents.

'What does this Zesiro name mean?' he asked her.

'I don't know, and because of that your father and I decided to name you Jelani instead.'

He felt as though he was not one, but two boys; two boys with different names. Two boys from two different worlds. It made him feel even more unusual than before; and he turned his attention to the second troubling matter.

'Then is the one who brought me here my mother?' he asked.

His mother said she thought not, because she could see no resemblance, but the woman couldn't say who his real mother was because she was sworn to secrecy.

'And who is my father?'

Again she said she didn't know. 'But I think, maybe he was a white man in an important position,' she said. 'Maybe he loved your mother but couldn't keep you because he was ashamed that people would not respect him because he fell in love with a black woman.'

Jelani became very anxious at this. He already felt different, and for his whole young life his difference had caused him trouble. It was bad enough that he was the child of another woman — a stranger. But to be the child of a white man would make the taunts much worse. He told his mother he would not be the son of a stranger *and* a white man.

His mother hushed him and said it didn't matter who his parents were: she and his father were his family now, and they loved him.

But Jelani would not be comforted by such a story.

'Wait,' his mother said. 'The one who brought you to us left me a gift from your mother.'

She went to an old woven basket that hung above her bed; she used it to hold the few personal items she possessed. From it she took a leather thong attached to a large tooth.

'What is it?' he asked.

'I don't know. Your father thinks it's a broken lion's tooth.'

Jelani turned it over in his hands. The thong threaded through a silver clasp fitted to the fang. It was the type of ornament he'd seen the warriors wearing. He asked her if he might wear it.

'It is why I have kept it all these years,' she said. 'Keep it.'

He felt better now that he had the pendant as a gift. Even so, he pleaded with her not to tell anyone. Finally, she and his father agreed to keep their idea of his true parents a secret.

This didn't stop the boys in the village from teasing him. He'd dash at those who called him a half-caste, throwing his arms about in rage. Consequently, he received many beatings, but eventually he became big enough and skilled enough to put down anyone who dared to accuse him of being partly white.

He knew he should confide his story to Beth, and had on a number of occasions started to tell her, but lost his nerve.

One day, soon, he must do it.

*　*　*

Three large fires sent shadows snaking over the packed earth, climbing the mud-daubed walls and lighting the thatch-roofed huts encircling the centre of the village.

The elders sat in dignified silence around the fire; behind them were the old women — their shaved heads gleaming with fat and red ochre.

There was a mood of subdued expectancy among them. The gathering was part of the celebrations for the newly initiated warriors, but they knew that many in the village did not condone what the leader of the African Inland Mission outpost of Embu, the Reverend Fenton Farley, would describe as an unholy gathering. It was because of the rift between the *kirores* and the *aregi* that the elders among the *aregi* felt the need for circumspection that night.

The cautious mood didn't extend to the *nditos* — the young unmarried and uncircumcised girls — who congregated in small groups in preparation for the start of the dancing. They wore short leather aprons and hid their giggles behind their hands. Their firm pointed breasts showed through garlands of their finest beads.

Jelani spotted Beth among the *nditos* and his heart thumped in his chest. He had pleaded with her to join the young women for the dance, but she was afraid of her parents.

'It is forbidden,' she'd whispered to him as they discussed it. 'Reverend Farley says the *ngoma* is a dance with the devil.'

But she was there, and it made him so pleased he wanted to catch her eye and let her know how much he loved her for it, but it was expected that a warrior should remain aloof so, with a great effort, he restrained himself.

Beyond the throw of the firelight were the warriors. They gathered in the darkness, naked except for brief loincloths, elaborate headdresses of ostrich plumes, and leggings of black and white colobus monkey fur.

His age-mates had given Jelani the honour of being the leader of the first group of dancers because he had so bravely and eloquently argued the case for their initiation with the Kikuyu man from the Legislative Council.

He now boldly led them from the darkness into the circle of light around the fires.

The choir sat in their own cluster and, immediately the warriors appeared, began to sing.

The *kehembe* players beat a furious pace on the leather-covered drums. Large and small rattles added to the drums and kept the singers, who were gathered close to the musicians, in time.

The warriors strutted and gyrated, leaped about and waved their feather-tipped staves in the air.

Jelani's group was joined by others and they formed three circles around each fire, chanting and grunting. They made fearful cries and struck the ground forcefully with their long decorated staves. Rattles tied below their knees added emphasis to their movements as they stamped their feet and circled the fires. During the circling, and responding to a hidden signal, a dancer would break from the formation and, with a wild shriek, leap over the flames.

Among the dancers, and the most awesome of them, were those with white-ochre coating their bodies. They looked like the ghosts of warriors who had long ago passed into the afterlife. They received the most enthusiastic cries of *ohh* and *ahh* as they joined the others.

When the *nditos* came from their concealment to join the warriors, the music and singing reached a new height. Soon the encircled warriors broke formation and mixed with the colourful *nditos*.

Jelani moved quickly to Beth and he doubled his efforts, leaping and high-kicking around her. Beth's eyes were turned shyly towards the fire, as was the custom, but she flashed him a smile whenever she dared.

The audience, enlivened by calabashes full of honey beer, began to chant and ululate; there was a deafening dissonance of drums, voices and rattles.

As the dancing progressed, new dancers took the place of the exhausted ones, adding fresh blood and new steps to the performance.

An old woman climbed to her feet, waving her calabash above her head. She made an obscene exaggeration of the body thrusts the young people were performing, raising a chorus of support from her companions. Soon another wizened old woman joined her and they pantomimed lovers coupling to roars of approval.

The noise reached a crescendo, and the audience had lost all inhibition, boldly forming their own dancing groups among the huts.

Suddenly, the music changed. The drums beat slowly but powerfully. The rattles became muted in accompaniment, and the *nditos* placed their feet on top of their partners', clasping them around their waist to keep balance. The warriors raised their spears behind their *nditos*' heads in a gesture signifying the protection they offered the women of the tribe against harm from others.

The chatter and laughter from the audience subsided and stillness took the place of the raucous noise. The night held fast and thin white clouds scudded across the face of the moon.

The silence was shattered by shouting and the screech of a whistle.

Jelani and the other warriors immediately sprang to the front of the dancing crowd, spears and staves at the ready.

From the darkness came a group of four black *askaris* and three whites, led by the Reverend Fenton Farley. He carried a flaring lantern that illuminated his pale face, and reflected from his rimless glasses, giving him the eyes of a man returning from the spirit world.

The *askaris*, whom the administration had placed under Reverend Farley's direction, were from the Kamba tribe — traditional enemies of the Kikuyu.

'*Out!*' Reverend Farley screeched. '*Be gone!* Fornicators and sinners. Go to your homes. All of you!'

There was a moment's hesitation as the dancers and spectators recovered from the shock of the interruption.

'*Strike them!*' Farley ordered the *askaris*. 'Drive them from this horrid place.'

The Kamba *askaris* needed no encouragement. They charged through the village, recklessly swinging their long night sticks.

Women shrieked and fled with their children.

Jelani searched the darkness for Beth, but the *nditos* had scuttled into the night as did most of the warriors, and the elders were put into an undignified retreat.

With their backs to the fire, Jelani and a handful of warriors paused, momentarily defiant against the attack. He was torn between his warrior's instincts to defend the village — to fight — and the certainty ingrained from infancy that resisting the strong arm of white authority was futile.

Suddenly he was facing Reverend Farley, whose eyeglasses now reflected the flames of the fire. In the next instant they cleared to reveal the zeal of the righteous in Farley's eyes. His nostrils flared and tiny bubbles of froth formed at the corners of his mouth as he panted and fumed.

'*You!*' he snarled. 'How dare you stand there with your pale face and light eyes — the very proof that the devil has been at work. When your mother fornicated with a white man she lost her everlasting soul, and left you — the spawn of the devil — as the proof of his lust.'

Jelani let out a roar of anger. He grabbed Reverend Farley and, against all his instincts, slung him forcefully to the ground. Standing over him, with his fists clenched, he had tears of rage in his eyes, but the words he desperately needed to defend his honour in front of his brother warriors would not come.

In the next moment he was on the ground, felled by the blow of one of Farley's enforcers. He tried to regain control of his limbs, to gather himself and get to his feet, but the reverend raised his walking stick and struck him a blow to the side of his head that sent him falling into a black void.

When he recovered, Reverend Farley and his *askaris* had gone. He thought his head would burst with the pain, but worse than any physical pain was the agony of humiliation. Not only had his reputation been dealt a brutal blow, but that of his mother — a mother he'd never known. In Kikuyu society, a warrior was only worthy to defend his people and his village if he and his parents were pure of heart. In one foul blow, Reverend Farley had torn away his place in his tribe.

* * *

It wasn't only theology that convinced the Kikuyu to join the Christians. Many hoped to gain education and personal advantage by their association with the Europeans. Others saw it as a way to escape the influence of the chiefs, who sometimes took advantage of their positions by seizing more than their fair share of the food grown by their villagers. Some chiefs also collected young wives from among their people — even when the girls were already betrothed.

Chief Muraimu had been the chief of Kobogi and the surrounding district for as long as Jelani could remember. In fact, he'd been chief for thirty years. Some of the elders recalled the early days of his rule when, as a young man, he had been a firm but fair leader. As the years passed, he had assumed more and more power and, with it, a grand sense of self-importance. He strained the boundaries of propriety by the manner in which he extracted his levies and fines. He once appropriated a goat from a man who dared to cough while he was making one of his many speeches. He was known to confiscate land, the most cherished asset in Kikuyu life, for nothing more than late payment of taxes. By these means and others, such as simple extortion, he accrued wealth at his subjects' expense.

There were many who would have liked to see the chief removed from his position of power, but he was favoured by the administration because of his zealous tax collecting, so no one dared to move against him.

* * *

'*Jelani!*'

The urgent whisper came from outside the thatched wall of his bachelor's hut. He quickly rose from his bed and slipped out the opening.

'Beth!'

Her voice was unmistakeable, but he couldn't dare to hope that she'd changed her mind about making love with him.

She took his hand and led him to a quiet place, some distance from the warriors' huts.

'Beth, you're here —' he began, but she shushed him.

'Jelani, we must get away from here.' She was tightly gripping his hand and she had a panicked look in her eyes. He started to worry.

'What is it?'

'The chief ...' she said, before burying her face in her hands.

'What is it about the chief?'

'He ...' She dared to look at him. 'He ... wants to take me as his wife,' she said, stifling a sob and covering her face again.

It took Jelani some moments to comprehend, then the hideous notion struck home. The chief was older than his father. There had to be an explanation, but in his heart he knew it was possible. The chief had become obsessed with finding young women for his bed. Over the last year or so he'd acquired three girls to add to his collection of wives.

'But he can't ... What does your father say?'

'He told the chief's man to thank Chief Muraimu for the great honour he has paid his family and that he will await the formal offer.'

'But what is he going to do?'

'He said there is no need to worry. He will think about it.'

'He will think about it? What does that mean?' Jelani asked.

'Papa says he will speak to the Reverend Farley. He said the reverend can't allow it.'

'Will he really speak to the priest?'

She appeared uncertain. Her tongue touched her top lip. 'I think so ...'

Jelani's mind raced.

'We will leave here,' he said.

'Yes, but go where?'

'Anywhere. Away. I will find a place where we can stay together.' He tapped his head, willing his brain into action. 'My father's brother! In Meru. It is far, but he will help us. I'm sure. The day after tomorrow. I will come for you before dawn.'

But Jelani wasn't confident about it. He was not of anyone's blood. Why would a distant and seldom-seen relative give refuge to the light-skinned child of a stranger?

* * *

Jelani crept through the bush to the outskirts of the gathered huts where Beth and her family lived. The shadows had already softened and the sky was turning from purple to green. Soon the old women would come from their beds to feed the lambs and kids.

He hid among a cluster of shrubs and waited.

He watched the women feed the livestock and when the sun was up, turn them over to the younger boys to care for them through the day. He waited as Beth's mother went to the millet store and watched as she returned to the hut to prepare her husband's breakfast.

The sun was up when Beth's father came from his hut and stretched. Jelani was now very anxious and could wait no more. He came from his hiding place and confronted him.

'Where is Beth?' he rudely demanded.

Her father baulked and was at first incensed by his ill-mannered approach, but then his shoulders slumped, and he took a deep breath.

'She is gone,' he said.

'You let the chief take her?'

'No. I sent her to Reverend Farley.'

'The priest? How could you do that?'

'To save her from the chief, of course,' he said, his anger returning. 'Am I not her father?'

'But if the chief wants her, even the Anglican mission can't save her.'

'Reverend Farley said he will send her away. Somewhere safe.'

Jelani had only had half a plan to save Beth, and in some ways it was a relief to be free of the immediate danger. When she returned he would assume responsibility and take her away forever. In the meantime, he had to know where she was.

'When will she return?' he asked.

'I don't know. Not for a long time. Maybe never. Even me, I cannot see my own daughter.' He turned his head away, unable to continue.

Jelani clenched and unclenched his fists. Swallowing a lump in his throat, he said, 'I must see her. I promised.'

'Did you not hear me?' her father said, his voice rising. 'Nobody must know where she is. Reverend Farley said it must remain a secret, and he is right. The chief would find her.'

Jelani could sense Beth's family members gathering at the edge of his vision, watching in silence, knowing they had never trusted him — the light-skinned *aregi*.

Regardless of how Beth's family felt about him, he had always respected her father, who could not now meet his eyes. He wanted to tell him that he loved his daughter and that they had planned to marry.

'How ... how could you let him take her with no idea when she would return?' Jelani whispered, his voice coarse with suppressed anger.

Silence.

Jelani now despised him for his weakness. 'What about your religion?' he demanded. 'What does your Bible say about giving away your child?'

Beth's father now lifted his head. 'What can I do?' He shrugged. 'It was either the chief or the church.'

Jelani wanted to strike him. 'What kind of Christian are you?' he demanded.

The older man had no answer. He simply stood there, shaking his head. 'What can I do,' he repeated, and walked back to his hut.

Jelani grabbed handfuls of his hair and tugged until it hurt. He tore at his face, drawing thin white stripes on it that soon dripped blood onto his chest. It was the Kikuyu custom when dealing with extreme grief; and Jelani knew he must grieve, for he had lost the love of his life.

CHAPTER 34

After the rain came and the crops were planted, but before the harvest, and the traditional celebratory feast, the chief called all the people of the village together.

Whenever more than a handful of Kikuyu came together it was normally an excuse for much joking and storytelling, but on that occasion there was none of the chatter that usually accompanied such a congregation. Somehow the people of Kobogi had determined there was bad news coming. Those who dared to break the silence made only brief and circumspect remarks.

Jelani stood with the warriors, trying to read the mood. On the other side of the gathering that encircled the chief, his father stood with the other men. They eyed the chief, standing among his *askaris*. Perhaps it was the presence of so many grim-faced armed men that made the atmosphere tingle with tension.

The chief made a few opening remarks about his duty and his position of authority. He made much of his connection with the District Commissioner and the honour that such a friendship conveyed on the village and all the surrounding villages.

As he droned on, Jelani watched the tight, closed faces around him. Nobody stirred. There was no shuffling of feet and no scratching of ears or sucking of teeth.

Suddenly the point of the chief's speech emerged. There was disbelief, shock and anger on the faces around him. The older men were alarmed. His fellow warriors were mumbling audibly. The elders left fingernail tracks down their cheeks.

He found his mother in the crowd of women wringing their hands at the edge of the gathering. Even from that distance he could see her tears roll down her cheeks.

* * *

It had taken months for the village to empty. For a long time nobody could believe they had to go, so everybody waited for someone else to move. Nobody did.

Even the chief was unable to convince them to go. He came with his *askaris* and ranted at them, but that was the extent of it, thereby confirming to the villagers that if the chief took no stronger action, then even he couldn't believe they had to abandon their ancestral homeland. The people were relieved and life went back to normal.

When the District Commissioner came, he had twelve *askaris* with bayonets fixed to their rifles and a white officer in charge.

Again he told the people of Kobogi that they must leave their land, because the government was alienating it for private sale.

Alienate. It was a word Jelani had never heard before, but he and everyone in the village had no doubt what the District Commissioner meant when he gave them two options: they could go to the Kikuyu Reserve where they would have enough land allocated to them for their needs, or they could become resident workers on a

European farm. They had run out of time. They must be gone within the week or his *askaris* would move them on by force.

The elders sent out scouts to the reserve to assess the quality of the land there. Others went to the nearest white farms to see for themselves what conditions would exist for them.

The report on the Kikuyu Reserve was not good. The land was uncleared and the quality of the nearest food gardens was not as good as that around Kobogi.

Those who had gone to the white farms had no luck. The owners said they had as many squatter-workers as they needed for their crops and stock. Further afield, they found Mr Cook, who was a new settler with a need for labour.

He said that each man could use a piece of land for a food garden, and would be paid enough shillings for the poll tax, but in return must work Cook's land for half of the year.

The old people were the last to leave Kobogi. Many laid down and died there, rather than live their last days in a strange place.

* * *

Mr Cook's property was a dusty place far from water. Even Jelani understood the difficulty of growing enough food in such soil on top of having to work in Mr Cook's fields, planting his wheat, reaping his sorghum, and clearing the bush for new crops.

What was once the village of Kobogi was taken for white soldiers returning from war; they mostly had little or no experience of farming, let alone in the highlands of

Kenya, but they were desperate enough to try anything to avoid the grim future they faced in war-torn England.

The Kikuyu were permitted to return to Kobogi to harvest their crop, but it would be their last. Thereafter, they would grow whatever they could on Cook's farm in the small plots adjoining their huts. The drought had taken a heavy toll on the crop. Although a harvest was always a cause for celebration among the Kikuyu no matter the yield, the last harvest in Kobogi was a grim affair. People went about their work with an air of sadness. Many of the women could not contain their tears, which fell silently to the good red earth they were leaving.

After the last baskets of maize were loaded onto the handcart, Jelani went to see his village for the last time. There was nothing there, just a patchwork of ash where the huts once stood.

* * *

Jelani found life difficult at Cook's farm. He hadn't been happy following the incident at the *ngoma*, when the Reverend Farley called him the spawn of the devil. He'd lost face among his fellow warriors. He might have stayed if Beth was there, but now that she was gone, there was nothing to keep him.

He told his parents he would leave Cook's farm to find work in Nairobi.

His mother immediately began to cry.

'You are a man and a warrior now,' his father said. 'It is for you to decide these things, but what is it that makes you want to leave us?'

Jelani found it difficult to explain his reasons. 'It makes me angry every time I think of the way we were chased away from Kobogi. It was our place, our home. Our land. What is here for us on Cook's farm? It is not our place. There is nothing here for me, so I must go.'

His father nodded his understanding. 'If I were a young man I would also find it difficult, but your mother and I, well ...'

His mother had her face in her hands and was softly weeping.

'I will bring money home to buy food,' Jelani said, but she didn't stop crying.

* * *

He walked all day and all night, following the murrum road by the light of the moon. A pack of hunting dogs stalked him for a mile, but he threw stones at them to keep them at bay, scoring a direct hit that sent the pack scampering off into the night.

Seventy miles away from Cook's farm at Fort Hall, he climbed aboard a freight car and hid in a consignment of timber bound for Nairobi.

He awoke next morning feeling there was something wrong. He lay in his half-awake state within the timber stacks and realised the train had stopped rocking.

He peeped out of his hiding hole and gawped at the town beyond the railway siding. It bustled like a beehive.

He scampered across the tracks and joined the throng. There were people of many tribes and nationalities. He saw an Indian man driving a donkey loaded with bundles of silks with his many black-veiled wives trotting behind. There was a pair of spear-carrying Maasai warriors who gave him a curious glance as they passed. And two small boys were pushing and pulling a large white woman in a wheeled carriage. There were stores large and small. Some sold fragrant spices. Others had fresh meat hidden in swarms of flies, and still others sold tools and shiny cooking implements. He passed a bakery and the aroma of fresh bread made his stomach churn. He'd not eaten for thirty hours.

He wandered the streets until he found the market, where he tried to find work in exchange for food. No one was prepared to offer him a chance.

In desperation, he collected some spoiled fruit and vegetable leaves from the sweepings; and he spent his first night in Nairobi with a pain in his stomach, sleeping under a couple of burlap sacks among a pile of fruit crates.

He had never been so alone.

*　*　*

After a month of near-starvation, when Jelani had to beg to survive, he finally had some luck.

While scavenging among the refuse in the foul-smelling town dump, he found a discarded boot-cleaning kit. He'd seen the boys earning tips by cleaning shoes outside the hotels and business houses. He saw it as a sign of a change of luck, and searched nearby and found a wooden stool. He took the kit away with him. Now all he needed was shoe polish to get started in what he hoped would be his lifeline.

He had no idea where he could buy shoe polish and wandered the streets in search of a store that sold it. He found a pile of shoe polish tins — black, tan and brown — in an Indian *duka* off River Road. The proprietor was a large Sikh — a people respected by all for their aggression, and who for that reason were often employed as guards. He already had his eye on Jelani when he entered the store, but Jelani had by that time calculated the head start he'd need to outpace the heavily built Indian.

He strolled around the store looking with interest at a number of items, avoiding the shoe polish and touching nothing. The Sikh hovered.

A prospective customer entered and the Sikh's attention was momentarily diverted. Jelani leaped into action. Grabbing three tins, he bolted for the door, but the Sikh was more nimble than Jelani had imagined. In an instant he planted his considerable bulk across the doorway, legs asunder.

Jelani made a dive through his open legs and, before the big man could turn, had regained his feet and dashed away with the Sikh's enraged insults following him down River Road.

* * *

With his stool, shoeshine box, new tins of polish and some cotton cloths salvaged from a tailor's shop, Jelani set up outside the New Stanley Hotel and waited for customers.

Around lunch time a well-dressed man in a wide felt hat came around the corner from Standard Street and stopped beside his box.

'How much for the shine, boy?' It was English, but he had a strange accent.

Jelani hadn't considered the question of price. Now he was so excited to get a customer, he couldn't speak. The only word that came to mind was brown — the colour of the shoes.

'Well, speak up kid. What's your price for this here pair?'

Jelani continued to stare at the shoes. Even he could see they were of good quality leather. Finally he spluttered, 'A-a-as you wish, sir.'

'Hmm ...' the man said. 'Can't argue with that.'

The customer took a seat and pulled his trouser leg up to reveal not shoes, but boots that reached his knees.

The man laughed at Jelani's expression.

'Lucky you didn't fix a price on these babies,' he said. 'I figure you'd have come out at a loss.'

Jelani tried to smile, but he was awed by the boots. Even in his ignorance of shoes, boots and leather, he could appreciate their beauty. In their unbuffed state they had a depth of colour, almost a translucency.

With an intake of breath, Jelani set to work. He peeled the top off the brown can of polish. It was wrong. It couldn't do justice to the colour of the boots. They had a lighter tone. He was afraid to start in case his polish changed the highlights in the leather. He levered the top off the tan polish. It was too light.

He'd never considered the possibility that his three different colours wouldn't be sufficient for all leathers. Perhaps if his first customer hadn't been the boot-wearing white man with the strange accent, he might have gained confidence in his new craft.

Why couldn't his first customer be a dusty settler-farmer, with scratched and bruised black work shoes such that anything done to them would be an improvement?

Maybe any brown polish would suffice for any brown shoe, but he didn't know if that were true. And now this man, wearing this pair of beautiful boots, would be his means of discovery. Jelani sighed. Why couldn't they at least be black?

Aware that he was taking far too long to start, he scooped up a dab of brown polish on his finger, and smeared it on the leather. He was right, it was too dark.

Without hesitation, he then dipped his finger into the tan and added it beside the other.

He could feel the owner's eyes on him. Without considering the consequences, he mixed the two colours and smeared them all over the first boot. The result was a ghastly mess, but he continued to spread and mix the colours, here and there adding a touch more of one then the other.

He massaged the polish into the leather, and then rubbed the boots with a cotton pad as if his life depended on it. The first cloth became clogged with polish, and he took another. After five minutes the high part of the first boot was cleaned of its excess coating and he buffed it until it was a deep, burnished brown. He worked downwards to the ankle, the toe caps, then repeated the performance on the other boot. Finally, he scrubbed the soles and heels.

When he sat back on his haunches, the sweat trickling down his cheeks, he studied the result of his efforts. The boots had a rich lustre and depth of colour beyond imagining.

The customer shook his head in wonder. 'Wow,' he said. 'Ain't that the goddamnedest shine you ever did see?'

Jelani smiled; he became aware of a small group of passers-by who had stopped to watch the boots' transformation.

The man stood and took something from his pocket.

'Here you go, son,' he said. 'That's about the best shoeshine I ever did see, anywhere.' He dropped a coin into Jelani's hand.

It was a shilling! A fortune! A brand-new shilling shining as brightly as the boots.

* * *

Jelani won more customers from the group who saw him work on the American's boots and his clientele grew steadily over the following days and weeks.

One morning, a Kamba man arrived with his own shoeshining tools and said the New Stanley was his territory and that Jelani must move on.

'Where have you been all this time?' Jelani demanded, not prepared to start again somewhere else. 'There was no one working here when I started.'

'Never mind that,' he said. 'I'm here now, *white face*, and you better go before I smash you and your shoe box.'

Jelani stiffened at the taunt and sized up the man. He was tall, solidly built, and in his eye there was the look of a man accustomed to getting his own way, using his size to bully others out of what was theirs.

Jelani retired, angry with the loss of his prized position and at the Kamba man for his thuggish manner, but infuriated by the reference to his appearance.

* * *

Jelani's new place of business, outside the entrance to the market in Stewart Street, was very busy, with shoppers swarming past his shoeshine box every moment of the day. But business was very slow.

When he abandoned his position outside the New Stanley to the big Kamba ruffian, he felt confident he could start afresh elsewhere without difficulty, but before the first day had ended, he realised it wasn't the quantity of people passing him that was important, but the quality of their footwear. Most people attending the market wore cheap sandals or no shoes at all.

Now he regretted his cowardly retreat from outside the hotel. There his strategy to allow his customers to set their price had worked handsomely, and they gave him good tips.

It was also the principle of the matter. He had worked hard to secure a loyal set of clients. He had managed to earn a better return on his skills because of his diligence so why should someone else profit from it?

As he sat on his stool mulling over these thoughts, he didn't notice a pair of fine leather shoes that stood before him until a voice drew his attention to them.

'Can you do something to these old brogues for me?'

Jelani whipped the stool from under him and slid it towards the customer.

'Certainly, *bwana*,' he said, diving into his box of rags and polishes.

'You can call me Sam if you wish,' he said.

The accent had deceived him. It was the Kikuyu man who had visited Kobogi. Jelani remembered him because he'd done what he'd promised to do — returning to the village with bags of maize to help the village survive the drought. Jelani also suspected he'd spoken to the chief to allow the initiation ceremony to go ahead.

Sam took his seat on the stool, and nothing was said as Jelani smeared polish on the well-worn but fine quality shoes.

'Weren't you working outside the New Stanley?' he asked.

Jelani nodded. 'Yes. I was.'

'I thought so. Now there's a Kamba in your place. Why is that?'

Jelani buffed the shoes vigorously. 'He said it was his place before I came there.'

'Do you believe him?'

He paused. 'No.'

The man said no more as Jelani worked the polish into the leather while again stewing about the Kamba.

When he stood, Sam asked, 'Did you complete your initiation?'

'Of course I did,' Jelani said, miffed by the inference that he was not yet a man.

'It's not only in Kikuyuland that you must go to battle. In the city there are also good causes for which to fight.' He paid Jelani. 'Stand up for what you believe is right.'

* * *

Jelani returned to the New Stanley early the next day, determined to regain his position, but the Kamba man was already there.

Jelani put his stool down beside the Kamba. 'Go,' he said.

The Kamba laughed at him.

Without further preliminaries, Jelani lifted his wooden stool, and struck the other man on the head.

The Kamba fell to the ground and, as Jelani stood over him with his stool raised ready to strike again, the bigger man crawled away to safety, holding his hand to his bleeding head.

Jelani carefully set out his equipment, and awaited his first customer.

* * *

After he finished one customer's shoes and collected payment, Jelani raised his eyes to the next man standing in line. It was the Sikh from River Road!

Sitting on his stool beneath the towering Indian, Jelani knew he had no chance of escape. He would be crushed like a *dudu* — an insect — at any moment.

The Sikh looked down at him, nodded, and walked away, leaving Jelani stunned by his good fortune.

The incident played on his mind for the rest of the day. In a world that had generally dealt him more than his fair share of bad luck, the Sikh's actions made no sense.

That afternoon, Jelani went to River Road. The Sikh nodded as he entered his *duka*.

'Why did you do it?' Jelani asked.

'What did I do?' He shrugged. 'I saw you working on the street. I walked away.'

'You remembered me. Why didn't you call the *askaris*?'

'*Poosh*. What would the *askaris* do?'

'Then why didn't you do something? I stole from you.'

'Why did you steal from me?'

Jelani thought the answer was so self-evident it was hardly worth the response. 'Because I needed the polish,' he replied.

'Yes. Polish. I knew you were waiting until I turned my back to steal something, but I didn't know what it was until you ran away. Polish. You had no shoes. *What would you want with polish?* I asked myself.'

Jelani shrugged. 'I needed the polish to do my shoeshines.'

'You needed polish to shine shoes. Exactly. But I wasn't sure. That is why I went to all the places I thought a boy like you might sit to shine shoes. And there you were. Doing honest business. I like that. You started as a thief and finished as a businessman.'

Jelani smiled. 'If I pay you for the loan of three tins of polish, am I still a thief, or just a businessman?'

'Come,' the Sikh said. 'Show me your money, and I will give you a discount — one businessman to another.'

CHAPTER 35

1947

'How long have you been shining my shoes, Jelani?' Mr Singh, the stationmaster, asked.

Jelani kept buffing the heavy black shoes as he considered the question. 'I think nine months; maybe a year.'

'That was how I am thinking,' Singh said, nodding. 'And you know, my wife still knows when I've been to see you during my lunch break.'

Jelani smiled. 'Of course. Because she can see her face in your shoes.'

Singh, one of Jelani's best customers, was a friend of the Sikh *duka*-owner in River Road. His black uniform with epaulets and brass buttons was always spotless and he was a striking figure with his huge white turban and white beard. Jelani enjoyed shining the footwear of well-dressed people. It somehow made him feel part of their success.

'You are perfectly correct, my young friend,' Singh replied. 'And that is a compliment to your fine shoeshining.'

Jelani's puzzled expression caused Singh to elaborate.

'After one year, you have not slackened in your energy. Same hard work. Same good shiny shoes. I have seen many in your position, Jelani. Oh, yes. After a while, they let a little bit go. Maybe a little slower. Maybe not so much polish-polish, busy-busy. But you, you are the same.'

Jelani was embarrassed by the praise, and mumbled his thanks.

'So you must come and work for the railways,' Singh said, with a decisive nod of his turbaned head.

Jelani looked up from his work.

'Shining shoes?'

'Ach, of course not shining shoes. Cleaning carriages. Cleaning station. There is plenty to do without shining shoes.' He waved his hand at the collection of cloths and polishes. 'You can throw all that away.'

Jelani looked from Singh to his kit and back again.

'I know you have nowhere to sleep,' Singh continued. 'You've been making do in a market stall on Stewart Street, or somewhere in Jeevanjee Gardens. No, that is not good. You work for railways, you get bungalow. Well ... maybe a small room, but it has a door that closes and a roof that keeps off rain.' He nodded again for emphasis. 'So, you come to my office and we talk about pay, all right?'

Jelani thought about it for just a moment. He didn't know how he knew, but Singh was right. Although he'd been earning enough from shining shoes to feed and clothe himself, he couldn't afford to rent a place to sleep. More than once he awoke to find rats crawling over his body; and on another occasion he had to fight off someone trying to steal his shoes.

'I think I would like to finish with the shoeshine business,' he said.

'Very good. Now come, we talk.'

Jelani looked down at his stool and equipment. He wouldn't need it any more.

As he turned to leave, Singh said. 'Better bring little bit polish. My wife, she will not like me to go home with dirty shoes after all this time.'

* * *

Jelani's concrete box in the East African Harbours and Railways compound was, as the stationmaster had warned him, small, but it was the first place he could call home since leaving Cook's farm over a year before.

For most of the next year, he cleaned the carriages, station, and station outhouses for a few shillings a month.

When the Nairobi Points Inspector's offsider went missing, Singh nominated Jelani for the promotion. He was the only candidate and joined Harry Johnstone out on the tracks. Harry had been with the Uganda Railway for nearly fifty years — the last thirty-nine of which had been as a points inspector.

One day they were sitting in the shade under the signals box. It was tea break time — an occasion of almost religious significance for Harry.

'Yah, been here so long they've forgotten I'm past retirin' age,' he told Jelani as he dived into his Gladstone bag for his tea paraphernalia. 'And I hope they never twig to it, either. What am I gonna do if I retire? Eh? If I hang up me oil can I reckon I'll just roll over and die.'

He lit a roll-your-own and parked it in the corner of his mouth.

'Yes, I was a boy even younger than you, Jelani,' he said. 'Age of fifteen years I was when I joined the platelayer's crew at mile 325 ...' His eyes were almost screwed shut to avoid the sting of tobacco smoke. '... In the place that is now called ... the city of Nairobi.'

Jelani had heard the story several times before, but he hadn't the heart to stop Harry in any of his repeated renditions. He enjoyed hearing them almost as much as Harry enjoyed telling them.

Harry nodded. 'Been with the railways, man and boy, for nearly fifty years.' Pleased with himself, he returned to preparing his cup of tea.

They had been working together for over a year. Harry had obviously decided to take Jelani under his wing, as he had done with all his young charges over the years. Jelani had to reconsider his animosity to all white men now that he'd met at least one who treated him as a human being.

Harry poured tea from a Thermos flask that might have been as old as the man himself. He could make a real ritual out of drinking a cup of hot tea. First, he would blow on it for a few minutes — little thoughtful puffs from his pursed lips as he curled the cup between both hands. Then he'd commence drinking it. But because it was still too hot, he'd whistle it up into his mouth with such a loud slurping sound that it reminded Jelani of a mule trying to pull its hoof out of one of Nairobi's notorious black-cotton bogs.

'There we go,' said Harry with a sigh. It was another ritual, this time to signal the end of morning tea. 'Hello, hello,' he said, packing up his tea things then taking a sheet of paper from his bag. 'I forgot about this.' He waved it in front of Jelani. It was a circular letter from Railway Headquarters. 'The stationmaster reckons I should take a look at it.'

He pulled his spectacles from his jacket's top pocket and popped them on the bridge of his nose. 'It says here: *Expressions of Interest. The Uganda Railway invites expressions of interest from all staff, in pursuance of the Railway's ambitious training program in the application of the sciences in railway management, who might be so inclined as to enter into training for the purposes of engaging such training for personal advancement.*

'*In preparation for such modernisation that the sciences of electrical and electro-magnetism might offer in such modernisation, applications for a study period of two years, with pay, are invited forthwith.*'

'What do ya reckon about that?' he said to Jelani as he slipped his glasses back into his pocket.

'Very nice, Harry,' Jelani said, smiling, although he wasn't happy at the prospect of losing Harry as his boss. There were many supervisors in the railway that Jelani would fear to work for. Harry was a little odd, but at least he was fair.

'That's what I was thinkin'.'

'What does it mean, *modernisation*?'

'Well, modernisation is them electrical point things they're talkin' about puttin' in. So the stationmaster says. They won't need the levers and rods no more.'

Jelani gave it some thought. He knew very little about science, and was surprised that someone of Harry's age would be interested to learn such complicated new skills.

'I am sure you will find it very interesting to work with these new electrical things,' Jelani said.

'Me? Hell no!' he said. 'It's you the stationmaster had in mind. Not me.' He cackled. 'Gawd, what a laugh.'

'Me?'

'Yes, me boy, you. Stationmaster reckons you got the spunk to give it a go. And I do too.'

Jelani stared at him. Harry had said the training would lead to promotion. His imagination went into a spin. He could see himself among electrical things, whirring and sparking. A position of importance far beyond his expectations.

'So,' Harry pressed him. 'Want to give it a go?'

Jelani's smile spread. 'Yes, I would, Harry. Very much.'

1950

Mombasa was a jewel lazing on the shores of an opalescent harbour sitting snugly in a nook in the Indian Ocean coast. The harbour lapped at the back walls of Arab shop-houses whose coral-stone footings were already oyster-encrusted when Vasco da Gama dropped anchor there in 1498 to a chilly but largely uneventful welcome. He left Mombasa in peace, but two years later his countrymen laid siege, which was not the first sacking the island town had suffered in its history — and nor would it be its last.

During the following centuries, the strategic port was caught in a tug-of-war between Portugal and Oman until finally, late in the nineteenth century, Britain sent a gun ship to the East African coast and settled the matter. The locals had named the place *Kisiwa Cha Mvita* meaning *Island of War*, which was appropriate, but it was a version of the Arabic name, *Manbasa*, that had endured.

The old Arab town and its beautiful port were initially very strange to Jelani, but he'd been there almost two years and had learned to find his way around the claustrophobically narrow alleys crowded with eating houses and trade stores selling spices, exotic food and tropical fruits. Jelani had seen nothing like them in the high dry interior, nor the thousands of trinkets, baubles, weavings and works of art available in the town's many coral-built shops.

The school was situated near the port of Kilindini on the outskirts of the town. Its purpose was to train the semi-skilled workforce needed to fill the ranks of the growing colony's transport infrastructure.

Slowly the mysteries of electricity and magnetism unravelled for Jelani and his African and Asian classmates. Initially, he was afraid of the hidden forces within an electrical current and, after several jolts from low-voltage systems, he soon understood to treat them with respect. He learned about electrical relays that used the principles of electromagnetism to control events in multiple locations. He learned about motors and magnetos, pumps and signal points.

But the East African Harbours and Railways trade school staff were not content to churn out mechanics to merely build and repair electrical devices: they insisted students also know how to complete the mountain of paperwork demanded within its massive bureaucracy. The proper use of the English language, both written and spoken, was an important part of the course.

Jelani had enjoyed learning his craft and would soon complete his training and join the ranks of real railwaymen, inspecting points, repairing signals and wiring new works.

It was a Friday, the Muslim Sabbath, when Jelani ran into Peter Gikuri in the market. He'd come to Mombasa from Cook's farm in search of work on the wharves.

Gikuri and Jelani had never been close friends, but finding each other far from home and in such an exotic location, they immediately bonded like brothers.

Jelani remembered Gikuri as a prankster at the government school. He was always receiving a thrashing from one or other of the teachers because of his practical jokes.

After finding out that Gikuri had only just arrived, Jelani asked about his family back home.

Gikuri became solemn. 'Your father, Karura,' he said. 'They took him to gaol.'

'Gaol?'

He couldn't believe it. His father was a loyal supporter of the white's rule of law. Even after the government took away his farm, he maintained that the years following the whites' arrival were the most peaceful that he, or any of the elders, could recall.

'Who took him to gaol?

'The administration police,' Gikuri answered. 'He did not pay his poll tax.'

'But he always pays his taxes.'

'There was much sickness in the village at that time. Even your mother and her sister-wives had been poorly. Your father had no crop to sell and could do no work for many weeks, so when the collector arrived, he could not pay.'

'What of Mr Cook? Surely he could help until my father was well?'

Gikuri shook his head. 'He said there was already too much indolence.'

'What is indolence?'

'I don't know. I think it means not paying tax when you should.'

'Then what of our friends? Our neighbours? Could they not help my parents?'

Gikuri shrugged. 'Nowadays people only seem to look after themselves. Not like when we were all in the village together.'

Jelani was disgusted with his former neighbours and felt bad about himself. In the three years since leaving Cook's farm he'd not returned home to give them the money he'd promised. When he was cleaning shoes in Nairobi he had no money for anything; and when he was with the railways there, he had no leave. Now, in Mombasa, he had excused himself by saying it was too far to travel. But he had managed to save a little. He would find the time to take some money home.

'It is shameful that we Kikuyu can't help each other as we did in the old days,' he said. 'Is my father at home again?'

'I don't know. My family sent me here soon after the *askaris* took him. They are also worried about paying their taxes. They hope I can find a job to send money to them.'

'Have you found anything?' he asked.

'No. Nothing.'

'How do you live?'

Gikuri nervously shifted his stance. 'I have nothing, and I was hoping that you might ... might help me until I find something.'

Now that he'd roundly condemned others for selfishness, Jelani could scarcely refuse, but it meant his mother and father would have to wait a little longer for their money.

* * *

Jelani discussed Gikuri's situation with his dormitory mates at the East African Harbours and Railways school. They agreed to have Gikuri sleep under Jelani's bed so long as they were not implicated in the scam, but as soon as Gikuri took up residence he was an immediate favourite. He had amazing mimicry skills and, within a couple of days of moving in, he could impersonate everyone in the dormitory.

His favourite subject, and that of his dormitory audience, was Nasar Visram — the Indian gang leader on the railways' wharf at Kilindini. He was a huge man and one with a very short temper. Gikuri would mimic Visram's ambling gait and out-thrusting belly as he strutted up and down the wharf. It took Visram some time to discover why the young trainees were laughing at him. When he spotted Gikuri in action he flew into a rage and chased him all over the wharf. Gikuri would let him almost reach him before he eluded him, to his friends' even greater amusement.

Jelani warned Gikuri to take care. 'If he ever catches you, you will be in trouble.'

'Catch me? That fat fart. He couldn't outrun a turtle.'

Jelani liked Peter Gikuri. It was impossible to offend him, and he could always find the bright side of any situation.

When he wasn't taunting the likes of Visram, Gikuri carved wooden images and strung together coloured beads with the intention of selling them at the market.

When he'd stockpiled what he deemed to be a suitable collection, he showed Jelani and asked him his opinion.

'Of your carvings, or your bead work?' Jelani asked.

'Both.'

'Hmm … Well, your carvings are interesting. I like that one of an elephant.'

'It's a rhino.'

'Really? Doesn't a rhino have only one horn?'

'That's his ears.'

'Oh, well.'

'Maybe I need to do a little more carving to make the ears smaller.'

'That would help.'

'What about my beads?'

'I think you had better concentrate on your carvings.'

'You don't like my beads?'

'Your carvings are bad, but your beads are worse.'

Gikuri spent the next week improving his work and took it to town the next market day.

Later that day he came back with the same items he'd carried in that morning, but as usual, he was not discouraged. He soon had his friends in the dormitory laughing as he recalled in detail the many insults he received about his carvings and beadwork.

* * *

Nasar Visram grabbed Jelani by the arm as he was on his way to class.

'You,' the big man hissed. 'Listen to me. Your little Kikuyu friend is very funny. But you tell him that if I catch him he will not be laughing for long. He will be very, very sorry.'

Jelani looked up into his eyes and had no doubt Visram meant it.

Later, he told Gikuri what had happened.

'Laugh? Who does he think he is to tell me not to laugh? I will always laugh. I will laugh in his face if he comes near me. Does he think he can make me afraid of him? The big fart. No.'

Jelani's language skills won him a part-time clerical position in the administration's head office on his days off training. He sorted and filed management correspondence circulating to and from the many outposts of the railways' network.

The job also gave him access to the railway administration's reports on current events affecting railway operations. As such, it was a good source of economic and political commentary — topics of increasing interest to Jelani, who still worried about his parents' life on Cook's farm.

Kenya was undergoing many changes in both the rural areas and urban centres. In the cities and towns it was a period of industrial unrest. During the previous years, Indian and African leaders emerged to voice their discontent — and that of their fellow workers — about the harsh employment conditions forced upon them in city-based industries. Many of the African workers were struggling to earn enough to pay their way in the cities and at the same time support family members back home in the villages.

The city workers had a lot in common with young men — like Jelani — from upcountry, who had seen their families forced from their traditional homes to become landless squatters on farms largely owned by poor white soldier-settlers. These mainly British newcomers needed cheap labour to wheedle a living out of their small, inefficient plots; and many imposed unreasonable working and pay conditions upon their squatters.

Jelani started to take notice of the union men who occasionally came to the training institute at lunchtimes to drum up support for their cause, but it took an issue unrelated to wages and conditions for Jelani to become more involved in their activities.

* * *

Peter Gikuri had found some casual work on the wharf and left one afternoon to do two hours' cleaning at the warehouse supervisor's office. When he hadn't returned by ten o'clock, Jelani became worried and walked the short distance to the wharf under the light of the half-moon.

He easily eluded the *askaris* guarding the gate, and headed to the warehouse. The lights were still on in the cavernous building, and Jelani softly called Gikuri's name. There was no reply. Jelani imagined he had waited for the last of the warehouse employees to leave, then found a comfortable hiding place to take a nap. He called louder.

Nothing.

He searched the aisles piled high with bagged produce, boxes and crates until he found Gikuri lying on the stone floor, his broom beside him, in a pool of blood.

Jelani could barely recognise him. His face was bloodied and broken and he moaned when Jelani lifted him to his feet.

'Who did this?' he asked.

One eye oozed blood and was swollen shut. Gikuri smiled, revealing broken and missing teeth.

'You wouldn't believe it, but that fat fart can move like a cat.'

Gikuri tried to laugh and then winced, holding his ribs. They staggered together for a hundred yards before Gikuri could go no further. Jelani hoisted his arm over his shoulder and half walked, half carried him to the gate. The *askaris* refused to help him find a doctor.

'But he works here,' Jelani insisted.

They turned their backs.

By the time Jelani and his three friends from the dormitory got Gikuri to the hospital, he was unconscious.

Jelani sat in the semi-darkness of the emergency ward and tried to put together what might have happened. Visram obviously arranged or found out about Gikuri's cleaning job, and ambushed him. Jelani could imagine Gikuri taunting him as the big man beat him, refusing to give him the satisfaction of victory. From the appearance of his injuries, the attack had been prolonged and vicious.

Jelani sent the others home and sat through the night, waiting for a report of his friend's condition. Nobody came to him so around seven the following morning, he found a doctor, who looked up the medical report from the previous night.

'Your friend has internal injuries. Ruptured spleen, three broken ribs, a punctured lung. Multiple contusions.' He flicked the page and looked grim. 'Was he involved in a car accident?'

Jelani shook his head. 'No. Will he be all right?'

The doctor shook his head. 'It's hard to know. He has a haematoma, bleeding in the brain. We need to see him awake to determine the extent of any brain damage. All we can do at the moment is wait.'

A week later, with Jelani at his bedside, Peter Gikuri died. He had never regained consciousness.

CHAPTER 36

The small item on page five of the *Mombasa Post* caught Jelani's eye.

> *The Coroner's Court on Thursday 21st September ruled that the death of Mr Peter Gikuri, lately of Embu District, was caused by misadventure. A spokesman for the East African Harbours and Railways Authority advised that Mr Gikuri had made an unauthorised entry into the Kilindini warehouse with the intention of committing theft of goods. He had fallen while trying to elude the security personnel.*

That night Jelani couldn't get the words *unauthorised entry* out of his head. Now he could see that Nasar Visram had planned the whole thing. He knew Gikuri would be in the warehouse and, when he'd cornered him and beat him almost to death, he reported the incident as an attempted robbery. It was the reason why the *askaris* on the gate would have nothing to do with Jelani when he asked for help.

The next day he skipped his classes and, with a friend's help and two hours in the headquarters' print room, they produced fifty posters promoting a rally and memorial service for Peter Gikuri.

Jelani spent the rest of the day distributing his posters, nailing them to posts and walls all over the wharf area and the East African Harbours and Railways compound.

Late that night he planned his speech and grew cold at the thought of standing in front of so many people. He'd always been self-conscious about his colour and never craved attention. For a brief moment he regretted his rash decision to hold a rally, then remembered Gikuri's battered face and terrible injuries: he resolved to carry it through for his friend.

* * *

Jelani climbed onto a table placed in the centre of the dormitory compound for him. Surrounding him was the entire student population, a group of stevedores, and a few whites, who stayed well away from the centre of the gathering.

'You have all seen the newspaper report,' Jelani said in a loud voice, brandishing a page of the *Mombasa Post*. '*Death by misadventure*, it says. And, *Gikuri made an unauthorised entry to steal goods*. Did you hear that? *Unauthorised entry*. Isn't it enough that they allow Gikuri to be beaten to death, without making him into a thief?'

A torrent of angry voices arose from the crowd.

Jelani returned to the article. '*He had fallen while trying to elude the security personnel*. I was there that night, my friends. We all know the *askaris* stay sitting at their gate. But someone came up to Peter Gikuri, who was legitimately working that night, and murdered him.'

He'd strayed from his prepared speech, which was more of a eulogy, but his fury and resentment swept him onwards.

'We all know Peter, and we all know he had one enemy. Before he died he told me the name of the person who beat him to the point of death. Will we stand for this?'

A roar went up.

'Are we going to allow them to do this to our friend Peter Gikuri?'

'*No!*'

Now he had no idea how to bring the rally to any other conclusion than to bring Visram to justice.

'Will you march with me to the house of the murderer?'

'*Yes!*'

Jelani waved them to follow him and, before leaping down from his platform, noticed that the white men at the back of the crowd had gone.

*   *   *

When Jelani's crowd of students and sympathetic workers arrived at Nasar Visram's house in Owen Road, they found another group of protesters already there. According to their banners and handmade placards bearing scrawled slogans, they were members of two groups: the Labour Trade Union of East Africa and the Kenya African Union.

A short but strongly built man with a rimless beaded hat was addressing the crowd in Swahili through a loud-hailer. Jelani could sense the tension in the gathering. The line of administration police forming a cordon around the house appeared to be very nervous.

'It is not enough that the government denies our just calls for a fair day's pay for a fair day's work,' the man in the beaded cap cried. 'But now they deny justice to our fallen brother — a young man not long from his home and now murdered by one of his supervisors.'

He gave a surprisingly accurate summary of Gikuri's life in the village — he'd obviously prepared well for his address — and described how difficult it was for Africans in rural areas to survive under the heel of the colonial government.

'And these people,' he went on, 'in the reserves and villages, or in the squatters' camps now spread all over what was once their land, can barely survive on what they can grow. They must spend time working for the white owner so they can pay their taxes. And if they don't doff their cap and say "please, *bwana*, thank you, *bwana*", he can put bad words on their *kipandes*, and chase them away.'

Here he held up the small metal box containing his own papers.

'And that means they may never get another job, or never be able to find a place to stay.'

He paused, his fierce eyes glaring out at the crowd. 'Should that be allowed?'

'*No!*' came the loud reply.

'Is it justice?'

'*No!*'

'Will you stand aside and let such injustice go unanswered?'

'*No!*'

Jelani was touched by his eloquence. Here was a master at work. His own attempts to motivate his fellow students paled into insignificance. The man, a Kikuyu by his accent, had captured the imagination of the crowd. They clung to his every word. When he evoked anger, they grew angry. When he wanted them to lift their voices in protest, they did so. If he needed silence he only had to lift one finger and the mob became as quiet as churchgoers. He was more than a orator: he was a maestro commanding the emotions within the crowd.

What had begun as a protest about the death of a worker had been transformed into a powerful political event without anyone noticing. Just as suddenly he was again railing against the murder.

'Are we going to let these people beat us and kick us until, like our fallen friend, we are lying bleeding on the ground?' he cried.

'*No!*'

Abruptly returning to his political message, he drew upon experiences in his early life to illustrate the callousness of white authority. He spoke of how the white missionaries had destroyed native Africans' traditions and religions, and in the process forced them to Christianity and capitalism. He told of land seized and villages stolen. The stories resonated in Jelani and within the crowd. Discontent and anger grew with the number of the white invaders' atrocities.

A chant commenced within the ranks of the mob. '*Jomo! Jomo! Jomo!*'

As it grew in intensity the speaker raised his voice.

Finally, he delivered the challenge: 'Will we stand for this injustice?'

'*No!*'

Jelani could hardly hear or recognise his own voice, added to the thunder of voices surrounding him. It wasn't a human sound, and he couldn't identify it as his own — it was more akin to the roar of a savage beast.

The mob surged past him, towards Visram's house. Jelani was at the rear of the crowd and followed, chanting *Jomo! Jomo! Jomo!* with everyone else.

The police held their lines against the push, using their riot sticks to belt the first line of men. Unseen by the police reinforcements observing from the other side of the square, Visram appeared at his door with an ancient blunderbuss in his hands and waved it in the air before releasing a panicked volley over the men's heads.

Hearing the shot, the officer in charge fired his revolver. From their hiding places behind the house, two columns of reservists mounted a baton charge against the crowds' flanks.

The battle raged for ten minutes.

Jelani and his friends ran to safety before the police could arrest any of them. Others were not as lucky. Twenty men were hospitalised, and one man died from his head injuries.

The brutal bashings of his fellow students and others present shocked Jelani. But the abiding memory he took from the day was that of the speaker who had, in a short time, changed Jelani's view of matters he had previously accepted as part of life under British law. The speaker was right: the British had no right to take away land belonging to Africans. Strangely, as they repeatedly preached the need for law and order, they had behaved in a manner simply unjust.

The gnawing pain of this injustice kept him awake all that night.

*   *   *

A week after addressing his fellow students in the compound, Jelani was called into the school's head office. There were two other men present, but they were not introduced. Jelani was invited to take a seat.

'Mr Karura,' the principal began. 'These gentlemen here, from our security department, have informed me that you addressed a group of students in the compound last Saturday night. Is that so?'

The principal, Mr J V Pavitt, had been involved in education since arriving in East Africa from Gujarat thirty-five years before. He was a mild-mannered man, much respected among the students in the trade school. 'Jelani,' he added with a smile, 'you don't have to answer if you don't want to.'

Jelani looked from Pavitt to the two other men. They were hard-faced, clearly more accustomed to breaking heads than educating them. He imagined they were among the white faces he'd spotted at the back of the crowd that day.

'I was there,' he said.

'And what was the purpose of the gathering?'

'It was about Peter Gikuri.'

'A commemorative meeting?' Pavitt offered.

Jelani didn't understand the term.

'A meeting to farewell your friend, Mr Gikuri.'

Jelani nodded.

'And what 'appened after that, eh?' It was the closest of the other two who spoke.

Jelani hesitated.

Pavitt sent Jelani an intense look, indicating he should be cautious, but Jelani didn't know how and wasn't sure why.

'You took your gang down to Nasar Visram's house, didn't you?' the second white security man demanded.

Again Jelani kept silent.

The man leaned forwards in his chair. 'Just because one of your friends — a cheeky black bastard — gets what was comin' to him, you get all upset about it. Ain't that so, eh?'

Jelani bristled.

'If I had my way, I'd have a few of my lads into that dormitory of yours and teach you a lesson about obeyin' the law. As for your little mate, well ... he got what he deserved, he did. The thievin' little prick!'

'He was not a thief! He was working and Visram beat him to death.'

'And you decided to do something about it.'

'Yes, we marched to his house to show he can't get away with it. Nobody can.'

'So you led the march?'

'Of course. What else could I do? He was a friend.'

The security man nodded, smiling.

Pavitt looked ill and let his shoulders slump.

* * *

As Jelani packed his handful of belongings into a burlap maize sack, he tried to imagine his future. The man from the Harbours and Railways security department spitefully told him that his name would be circulated throughout Mombasa, and nobody would employ him now. There was no opportunity to return to Nairobi and his previous job in the railways, and he couldn't face going back to his shoeshine business. An ignominious return, empty-handed, to Cook's farm appeared to be his only option.

A man appeared at the door and spoke to the nearest student.

'That's him, there,' the student said, pointing to Jelani.

The man introduced himself as Chege Muthuri, and asked Jelani if he could talk to him in private.

Jelani shrugged and followed the man into the night, making a gesture to the other members of the dorm that said *I have no idea*.

Outside, Muthuri came to the point.

'I've heard you've been sacked,' he said in Kikuyu.

Jelani looked at him, wondering how he knew.

'Don't worry,' he said. 'I'm the secretary of the Transport and Allied Workers' Union. We have friends here. There's not much that happens in the railways that I don't hear about.'

Jelani shrugged. 'I've been sacked for conspiracy to damage railway property.' It was still painful to talk about it, knowing that his hopes of becoming a qualified electrical mechanic were at an end.

'What property?'

'Visram's house.'

'Were you the one who spoke to the students that night?'

He nodded.

'Incitement. That's how they brought the conspiracy charge against you — it's instant dismissal. And that's the reason I came to see you. The union can use your help.'

'Me?'

'We're looking for young leaders. People who can speak to other young people.'

'But what do I have to say?' His old worries about drawing attention to himself returned.

'Only what you want to say. You could speak about your friend who died. You can speak about your life in the reserve or on someone else's farm. It's usually one or the other. You'll be speaking to people who are looking for freedom.'

'Freedom from what? All we want is food and a place to farm it.'

'Freedom gives you that. Freedom from the imperialist British.'

Jelani looked at him. Muthuri truly believed what he said.

'How is that possible?'

'Listen, my friend,' the union man said. 'The black Africans are forming strong groups to take over when the whites leave. Yes, you think it is a strange thing to say, but even now we have many men, educated men, strong men, who are preparing for what will come. They are in the unions and political parties like the Kikuyu Central Association and the Kenya African Union. One day the KAU will be in government.'

He paused to allow Jelani to absorb the images, before adding, 'Join us. One day, you may be a part of that government.'

CHAPTER 37

The *dak* bungalow at Kibwezi had served train travellers to Mombasa for half a century. Based on the system of rest houses throughout India, *dak* bungalows provided basic food in sufficient quantities for passengers who wanted a quick meal while the train took on fuel and filled its water tanks.

Sam alighted with the other passengers, but didn't care for a meal. Instead, he settled into a cane chair on the veranda with a cup of tea. He was on a business trip to Mombasa, one that would take him away from Nairobi for just a couple of days. Scattered over the table beside him were some newspapers. It had been a few months since he was last in Mombasa, and he picked up a three-day-old edition of the *Mombasa Post* to see what was making news on the coast.

He read the front page story on North Korea's invasion of the south, then scanned a story about an American senator claiming more than one hundred known communists were in government employment, to the local news with the headline: *Rioters Routed in Kilindini.*

Yesterday, police fired shots and used night sticks to break up a large and unruly crowd in Kilindini.

It was not immediately apparent why the rioters gathered at the house of a Harbours and Railways supervisor. Witnesses say that it was a gathering of mainly Indian and native employees, but there was no knowing whether it was prompted by demands for better pay — a situation increasingly common in the colony these days — or other matters.

One witness, who wished not to be named, said that a local political firebrand — a Kikuyu going by the unlikely name of Jomo Kenyatta — was the cause of the ruckus. Our informant confided that the speaker inflamed the mob's passions by inciting them to violently protest against various decisions of the administration in so far as they affect natives and their holdings of farmland.

It is this writer's opinion that these native upstarts be shown no mercy. If they cannot enjoy the generous benefits afforded them by His Majesty's British government in peace, and would rather incite their brothers to violent protest, then they should not be given such benefits, but rather be shown the full measure of the law.

One officer received minor cuts and bruises and was treated at the scene. Twenty native men received injuries, one of whom was seriously hurt while attempting to flee and later succumbed to his injuries in Mombasa hospital.

Sam thought it odd that the *Mombasa Post* reporter had not previously heard of Jomo Kenyatta. Sam had no urge to follow his political career but as he was a member of the Legislative Council who needed to keep abreast of current events through the newspapers, it was impossible not to occasionally see his old rival's name in print.

Kenyatta had risen quickly to prominence in the Kikuyu Central Association. A few years later he was sent back to London to lobby on behalf of the organisation's aim of winning land rights for displaced Kikuyus. While there, he received financial assistance from the communist party to study economics in Moscow. He then attended the London School of Economics and wrote his thesis, *Facing Mt Kenya*. It was an exposition of Kikuyu culture and the need for it to remain intact. He conceded that the British had a lot to offer Africans, but asserted that they had withheld most of the material benefits while removing the African from his land — the pillar of his culture and his means of sustenance — so as to exploit his labour.

Sam had read the book and found he agreed with most of its contents. Kenyatta's recent utterances, however, confirmed Sam's impression that while he and Kenyatta might agree about the importance of land in Kikuyu culture and the immoral nature of its confiscation, they differed on the means of resolving the problem. Kenyatta appeared to be following the communists' solution of an armed struggle. Sam had faith in the system, and believed change would come by engaging the whites in a political debate. To do so effectively, Sam knew that Africans would have to broaden their awareness of the European system of democracy so they could beat the British government at its own game.

Expanding young Africans' view of the world and its social structures was important in winning the debate in favour of equality. Assisting in that process was the main reason Sam was travelling to Mombasa.

* * *

Sam stepped from the carriage to the platform and loosened his tie. He squinted up into the bright morning sunshine. He'd forgotten how hot Mombasa could be.

At the end of the platform he hailed a driver from the line of waiting taxis then slid into the rear seat.

'Court Chambers building,' he said, and the taxi jerked into motion.

When the Governor nominated him to the Legislative Council, Sam had hoped to convince his fellow members to establish a government-funded program to select black Kenyans who showed leadership qualities, and develop them for the day when Kenya became independent. It was the subject of his maiden speech to the council, which received a cool, but generally polite hearing, although some of the settlers' representatives were openly hostile, saying he was a dreamer: why would the taxpayers of today pay for something that was clearly decades away. Sam persevered for a time, then gave up trying for official support.

Instead, he decided to establish a fund himself, but his finances were insufficient for what he had in mind, so he sold some of his shares in Ketterman Industries. He felt it was consistent with Ira's wish that he make use of some of his inheritance to help his fellow Africans overcome the restrictions of poverty.

He found the offices of White and Webb on the first floor of the Court Chambers building, and introduced himself.

Graeme White shook his hand and led him into his office. He was balding, with projecting, fly-away tufts of hair reaching out over his collars.

Sam sat opposite him, reading the papers White had prepared for him.

'I think you'll find all the instruments of the trust are as you intended, Mr Wangira,' he said when he'd finished.

Sam nodded, returning the papers to the lawyer's desktop. 'Thank you, Mr White. It all appears to be so. I'll instruct my bank to transfer the funds as soon as I get back to Nairobi.'

'Excellent. Is there anything more we can do for you?'

'No. Thank you again.' He stood to leave.

'One more thing, Mr Wangira, if you don't mind. Not that I'm complaining, but I'm curious as to why you have chosen White and Webb rather than one of the Nairobi law firms. I should think they would be far more convenient for you.'

'Perhaps, but if you'll recall our first telephone conversation, I wanted to keep this matter strictly confidential.'

'I see. You believe the Legislative Council might think you a little, um —'

'I think the expression is *uppity*, Mr White.'

White smiled, a little embarrassed. 'Well, I hope it all goes as you intend it, Mr Wangira,' he said, extending his hand.

Sam took it and wished him good morning.

* * *

Sam caught a taxi to the station, but since he had plenty of time, decided to detour via Kilindini. He'd been intrigued by the report of the riot and wanted to see for himself what the working conditions might be at the port.

The taxi waited outside the gate as Sam strolled onto the wharf to watch the last of the cargo being loaded onto a very rusty ship, the MV *Mogadishu*.

The name evoked strong memories of his visit almost exactly nineteen years earlier, when he was just a young man of thirty-four.

As if it were yesterday, he saw himself hurrying along this very wharf, in his last desperate bid to find Dana before she embarked for England.

He stood there letting the memories wash over him. In his desperation to find her, he had almost taken a *dhow* to the island of Lamu, where some demented old fool had said she'd gone. The world had seemed to stand between him and what he believed was his one great love back then.

For a long time after that, his life seemed to have no point. Even when he had the best intentions, fate turned against him as it had when he formed his rural bank. Of course there were other times when he had acted selfishly and caused others pain.

He felt bad even now when reflecting upon Sister Rosalba's love and affection. He always found reasons for not replying to her letters when he was in New York. He didn't appreciate how much they meant to him until they stopped; and even then, he didn't trouble himself to enquire why.

And Ira. He never properly thanked him for his generosity of spirit. Only when he died did Sam realise that Ira loved him in a special way. His defence was to ignore that love, when a simple acknowledgement of it would have meant so much to his dear friend.

And if he'd only recognised his feelings for Dana on that last day at Muthaiga, or at least understood that he needed to consider them properly, his life might have turned in completely different circles.

He wondered about Dana and where she might be. He wondered too if she ever thought of him, and what her life had become.

CHAPTER 38

The butler knocked once then entered the bedroom carrying a silver tray, a white china teapot and two cups. He placed the items on the little round table in the bay window beside Dana, and poured the tea while she gazed out over the sun-dappled garden. The gardener was tending the espaliered pear tree on the back wall. It was in full flower and would soon fruit. She remembered the day, shortly after she moved into the Mayfair house, when she'd planted it. It seemed a lifetime ago.

The memories weighed her down. She'd slept poorly, and when she looked into the mirror earlier that morning her puffy eyes confirmed it.

Oswald came in from his adjoining bedroom. His eyes were also puffy, but that was not so unusual for him. He was approaching seventy-five, and looked it. His belly protruded over the waistband of his pyjamas and his heavy jowls tumbled over the collar of his robe.

He took the napkin from his seat and sighed as he lowered himself to his chair.

'Sleep well, my dear?' he asked.

Dana took a sip of tea. 'Well enough, darling. And you?'

'Quite well.' He loudly cleared his throat. 'We should have a good crop of pears this year,' he said, admiring the tree on the back wall. 'Do you remember when we planted it? It must be eight or nine years ago.'

'Eleven,' she said. 'But yes, I agree. A good crop this year.'

They sat in silence. Oswald reached for the morning's edition of *The Times*.

Eleven years. They'd been tranquil if somewhat humdrum. She had known from the outset they would be, but it was for a good cause.

It was not always helpful, and she tried to avoid it, but her life with Edward in Kenya occasionally intruded. She could scarcely recall the person she'd been back then. As if she was watching a racy film of someone else's life, she'd see herself making love, sometimes with two men at once. There were titillating parlour games as the voices of Al Jolson and Bing Crosby sang the music of Oscar Hammerstein and Cole Porter.

Everyone in the Zephyrs knew it couldn't last — and perhaps it was that excuse, and the fact that they were all outcasts in the furthest corner of the Empire, that allowed them to act so outrageously.

During the years following her departure from Kenya in 1932, Dana had found it difficult to settle down in England. She missed her beautiful farm in the White Highlands. In those first days back home, while driving between London and Edward's country residence, she found herself idly scanning the fields for giraffe. Jersey cows were eland, and frolicking lambs were little Thommies. Even the best of days in the Midlands lacked the sparkle of the Kenyan highlands.

She lavished upon her daughter all the love and affection denied any other outlet and although she found great joy in seeing her child blossom and grow, it wasn't enough to overcome the tedium in other aspects of her life.

She turned once again to the thrill of extramarital sex and found one man after another. Edward stormed and raged, but she didn't care. When he engaged a private detective, who ultimately found her *in flagrante delicto* with a young member of the golf club, he demanded a divorce.

Dana's main concern was for the life she and her daughter would lose if Edward carried through on his threat, and chided herself for not getting evidence on his philandering before he did. She felt she had endured enough during the marriage to justify a sizeable settlement. Edward held other views.

The court case was messy; the private detective's evidence graphic and damning. Dana pleaded for support for their daughter, which finally softened Edward's heart, although his lawyer made it impossible for Dana to have access to the trust account.

It was only when she divorced him that she realised her stupidity. She was alone and vulnerable again.

With the single-minded determination once devoted to finding sexual pleasure, she set about finding another rich husband.

Oswald Middlebridge was an irascible bachelor, and even older than her first husband, but he was rich: very rich. Dana was again safe. But at a cost. Sex with Oswald was unexceptional at best, and often failed completely. After a few months he moved into an adjoining bedroom and soon gave up any idea of sharing hers.

Dana locked away her libido. There could be no dalliances. Oswald would not tolerate her casting even a sideways glance at another man, and she knew if she strayed even once, it would be the end of her marriage.

Being a dutiful wife wasn't as hard as she'd imagined. She'd enjoyed a passion with Sam that she'd been unable to replicate with others, and rationalised that in the absence of a similar obsession she could tolerate her enforced fidelity. It also helped to remind herself of the reason she'd entered into marriage with Oswald in the first place.

She'd denied herself a son and a lover to retain security for herself and her daughter, only to throw it away in a bewildering procession of beds.

She would not allow that to happen again.

CHAPTER 39

Jelani moved into a hut in Likoni, a ferry ride and long walk from the office of the Transport and Allied Workers' Union. His main job was to compile the union's newsletter, the Kenya Worker, from material prepared by Chege Muthuri. At other times he folded pamphlets and ran errands. His wages were small, but enough to survive.

He also tried to understand the aims of the Transport and Allied Workers' Union — and indeed those of the union movement in general. He couldn't see how the union could possibly make the improvements to pay and working conditions that they promised. From Jelani's perspective, and he kept his opinions to himself, the entire movement was powerless to alter the present situation where the government and employers had complete control. This impression, however, was challenged some months later.

During 1950, Mombasa's industrial unrest escalated to unprecedented levels. Workers and strike-breakers fought in the warehouses and factories on an almost daily basis. The situation was nearly as bad in Nairobi, where a large group of squatters from the farms around the neighbouring towns swarmed onto the lawns of Government House in Nairobi to demonstrate against the settlers' harsh employment conditions. A bloody battle ensued. The Governor promised to investigate the protestors' claims, but did nothing.

Finally, a general strike was called, and three-quarters of Mombasa's twenty thousand workers walked off their jobs. The strikers came from all the crafts and industries and were joined by domestic workers. The city came to a standstill and widespread rural protests arose in sympathy.

Jelani was with Chege Muthuri at the head of a march through the centre of Mombasa when the strikers faced police lines four deep. The officers carried batons held across their chests. In the rear were others mounted on horseback.

Muthuri leaned close to Jelani's ear. 'Go,' he said.

'What?'

'I said, go. You will be needed at the office if I get arrested.'

'But ...'

'And if I get arrested, you will find me for your orders.'

A whistle sounded from deep in the police ranks.

'Go!' Muthuri said, pushing Jelani away as he and the leaders at the head of the march roared defiantly, and surged towards the oncoming baton charge.

Jelani ran into an alley and climbed onto the roof of a building facing the street to watch the battle.

He watched as the batons rained onto the leading rows. The horsemen pressed their panicked mounts into the ranks while lashing out with long thick canes.

* * *

In the aftermath, four hundred people, including many union leaders, were arrested and thrown in gaol without charges being laid.

Jelani eventually found Muthuri in the old gaol.

'How did you get here?' Muthuri asked when Jelani stood on the other side of the barred gate. Behind him were scores of men milling in the open compound.

'Everyone likes a little tea money.'

'Hmmph ... Now this is what you must do,' he said and rattled off a string of instructions.

'But I know nothing about unions,' Jelani protested.

'There's no one else, Karura. Everyone's in here. Do what you can and report to me. Save your tea money and ask for Sergeant Obare — he's one of us. Keep the newsletter going, whatever you do. If we can't keep the members aware of what's happening, we're finished.'

The detentions didn't stop the union members' actions. They rallied again, and again the police retaliated with vigour, this time killing three and severely injuring thirty others.

An uneasy peace simmered through the doldrums — the weeks between the *kusi* and *kazkusi* trade winds when not a breath of air stirred the long tendrils of bougainvillea in the trees above Jelani's office. From the membership network came a constant string of complaints against employers, which Jelani duly noted. Women and children were being forced to work in difficult or dangerous situations; domestic servants were physically and sometimes sexually abused; local chiefs exploited their position of authority to extract free labour from their communities; administrative police extorted money or livestock from impoverished squatters. It took a groundswell of outrage to compel the normally placid Africans to complain to the authorities, but when they did, it came with a flood of pent-up fury. When these protests failed, and they often did, they had nowhere else to turn, except to the union.

As instructed by Muthuri, Jelani reported all in the *Kenya Worker.*

* * *

While the industrial campaign raged in the cities, another group had appeared in Kikuyuland and was building a reputation for helping the oppressed. They had no name, but Muthuri thought they might be potential rivals to the union and told Jelani to go to Nairobi to find out more.

A member brought a man to the lean-to in Bazaar Street that served as a union office. He was a Kikuyu squatter-labourer from the rolling hills below Mt Kenya; he seemed a little awed by his visit to the city.

Jelani asked him about the group.

'They are called The Movement, and they have been helping many of us squatters up there near Kirinyaga,' he said.

'And how have they helped you?'

'In Naro Moru where I stay, there is a farm owned by a man called Botha. He has many, many squatters working his farm. It is big. He works us very hard. Too much. When we complain, he beats us and threatens to chase us away. But these people, The Movement, they listen to us. They say we must join them and they will help us. So we join. Then they come to Naro Moru.'

'What did they say to this Botha?' Jelani asked.

'They say nothing. They did not meet him.'

'Then how did they help you?'

'They burned down his house.'

Jelani returned to Mombasa knowing little about the new group who appeared more like vigilantes than negotiators. They did, however, also sound capable of attracting supporters who might otherwise turn to the unions.

It wasn't an ignorant Kikuyu farmer who presented the most compelling argument that something strange was happening out in the rural areas surrounding Mt Kenya, but a district officer.

Jelani stumbled upon the DO's comments among documents given to him in Nairobi by a disgruntled office clerk. They were closed files detailing numbers of Africans employed in the districts by the administration and so were of interest to Jelani. The comments came in a footnote to the DO's annual report to his boss, the District Commissioner.

He wrote that local white farmers had complained about suspicious livestock losses soon after rejecting petitions from their workers for better pay and conditions. The whites expressed concern about what they called a secret society formed from mainly young Kikuyu men intent on stirring up trouble among their squatter-labourers. This society argued that the squatters' problems could only be solved by expelling all whites from the fertile highlands — the traditional home of the Kikuyu people. It was a step too far.

The District Officer suggested to the DC that he might ask the white farming community to become more aware of their resident squatters' concerns and take some time to understand their point of view. He said that too many were inclined to bully their workers into submission and that they quite often chose to use a fist of iron rather than a helping hand.

The DO said there were many names for the secret society including The Movement, the Freedom Struggle Association and, more ominously, the Land and Freedom

Army. However, he thought the most commonly used name was Mau Mau.

Jelani flipped from the report to a file note where he found the District Commissioner's succinct and dismissive comment: *Noted.*

On his next visit to the Mombasa gaol, he raised the matter with Chege Muthuri, who nodded his understanding, but said no more. On a second occasion he brushed Jelani's concerns aside, saying the stories about the group who promised land reform and an end to the white's domination were merely wishful thinking on the part of ignorant farmers.

'They would rather invent a mysterious saviour than to join the union's ranks and fight for better conditions,' he said. 'Ignore them.'

* * *

Muthuri and the other leaders were released after a prolonged industrial campaign. Eventually it was the whites — farmers and factory owners in the main — who demanded they be released: their businesses were suffering.

Jelani was rewarded for his conscientious work by being given the job of editor of an expanded newspaper — *Uhuru*, or *Freedom*. Muthuri said it would be the backbone of the new independence movement.

Jelani was flattered, but thought it unimaginable that a small newspaper could halt the whites' changes to the African way of life.

As part of his induction to his new role, Jelani accompanied Muthuri to the Rift Valley town of Nakuru where the union secretary planned to hold the first of a series of meetings with his members. He wanted Jelani there to take notes. Thereafter, he would continue on a whistle-stop tour to Kisumu. Jelani would return to the Mombasa office to write up the meetings for the next edition of *Uhuru*.

They sat in the second-class carriage, Muthuri at the window, as the train climbed towards the Mau escarpment, north of Nairobi. Muthuri talked about his plans for the coming months. He said he wanted to spend more time away from the coast.

'This is where we will begin our big push,' he said, pointing out the window at the rolling hills around Limuru. 'Here in Kikuyuland, and it is the Wakikuyu who will be our warriors in the battles ahead.'

Jelani followed his gesture. Food gardens climbed the slopes of red volcanic soil to tea and coffee plantations along the ridges. It was late morning and Kikuyu farmers dotted the landscape tending their plots — or more likely, the acres of the white land owners. It was an outlook similar to that from his home on the slopes of Mt Kenya.

'That is why I'm moving my office to Nairobi,' Muthuri added, then turned to peer out the window as the train snaked its way along the contours into the next valley. Here another patchwork quilt of crops coloured the hillside. Cassava, maize, chick peas, beans, sorghum. The squatters grew everything they could, but not the cash crops — coffee, tea and wheat — that were the exclusive preserve of the whites.

Shortly after passing through the village of Kikuyu, the train driver tooted as the line crossed the road through Sigona Country Club, where groups of golfers strolled the green fairways hitting then foolishly following little white balls. Black boys carried their heavy golf bags.

Here and there were thatched villages sitting in the folds of the land or down on the flat beside a stream.

The train clattered across culverts covering the leaping waters of streams that dashed down to the tributaries of the Mathare or Nairobi rivers, depending upon what side of the watershed the tracks were situated.

'I've been thinking, Karura,' Muthuri said after some time. 'I would like you to move to our Nairobi office too. I will need your help as our work there increases. The union has a small bungalow among the railway workers' huts. Do you know the place? It's near the Nairobi station.'

'Yes, I had a place there years ago.'

'It's a small place, but enough for you and your wife.'

'I'd like that, Chege. But I have no wife.'

'Good. That's good. A wife could become a problem.'

Jelani would have liked to ask why, but his boss continued.

'When you get back to Mombasa, pack your things and come back to Nairobi as soon as you can. There is much to do.' He glanced at Jelani. 'Yes, we need more people in Nairobi these days. Can you drive a car?'

'No.'

'Hmm … Well, I think we should give you some lessons in these things.'

Jelani was excited about learning to drive, but tried to remain casual. There were weightier matters to discuss.

Muthuri continued: 'I want you at Nakuru as I have invited a fellow called Kenyatta to join me. Have you heard of him?'

Jelani thought he had, but couldn't recall the context. He shook his head.

'Kenyatta ...' Muthuri said derisively. 'What kind of name is that, ah? And Jomo — they say it means *burning spear*. I've never heard of it. But he is making a big name for himself. He is popular with we Kikuyu; and he has some connections with the Maasai. I'm not sure, but I think he lived in Narok for some time. Anyway, I want him to address the meeting. And I want you to speak to as many people as you can afterwards. I want to know what people think of him. If he can make an impact on these simple fellows up in Nakuru, I might invite him to join our movement.'

* * *

The town of Nakuru spread east from the railway station through a dusty stretch of flat country dotted with Indian trade stores, farming equipment suppliers, horse traders and stock and station agents, into a sweep of lush grass that climbed past a number of large farms and ranches to the top of the Great Rift Valley. There the eye could travel for forty miles before it again met the same level of the land on the far side.

Below the railway line Nakuru fell away through a series of squalid little huts and *dukas* to the lake and its enormous flocks of flamingos and water birds. Not more than two hundred yards from the line was the produce market's array of local eating places that offered Jelani's favourite meal — *nyama choma* — and a slab-top table to sit at while eating it.

Jelani did just that the first time he had a free hour and was soon in conversation with another customer —

an older Kikuyu man — also enjoying the barbecued meat.

'Mombasa,' Jelani told him, when asked where he lived.

'So far from home,' the man said, shaking his head in sympathy. As a brother Kikuyu, he recognised the difficulty of leaving the homeland.

'But soon I will be moving back to Nairobi,' Jelani added.

The older man nodded, unconvinced it was much of an improvement on the situation.

Neither of them was in a hurry and they spoke at length about home and, as people do when meeting a countryman, explored the possibility of mutual acquaintances. They identified a few distant cousins; and the conversations became more personal.

'How is it for you here in Nakuru?' Jelani asked.

The other man shrugged. 'In the Rift Valley there is not enough land. My family of seven and I ... we have a small plot. But we are always fighting with the Maasai, who think they can graze their cattle wherever they please.'

'So I have heard,' Jelani responded. 'But what can be done?'

'Land reform.' The farmer spoke the words reverently, as if in themselves they held the answer to the problem.

Jelani waited for further explanation. It didn't come.

'But how?' he asked.

The man hesitated, perhaps assessing how much he could say to the relative of a distant cousin, who lived in faraway Mombasa.

'The Movement,' he said at last.

'You mean the Mau Mau,' Jelani said in equally lowered tones. 'I have heard that they make their supporters take an oath.'

'You make it sound unusual. Surely you know of the power of an oath.'

Oaths were in common use among the Kikuyu. Just as a white would swear on a Bible, a Kikuyu man would take an oath.

'I have, but if the cause is good, why is there a need for an oath?'

'Everywhere there are traitors. An oath-taker will not betray. Who knows what the whites can do to force someone to report on his friends?'

'And what can we gain from these Mau Mau in return for our oaths?'

'They are trying to help us win some land.'

'How do they do that?'

'They are making it difficult for the white farmers. They destroy their fences. They poison waterholes. They hamstring their cows.'

'Hamstring their cows!' Jelani said, horrified at the thought of such cruelty. 'How can that help their cause?'

The man shrugged. 'Anything that makes life difficult for white farmers will make it easier for them to leave our land to us. Or so some of the big men say.'

A big man was anyone with power and influence.

'But who?' Jelani pressed him.

'I know of one man, Kenyatta by name.'

'Is he one of the Mau Mau?'

The man nodded. 'Yes. I think so. Like them, he speaks of land reform. He travels all around the Rift Province, telling the people to be ready.'

'Ready for what?'

'I don't know. He doesn't make it clear. But some say he will lead an army to throw out the whites.'

*   *   *

The union meeting was held in the open space at the centre of the produce market. The space was lit by paraffin torches that smoked and flickered, sending shadows dancing across the faces of the crowd. Some sat on the emptied produce benches surrounding the square; others stood behind them, four deep in places.

Muthuri opened the meeting and spoke about the need for solidarity now that the business leaders and the administration had formed a united block against them. And he appealed for new members to shoulder the financial burden of continuing the fight.

Jelani frantically scribbled his notes, not daring to lift his head. At the end of his speech, Muthuri received only lukewarm applause. Then he introduced Jomo Kenyatta.

Carrying his elephant-headed ebony walking stick as though it were a ceremonial sceptre, Kenyatta strode to the centre of the crowd like a monarch about to conduct an audience among his subjects. He was a short, stocky individual with a pointed goatee beard. He wore flannel trousers and an opened leather jacket that revealed a beaded Maasai *kinyatta* belt around his sizeable girth. Perched on his massive head was a colourful embroidered Luo hat. But it was his eyes that commanded everyone's attention. Even in the dull light of the lanterns, they shone like burning coals in the heart of a brazier. They demanded attention and the crowd gave it willingly.

Within a few minutes, Jelani recognised him as the speaker at Nasar Visram's house in Mombasa; he abandoned his notebook to watch enthralled as Kenyatta roused his audience with compelling words and dramatic mannerisms. He spoke in Swahili, which was not fluent, but he used simple words to carry his meaning. Occasionally he would inject a few more sophisticated English words to perhaps indicate his higher education, but he never obscured his message: Kenyatta was a man of the people; he understood them and was a champion of their causes.

He reminded the gathering that they should not forget their origins, no matter to what tribe they belonged. He said that the whites knew that they had to first sever the connection between Africans and their ancestors before they could break them in as common labourers and servants. He warned them about trusting the missionaries who came with lofty talk of God and salvation, but with the implied threat of hellfire and retribution unless they followed their rules.

'When the missionaries arrived,' he said, 'the Africans had the land and the missionaries had the Bible. They taught us how to pray with our eyes closed. When we opened them, they had the land, and we had the Bible.'

Then he turned his attention to the people in his audience who worked the land and had come to hear what the union and others might say on their behalf.

'I know that many of you squatter-labourers have been put in a bad place. You have lost your land and been offered a pittance to work it on behalf of the new white owners. I know you work on that land every day of the month, with your women and children beside you at times, for no more than twelve or fourteen shillings. I know that you must pay twenty of those shillings in poll tax every year. For what?' He glared into the faces staring at him from the gloom. 'Do you get to vote for the men who impose these taxes and conditions upon you? No. Do you get the right to better yourself by planting cash crops? No. If you are lucky, the farmer will allow you to plant some maize on the acre he offers you — an acre you may have once owned. But can you sell it in this very market?' He waved his arms to indicate the empty stalls. 'No. The government says you must sell it to the white farmer for fourteen or fifteen shillings a bag, and then another foreigner — perhaps a *Mahindi* in his Indian *duka* — sells it back to you for thirty-two!

'And what does your half shilling per day buy you in the white man's store or the Indian's *duka*? Nothing. A cheap shirt costs you four shillings. An axe to cut your firewood, six or eight.

'We Africans are paying taxes to the white man to keep his fine house and his fine life. Will we continue to tolerate this?' he asked, his voice rising in volume.

There was a rumble of discontented voices.

His voice dropped to a whisper, but one that could be heard to the back row of his audience. 'Then I say to you, my friends: prepare. Prepare to fight for the return of your land; the return of your livelihood; and the return of your dignity.'

Jelani looked around him. Nobody spoke, but there wasn't a person in the audience not contemplating the vision that Jomo Kenyatta had dared to reveal to them.

CHAPTER 40

The fifteen-year-old Model B Ford the union used to ferry officials around Nairobi's employment sites was not one of the very handsome black models Jelani had seen in American films, with high pointed bonnets and sleek mudguards and running boards. It was narrow and boxy and one of the windows wouldn't wind up. It was also hard to start and Jelani often had the demeaning task of cranking it. But driving it was about the most exciting experience he'd had since he was a boy taunting buffaloes for the sport of having them chase him up a tree.

He loved the subtle power he felt emanating from under the bonnet. The mysteries of the internal combustion engine enthralled him regardless of his ignorance of its workings. When there were no others in the car he would hang his head out the window to feel the air rush through his hair. He washed and polished the duco until it gleamed.

While returning to the Nairobi office after driving one of the organisers to a meeting, Jelani saw an African man sprinting down the centre of Government Road in the vicinity of Central Police Station. Two policemen were running after him. Three more followed half a block behind.

The fleeing man shot past Jelani, who had, like most

other drivers on both sides of the road, stopped to watch the drama unfold.

The man was a Kikuyu and the fact that so many police were chasing him probably meant he would be in serious trouble if caught.

The escapee turned down Gulzaar Street and Jelani made a left at the next street to continue to watch the action.

He saw the man emerge from Gulzaar and make a short dash along Stewart before turning into Bazaar Street. A good manoeuvre, thought Jelani, who by now had developed some sympathy for this lone person escaping from superior forces. His detour into Bazaar Street with its maze of Indian shops and alleys behind was exactly what Jelani would have done in the same circumstances. And Bazaar Street was only a block away from the produce market, which is where he would go and guessed the running man would too.

He could identify with the escapee. He and many of his family, friends and acquaintances had had similar run-ins with the police. From childhood they'd been the enemy; and since then he'd heard and seen many instances where the law had not acted fairly nor honourably.

By now he had become enthralled by the chase and he drove to the market and parked the car at the rear among the vendors' trucks and hand-trolleys. It was as if he was part of a Hollywood film and he was the hero's trusty sidekick with a getaway plan unknown to all but himself. So when the man appeared in the parking area, Jelani flashed his headlights at him without a second thought.

The man saw him, but hesitated.

Jelani opened the door and waved him over.

'Brother!' he shouted in Kikuyu. 'This way!'

The man dashed to the car and dived into the passenger seat.

When the adrenalin had subsided, and Jelani and his rescued escapee were driving down Ngong Road, Jelani suddenly realised what he'd done: he'd used the official vehicle of the Transport and Allied Workers' Union to assist a fugitive to escape custody. If the Trades Union Council heard of it, he would be finished with the union.

Jelani glanced sideways at his passenger — the man might be a murderer, or a madman. His breathing had returned to normal, but he still had the look of a wild animal, with tangled hair, tattered clothes and blazing eyes.

The man must have felt Jelani's gaze, and turned to him. Jelani returned his attention to the road, which was almost devoid of traffic through the Ngong Road Forest.

'Keep driving towards the Ngong hills,' the escapee said.

Jelani nodded.

'I am Dedan Kimathi,' he said. 'Field Marshal Dedan Kimathi.'

Jelani nodded, unsure of what he meant by *field marshal* — Kimathi was only a little older than he was.

'... of the Land and Freedom Army.'

Mau Mau, Jelani thought, confirming his worst fears. I have rescued a terrorist escaping from the government.

Kimathi read his mind. 'You are a Kikuyu,' he said. 'You know of the Mau Mau. You know our work.'

'Um ...' Jelani said.

'Surely you know how many of us have been thrown from our land?'

'I do,' Jelani answered, keen to find common ground. 'Even my own family were put off our land and sent to a white man's farm.'

'And what did your father do about it?'

'Well ... what could he do?'

'*Correct!* Nothing!'

Jelani glanced in Kimathi's direction again. He had the crazed expression of a fanatic. He wished he hadn't agreed to drive him out of the city.

'Correct,' Kimathi said, more moderately. 'He could do nothing alone. That is why we have formed our movement. Kenyatta and Harry Thuku are talking to people. They talk about peaceful protest and negotiations, but what have they achieved, ah?'

He turned to Jelani, who made a great show of careful driving, keeping his eyes firmly on the road ahead and the steering wheel in the vice-like grip of his hands.

'Nothing,' Kimathi said, answering his rhetorical question. 'Nothing but talk. That is why the movement is there — for when Kenyatta and Thuku and all the rest fail, we will act.'

Jelani felt compelled to speak. 'You will fight for our land?' he asked.

'And die if necessary,' Kimathi answered. 'As will many who follow the cause of the dispossessed Kikuyu landholders.'

Jelani felt a vague sense of guilt for not taking more of a stand against the chief and others when he and his family were unceremoniously marched off their land.

'We need many loyal warriors. Will you join us?

Jelani shot a glance at him. The question wasn't coercive but a genuine invitation; he sensed no threat from his passenger. He thought about it. Why shouldn't he fight with his fellow Kikuyu for what was right? Isn't that why he had so strongly identified with the union cause?

A roadblock came suddenly into view as they rounded a corner.

'Police,' Jelani said, easing off the accelerator. There was nowhere to turn.

'Let me out, I will run.'

'No, wait.'

The surrounding forest was dense and he had a good chance of getting away, but that didn't solve Jelani's problem. If the police spotted a man fleeing from his car, he would have some explaining to do.

It was just a routine control point, which the police often set up to check licences and other trivial details. Jelani had passed through many similar. The police were generally a sleepy lot, angling for small bribes from those without proper vehicle registration or who otherwise had something to hide.

Jelani made his decision. 'I'll drive through it!' he said, barely believing he could even consider it, but he was already implicated in the escape of a leader of the dreaded Mau Mau. What else had he to lose?

Jelani pressed the accelerator and the V8 engine responded.

He swung the car onto the verge, avoiding the car already at the checkpoint, and powered past it. The police shouted.

In the rear-view mirror he watched as they waved their arms, and then ran towards their parked police car to give chase.

Jelani's mind tumbled through the consequences of what he'd done. His whole life was now on a knife's edge. Disgrace, the sack, and gaol loomed as the likely outcomes.

'There is a small road on the left over this next hill,' Kimathi said.

The road was clear behind him and Jelani was now almost too despondent to care. He turned onto the track.

The car bumped and rocked for a few hundred yards before coming to an enormous fallen tree that blocked further progress.

Kimathi didn't seem concerned, and indicated to Jelani to cut the engine.

Jelani's heart pounded as they sat in silence. They heard the pursuing vehicle approaching then receding down the tarmac in the direction of Ngong town.

Jelani was able to breathe again; and Kimathi began to laugh quite loudly.

'Ah, my friend, you have saved my life. Do you know that they would hang me if they could?'

Jelani thought he was joking, but when he looked at Kimathi, his eyes were blazing. He laughed again: this time it was high-pitched and forced.

'Come,' Kimathi said after taking a moment to regain his self-control. 'The house is not far. I will introduce you to my fellow warriors.'

Jelani was tempted to follow, but he felt he'd narrowly avoided a catastrophe and was not ready to take any further risks.

'No, I'd better be getting back.'

Kimathi stared at him. It was impossible to read what thoughts lay behind those wild eyes. After a long moment he laughed again.

'Of course, my friend. You have work to do.'

He made a move to open the door, but turned back to Jelani.

'Let me tell you this before I go. I have seen inside your heart. I know you, my friend. I know there will come a time when you realise too much injustice has been done to you. You will become angry and you will shake with shame because you have let too much happen. It is then that you will want to strike out. You will remember all the wrongs committed against you and your family. You will want to fight. And you will be defeated, because one man cannot defeat the British invaders. That is when you will come and join us. The Land and Freedom Army. That is when you will come to us.' He nodded down the track. 'And be welcomed here — up this road — with our other recruits.' He smiled and nodded. 'I know this about you.'

Jelani said goodbye and drove back to the city.

In the car park at the rear of the union's rented office, he turned off the motor and explored the thoughts that had played in his mind on the drive back.

His rescue of Kimathi in the market and their escape from the police had been very exhilarating. But it was more than the excitement of the moment that had lifted his spirits. For the first time in his life he felt he was doing something to strike back at the authorities that had been responsible for so much of the injustice he had seen and experienced. His act of defiance that day had gone some way to even the score, and it made him feel good.

However, he knew it wasn't enough because Kimathi's parting words had left him feeling unsettled: 'You will shake with shame because you have let too much happen.'

* * *

When the Kenyan government applied to the Colonial Office to grant a Royal Charter to the city of Nairobi, rumours spread that it was an attempt to expand the boundaries of the city to include the surrounding districts. One of those districts was the White Highlands, so named because only whites could own land there. The fear among those agitating for a return of their land was that Nairobi would become a whites-only city — even further entrenching the colonial grip on native land.

Chege Muthuri sent messages to all the Transport and Allied Workers' Union representatives all over the country to call on the membership to attend a mass rally in Nairobi to protest against the granting of a Royal Charter. He stressed the need for numbers so that the administration would not have the nerve to arrest the rally leaders.

Two days before the rally, Muthuri gave Jelani a copy of his speech to include in the edition of the *Uhuru* newspaper that would be made available on the day of the rally.

Jelani went to Muthuri's office before he'd completed the transcript.

'Chege,' he said. 'You can't say these words.'

Muthuri looked up at him from his desk, which was covered in papers.

'They need to be said,' he replied, then returned to his papers.

'Asking for land reform will anger the government. They will be prepared for that. But calling for independence will have you thrown in gaol.'

'They won't dare to touch me in front of a mass rally.'

'Do you really think that our members out there in Nanyuki and Eldoret and Voi will come to Nairobi because of something like a Royal Charter?'

'They will come. It is important.'

'Chege, they won't come and you cannot say these words.'

Muthuri sat back in his chair and placed his pen on the desk. He sighed. 'Karura, have I taught you nothing? Ah? Have you heard nothing I've been telling you these last few months?'

'It's been more than a year, Chege, and yes, I have heard everything you've told me. But this is madness. You know they will arrest you. They will have no choice.'

'The whites have been asking for independence for some time,' he said, returning to his papers.

'That is different. The white Kenyans think they own this country. And they are quarrelling with their own back in Britain when they demand this and demand that. But if you say something similar, they will be afraid of our millions against their thousands. Their fear will force their hand.'

Muthuri nodded; a smile slowly spread across his grizzled, unshaven face. 'Ah, Karura ... you have been listening after all.'

'So why are you doing this?'

Muthuri stood and came from behind his desk to sit on the edge of it, facing Jelani. He folded his arms.

'When you have done everything that you think is right to make the other side understand — when even your own people turn against what they know is right so as to please their masters — *then* it is time to force the issue. Then it is time to act.'

'But how will going to gaol help?'

'There has never been a good cause won without a fight. Soon there will be many like me in the gaols. Then the British, and the world, will take notice.'

Chege Muthuri stood on the platform erected on the flat bed of a borrowed truck, and addressed the crowd scattered around the City Council forecourt. There were perhaps no more than three hundred people present, but if Muthuri was disheartened by the numbers, he didn't show it.

He had none of the eloquence of Jomo Kenyatta, but there was no doubting his passion as he railed against the administration's heavy-handedness and the dangers if the city were allowed to declare a charter covering the surrounding districts.

Following Muthuri's orders, Jelani kept apart from the crowd. 'I don't want you arrested if it comes down to it,' he'd said. 'Someone has to keep the office open if I and the others are taken away.'

Around the perimeter of the quadrangle was a thin line of administration police, most of whom were black Africans. There were only three or four white officers in sight. Clearly, if there was going to be any physical force applied, it would not be by white officers. It didn't look good from the very start.

When the rally commenced despite the low attendance, the police gathered into small platoons. The white officers moved among them, issuing orders. Jelani wanted to rush to Muthuri and warn him, but he knew it was too late. He also knew Muthuri would not thank him.

At a signal, the police charged into the centre of the rally, wielding their batons, and scattering the crowd in a panic. They cut through the small knot of union officials standing around the truck, and hauled Chege Muthuri from it.

The last Jelani saw of his boss, he was being dragged away by two heavy Kikuyu policemen — two of the people he was trying to protect from exploitation.

* * *

The Trades Union Council acted swiftly and called a general strike in protest against the union officials' arrests. Large numbers of black workers stayed away from their places of employment in spite of their employers' threats of fines and dismissals.

The government was rattled by the unexpected show of solidarity by the black Africans. Newspaper headlines shrieked *Anarchy*, and business and political leaders harangued the strikers.

Days passed without either side conceding ground. Meanwhile the union leaders remained in gaol. The Trades Union Council decided to increase the stakes and called for a massive show of strength. Convoys of trucks and buses ferried hundreds of rural workers to the city where they joined thousands of their urban counterparts.

The demonstration quickly turned violent; police were unable to quell the spread of the disturbances as the more extreme groups, without the knowledge or approval of the march organisers, broke from the main crowd and attacked shops and places of business. They smashed windows and set fire to a number of buildings.

The police chief called in members of the armed forces who were stationed a short distance from the city centre. Their reaction was swift and brutal.

The soldiers barricaded the road to Government House with their vehicles, standing behind them in a show of strength. Jelani was among the union officials in the first rows of the march. When they rounded a corner they saw the barricade for the first time. There were black faces among those manning the barricades, and the union leaders called on their followers to proceed in a peaceful show of solidarity.

When the first shots rang out, the marchers faltered, but the volley flew well over their heads. They pressed on.

Suddenly the man next to Jelani fell to the road. Jelani hadn't even heard the shot that felled him. There was a scream from somewhere behind him; more shots rang out. Men were falling all around him, some crying in agony, others dropping without a sound — dead before they hit the ground.

Jelani was frozen in shock, but a moment later he and the others were bolting away in terror, crashing through fences and gardens, running for their lives.

Tears of anger and outrage streamed down his face.

* * *

The matatu rattled along the rutted, potholed road towards Ngong town. When it reached the track leading into the forest where he'd left Kimathi some days before, Jelani called on the driver to stop.

It was late afternoon and the forest was dark, made more ominous by the flat sky that had hung like a grey blanket over the city all day.

An armed guard met Jelani on the track, then after checking his *kipande*, led him deeper into the forest to a group of a half-dozen or so other men standing and sitting in the fading light. Several looked as though they had been waiting in the clearing for a long time.

Nobody spoke.

After a lengthy silence, one of the men nodded a greeting to Jelani. He asked Jelani where he was from.

'Nairobi,' he said, then realised he'd meant what district. 'Kobogi. Near Embu.'

The man nodded. 'Meru,' he said.

They didn't exchange names, but their home villages were widely separated and this seemed to give them freedom to exchange information while keeping their identities safe.

Jelani learned that the man had decided to join the Mau Mau after his local chief had confiscated most of his maize crop for an invented misdemeanour. When the man protested the chief had the tribal police throw him in gaol. While his wife was bringing him food, the chief invaded his house and raped his oldest daughter — a girl of twelve. His complaints to the district office went unheeded, however the local Mau Mau leader took revenge on his behalf: he had the chief's legs broken. It was then that he decided to join the movement and to convince his other male family members to do likewise.

Jelani said that his story was pale by comparison. He told him about his Kikuyu friend who had been murdered by a vindictive manager and that, more recently, he'd been in a march where peaceful protesters were shot down like dogs.

There was more to it than that, but Jelani didn't want to appear too philosophical. He'd thought long and hard about his decision to accept Dedan Kimathi's invitation. The violent reaction to the march was simply the catalyst.

He knew that orators were respected in times of peace, and were heeded on social matters, but in times of war the Kikuyu people always turned to the strongest among them. Jelani believed that no matter how eloquently Muthuri or Kenyatta spoke, unless they were prepared to show aggressive leadership, they would be ignored by the Wakikuyu. He also knew that the Kikuyu were the largest tribe in Kenya and, since the leaders of the Mau Mau were Kikuyu, they were the best able to mobilise the numbers needed to challenge the white government. Jelani had come to the enclave the previous day, hoping to be allowed to take his oath at the next ceremony and so make a real difference for his people.

After a further fifteen minutes, the guard returned and led them through the darkened forest to a wattle and daub house with a large *makuti* roof and shuttered windows. A newly constructed hut of bush materials stood at a short distance. A goat, making an occasional nervous bleat, was tethered to a stake inside the hut.

The men filed through the doorway into an interior empty of any furniture and well lit by smoking lanterns. An arch made of vines and flowers stood at one end. It was similar to ones Jelani had seen used in ceremonies back home in Kobogi.

There were three men already in the room. Two were sitting at a large table, the other stood at the window. Jelani could vaguely recall seeing the seated two at Nairobi rallies. He recognised the third, bearded and wearing metal-rimmed spectacles, as Bildad Kaggia. According to the daily newspapers, Kaggia was the Nairobi leader of the Mau Mau and principal oath-giver. After glancing around the group, Jelani turned his eyes back to the window opening outside which, by the sounds coming into the hut, the goat was being slaughtered.

Kaggia gathered all of them into a circle, then the assistant who had slaughtered the goat came in from outside carrying a long strip of bloodied hide. Kaggia made a circle of it on the floor and the initiates entered the sacred space that it made.

Bildad Kaggia made a long speech about the Movement. He told them that it represented the Kikuyu people and would fight their battle to regain their land. In the process they would also gain independence from the British, who had kept their booted foot on the throat of Africa for too long. He reminded them of the importance of a Kikuyu oath; how oaths had been used throughout their history as a means of solemnising undertakings and promises.

'In the most serious situations a broken Kikuyu oath can condemn the taker to death,' he said. 'Such is the case in the oath you will be swearing tonight.'

Jelani felt a growing apprehension. He couldn't say exactly what he had expected that night, other than a promise to keep the rules of the organisation, but as Kaggia continued his tirade against the government, the white settlers and all who would oppose the Mau Mau, his unease grew.

Kaggia circled the men, staring at each in turn, as he spoke. When he paused in front of Jelani, he felt Kaggia's eyes burning into his. Jelani had the almost irresistible urge to blink or look away, but he held his nerve until Kaggia passed.

Kaggia's assistant reappeared carrying a wooden platter upon which were a pot and lumps of raw meat. He set them down in front of Kaggia, who then indicated that the man two ahead of Jelani should step forwards to take his oath.

The first man swore the oath then took the pot from the assistant, lifted it to his lips, and drank. He then sliced off a piece of the raw meat and swallowed it before moving on.

The next man stepped up and Jelani could then see that the meat was the goat's heart, liver and lungs. With a lurch in the pit of his stomach, he realised that the pot held the goat's blood.

Standing under the harsh gaze of Bildad Kaggia, Jelani had no doubt that if he decided to renege at the last minute, he would not make it back to Nairobi alive.

Kaggia intoned the words of the oath again and Jelani repeated them.

'*If I ever argue when called, may I die of this oath.*

'*If I ever disobey my leader, may I die of this oath.*

'*If called upon in the night and I fail to come, may I die of this oath.*'

Jelani took a deep breath and sipped warm blood from the pot then gulped down a slice of the heart.

His initiation was complete.

CHAPTER 41

The following morning, the sun rose clear and bright in a brilliant blue sky.

As Jelani waited for the gaoler to lead Chege Muthuri into the visitors' meeting room, he wondered about Kaggia's almost primeval antics of the previous night. Although the oathing was quite bizarre, he had no doubts about his decision to join the Mau Mau.

The gaoler led Muthuri into the visitors' room then backed out. The unionist looked pleased. 'Ah, what a wonderful day, my young friend,' he said, beaming.

'Haven't you heard about the riots?' Jelani asked, surprised.

'I have. We are very close to victory.'

'I don't see how you can say that. The army are helping the police.'

'Excellent. It means they are worried. And when I heard they'd used tear gas, I knew we'd won.'

Jelani merely shook his head, thinking Muthuri had become delusional.

'You don't understand, do you?' Muthuri said. 'Let me explain. The administration has never before used tear gas in Kenya. It's unprecedented and, as someone said about empires, *what is unprecedented is not permitted*. This story will be in all the London newspapers. The Colonial Office will have a fit.' He was beside himself. 'I give them two or three days before it is all over. And I will be out of this place. Now, to business.'

Muthuri detailed what needed to be done in preparation for his release. Jelani scribbled notes, still not convinced Muthuri wasn't deceiving himself. When the union matters were completed, Muthuri asked about his scholarship.

'What do you mean?' Jelani asked.

'I've put you forward to the Trades Union Council. Didn't I tell you this?'

'No, not really.'

'For a place on the government's scholarship program. Someone in the Legislative Council is running it.'

'A scholarship? What is that?'

'A training program. In your case it would be six weeks in America with the Longshoremen's Union.'

'In America?'

'If everything goes as planned. They'll want to interview you, but that won't be a problem. You'll probably leave in a couple of months.'

'For America?'

'The person who you must see is ...' He patted his pockets and pulled a crumpled piece of paper from one of them. '... Sam Wangira.'

* * *

Jelani crossed the quadrangle on Queens Way. It was still littered with the detritus of the most recent fracas — stones and empty tear-gas canisters lay scattered around the grounds.

There was a large crowd inside the administration building. Jelani had never seen so many excited white people — businessmen from the look of their expensive suits. He guessed many were there to lobby the politicians to choose one of the solutions to the industrial situation suggested in the press. There was also a small number of black Africans. All were trying to gain access to the information desk where two quite harassed black public servants were attempting to answer questions and direct people to the appropriate person or department.

Jelani took his place in line behind a young woman wearing a white broad-brimmed hat, pleated brown skirt and white gloves.

After some time waiting in line he was getting no closer to the counter and realised that the woman in front of him was allowing others, particularly the businessmen, to push ahead. It annoyed him that they always considered their business more pressing than any others, but he thought it quite unusual that they ignored the usual protocol of allowing their women to go first.

When she finally reached the top of the queue, he understood why the men had ignored her. By her fluent use of Swahili, she was a black African. Her subdued European outfit had deceived him.

He could overhear her request for information about the two *askaris* promised to her village. She had a soft, lilting voice. Her Swahili was also quite proper and without any accent. It was the Swahili taught in good schools and used by quite educated Africans.

The clerk gave her some forms to complete and, as she turned away, she stepped on Jelani's toes and dropped her papers.

'Oh, I beg your pardon,' she said, stooping to retrieve the forms.

Jelani bent to help too, and when they stood they were face to face.

She had curving black lashes framing the most beautiful dark brown eyes, which now widened in surprise. Her lips parted, and her tongue lightly touched her top lip.

She was more beautiful than ever.

'Beth!' he whispered.

* * *

It wasn't the most romantic venue Jelani might have chosen, but the tea shop at Nairobi station was at least a respectable one and, since Beth appeared to have grown into a very proper young lady, with pleated skirts and white gloves, he thought she would be more comfortable there.

He sat listening to her beautiful voice and simply couldn't stop grinning.

She told him about her job working with Chief Luka in the district of Lari.

'Lari? You mean up past Limuru?'

'Yes.'

Jelani knew of it. It was a small farming community in the fertile high ground at the edge of the Rift Valley.

'I work helping Deacon James in the villages around Lari.'

He asked her if she'd like tea and she said she would — with milk and sugar. But when he reached the counter he realised he'd forgotten her order, and three minutes later he was back to ask again.

He felt no desire to speak, preferring to watch her face as she talked. He loved the way she touched her cheek as she tried to recall a detail and how her eyes sparkled when she smiled. He asked about her life since she left their village five years before.

'Reverend Farley sent me to the Anglican Inland Mission school in Voi. I studied there for four years. I learned about the work of the mission in Kenya, of course, and secretarial work, and I learned dressmaking and cooking.'

He listened patiently as she listed her academic subjects, but she was not telling him what he most wanted to know. 'Are you married?' he asked, impulsively.

Beth looked surprised, then shy. 'No,' she said. 'Are you?'

'No. Never. I mean … when you went away, I knew …'

Now he regretted choosing the railway station café. He reached across the table to take her hand in his.

'I knew I only ever wanted you, Beth.'

* * *

Back at the administration building, still buzzing with love and delight, Jelani found Sam Wangira's office at the far end of the corridor, with only the number on the door to indicate he'd found the right place. When he opened the door he was surprised to see Wangira himself sitting at a secretary's desk; he looked up when he arrived at the doorway.

'Oh,' Jelani said. 'I'm sorry to have barged in.'

'Not at all,' Wangira said. 'Come in.'

Jelani did so, closing the door behind him.

Wangira smiled. 'I suppose you expected a secretary to be sitting here.'

'Um … yes.'

'Well, there's just me.'

He sat back in his chair, appraising Jelani.

'I've seen you somewhere before. Ah! The light-skinned kid with the shoeshine box. A few years ago now.'

Jelani squirmed. He didn't want those days to figure on his résumé. 'I came about the scholarship,' he said frostily. 'I'm Jelani Karura.'

Wangira nodded. 'A Kikuyu.'

He studied Jelani in a way that made him uncomfortable. Or maybe it was because he had referred to his skin colour.

'A lot of people around here will question why I want to give a scholarship to a Kikuyu,' Wangira continued. 'They think we're all members of the Mau Mau. Wrecking farms. Butchering livestock. Maniacs, the lot of them. I don't suppose you'd admit it if you were one of them.'

He waited a moment, but Jelani again said nothing. The Mau Mau were a banned organisation. He'd be mad to admit to membership.

'Let me tell you what this is about, because my guess is you have no idea,' Wangira said, leaning back in his chair. 'The government of Kenya is preparing for the day when this country becomes independent. We are looking for young people who are showing promise, and who might be trained to become future leaders.'

Wangira explained that there were only limited funds at present, but that after a trial period, when the success or otherwise of the program could be assessed, more funds might be allocated.

'I only have a few places available, so I have to be choosy.' He glared at Jelani from the other side of the desk. 'I don't want anyone who'll mess up.'

Jelani held his silence, not daring to make the response he would have liked to give.

Wangira then went to the single filing cabinet standing against a wall.

'Here,' he said, handing a page to Jelani. 'Fill that in.'

He waited as Jelani completed the form and slid it back across the desk.

'Cook's farm. Up in the Embu region,' Wangira said, reading from the form.

He studied Jelani yet again. 'I was up there a few years ago, delivering a pick-up load of maize. Yes … I remember you from then too. It's your colour. Very distinctive.'

Jelani had had almost enough of him. He asked through tight lips if Wangira had all he needed from him.

'You can go. I'll let your boss know if you're successful.'

Jelani stood to leave, but at the door Wangira had more to add.

'I wasn't just joking about the Mau Mau,' he said. 'I know they're out there recruiting everyone they can. Using threats and promises. They call themselves freedom fighters, fighting for land reform and independence. Heroes, if you'd believe them. But they're not. They're becoming increasingly desperate, and they're not doing the cause, our cause, any good. If they approach you, don't get involved.'

Jelani closed the door behind him.

* * *

Sam watched Jelani Karura close the door to his office. He had handled himself very well during the interview. Even goading him about his skin colour, an issue Sam suspected was a sensitive one for him, had failed to provoke an angry response.

He'd been impressed by the young man since encouraging him to defend his shoeshining turf against the big Kamba and, although Sam was no great supporter of the trades union movement, he'd followed Jelani's ideas as editor of *Uhuru*.

He reached for a sheet of letterhead paper and used it for a note to Chege Muthuri, confirming the scholarship for Jelani Karura to attend the offices of the International Longshoremen's Association in New York. He paused there, again wondering if he'd acted wisely in allowing Muthuri to have his way on the choice of the ILA. Sam wanted the scholarship to be with the *New York Times*, but he felt he needed to be conciliatory on this, the first occasion his trust would be used. In future he would exert more pressure to get his way.

He reached into his desk drawer for an envelope and also took out the letter he'd received from General Motors. It was hedged in complicated legal terms, and obviously written by their highly paid lawyers, but it was clear to Sam that the company wanted to discuss a business deal.

General Motors had long ago purchased Cadillac — the car manufacturer to first use Ira's electric starter motors — and now wanted to buy the patents of which Sam was the nominal owner.

The money from the settlement was likely to help Sam continue and expand his training scholarship program a few more years. It would mean going to New York to discuss the details.

New York. The thought of the city drew mixed emotions.

Although it wasn't convenient or pleasing to be returning to New York — he dreaded the sea journey — in some ways he welcomed it. He could arrange his trip to coincide with young Karura's scholarship so he could keep an eye on him.

It would also draw to an end his involvement with Ira's legacy. It was time to put that painful part of his life finally to rest.

CHAPTER 42

The general strike that was called to protest the arrest of Chege Muthuri and others lasted eighteen days, during which time the member unions of the Trades Union Council demonstrated and marched in all the major towns, particularly in Mombasa and Nairobi — the two largest. As Chege Muthuri predicted, the administration didn't proceed with the planned expansion of the city boundaries and the union men were released without charges being laid.

A few weeks after the strike, Muthuri became the leader of the Trades Union Council while retaining his role as Secretary-General of the Transport and Allied Workers' Union. It made him one of the most powerful men in Kenya — and put him in direct competition with Jomo Kenyatta and his political party, the Kenya African Union.

Jelani was filing papers in the archives room adjacent to Muthuri's office when he heard the unmistakeable voice of Jomo Kenyatta through the open door to the Secretary-General's office. Their heated conversation had obviously commenced before they entered Muthuri's office and neither of them were aware of Jelani's presence.

He was about to close the door when he heard Kenyatta mention the Mau Mau.

'It's no wonder these young men get swept up by Kaggia's thugs,' Jelani heard Kenyatta say. 'The mission schools have enticed them away from the traditional Kikuyu culture to make them good Christian boys. Then, having broken traditional ties, they join the Mau Mau.'

'They join up because they are gullible young bucks, not because they believe everything they are told at mission school,' Muthuri said.

'Of course they don't, but they are happy to go along with it because the missions have convinced them that if they give up the circumcision and warrior ceremonies and become Christians, they'll get a good office job. They let them believe that if they dress and speak like an Englishman they'll get a job like an Englishman. Then they find there are no jobs for them; they are stuck, neither Kikuyu nor Christian. That's when the Mau Mau find it easy to pick them up.'

'You worry too much. The Kikuyu have always used oaths.'

'No. The Mau Mau coerce people into this oath. That is not our way. They corrupt our Kikuyu culture with their oathing ceremonies. They are taken secretly and at night, not, as our culture demands, in front of witnesses and agreed to by all the family.'

'They might attract a few ignorant villagers, but do you seriously believe that a young educated Kikuyu fellow would join such an organisation, with its mumbo jumbo and black magic nonsense?'

'I know they're finding recruits among returned servicemen. Men who have learned how to use modern weapons. I tell you, Chege, if the Mau Mau can find a source of arms they will be very dangerous. They're an abomination.'

'Rubbish, Kenyatta. You're overly imaginative.'

'The Mau Mau are not right for us. They deliberately lie when they say we can win by force of arms. How can a few thousand ignorant tribal people with *pangas* and spears attack the British army?'

'Thankfully, that won't happen and, even if it did, they wouldn't have to fight the British army,' Muthuri said. 'Just the Kenya police and a few reservists.'

'I'm not at all sure of that. If the Mau Mau continue to grow, and goes the way I suspect it will, the Kenyan government will have no choice but to call for assistance from the defence forces. Then there will be real trouble for all of us. And we'll not see independence for decades.'

'It won't go that far,' Muthuri insisted.

'No? Already they're in a panic. They've closed down all the Kikuyu schools in the reserves. There's talk about concentration camps like they had for the Boers.'

'Nonsense,' Muthuri said dismissively. 'They wouldn't have the nerve.'

'I'm telling you, if the Mau Mau don't get what they want by poisoning watering holes and mutilating farm animals, they'll turn to murder. Then we'll have a hell of a battle to keep our people out of a full-scale war.'

Jelani quietly closed the adjoining door.

Kenyatta's argument surprised him. He'd not considered the Mau Mau to be anything more than a militant protest group, and he'd certainly never considered taking up arms with them.

Jelani's view was more in line with Chege's — that the Mau Mau would be a pressure group, harassing the administration in hit-and-run operations. He went back to his filing work, but Kenyatta's words niggled at the back of his mind.

* * *

Muthuri casually mentioned to Jelani that he'd received confirmation of his trip to America. Jelani could hardly contain himself and, when he met Beth at the bus station a few days later, he started jabbering the news the moment she stepped out of the vehicle.

He bought two roasted maize cobs from a street vendor and they took them to Jeevanjee Gardens, where they sat on a stone away from the traffic noise on nearby Government Road.

Jelani told her the full story.

'Oh, Jelani,' she said. 'That's wonderful. You must be doing very well in your position.'

He tried to be modest, but he mentioned Muthuri's opinion that he could be a future leader of the union, or even in a higher position.

'But I'm not sure I want to go to America now ... now that I've found you again.'

She took his hand; hers was warm from the maize cob.

'Five years ago, we had no say in our separation,' she said. 'Now we have our lives in our own hands.'

'Beth, I missed you every day of those five years.'

'My love, we have the rest of our lives together. We'll make up for the days lost. No one will force us apart again.'

'That's why I don't want to leave you. Not even to go to America.'

'But you must. It's your future. Mr Muthuri's right. We need people like you in the important positions. And people like Chief Luka. He's a wonderful old man, and very loyal.'

'Loyal? Loyal to who?'

'Why, loyal to the government, of course. There's a lot of talk about this Mau Mau thing — how they are making people take an oath, and causing a lot of trouble everywhere. Chief Luka is fighting very hard to keep the young men away from them. And Deacon James and I are helping him.'

'What do you know of the Mau Mau?' he asked.

'They're terrorists. And murderers.'

'I haven't heard about murders.'

'Chief Luka says they're murdering our brother Kikuyu in villages out in the bush; we just don't hear about it.'

'I don't believe it.'

'Deacon James says it's true.'

'A priest. What does he know about the Kikuyu?'

'I think he knows a lot about us. And the Mau Mau. At Lari we're in the middle of everything.'

Jelani took a breath and held it as he tried to remain calm. When he was thirteen, he and Beth had disagreements about what was the right way of life for them: was it the Kikuyu's traditional customs as he had been taught by his parents and grandparents, or those introduced by the missionaries? Back then he had been prepared to forgo his beliefs if that was what was required to marry Beth. Now, at eighteen, he felt strongly that the Mau Mau were the Kikuyu's best hope of regaining the rights to their land, and eventually a say in their own government. He put the worrying similarities between Beth's stories and Kenyatta's anxieties out of his mind and wondered how far he could now bend his principles to hers.

He loved her, but this time he felt she should be guided by his better knowledge of the situation. He would explain what the Mau Mau were attempting to achieve for all their people — Kikuyu and other tribes — religious or not.

But not yet. Their recently reinstated love must be given time to strengthen before he tackled the inventions of her Christian upbringing.

*   *   *

Dedan Kimathi told Jelani he was more useful to the movement by writing and printing information sheets to be distributed among the villages than getting directly involved in their activities.

'In good time, my friend,' Kimathi told him. 'We have many hands in the bush, but few who can do what you are doing for us.'

So in the weeks before he packed his bag for the USA, Jelani spent his spare time with Kimathi at the house in Ngong Forest.

During this period, stories of the Mau Mau's senseless acts of cruelty appeared almost daily in the Nairobi newspapers. Cattle were mutilated, usually by hamstringing them, leaving the poor animals kneeling on their useless rear legs. Others were disembowelled and left to die in agony. Barnyard animals were maimed or slaughtered in increasingly bizarre rituals.

It unnerved Jelani to see the organisation so savagely attacked in the media. He suspected their methods had been exaggerated by the authorities to discredit the organisation. He put his theory to Kimathi.

'No, they are accurate enough, my friend,' Kimathi said. 'It is good, ah?' The gleam of excitement shone in his eyes.

'Um, but why do we do this?' Jelani asked, keeping the surprise from his voice.

'It shows the *wazungu* that the Mau Mau are pitiless and can reach out and strike the white farmers whenever and wherever we wish. It shows we are strong and our members will do anything we ask.'

It seemed to be working. Jelani had noticed an air of tension around the city. For once he was glad to have lighter skin. Most of the Kikuyu came under close scrutiny by the police, the Home Guard and even native *askaris*.

Kimathi also told him that Bildad Kaggia had recruited a number of trusted union leaders in Nairobi. John Mungai's taxi drivers' union provided logistical support and transport for the Mau Mau hierarchy. In a sign that the organisation was not about to wage a purely psychological war, metal workers covertly forged swords and lethal cutting weapons on the machines of unsuspecting factory owners. And four hundred of the city's prostitutes took the oath and started charging ammunition — between one and ten bullets depending upon the client — in payment for their services.

Muthuri told Jelani that Jomo Kenyatta was quietly negotiating with members of the union movement to break with Kaggia and his Mau Mau.

'He doesn't have to worry about us. Our members won't support the Mau Mau, but Kenyatta wants everyone's allegiance,' Muthuri said. 'But he must be careful. If the Mau Mau leaders find out he's trying to drive a wedge between them and the unions, they will be furious. He walks a fine line.'

It appeared to Jelani there were two conflicts arising: one between white and black, and the other between

Kikuyu and Kikuyu. This wasn't how he'd imagined it would be. Surely the aim was to unite all black Kenyans behind a common cause?

Then, just a few days before departing for the USA, Jelani received the strongest indication that he was being groomed for a higher position within the Mau Mau.

'Kaggia wants you to attend an oathing ceremony,' Kimathi told him.

'An oathing ceremony … Yes, of course.'

He accepted the invitation with some trepidation. His union had publicly stated that it was implacably opposed to the Mau Mau. He had to rely on the oath of secrecy, because if Chege Muthuri discovered his involvement, it would cost him his job and, presumably, Wangira's scholarship.

The ceremony was scheduled to take place in the Mathare slums — a place avoided by the Nairobi police force after dark.

They met at the bus stop on Outer Ring Road.

Kimathi said nothing, but Jelani followed him at a distance to a clearing among the hovels. It was alight with paraffin lanterns and had been decorated with palm fronds and stalks of sugar-cane and arrowroot. As usual, a goat had been slaughtered and skinned, and the hide cut into a single long strip that lay on the ground in a circle.

Jelani had not had time to eat before meeting Kimathi, and he eyed off the troughs of traditional food placed among the decorations and lanterns. On closer inspection, his stomach turned. The food had been fouled with blood, filth and goat faeces. He almost gagged.

Kimathi spoke for the first time. 'It is good you are here. You will find tonight's ceremony interesting.'

Somebody struck a gong, and a dozen nervous recruits walked into the circle of goat's hide and, lifting it, faced outwards with the hide encircling them.

A figure dressed in a long white robe came from the darkness beyond the throw of the lanterns. His head was bowed, but when he looked up, Jelani took a sharp intake of breath. It was Chege Muthuri.

Jelani was at first alarmed, then realised that Muthuri must have known all along he had taken the oath.

He felt he had successfully passed another test.

* * *

After the oathing ceremony, as the other Mau Mau and their new recruits disbanded, Muthuri came to Jelani and slapped him on the shoulder.

'Many people have no idea how strong the Mau Mau is,' Muthuri said. 'Now you know we are everywhere.'

Jelani could only nod, relieved that he'd overcome his urge to discuss the Mau Mau with Muthuri and thereby break his solemn oath.

'Come,' Muthuri continued. 'We must talk about your visit to America.'

They went to a small bar for a generous serving of *nyama choma* and a few Tusker beers. Jelani took his lead from Muthuri, who drank slowly. Even then, by the time they'd eaten, Jelani felt the effects of the alcohol.

They sat at a table in the open area at the back of the bar.

'Now, Jelani, my friend,' Muthuri began, glancing around the space, which was almost empty except for a group of loud drunks sitting under the sole light. 'We must talk, ah?' he said. 'This Wangira fellow, he wants you to study things that will make you a better stooge of the government. He says it's for you to learn how to be a leader. Well, the union movement needs leaders too. And so do the other friends we were with tonight, ah?'

Jelani nodded. Muthuri turned many of his statements into questions.

'You will visit the Longshoremen. They are becoming very powerful. You will observe them carefully. You will study their methods of organising their membership. They have thousands of members.

'The Longshoremen's Union is pushing hard these days,' he continued. 'Now that the war is over they can fight the businessmen and the governments. They are going to push, push, for better pay and safer working places.' Muthuri lowered his voice. 'I want you to know all their tricks. How they think. I want you to find ways that we can organise thousands of people. Tens of thousands.'

Jelani drained his beer. It was warm and flat, and caught in his throat. He knew Muthuri was no longer talking about union members.

'As our numbers grow,' Muthuri continued, 'it will become more difficult to conceal the extent of them. We must eventually prepare for open warfare, but until that time, we must remain hidden.'

The recent oathing ceremony was still etched in Jelani's mind. The procedure had changed markedly in the short time since his own. He was still disturbed by memories of the new initiates dripping blood from the seven cuts on their arms into the fouled food bowls.

The alcohol prompted a question he'd otherwise not ask. 'I understand it's important to keep our membership secret, but why do we need all that blood and filth?'

'Already I am thinking we must change our ceremony. The cuts leave scars. There are other ways to bind our brothers closer to us.' Muthuri smiled thinly. 'It is important to make the oathing ceremony vile and disgusting. That way no one will admit to being a member. It will separate them from everyone else, except us. The Mau Mau becomes their only family.' His smile broadened.

'Then how will we get new members?' Jelani asked. 'No one will want to join us if the ceremony is so disgusting.'

'That will not be a problem,' he said. 'Soon we will be like an army in times of war.'

'What do you mean?'

'I mean we will have compulsory membership.'

'But not every Kikuyu will agree with us. They will want a choice.'

'They will have a choice — they will either join the fight, or die.'

CHAPTER 43

As the day of his departure for America loomed closer, Jelani became overwhelmed by the countless tasks facing him — each one a hurdle and potential stumbling block to boarding his ship.

The only person able to advise him was Chege Muthuri, but he was seldom available. It was therefore only by chance that his boss was around to mention a very important matter — he needed travel papers before he could set foot in America, or anywhere else in the outside world.

'You need to go to the admin office with your *kipande* pass,' Muthuri said. 'Find Joe Mbale. He will help you.'

'Who is Joe Mbale?'

'A Ugandan friend of mine. And don't worry, he is easy to find. Look for a man with a moon face and a big belly.'

Muthuri was right. Joe Mbale was a big man with, improbably for a government employee, a big smile — after Jelani introduced himself as a friend of Muthuri.

Mbale said, 'And how is my good friend Chege? Why is he such a troubled soul and always fighting with everybody?'

'He is very well, thank you. And I'm surprised you ask why he is fighting. I'm sure that even in Uganda you are facing the same struggles as we are here in Kenya.'

'Ai, ai!' Mbale said, his smile unaffected by Jelani's outburst. 'I see you are from the same *kali* tribe as your boss.'

'There is much to be angry about,' Jelani said, trying to remain calm.

'Mmm, but not for you,' Mbale said, turning his attention to Jelani's papers. 'I see you are going to America next week.'

'I am. If I can get my travel papers. Can you help me?'

'I'll try. Give me your *kipande* and I'll fill in the form for you.'

Jelani slipped the cord over his head and opened the small tin box containing his *kipande*.

Mbale took it and commenced to fill in the details. 'This is your full name?'

'Jelani Karura. Yes.'

'No other names?'

'No.'

'These British.' He shook his head. 'They like to see many names.'

'Why?'

Mbale shrugged. 'Who knows? It is their way.'

'I see ... Maybe you can add Zesiro. It was a name I had as a child.'

'That is very good. See, it fills the space nicely.'

With Jelani's help, Mbale worked his way through the form. 'There, it is done,' he said, running his finger over the entries, but stopping at the name box. 'This name, Zesiro: it is a Ugandan name.'

Jelani's childhood discomfort surrounding his appearance and his name fleetingly returned, but now he could put it aside. 'Yes,' he said. 'My mother's friend was Ugandan. She suggested the name.'

Mbale nodded, and continued checking the form.

'It is all done,' he said. 'Come back in three days for your papers.'

Jelani thanked him.

'By the way,' the big man added as he clipped a cover note to Jelani's form, 'does your twin also have a Ugandan name?'

'My twin?' Jelani asked, puzzled. 'I don't have a twin.'

Mbale smiled. 'Surely you have ... otherwise that Ugandan lady has been having a big joke on you, my friend.'

Jelani made no attempt to hide his annoyance. 'What do you mean?' he demanded.

'Your name ... Zesiro.' Mbale's belly wobbled with his suppressed chuckle. 'It is a popular Ugandan name. It means *first born of twins.*'

Jelani felt the blood rush to his face. He snatched his *kipande* from the desk and stormed from the building.

Once outside, the full significance of his name hit him. *First born of twins.* Could it be possible that he had a sibling, a twin, somewhere? Surely his mother would have told him if she knew. She'd said that they dropped the name Zesiro because they didn't know what it meant. They also said the Ugandan who had brought him to Kobogi wouldn't give any details of his birth mother. What could it mean?

It seemed to him that the mystery of his birth had just doubled in size.

With all the uncertainty of his identity returning, his thoughts and dreams for his life with Beth came into sharp focus. How could he hope to hold onto her — a beautiful young educated Kikuyu woman of a good family — when he was a half-caste; a nobody?

* * *

Jelani met Beth at the River Road bus station on Sunday afternoon; they again walked together to Jeevanjee Gardens. The sun shone from a clear, pale blue sky and the park was crowded, but they found a bench seat under a tree where Jelani took Beth's hand in his.

'I thought about inviting you back to my house, but ...'

She smiled and gave his hand a squeeze. 'It's nice here,' she said.

Jelani looked about them. There were family groups picnicking and young people like them with their heads together, talking and giggling. A small boy collected empty drink bottles and put them into a woven fruit sack held by a friend.

'Beth, I'm leaving in three days.'

'I know,' she said softly.

'Will you miss me?'

She looked at him and her beautiful eyes made him melt.

'You know I will.'

'Do you also know how much I loved you when we were kids?' he said, now taking both her hands in his.

'Were we kids? It was only five years ago,' she said, dropping her eyes to his hands resting in her lap. 'But yes, I know how much we both felt.'

'And now?' he dared to ask.

She took her gaze from his hands and looked into his eyes. 'I haven't changed my mind over these five years. Have you?'

'No. Never once.'

He swallowed. The time was perfect. His intention was to tell her of his love and then to raise the subject of his involvement in the freedom movement. It was important that he tell Beth of his passionate wish to help to change their world to one that was better for their future together, but he didn't want to risk losing her over an argument about politics. Beth had already indicated that she agreed with the missionaries' view, and he'd heard that they were using the pulpit to turn their congregations against the Mau Mau.

He weakened, and simply said, 'We have a lot to talk about when I get back.'

'I'll be waiting,' she said.

* * *

The engine roar grew louder. Vibrations, which began at his feet, continued up Jelani's legs until he felt them in his chest, pounding and juddering among his ribs. The whole cabin of the Solent flying boat shook and rattled. Whatever fear he felt was subjugated by a great rush of excitement as the plane moved forwards.

Above his window he could see two of the four engines, their propellers a blur. They turned the water below them on Lake Naivasha into a flurry of flying droplets that hit his window and trickled down it in rivulets rainbowed by the morning sun.

Gathering speed, the vibrations merged with staccato bumps coming from below as the keel pounded the wavelets.

The plane struggled to overcome the lake's persistent drag; Jelani hoped the engines would win the battle. They slowly did so as the plane's momentum gathered, and the surface of the lake melted into a blur of blue and white. The bumping stopped, the spray disappeared and the roar of engines increased as the sea plane defiantly hauled itself skyward against the drag of water and gravity. Below them the papyrus and fever trees flashed by, then farm houses and villages. They climbed to the level of the Rift Valley escarpment and Jelani could see the grasslands rolling up to the distant and densely wooded Aberdare Ranges.

He turned his attention to the thirty or so white passengers inside the aircraft, all of whom had regarded him with suspicion as he boarded the plane. They seemed uninterested in the miracle that was evolving around them; most now had their heads buried in newspapers.

Below him was another lake, this one fringed with a filament of pale pink flowers. While he watched, a strong wind seemed to lift a cloud of pink petals from the flowers and send them whirling over the lake surface, but then they wheeled and spread and he realised they were flamingos — millions of flamingos. The vision flashed in and out of view as the Solent bumped through the clouds, until the plane was totally engulfed in white fluff.

He sat back and closed his eyes, reflecting again on the night at the bar in Mathare discussing the purpose of his visit to New York. He was to absorb all he could of the protest movements in the union organisation and elsewhere. The impression Jelani gained from Chege Muthuri was that when he returned, he would be given an important position within Mau Mau. One that would bring him into close contact with the enemies of the organisation — the police and the government members who opposed true freedom.

And from what he'd already witnessed of Mau Mau tactics, he knew the leaders expected him to fight their enemies, not by words as he'd done in the union, but with violence.

He knew it was not the life that Beth had in mind for them. But was Beth's vision of their future realistic? Even if the two of them were somehow exempt from the injustice visited on black Africans by the Europeans, how could they find contentment and happiness while the white government continued to force the Kikuyu and others into native reserves, or to condemn them — the rightful owners — to become squatters on their own land?

PART 4
EMERALD

CHAPTER 44

1951

Emerald Kazkusi Northcote-Middlebridge strolled down Piccadilly swinging her hips, aware that the cab drivers outside the Park Lane Hotel were watching her. She had her mother's olive complexion and startling green eyes, which she accentuated with a little eyeliner uplifting the corners so that she had a touch of the feline about her. But her curves were more rounded than Dana's, which made her look older than her nineteen years.

The outfit she'd chosen that day suited the May afternoon with its hint of spring in the air and low western sun struggling to break through London's nondescript sky. Her suit was navy blue — a popular colour that season. The skirt hugged her hips and the short flared jacket emphasised them. The cuffs and collars were turned back to reveal a leopard-skin print. A loosely tied scarf of identical material and a three-row choker of pearls circled her elegant neck. Her hat, perched perkily towards the back of her head, matched her ivory-coloured gloves.

One of the hotel's boys gave a low whistle. She ignored it, of course.

She could have been going to a tea party in Mayfair, but instead she was taking a bus to Chelsea for her friend's twentieth birthday do. It was in a marquee in the grounds of Chelsea Hospital, adjacent to the flower show.

Emerald's mother had almost insisted on driving her, but she would have none of it. At nineteen, Emerald told her, and in that day and age, she was quite capable of going to a late-afternoon party on her own. What she didn't tell her mother was that she had arranged to meet a very nice young man at said party. She and her girlfriend Fiona had met Peter and his friend Michael at a boat race in April. They were in the Oxford Blue's reserve boat, and the girls had enjoyed two rendezvous with them since.

Peter was a tall young man, square chinned and broad shouldered. She had chosen him over his friend Michael because of his mop of fair hair and cheeky smile.

Emerald was quite taken with her first conquest. The thought of seeing him again made the nape of her neck tingle with excitement.

* * *

Dana had only reluctantly agreed to allow Emerald to go to the party in Chelsea on her own. She trusted her daughter, but she didn't know the Parke-Hollaway family and wondered if they were the right type. Fiona seemed a rather quiet, introverted young person, in contrast to all Emerald's other friends, who appeared to be more sophisticated and worldly than her daughter. But Dana still had her concerns. Emerald had shown indications she was developing an awareness of the many young men in her social life, and Dana could well remember what had followed that revelation in her own life.

Dana's teenage pregnancy may well have been kept a secret, but she didn't want a similar episode to risk Emerald's chances of inheriting the Middlebridge fortune.

Oswald had inherited the Middlebridge collieries in Lancashire. Unfortunately, he was childless, and the family had only ever entrusted one of their own to take the reins. His options were to anoint either his brother's idiot son or his stepdaughter Emerald as his successor. If Emerald were to get involved with the wrong boy, she would risk losing Oswald's confidence — and control of his family fortune after his death.

Emerald had no shortage of distractions from the opposite sex. At first it was her interest in the latest fashions. She would drag Dana through endless stores, seeking the right outfits for the many society events she had begun to attend.

Then it was the theatre. Although Dana preferred the more expensive seats, she agreed to attend a Henry Wood concert at the Royal Albert Hall and join the *prom* — the milling crowds in the cheaper seats. It was while *promming* with Emerald that Dana realised her daughter was too rapidly growing up. She turned a lot of male heads, which was understandable given her eye-catching gown, but it was the way that Emerald handled those glances that surprised Dana. She realised that Emerald already knew when a man was looking her way. Furthermore, when Emerald wanted to take a closer look at an admirer, or to send him an encouraging signal, she would turn and bend as if to see if her stockings were straight, or she would touch the brim of her hat and steal a glance, or simply take a sweeping scan around the crowd without making obvious eye-contact with the person who took her interest.

She also sent signals, ranging from a brief glance, to a twitch of amusement on her lips, to an alluring smile. They all seemed to find their mark as a constant stream of young men presented themselves to Dana, begging to be introduced. Dana felt it had been only moments since young men had clamoured for her attention too. At fifty-one, she felt extremely old in comparison.

The following week they would attend the Royal Windsor Horse Show, were already booked for the Royal Academy Summer Exhibition, and were considering Wimbledon. Emerald wanted to see the Henley Regatta on the Thames, but at this Dana had baulked. Standing in July sun was not a prospect that enthralled her. Unless they had an invitation from someone with a comfortable barge or a riverside lodge, she would not attend.

Oswald showed no interest in any of the season's social events, and none of the sporting events except for the cricket. This year it was the South Africans, and Oswald said they would see the second test at Lord's.

But Emerald was not content with even this whirl. She insisted it was time for her official *coming out*, when she would be presented to the King. Dana knew it would be difficult to postpone this for much longer as she and Oswald had always indulged the girl. She could see through her daughter's plan, though: once Emerald had made her debut, she would expect to have more freedom than her mother presently allowed her. Dana hoped nevertheless to prevent what she feared was her daughter's journey down the same path she had herself taken so many years before.

* * *

Emerald knew most of the girls at the party — there must have been thirty of them — either from school or through her school friends. Many had escorts: either male relatives foisted on them for the occasion or boyfriends.

Emerald and Fiona had colluded with Clarice, the birthday girl, to have Peter and Michael added to the guest list because neither had yet told their parents they'd commenced a friendship with Oxford boys — who in some circles were considered characters of dubious reputation. In Emerald's case, she wasn't sure if her relationship with Peter could be called more than a friendship because there'd been very little physical contact. From what she'd heard exchanged in confidence among her closer girlfriends, a certain amount of caressing, either attempted, permitted or encouraged, had to occur for a relationship to exist.

'Hello, Em,' a girl in a floral dress said.

'Oh, hello, Miriam,' Emerald replied, thinking the cut of the floral number emphasised her friend's ample breasts. She wondered if she should add some padding to her own bra.

'Wasn't this simply divine?' Miriam went on. 'People are starting to leave. But it has been nice, hasn't it?'

'It has. I suppose we'll be leaving soon too.' Emerald avoided adding that her mother had insisted she send the driver to collect her at nine.

'It's been ages. What have you been doing with yourself?'

'Not much. Switzerland.'

'Lovely,' said Miriam.

'Not really, but I did have a chance to practise my watercolours.'

'Oh, you too! Isn't it fun?'

'It was,' Emerald said. 'But now I'm back Mother has insisted I do something *noble* for a couple of days a week.' She rolled her eyes.

'What do you mean *noble*?'

'Oh, you know, charity work and such. She's insisting I go down and volunteer for work at the Red Cross.'

'Ghastly.'

'And how about you, Miriam? How's life?'

'The usual. We went to the Cotswolds for three weeks. The weather was abysmal.'

'I simply hate the Cotswolds.'

'Quite. Well, must dash, but I'm glad we've had a chat. I've been trying to catch your eye all evening, but you've been busy. I have to ask — who's the handsome man who's been taking up all your time? Did you come with him?'

Emerald understood that arriving with a boy at a social engagement had its own connotations. Definitions were important.

'Peter? He's ... a friend. He's getting me another drink.' The *friend* label was sufficiently ambiguous to avoid a detailed discussion about him, but was proprietary enough to dissuade all but the most predatory of competitors. 'What about you? Are you with someone?' Emerald countered.

'Me? No, I've been going with a chap for a while, but ... you know how it is.'

'Quite,' Emerald said, nodding, but having no idea.

Fiona and Michael returned to the marquee and Miriam, having exchanged brief pleasantries with them, wandered off.

Emerald discreetly picked a sprig of greenery from Fiona's blouse.

Fiona giggled. 'We've been in to see the Chelsea Flower Show,' she said.

At that moment, Peter returned with the drinks and the four began to discuss attending the Henley regatta.

'What do you think, Emma?' Fiona asked. 'Can you make it by mid-afternoon?'

'I'm not sure I care to go,' she replied, taking a sip of her drink.

'You're not?' Peter asked. 'But I thought you had arranged it. We'd even spoken about where to meet on the Thursday.'

'I know, but I'm actually still thinking about it.'

She couldn't admit that she'd been unable as yet to convince her mother to allow her to go, and decided to change the subject.

'Come, Peter,' she said. 'Let's take a walk in the flower show.'

She led him from the marquee to the hospital grounds, where they spent a few minutes admiring the flower displays. Then she found a narrow path leading from the main area into the shrubbery.

'Emma, what are you doing?' he asked.

She turned to him and put a finger to her lips. 'It's a secret,' she said. 'Just follow me.'

In a grove of trees, surrounded by camellias and rhododendrons, she stopped.

'Is this it?' he asked.

'Yes. They're pretty, aren't they?' she said, nodding at the flowers.

'Yes ... But they're not part of the show, are they? I mean, they're nice, but there are others far more beautiful in the exhibits, don't you think?'

'Perhaps, but this is our private show.' She made a performance of studying the camellia's petals. 'And I thought you might want to be alone with me.' She gave him a coy smile.

Peter moved close to her and placed a hand gently on her elbow.

'I do …' he said, but remained where he stood — half a pace away from her.

'I thought you might want to … you know … kiss me,' she said.

'As a matter of fact …' He moved towards her, lifting his right arm as she lifted her left. There was an awkward moment as they shuffled their feet and shifted positions. They seemed to have too many limbs between them and nowhere to put them.

At last, he wrapped his arms around her slim waist and she ran her hands up to his shoulders before clasping them behind his neck. She raised her face to him and closed her eyes.

When Peter's lips met hers she was transported. It was the most exhilarating feeling she'd ever experienced. At that moment, as her head whirled and her breath caught in her chest, she knew she would remember that kiss for as long as she lived.

He continued to press into her until their teeth grated together and it was hard for her to breathe. Finally she had to break away. She clung to him, gasping. His arms were strong around her waist and she could feel his hips pressing his lower body to hers. Something other than the earlier euphoria claimed her. She was now very conscious of his body on hers. She could feel the press of his thighs and the thrust of his groin. A flush of warmth rose from her shoes through her thighs to her breasts.

Peter was taking quick, shallow breaths and muttering to her that he loved her and wanted her.

She didn't know what to do or what to say. But she felt a power over Peter that until that moment she'd never known existed.

* * *

When the policeman rang the bell in Belgrave Square and Dana found him in the doorway with his bobby's helmet in his hands and a nervous look on his face, she knew it could only be bad news. She also knew it wasn't as bad as it could be, as Emerald was standing behind him and not dead.

'Afternoon, mum,' he said, lifting his chin and straightening his back.

'Hello, officer,' Dana said as calmly as she was able.

'I'm afraid I have some matters to report that might be distressing to your ladyship.'

The neighbourhood was bristling with diplomats and lesser royalty. The sergeant was having an each-way bet with Dana's elevation to the peerage.

'Won't you come in?' Dana said, stepping aside and not telling him she was no longer a countess.

As Emerald passed she tried to catch her eye, but her daughter kept her face averted.

In the drawing room, she indicated a Louis XIV chair, but the policeman gave it a look and remained standing.

Seeing this, Dana decided to take the initiative. 'What seems to be the trouble, sergeant?'

He cleared his throat. 'Well, mum, I'm not sure how to say it.'

'Come, come, I'm a mature woman. You can speak frankly.'

He coughed again. 'At about six o'clock this evening, I was patrolling the Chelsea Flower Show in the grounds of —'

'There's no need to go into detail,' Dana said with more edge on her voice than she intended. She smiled and continued. 'I think we all know where the Chelsea Flower Show is held. Can you please get to the point of your visit?'

'While patrolling the grounds of the ... while patrolling the grounds, I saw the young lady here being led into the bushes behind the —'

'He was not leading me,' Emerald said, interrupting. 'I was leading him.'

This caused the sergeant to pause and regather his thoughts. 'As I was sayin', I observed two persons leaving the main path by stepping over a rope line and removing themselves to the shrubbery behind the Agricultural Society's pavilion. I understood that the path led to nowhere in particular, so I followed same to inform them of this fact. When I got to where they were standing, I saw ... ahem ... the young man taking liberties with the young lady here.'

'Liberties?' Dana asked.

'Certain ... um ... liberties, ma'am.'

Dana turned to Emerald, aware that her face was as pale as her daughter's was flushed.

'We were kissing,' Emerald said. 'Actually, I was kissing him, and he, well ...' She giggled. 'He didn't know what to do.'

'Emerald!'

Her daughter dropped her head and shrugged. 'It wasn't anything ... bad,' she said.

Dana turned back to the policeman. 'And what did you do, sergeant?' she asked.

'I enquired as to his name and address, mum.'

'He gave him a nasty poke with his baton,' Emerald said, giving the sergeant a scornful look.

The policeman's top lip tightened a fraction. 'I thought it a very poor state of affairs, *mum*. He and the young lady an' all. The chap's up at Oxford. Ought to know better how to behave 'imself. And Miss Emerald 'ere is only a child.'

'I'm nineteen,' she said, pouting.

'Emerald. I don't want to hear another word from you.' Turning back to the policeman, Dana said, 'Thank you for your time, sergeant.'

'I thought it best to be discreet, mum, but I have the young man's name and address. That is, if you are wantin' to take the matter further.'

'I think not. Thank you again.'

Dana led the way to the front door, grateful for the fact that the butler had taken the day off to visit his ailing mother.

As she closed the door behind the policeman, she firmed her resolve. She had to take steps she'd been mulling over for some time. But first she had to talk with Oswald.

After Emerald went to her bedroom, Dana found her husband in his office, paddling among his papers. 'Darling, I'd like to have a word to you about Emerald,' she began.

Oswald looked at her over his glasses. 'Emerald? Certainly, darling. What's been happening in her busy life?'

'The usual, but I've been meaning to discuss taking her overseas with me for the season.'

'The season? Why, it's half over already.'

'I'm talking about the next season, dear. In New York. It opens in September with the Metropolitan Opera. And then there's the international debutante ball in December. It would be so good for her, Oswald.'

'How long would you be gone?'

'The season runs through to Easter.'

'Oh, but I shall miss her too much. And you, of course, my dear. What does Emerald think of the idea?'

'I haven't asked her yet. I thought it best to discuss it with you first.'

'Thank you; I'm glad you did. I really don't think she should be away so long. She's too young.'

'Oswald, she's going on twenty.'

'Good lord! Even so, another year or two shouldn't matter. Let's say you take her next year. Soon enough by far, if you ask me. Yes, when she's twenty-one will do.'

CHAPTER 45

The Red Cross office was a converted factory in Beddington. It had two rows of tables in the middle of an open space and benches around the walls where the applicants for emigration assistance sat awaiting their turn.

Elsie, the woman who showed Emerald around, had her grey hair tucked into a hairnet, and wore a pair of white elasticised cotton sleeves pulled to her elbows to protect her cardigan against wear. When Emerald met her that morning Elsie had expressed surprise at her youth.

'I thought all you young people would be working or at least looking for a job,' she said.

'I don't need to work,' Emerald said, then regretted it. Elsie let her surprise show, but resisted further questions on the matter.

Elsie was very thorough in her briefing, paying particular attention to what she called the professional distance needed between the Red Cross volunteers and the refugees.

'You know, my dear,' she said near the end of her briefing, 'the Red Cross aren't always able to find a country that will take these poor souls. And many times we can't reunite them with their loved ones. There are cases where people have disappeared during the war and we can't find hide nor hair of them. Vanished into thin air, you might say.' She looked over her glasses to deliver her next words. 'It would never do to become too involved, too friendly. It only leads to heartache.'

It was such a quaint sentiment, Emerald almost smiled.

'Well then,' Elsie said, 'you're ready to start.'

And she did, working through the rest of the morning and into the afternoon on emigration requests. Her tasks were simple enough: she helped the refugees complete their paperwork, checked their documentation and then, depending upon a set of guidelines Elsie had given her, stamped: *Approval Recommended* or *Approval Not Recommended* on the form. The final decision was made elsewhere, but she enjoyed the sense of power her part of the processing gave her. On her say-so hung the future course of many people's lives.

She was becoming quite adept, even bored, with the repetitive nature of the work, and she began to think of her trip to Henley and the regatta the following week.

Her mother couldn't be reassured Emerald would be safe — by that she meant chaperoned — until she called Fiona's mother, who told her that Fiona's older brother would be there to supervise matters until she herself arrived on the weekend. He was a sensible young man, she said, coming down from Cambridge with a few friends to see the races.

Naturally her mother didn't know that Emerald and Fiona had arranged to meet up with the Oxford boys before then. Emerald allowed herself a little daydreaming about what a few days alone with Peter might look like. It was electrifying.

Things continued in the same vein with the refugees all afternoon, until a young man, wearing a brown hat and a black coat too large by at least two sizes, came forwards.

Emerald ran her eye over the front page. He was Goran Papasov, age twenty-four, originally from Czechoslovakia, but now living in a refugee camp at Heathrow.

The subsequent pages of his application were largely incomplete.

'Are you having trouble completing the remaining questions, Mr Papasov?'

He shrugged. 'No,' he said.

'But you haven't filled in the section on which country you wish to emigrate to.'

'It is not important. I do not care where I go.'

'Do you have family members who have emigrated?' she asked.

'I have no family.'

'Then you have a choice. There are a number of countries taking refugees.' She consulted her notes. The Australian government were seeking labourers and skilled workers for something called the Snowy Mountains Authority.

'How about Australia?' she asked.

He didn't answer.

'Mr Papasov? Would Australia suit you?'

'Do they have Romany people in Australia?'

'Romany people?' She lifted her head from the form, but he did not meet her eyes; nor did he elaborate. He was a serious-looking fellow, dark eyes and hair, olive skin.

'I don't understand,' she said.

'Gypsies,' he said, and still he kept his face averted.

'W-why does that matter?'

He finally looked at her, and Emerald almost flinched from the intensity of it.

'Because we have been hunted to death everywhere else,' he said.

He looked angry. This situation had not occurred before. The confidence she'd built up during the day evaporated. She stared at him, lost for words.

'Have you heard of the Nazis?' he asked, then added, after reading her name badge, 'Miss Northcote-Middlebridge?'

'Of course I have,' she answered, indignant in spite of her unease.

'Then you would know of the Jews and the Holocaust.'

'I don't see what the Nazis and the Holocaust has to do with your application to emigrate to —'

'But you haven't heard of the persecution of the Romanies, have you?'

She hadn't, but refused to surrender any further ground.

'Up to four million gypsies were exterminated during the war, but nobody really knows because most were illiterate and not registered in the camps. Nobody cared enough to count them.

'You see, Miss Northcote-Middlebridge, Himmler also had a *Final Solution* for the gypsies. My family was sent to Auschwitz, to a special *Gypsy Family Camp*. A nice name, ah? Even better, my little brother was put in Dr Mengele's dormitory they called *The Zoo*. We never saw him again.

'My father was part of a sterilisation experiment. He was bombarded by X-rays from two powerful machines day after day until the skin peeled from his private parts.

My mother tried to save him from the infection that was killing him by cutting off his genitals.' He paused, watching her reaction. 'Of course, he died.

'Few people know the Nazis' persecution was not the first, or the last of it. Do you know, for example, that here in England, the enslavement of the Romanies was only abolished in 1856? In France we were *branded* and our women's heads were shaved? Elsewhere we had our ears cut off so people would know a gypsy when they saw one.'

He sat back and folded his arms across his chest. 'That is why I don't care where I go.'

Emerald felt ill and couldn't think of a response. Was there anything she could say to him to express her utter dismay?

'But that's ... that's terrible. Why haven't I heard of all this before?'

'Because we gypsies are not rich, and we have no powerful friends to represent us. We are like nothing.'

Papasov dropped his head into his hands. Now that his anger and hatred had been spent, he went limp like a rag.

Emerald reached a hand to him, but stopped short of resting it on his shoulder. She felt useless, ashamed of her ignorance, and guilty because of her sheltered position of privilege.

She wondered if that was what Elsie meant by *heartache*.

*　　*　　*

Emerald and Fiona took the train to Henley for the regatta, but had a two-hour wait at Twyford for the

463

connection. They took a stroll along the railway lines to kill time, and arrived at a field with dozens of carts and caravans.

'Oh, it's gypsies,' Fiona said in a lowered voice, although they were still fifty yards from the nearest of them. 'They swarm around Henley this time of year for the regatta.'

Emerald had seen gypsy camps before, but having met the gypsy refugee, she was now more interested in them.

'Romanies,' she said, more to remind herself than to inform Fiona. 'That's their proper name.'

'Awful, dirty people. Let's go back.'

'Look,' Emerald said. 'There's someone wanting us to come.'

An old woman with a red and white head scarf was waving to them.

'Come on, Emma, let's go back and wait at the station.'

'I wonder what she wants.'

'Your money, I suspect. Thieves, the lot of them. Don't look at her; let's just go.'

'Wait a moment, Fiona. I've learned a bit about these people. I want to see what she wants.'

'Emma, if you think I'm going anywhere near that gypsy camp, then you're quite mad. Now, I'm going back to Twyford station. Are you coming or not?'

Emerald looked at the old woman again. Even from where they were standing, her smile revealed few front teeth. She wore a tattered dark green cardigan and a blue apron.

Fiona was inclined to be bossy with Emerald. She decided to make a stand. 'You go, Fiona,' she said. 'I want to see what she wants.'

Fiona muttered something about rape and murder, and then stormed off.

The old woman smiled her toothless smile; and a scruffy toddler ran and hid behind her apron as Emerald approached.

'Ah, eyes like emerald,' she said. 'You very beautiful lady.'

'Thank you.'

The urchin poked his head out and looked up at Emerald. When she moved to touch his head he dived for cover.

The old woman cackled. 'Him not like English lady. You like fortune-telling?'

Emerald looked around the camp. It was empty except for a handful of tiny children and a few tethered horses.

'Where is everyone?' Emerald asked.

'Gone to Henley. You like me tell your fortune?'

Emerald looked back towards the path. Fiona was gone. Her fortune would be something to laugh about when they were together on the train.

'All right,' she said, and followed the woman to a table and chairs set beside the caravan.

Emerald laid her hand, palm upwards, on the table. The gypsy woman took it; her skin was as dry as parchment, but she held Emerald's hand as delicately as she would a bird. She lowered her head over the table and began to mutter inaudibly in a foreign language. After some minutes, Emerald began to grow bored with the old woman's charade of authenticity.

'Am I going to marry a rich and handsome man?' she asked, smiling.

The gypsy remained hunched over the table, mumbling.

'Well? I haven't got all day, you know.'

The woman lifted her head and Emerald recoiled. Her eyes had rolled back into her head: with only the whites showing, she was a ghostly sight. Emerald shifted her chair, ready to rise and flee, but her hand was caught in the woman's now surprisingly strong grip.

'I see … I … you. I see babies. Half black, half white.'

The white eyes stared at her, seeing but unseeing.

'Who are these babies? Are they my babies?' Emerald asked, not sure what she thought now. It was too bizarre.

'No. Black and white. Boy and girl. Black and white. Man and woman. They call … far away. They call you. I hear … *recha*.'

'*Recha*? What is *recha*?'

The gypsy was silent for a long moment.

'I hear *recha*.'

Her head nodded forwards. A moment later she sat up, eyes wide.

'Are you all right?' Emerald asked, startled by the sudden transformation from white-eyed sleepwalker to haggard old woman.

The gypsy blinked, and cackled. 'Two bob,' she said, her wrinkled hand turned up on the table.

'Two bob!'

It was outrageous, but Emerald had no recourse. Thieves indeed. She stood up in a huff, angry with herself for succumbing to the rort. She tossed the two shillings onto the table.

'Two bob for two minutes or so,' she muttered. 'Highway robbery if you ask me.' She was about to leave, but turned back. 'Anyway, what does *recha* mean?'

'*Recha*?'

'Yes, you said *recha*. What does it mean? In English.'

The old woman appeared puzzled. 'In English it mean … I don't know how you say.'

'Oh! Never mind.'

She stormed off.

* * *

Emerald arrived in Henley with Fiona, a day ahead of Peter and Michael. They found a group of about a dozen young men lounging about on their cottage porch. Fiona whispered they were some of her brother's friends from Cambridge. The young men pretended to take no notice of the girls, barely interrupting their conversations to be introduced by Fiona's brother, Laurence.

The men wore a mixture of the latest fashions: fedora hats, double-breasted pin-striped suits with wide shoulders and high-cut baggy pants in brown or navy. The wide trousers tapered down to very narrow cuffs sitting on spectator brogues in black- or brown-and-white, very popular for jitterbugging — the latest dance craze. Their short, wide ties were boldly coloured or striped. There were elaborate clasps to hold the ties and suspenders to hold up their trousers. Cigarettes hung from their mouths, Bogart-like, and their slicked hair was parted arrow-straight down the left.

They were all very sophisticated and similar, except for one, who wore what appeared to be worker's trousers of coarse blue denim and a polo shirt under an old knitted vest. He was tall, and had uncontrollable blond hair and an unfashionable moustache. His name was Raph.

'It means *wolf*,' he said to Emerald when Laurence left them alone after the introductions.

'I see,' she said, thinking that his face had something of an angular shape to it, wolf-like. 'I have no idea what emerald means.'

'Don't be fucking daft,' he said.

She flushed, but noted he was studying her closely. She controlled her response, which under normal circumstances would be to simply walk away, however she noticed there was a smirk lurking behind his guarded expression. She stayed, mainly because she didn't want to reveal she was shocked by such language.

'It's your eyes,' he continued after it was obvious she wouldn't respond to his crudity. 'Unless of course you were born in May, in which case you've been named after your birthstone. If you believe in that stuff.'

'You do,' she responded, 'otherwise you wouldn't know it was the May birthstone.'

'I don't believe in any of that bullshit.'

'What *do* you believe in?' she asked. 'If anything.'

'I believe in the struggle of the working classes.'

'What does that mean? Exactly.'

'It doesn't surprise me you don't know. You're one of the moneyed class. You have servants you couldn't give a shit about, with first names you don't know. You have a big house in town and a holiday house in at least one of the counties. Your father owns factories and pays the workers shit, and your mother does charity work for the poor who wouldn't *be* so poor if they got a decent wage in the first place.'

'What makes you think you know anything about my family?'

'I can tell by the way I shocked you with my use of the old-English word *fuck*.'

'You didn't shock me at all, just confirmed my low opinion of Cambridge men.'

'I'm not a Cambridge man, I'm proud to say.'

'I'm sure Cambridge would be pleased to hear that.'

He shrugged.

'Then what are you, if I may ask?'

'I'm an artist.'

'Really? What kind of artist?'

'A photographer.'

'Hmmph, I'm not sure photography qualifies as art.'

Fiona joined them and whisked Emerald away to help her make tea.

During the course of the afternoon, Emerald caught sight of Raph in deep discussion with others among Laurence's group of friends. He seemed very intense. He didn't seek her out and she certainly had no intention of renewing her conversation with him.

Fiona came to her late in the afternoon to excitedly whisper that a young man named Lance had invited her to a nearby pub to listen to some music. She asked Emerald to go with her.

'What about Michael?' Emerald asked.

'It's only an outing,' she said defensively. 'Anyway, it's not as if Michael and I are engaged or anything. Won't you come?' she pleaded.

Emerald didn't want to be left alone with the crowd of Cambridge men, and agreed.

She went inside to collect her coat.

Raph stopped her in the hall.

'It *is* art, you know,' he said. 'Photography, I mean.'

He surprised her by his conciliatory tone, but she wasn't about to drop her guard. 'If you say so,' she said.

'I'd like to prove it to you.'

'Oh? How is that possible?'

'I'll take you to an exhibition by one of England's best photographers.'

'You must be joking,' she said, and continued out of the house with her coat over her arm.

Fiona was in the garden, gaining the necessary assurances from her brother that he would say not a word to her parents about her outing. While she waited in the garden, a few of the young Cambridge men passed. They were leaving. Raph was among them.

'Day after tomorrow,' he said, barely pausing as he walked past her to the gate.

'I beg your pardon?' Emerald said.

'You heard. Day after tomorrow. Friday.'

'If you think I would go anywhere with you, after what —'

'Around four,' he added, then was gone.

* * *

Fiona and Lance led Emerald and four of the Cambridge men across the Hart Street Bridge to the Red Lion Hotel — a solid brick building of three storeys with several racy little sports cars parked outside its red-brick portico. From the street they could hear the sound of drums and some kind of reedy flute. It wasn't jazz or jitterbug music, but it had a compelling, almost savage rhythm.

They followed the sound down a long hall. The hotel's dining room had tables packed together around a tiny dance floor and a small bandstand where two black men were pounding large drums and another was playing the flute. A fourth black man, bare-chested and wearing a short leather skirt, was leaping high in the air, his black and white fur leggings flailing with every kick. His female partner was wearing a colourful loose-fitting cotton blouse and a thick grass skirt, which bounced as she gyrated her hips in time with the beat.

Emerald sat with Fiona and Lance while the others either stood against the wall or found what seats remained. She was fascinated by the spectacle. She'd been to many dances and loved the jitterbug and the bop, but this was like nothing she'd ever seen or heard before. The drums, which she now noted had two different tones, beat a constant accompaniment to the flute, which carried the melody. At first it was the melody that carried her along with the dancers as they leaped and gyrated, until she realised it was the unremitting drums that drove them. As when she heard the compelling beat of train wheels on a track, her heart, her mind, fell into tempo with the incessant rhythm of the drums. The more she listened to their beat, the more she was spirited away to whatever dark country they'd come from.

Suddenly, and with a final booming crescendo of drums, the music stopped.

A stunned silence fell over the crowd before a roar of applause went up. Cheering and whistling, the crowd demanded more, Emerald as much a part of it as anyone.

The sweating dancers smiled; and the drums began again.

This time the beat was slower, like a heartbeat, and sensual. The dancers came together with snaking arms and swaying movements like trees in the wind. The flute played in and around them, vying with the drums.

As the dance progressed it was obvious it was a story of seduction. The black man thrust his hips forwards and the woman retreated. He tried again and again with the same result until a subtle shift in the beat changed their rhythm and now they were synchronised: he thrusting and she receiving him. The couple were almost making love on the dance floor.

The air was thick with smoke in the crowded room. Emerald's lips were dry. She couldn't swallow. Someone should open a window, she thought. She needed a drink, but couldn't take her eyes from the performers. It was the most thrilling and exciting dance spectacle she'd ever seen.

When the group headed home across the bridge an hour later, they hardly spoke.

The drums had ended, but they remained inside Emerald's head; even while looking down into the swift dark waters of the Thames, she could feel their surge moving the blood through her veins in the same beat.

'Where do the dancers come from?' someone asked.

'I think it's the Belgian Congo,' another answered.

Emerald had no idea where the Belgian Congo was. She'd never been interested in Africa and, although her mother had told her she'd been born there, it seldom came up in conversation. On one of her weekend visits she'd asked her father about his life in Africa and he became annoyed. She never raised it again.

She decided she should know more about her country of birth. The dancers and their music had sparked something within her that needed to be explored.

CHAPTER 46

On Thursday, Peter and Michael arrived from Oxford. They were staying in a guest house rented by the rowing club, but Fiona and Emerald had invited them to dinner. The cook had done most of the work and gone home, and Laurence was out with his friends, leaving the house to the two girls.

They took the boys, who had brought two bottles of lager and a bottle of Riesling for the occasion, into the sitting room. The drinks were opened and Fiona passed the glasses around.

'Are you sure you won't have a glass of wine, Em?' Fiona asked her. 'It's really quite refreshing.'

'Go on,' Michael said. 'You only live once.'

'Just a half then,' Emerald conceded.

Fiona poured. It tasted awful, but she said it was nice.

Over dinner, talk turned to the boat races. The two young men would be in training on the following day, but the girls said they would go to watch them in their race on Saturday.

The dinner proceeded well. While the men drank the beer, Fiona poured herself a third glass of wine. Emerald sat on her half-glass and declined any refills.

Michael and Fiona, who had begun to giggle, went searching for a bottle of port, while Peter suggested he and Emerald go out into the garden.

The evening was warm. They strolled to the little vine-covered rotunda at the bottom of the garden. She still had most of the half-glass of Riesling in her hand. A cricket chirped from the shrubbery.

'Are you still angry with me?' he asked when they'd taken a seat.

The night air was still and the half-moon ambled among the drifting clouds. She placed her glass on the seat beside her.

'No.'

'I'm pleased,' he said, and turned towards her to slide an arm over her shoulders. His breath was warm and beery on her cheek.

Another cricket chimed in.

He shifted his position and slipped his arm further around her shoulders until his hand rested gently on her breast. 'You're a wonderful girl, Emma,' he whispered. 'A beautiful girl.'

After an initial rush of alarm at his incursion, she examined her feelings more calmly. It was a curious and pleasant sensation. There was something flattering about his interest in her, quite aside from the warm glow emanating from the pit of her stomach to where his hand now lay more resolutely on her breast. She could no longer pretend not to notice.

'Emerald,' he whispered. His fingers fumbled with the buttons on her cotton blouse.

He covered her mouth with his and thrust his tongue between her lips. The beer taste flooded into her mouth; she pushed him away. She had an almost unbearable urge to spit.

'Stop that!' she said.

'But you say I don't show you how I feel, and now, when I do —'

All she wanted was a tumbler of water to freshen her mouth. 'I think we should go in.'

'But Emma ...'

'I just want to go,' she said.

Emerald got to her feet and walked briskly to the back door. Peter followed.

'Emma,' he said. 'I think we should wait.'

Fiona was not in the kitchen where she'd left her.

'Fiona?'

They were not in the sitting room either.

She heard a loud thud from their shared bedroom. Alarmed, she went to the door and flung it open.

'Fiona!' Emerald said, looking from her to Michael and back again. The blood rushed to her face.

Fiona was in one of the single beds, the covers drawn up to her nose. Michael was sitting on the side of the bed, searching on the floor for his trousers.

'Emma,' Peter said, touching her on the arm. 'Come on. Let's wait outside.'

Outside in the kitchen, Emerald sat, stunned. She and Fiona had often talked about what they wanted to do with their boyfriends, but it had always been just talk. She had no idea Fiona was prepared to go all the way.

Peter tried to calm her by taking her hand and patting it, but she withdrew it. She wanted nothing to do with him or anyone else at that moment. She was mortified.

Fiona came into the kitchen, but Michael stayed in the doorway.

'C'mon, Pete,' he said. 'Let's go.'

Peter looked helplessly at Emerald. 'See you Saturday?' he asked.

Emerald didn't answer, and he followed Michael to the door.

Tears welled in Emerald's eyes. She didn't know why — surely her mother couldn't be right about her not being old enough to handle sex. But she certainly felt a ludicrously childish longing for her own room and her own bed.

After a few minutes Fiona asked if there was anything she needed.

'I'm quite all right,' she said, and took the glasses to the sink and began washing them.

'Em,' Fiona said. 'I thought you wanted to do it too. I thought that was why you went out into the garden with Peter.'

In spite of her discomfort, Emerald had an urge to know what had happened, but she couldn't form the question without appearing voyeuristic. It wasn't the details she needed, but the process of seduction that interested her. How did Fiona get to the situation where she could allow Michael to do ... that?

She turned from the sink. 'What happened, Fiona?' she asked.

'Oh, that Michael. He's never satisfied.' Her voice was harsh, but she was smiling.

'Did he ... Did you do it?'

'For goodness' sake, Em,' she said. 'There's more than one way to please a boy.'

Several thoughts ran through Emerald's mind. She'd heard things whispered among her friends about what boys liked. She felt a guilty fascination. 'I don't understand.'

Fiona sighed. 'Look,' she said. 'At first we'd play around a little and I used my hand, and it was all done. But that time when we left you at the flower show, he wanted to go all the way.' She shrugged. 'So it's been like that.'

Emerald swallowed: her kiss with Peter had been such an innocent act in comparison. She felt foolishly juvenile. Even his fumbling in the rotunda tonight had hardly been seductive. She tried to imagine what might have happened if she had allowed things to progress. She had enjoyed his hand on her for a time before the smell and taste of the beer spoiled it. She wondered how she might feel about Peter doing it at another time. Or how would she feel if it happened with someone else? Someone more interesting, and without beer breath.

Someone like Raph.

*   *   *

It was Friday.

Emerald hadn't really forgotten Raph's promise to take her to the photographic exhibition, but when he arrived just after four, she feigned surprise and indifference.

He looked at her, sucked the inside of his cheek and nodded.

'You're not going to go on with all that nonsense, are you?' he said.

'I don't know what you're talking about,' she countered.

'All that bullshit where you pretend to be disinterested, but at the same time you've put on a sexy dress and done your hair.'

'I do wish you wouldn't swear so. It's very crude.'

'It's the only way you Regent's Park types can get a real education.'

She was about to correct him and say *Mayfair*, but held it back.

'Well, I'm sure I don't need that kind of education, thank you very much.'

He laughed. It was quite disarming.

'Have it your way, Emerald with the beautiful green eyes. Now ... are you coming, or not?'

She could see herself spinning on her heel and slamming the door in his face, but she suddenly wanted to go with him very much.

'What is this exhibition all about?' she sniffed.

'You'll have to come along to find out, won't you? But if you do come, I promise it will change your perception of art. You can have your van Goghs and Turners: Ivanof is a real-world artist. When you see something that is real, unlike your paintings, where everything is intended to trick the eye, you'll be amazed at what you've missed in real life. Until a brilliant photographer makes you see the world — really see it — you don't have a clue. And after he shows you, you can never see that object in the same way ever again.'

As he spoke she watched his expression change. His piercing eyes softened and the tight line of his jaw relaxed, adding a fullness to his mouth she'd previously not noticed. Even his voice, which had appeared strident at their first meeting, had become more rounded and expressive. He was still intense, but now she could see the passion that impelled him.

'So what are you going to do, Miss Emerald Eyes? Do you want to remain stuck with your views of the world, or are you brave enough to let me challenge them?'

At that moment she thought Raph could have convinced her the fiery depths of hell were worth a visit.

She took a breath. 'Very well,' she said, and followed him to the front gate.

* * *

'I didn't know the exhibition was in Oxford,' Emerald said above the wind that had almost torn her hat out of her hand, and now flung her hair in every direction.

'Would it have made any difference?' he said, his voice raised to be heard over the wind.

'Well, for one thing, I would have worn a hat more suitable for a spin in a … a … What did you say it's called?'

'It's an MG TA. Made right here near Oxford. And in case you're interested, it's nearly 1300cc, overhead cams, and fifty horsepower.' He turned to her and smiled. 'Are you impressed?'

'I'll say,' she said, grinning.

Raph was a different person when he wasn't baiting her.

'How long have you owned it?' she called.

'I don't. Not yet. It's my brother Kelvin's. I'm paying it off. He left it with me when he went away to America.'

'I see.'

She couldn't imagine not immediately owning something that she wanted. All her life, even after her parents' divorce and before her mother's remarriage, she'd never wanted for anything. She was starting to realise the world was a more complex place than what she'd seen. Until she heard Goran Papasov's story, she'd had no idea of the prejudices levelled at the gypsies, nor the horrors of their life on the continent during the war. And until she met Raph, and he challenged her about it, she'd never given a thought to the poor in her own country.

She wondered about being the wife of a working-class man. She would have to be careful of her spending. No spontaneous trips to Harrods for a new outfit; no traipsing off to the Cotswolds for the summer.

She looked at Raph hunched over the wheel, the wind tearing at his rakish tartan scarf and flinging his untamed blond hair here and there, and wondered what it would be like to live in his world.

* * *

Raph led Emerald into the temporarily rearranged dining room of the Oxford Hounds hotel, where a small group of enthusiasts, some sipping champagne, strolled from one large photograph to another.

Emerald wondered aloud whether all the cultural events west of London were confined to pubs: surely there were ample proper exhibition spaces elsewhere in that part of England to accommodate them.

'It saves on costs,' was Raph's explanation. 'And Alexi can't be too choosy. It's not easy being a Russian in the west these days; but the publican's sympathetic.'

'Sympathetic to what?'

'To the cause.'

'What cause?'

'The socialist cause, of course,' he said.

'Socialist? You mean communism?' Her stepfather had often been apoplectic upon reading any reference to communism in *The Times*. 'Bloody reds!' he'd say. 'We should have let Hitler wipe them all out in the war.'

'No,' he said, patiently. 'I mean socialism. There *is* a difference, you know.'

She had expected derision, so his only slightly patronising words disarmed her. Now she wanted to know more, but they were interrupted by a huge man who came to Raph and swept him into a bearhug.

'Raphael!' he boomed. 'My friend. It is good to see you again.'

'Jesus, Alexi!' Raph spluttered as he broke the embrace. 'At least have a shave if you're going to kiss me, will you?'

'And look, you have found yourself a beautiful English rose,' the big man said, eyeing Emerald.

'Emerald, this is Alexi Ivanof,' he said.

'Wonderful,' Alexi said. 'She is beautiful.' He raised his hand to the waitress. 'Drinks! Over here, *mademoiselle*.'

The waitress arrived with a tray of champagne flutes.

Alexi handed them each a glass. 'A toast,' he said. 'To the revolution. No ... fuck that.' He laughed — a booming sound that filled the bare room. 'To the success of my exhibition.'

They clinked glasses.

Alexi drained his in a single gulp and called for another, forcing fresh glasses into their free hands when the tray arrived.

'Now, to the two of you. A happy couple.'

Raph shrugged and Emerald smiled.

'Raph tells me you're from Russia,' Emerald said.

'Russia, no. We call it Belarus. But me, I'm from everywhere.'

'Alexis claims he knows a dozen languages,' Raph said.

'That's me. I can talk bullshit in too many tongues.'

'Really,' Emerald said. 'Then let me test you.' She tapped her index finger against her bottom lip, trying to recall the word the gypsy used. 'Let me see, yes: what does *recha* mean?'

'Ah! That one too easy. From my home in Belarus. *Recha*, it means vibrate.'

'Vibrate?' Emerald tried to recall the context of the fortune-teller's message.

Alexi again downed the champagne. 'No,' he added. 'Better I say, echo. Yes, echo.'

He then disappeared to attend to a prospective buyer.

She replayed the gypsy's words again. She'd talked about black and white babies. Now echoes. It didn't make sense. She'd simply been swindled out of her two bob.

'How do you know Alexi?' she asked Raph, putting the matter from her mind.

'We spent time together in gaol.'

'*Gaol?*'

'Posing a public nuisance,' he said. 'It was a demonstration against the government's lockout at the mines a few years ago. We were locked up together for a couple of weeks because neither of us could post bail. Well, I could have, if I'd been prepared to ask my family. But it wasn't worth the heat, so I decided to sit it out. We were both convicted and released on time already served. You can get to know a lot about a person under close confinement like that. I learned he was a photographer, and I had always been interested in it, so we went from there.'

She finished the first glass of champagne and started on the second while Raph further charmed her with his enthusiasm for the art around them.

'It's not all about *f*-stops and depth of field. What Alexi has is creativity. He can see the shot in the landscape or the face or the animal. He can extract the essence of that scene and capture it on film.'

'Can *you* do that?'

He paused before answering. 'I try.'

'Do you have a collection like Alexi?' she said, indicating the work on the surrounding walls.

He ran his gaze around the room. 'Not like this.'

She wanted to ask him to show her what he had, but the moment passed when he asked if she cared to take a tour of the exhibits.

He led her to the nearest of Alexi's work — a study of windblown trees above a bleak stretch of coastline.

'Step up to it,' Raph said.

Emerald moved closer to the black and white photograph until it filled her field of vision.

'Now … step into it,' he added.

She glanced at him. He was watching her closely. It was hard to read his expression, but when he nodded encouragement, she tried to imagine herself in the scene.

She studied the picture with the branches of the tree nearest to the camera straining against the wind. Tiny droplets took flight from the leaves in a spray that flew horizontally across the print. Behind the tree, foam came from the sea, whipped into a froth that scuttled across the sand like startled white rabbits, then up into the dunes, where the grass waved and rippled in a vain attempt to resist the onslaught of the driving rain. She felt suddenly chilled and a shiver ran down her spine. When she turned back to Raph he was smiling.

'You felt it, didn't you?'

'It's amazing! I was actually on that hill, in the wind and rain.'

'Now, look at this one.'

He took her hand and dragged her across the room to a large photo of a black-maned male lion, its face turned full towards the camera.

'What do you see?' he asked.

'It looks a little quizzical. How did he get this shot?'

'Look again,' he insisted. 'What else do you see?'

She moved closer.

'It has a scar on its top lip.'

'Good. What else?'

'And tiny little flies around its mouth.'

'Bad breath,' he said, smiling again.

'Does Alexi make a living from his photography?' she asked.

He pointed to the price on the tag.

'Oh, I see,' she said. 'Isn't that rather ... expensive?'

'Not for people like you and your parents.'

Her impulse was again to defend herself, but she quickly realised he hadn't intended the comment as a slight. Since meeting Raph she'd become slightly paranoid about her parents' privileged position.

'It's the self-promotional game,' he continued. 'Nobody respects your work if you put a small price on it. Look at all the great masters in art. Many were penniless for most if not all of their lives.'

He paused to take a handful of peanuts from a passing tray.

'Today's artists have learned to value their work. Mind you, they have to make a start somewhere, which means for a long time they have to find another way to survive.

If they're lucky, it would be using some of their skills, like doing weddings and portraits.'

'Hmm,' she said. 'So, to be successful as a photographer you have to charge a high price for your work, but you can't charge a high price until you're successful. It sounds rather tricky.'

'It is. So everyone is out there trying to win some acclaim, or at least be noticed, then they can start to raise the price.

'How did Alexi get his start?'

'He found a rich widow,' he said, as he popped a peanut into his mouth.

Emerald stared at him; he wasn't joking. 'You don't mean ...'

'As a matter of fact,' he went on, 'that's his benefactor over there in black, with the wide-brimmed hat.'

The woman was in a dress at least a size too small for her grossly overweight body. She also wore too much make-up.

Emerald looked again at Alexi, smiling and in animated conversation with a couple who had apparently just purchased the silhouette of London Bridge.

'Do they ...?' she began, allowing her thoughts to escape and already regretting it.

Raph smiled. 'I don't think so. Unless it's for old times' sake.'

'Raph!' she said, shocked. Then had to smile with him.

They'd completed the tour of the gallery. Raph grabbed two more champagnes before leading Emerald out the door to a seat in the small garden adjoining the pub.

For the best part of an hour they chatted. At times he was the angry Raph, proclaiming the imminent demise of the capitalist system and the privileged classes generally, and Emerald's parents in particular. At other times he was almost lyrical as he talked about his hopes for success in his chosen art form. Then he'd make a joke at his own expense. Emerald laughed a lot.

She was on her third glass of champagne — or was it the fourth? — when Raph noted it was getting late.

The long twilight was ebbing and a pale moon hung overhead. Emerald didn't want the day to end. She'd become enthralled by Raph's wit and wisdom; had marvelled at his wide knowledge and experiences in a world she'd hardly realised existed. She wanted more. She wanted to know what he knew; to know more about his passions and his dislikes.

'Do we have to?' she asked, pouting, when he said it was time to go.

'I'm afraid so.'

'Bully,' she said and playfully tweaked his ear.

He gave her a quizzical look.

She frowned while trying to see the colour of his eyes in the fading light. He was rather too thin and not as tall as Peter. His mop of blond hair needed a good cut. Probably a shampoo. He wasn't even good-looking, when it really came down to it. But there was an air about him that she found ... very interesting.

'What colour are your eyes?' she asked.

'I believe they're brown,' he said. 'And I also believe you're drunk.'

She giggled. 'Really?' Then she put on a serious face. 'Do we really have to go?'

'Yes.'

Looking up at the hotel's second floor, she said, 'Do you suppose they have rooms here?

Raph's face was in shadow but she knew he wasn't smiling. The silence extended for a long, breathless moment.

'C'mon,' he said, and took her hand.

Emerald felt a flock of sparrows take flight in her stomach.

'W-where?' she stammered.

He said nothing, but led her through the garden, into the gallery, and out the front door to the MG.

* * *

The cool air, the breeze in her hair and the half-hour it took to drive back to Henley had cleared Emerald's head, but she felt a touch queasy in her stomach and considerably humiliated following her conduct back at the Oxford Hounds hotel. She didn't know what was worse: her disgraceful behaviour, or that Raph had not accepted her outrageous offer.

When Raph pulled up outside the cottage, he turned off the motor and they sat in darkness without a word for several minutes.

'I feel like such an idiot,' she said at last.

He took her hand.

'Don't worry. In the morning I'll probably feel the same.'

'I don't know how I …' She felt it hard to express her shame.

'Champagne can do that,' he said.

She went over the events in her mind again, trying to find a more reassuring excuse than the alcohol. She couldn't think of one.

'It's not often I have such an ill-timed attack of gallantry,' he said. He was smiling, and she could have hugged him for both bringing her home and apparently regretting it.

'Would you have ... you know ... would it have been different if I wasn't ... if I hadn't drunk so much champagne?'

'That would be telling, wouldn't it?'

'I suppose it would.'

She stared out the window at nothing in particular, hoping he'd say something. 'Well,' she said eventually. 'I'd better go in.'

Still he said nothing, so she opened the door, but remained in her seat. Turning to him, she said, 'Good night, Raph.'

'Good night, Miss Emerald Eyes.'

Dana loved the theatre. It was one of her most cherished distractions and, since deciding it was better to leave Oswald at home and avoid his constant grumbling complaints, one that she usually enjoyed alone. However, sitting with Emerald in the Bentley as Henry, her driver, expertly navigated the dark streets of South Kensington, she wasn't at all sure she should be attending this particular performance with her daughter.

It had been Emerald's idea, but considering the theme of the play, she was surprised that she chose it.

Dana knew about the play, *Native Son*. She'd discussed it with Oswald after she'd read the reviews. It had done very well in New York and was something of a sensation there as it dealt very frankly with issues of race and privilege. These two themes always left her feeling uncomfortable.

Against her better judgement, she'd agreed to take Emerald in an attempt to ease the tension that had existed between them over recent days. Since her return from the regatta, the girl had been somewhat subdued, but she was still increasingly determined to express her independence. Despite Emerald's apparently excellent behaviour at Henley — Fiona's mother had been delighted with her — Dana remained convinced that she was as yet ill-equipped for the realities of adult life.

* * *

Henry eased the Bentley into a space at the kerb, and immediately stepped out to open the rear door. He threw a snappy salute as Emerald climbed out, which as usual made her smile.

The theatre entrance was awash with lights. Emerald studied the first-nighters as her mother engaged in conversation with acquaintances. There was a fascinating flourish of furs, stringed pearls and diamante tiaras, but Emerald was particularly interested in those younger women dressed in more modern fashions.

A tall woman with her red hair piled on top of her head wore a full-length black dress with tight-fitted embroidered sleeves and bodice. A single, short circle of pearls was her only jewellery. In fact, every woman was very elegantly dressed in the latest styles. Her mother had often commented on how uneasy she'd felt wearing attractive clothes during and immediately following the war, but it was obvious from the fashions worn by the women milling outside the theatre that night that those days were long gone.

Emerald was pleased she had chosen her ballerina-length dress in vivid green velvet. It hugged her waist and the button-up bodice accentuated her breasts. Her long black gloves almost reached her bare elbows. She felt quite sophisticated, and wished that Fiona could see her.

Emerald knew her mother was not pleased to be there. She'd overheard Dana saying to her stepfather that she didn't approve of the *themes* in the play. This had piqued Emerald's interest, so when she read the review and learned it was about black people in America, she'd pestered her mother to go.

As the bells calling patrons to their seats rang, she made eye contact with an older man — he must have been thirty-something — who gave her a wink and a smile. Emerald flushed with embarrassment and excitement.

When the theatre lights died, the curtains parted to reveal a squalid room occupied by a family of four black people: a young man, Bigger Thomas, his mother, younger brother and sister.

It soon became clear that the family depended upon Bigger for their survival, and this responsibility weighed heavily upon him. He won a job in a wealthy white family's home, and was uncomfortable not knowing how to behave in that unfamiliar environment. He became even more confused when the family showed him kindness. With Raph's comments about class ringing in her ears, Emerald was only too aware of the vast cultural and social void between Bigger and his employer.

A series of accidents ended with Bigger fleeing, indirectly responsible for a young white woman's death. The accidental crime, however, made him feel *real*. He saw newspaper headlines about himself and his feeling of relevance grew. He overheard conversations about him and his crimes. The whites were full of fear and hatred and the blacks were furious that he had given their oppressors ammunition.

His deliberate crimes were far more brutal than his accidental one.

Bigger Thomas is caught in the final scene and, as the curtain falls, he dies a ghastly death in the electric chair.

As the theatre rose to its feet in applause, Emerald remained seated, stunned.

* * *

Emerald again sat in silence during the journey home. *Native Son* had a profound effect on her and she needed time to digest it. She also needed time to unravel the odd feelings it stirred in her.

The white employer was wealthy and privileged — much like her family. As a member of the Middlebridge dynasty she was one of the upper class. The similarities between her life and some of those in the play disturbed her. She had never questioned why she was so comfortable while so many were not. She vaguely understood that some people actually had no place to live and sometimes went hungry. Until seeing the play, the possible consequences of such deprivation had not occurred to her.

When Henry pulled up at the front door to let them out, Dana asked Emerald if she would care to join her in the kitchen for a cup of cocoa.

As Emerald waited for the cocoa to heat on the gas stove, the character of Bigger Thomas wouldn't leave her. She couldn't get his utter hopelessness from her mind. The Thomas family were decent people. Poor, but honest. Could the play be a true representation of how black people live in America? she wondered. And if so, could it also be the case in England? And what about Africa itself?

When Emerald was much younger, and had learned that she was born in Africa, she had been curious, but even at that age she knew her mother was reluctant to discuss those times. Perhaps her lack of interest in Africa later had been a result of Dana's attitude. The play had certainly reawoken her curiosity.

'Mother,' Emerald said. 'How long were you in Africa with Papa Edward?'

After a moment's hesitation, her mother said: 'Six years.'

'And I suppose you had plenty of black servants?'

'A few.'

'What are the black people like in South Africa?'

'It was not South Africa, Emerald,' she said. 'You were born in Kenya — quite a bit further north.'

'But what are they like?'

'They were nothing like the characters in *Native Son*, if that's what you're wondering.'

'Did they live with you?'

'Yes … No, they lived in their own houses … *bandas*.'

'Next to your house?'

'On the property. Emerald, what's all this about?'

'Just wondering. I imagine you got to know them quite well.'

Dana paused for a moment. 'I think so,' she said.

'Do you ever wonder how they are? I mean, if they are still there, after all these years.'

'Oh, I don't know. I suppose I do — once in a while.'

'Have you ever thought about going back again?'

Dana took her cocoa to the sink, and sipped it with her back to Emerald. 'No.'

'Perhaps we should,' Emerald said.

Her mother put her cup on the table. 'It's late,' she said at last. 'Time for bed.'

* * *

Dana could hear Oswald's snoring through the door to his adjoining bedroom. She slipped off her dress and hung it in her wardrobe, then took a seat on the Georgian chair to remove her silk stockings.

She was exhausted, and remained seated in the dim light of her dressing room, thinking about Emerald's questions. The girl had clearly found the play confronting.

Dana certainly had. Memories of her life in Africa now gathered at the edge of her mind; pressing upon her, demanding recognition; threatening to render her sleepless and regretful.

She got to her feet and completed her undressing, then slipped on her nightdress.

The moon threw enough light through the bay windows for her to find her way across the room and into bed. She lay awake for a long time, staring at the ceiling. Shadows formed there, moving under the influence of the breeze that played among the lacy curtains. Her imagination made dark shapes of them. Half asleep, she saw Jonathan and Benard working in the stable. And Ndorobo the syce and expert game tracker. It was quite by accident that she had discovered Ndorobo was not his name: he was Dorapata, of the Ndorobo tribe. In her ignorance, she'd confused the two, but he had never corrected her. Emerald had asked if she knew her African staff — obviously not as well as she should have.

Other memories beckoned and she could no longer deny them. She could see her black baby boy in her arms, blowing spit bubbles through his puckered lips; she felt him hungrily drawing her milk from her, squirming and wriggling with pleasure.

Emerald had asked if she ever thought of the people she'd left behind in Kenya. She'd answered, 'Once in a while.' The truth was that her last minutes with her son, before she laid him in another's arms and sent him out to an unknown place with unknown people for an unknown future, had been with her every day since.

CHAPTER 48

The Statue of Liberty appeared smaller, and the New York terminal quite a deal larger, than Sam remembered from his arrival in 1920. The hubbub on the wharf was as he recalled it, but instead of mainly horse-drawn vehicles awaiting passengers and their luggage, there were now only cars and taxis.

One passenger tried to hand his bag to Sam. 'Here, boy,' he said. 'Take this and find me a cab.'

Sam ignored him.

'Hey!' the man said indignantly, as Sam headed off to collect his own suitcase.

It took him some time to find a cab whose driver would accept him and even when he did, he had to load his luggage himself.

Some things don't change, he thought.

Fashions had. The pale grey suit he'd purchased for the journey in one of Nairobi's finer stores was high-waisted, baggy in the legs, and narrow at the ankle, with an oversized jacket. In New York he realised his outfit was starkly at odds with those worn by Manhattan's businessmen. Here, everybody dressed almost identically in dark blue, brown or grey flannel. Ties were narrower and jackets and trousers closer-fitting. Shoulder pads were gone as was the elegant fedora. The hats had narrower brims and higher bands.

Sam went shopping for a new suit; in the stores that would accept a black man's business, it took him time to find a suit that didn't make him look like a pimp or a gangster.

* * *

A day later, wearing his new navy-blue flannel, he went to the offices of Bradstreet and Gardiner — General Motors' lawyers in the matter of Ira's self-starter motor.

The firm's receptionist appeared surprised to see him, but if the pair of lawyers who greeted him in their plush meeting room were, they didn't show it. Both were wearing single-breasted, charcoal-grey suits.

'Mr Wangira.' They beamed, shaking his hand vigorously. They mentioned their similar-sounding names, which Sam promptly forgot, and proceeded to ask him trite questions about his health and wellbeing.

'And how is your accommodation, Mr Wangira?' one asked.

Sam said it was comfortable.

'Good. Good.'

'And your journey? How was the flight?'

'I don't fly. I came by ship.'

One nodded. 'Oh, very wise.'

'A sea journey can be so relaxing,' said the other.

They spoke to Sam in slow, measured tones, as if speaking to a child or to someone with limited language skills.

When the preliminaries finally ended, they slid a brief across the table to Sam, who read it as they continued to blather about their firm's long-standing association with General Motors and other important clients.

'Gentlemen,' Sam said, interrupting. 'This document has none of the agreements mentioned in your earlier correspondence.'

'Yes, well … they were just drafts. We've tidied things up a little in this final version.'

'And in paragraph six you've veritably accused me of stealing Mr Ketterman's intellectual property.'

'I can promise you, Mr Wangira,' one said solemnly. 'We don't intend to pursue that matter.'

'In return for you accepting our settlement terms,' added the other.

Sam glanced down at the document again. 'A cash settlement of ten dollars,' he noted.

'We will carry all the associated costs to transfer ownership to our client.'

'And we'll say nothing more about rightful ownership.'

Sam looked from one lawyer to the other. They wore identical smiles.

'So, what do you say, Mr Wangira? Do we have a deal?'

Sam stood. 'What do I say?' he said in his broadest American accent. 'I say, gentlemen, you can kiss my ass.'

And he walked out of their office.

He'd hoped his stay in New York would be brief. It was now clear it would not be. In Kenya he'd had some experience fighting situations he knew to be unfair. In America it would be more difficult. He didn't imagine many black people had challenged the workings of the white business world. But he would not go home without giving it a shot.

Sam knew nothing about the American legal system — a fact that GM's lawyers had obviously counted on when crafting their outrageous offer — and no idea how to find a suitable attorney to handle his case. Then he recalled the young lawyer who Ira had engaged as executor of his estate.

He wracked his brain and came up with the name Joshua Samuels, but there was nobody listed under that name in the telephone directory entries for lawyers. He made a dozen or so phone calls and found someone who knew him. He was now a senior partner in one of New York's biggest law firms.

* * *

Samuels had added thirty pounds and lost most of his hair since Sam last saw him, but he greeted him warmly in his office high above Fifth Avenue.

'Mr Wangira,' he said, coming around his desk to take Sam's hand. 'So good to see you again. Please, take a seat.'

Sam was pleased that he remembered him. After some small talk, Sam outlined his situation and showed Samuels the offer.

Samuels shook his head. 'Amazing. If I may say so, Mr Wangira, they obviously saw you coming. But you've done the right thing bringing it to us. If you'd gone to a small operator, B&G would have wiped the floor with you.'

'I didn't have much choice. I came to you because I remembered you from Ira's will,' Sam admitted. 'You're the only lawyer I know.'

Samuels laughed. 'Either way, you've made the right decision. Speaking of Ira, I tried to get in touch with you again some time after the settlement, but I think you'd left your hotel, or returned home. Anyway, the purpose was to ask what you wanted me to do with Ira's personal effects.'

'I thought we sorted all that out.'

'We did, but these things came to light later. I put them in my attic while I looked for you, then forgot all about them. About a year ago, I found them again. Yes, I know, it sounds strange. The fact is, I got divorced and my ex got the house.' He shrugged. 'I was about to throw them out, but they're real nice, and I thought you should decide what you want done with them.'

'What are they?'

'Photos and films. Quite a few of you.'

* * *

Sam carried the box up to his hotel room. He hesitated, considering whether he should open this passage to his past. He left it on the bed and sat in the armchair to stare at it for a further ten minutes before berating himself for his childishness.

The box contained a number of large envelopes, each enclosing a photographic print, and spools of film. He slid a print carefully from its jacket. It was a black and white study of a Maasai warrior. He opened more, arranging them on the bed and furniture in his hotel room. Soon he was surrounded by fifty or more photographs of various African subjects.

A sizeable part of the collection was Ira's studies of wildlife. There was a magnificent front-on head-shot of a black-maned lion, taken as the spark of alertness flashed into its intelligent hazel eyes. From experience, Sam knew that an instant later the lion would be in full charge at his quarry: in this case, the photographer.

In another towered a great bull elephant. Ira must have had his camera set low and only a few paces from the beast. A halo of dust framed the bull's raised trunk, flared ears and long sweeping tusks. He could almost feel the reverberation of its enormous pads and hear its trumpeting blast of alarm.

There were sweeping landscapes of the Mara savannah with long snaking lines of migrating wildebeest and zebra silhouetted against the sky as they climbed a hill; the wide expanses of the Great Rift Valley captured as if in watercolour; acacia trees at sunset; and a misty jungle waterhole with the muzzle of a waterbuck sending widening concentric circles across the silvered water.

There were many large prints of Sam as a young porter on Bill Hungerford's safari. In one he was proudly wearing his blue jacket, khaki shorts, boots and gaiters, with a red fez perched at a jaunty angle on his head, and an uncertain smile on his lips. On the back was written *Samson Wangira, August 1916.*

In another — a more detailed black and white study of his head and bare torso — Ira had used lighting that captured the bulge of muscle on his arms, shoulders and chest, and emphasised his taut abdominals in ripples of highlight and shade. Sam's hand went involuntarily to his midriff, where a thin layer of flab now covered the underlay of muscle.

The last in the series was a close-up. It was taken a few weeks after the first set, when Sam had become accustomed to the camera and was starting to take an interest in Ira's work. He took the print to the bedside lamp and sat on the bed to study it. His youthful eyes were wide and quizzical; he recalled that Ira was attempting to explain what the camera did to capture his image at the time.

In a mere twinkling of an eye, thirty-five years had slipped by.

He remembered there was a period in his life when he willed the sands of time to quicken their flow; to move him from child to boy; from boy to warrior. Now he wanted to give it no more encouragement, nor to be reminded of its passing.

He felt uncomfortable keeping Ira's body of African work. It was too personal. The photographs were not only of their subjects: by their presentation they portrayed the thoughts, the feelings, the emotions, of the photographer. It was like having Ira's ghost in the room with him. But if he couldn't keep them, he also didn't have the heart to throw them all away.

While walking past his old college, New York University, the previous day, he'd noticed an announcement of an upcoming photographic exhibition. He would donate Ira's collection and, if the art department didn't want to include these examples of early African photography by a talented amateur, they could do with them as they wished.

Sam knew it was a cowardly decision, but it meant he could avoid a painful choice.

* * *

Jelani was in a part of the city he'd not visited previously; he'd been directed there by Randolph, the rotund black man who had collected him at the airport in a black sedan with a high pointed bonnet, sweeping mudguards and a running board trimmed with chrome — just as Jelani had hoped he'd ride in when in America. Randolph was employed by the Longshoremen's Union and given the task of introducing Jelani to New York.

'You done arrived at the right time, boy,' he'd said. 'We's gonna have a big demonstration next week.' He pronounced *demonstration* as if it consisted of three separate words. 'Yessir. Thousands of our members are gonna be out on the streets, takin' on New York's finest.'

'New York's finest?' Jelani asked.

'The po-lice.' He laughed. 'Who you think? Li'l Red Ridin' Hood? The boss says you should come along. Good experience.'

The next day, Randolph began his induction program by telling Jelani: 'Get yo' ass down to Harlem, Jelani my man. See a part of New York what no visitin' white man sees.'

That was why Jelani was now on West 122nd Street, feeling oddly out of place. All the people were black, but none looked familiar. There was no Luo, or Kikuyu, or Maasai, or any other Kenyan tribe identifiable in the faces surrounding him on the crowded street.

Barefooted children played in piles of rubbish and old people sat on the bottom steps of three-storey brownstone buildings, some with paint peeling off in large curled flakes, watching him pass with idle curiosity.

On the steps of the Second Baptist Freedom Church — a flat-fronted two-storey building painted white at least a couple of decades earlier — stood a black vicar in a pointed white hat and a long white robe hemmed in gold lace. He was preaching in a babbling, rhyming voice that Jelani found difficult to understand. At first he wasn't even sure it was English, then a string of words caught his attention.

'Just brown, O Lord, not the black of Your Holy Word: sinners' wages, Jesus! Born of sin!'

Jelani stopped short in a sudden fury: he'd come halfway across the world and yet there was no escaping this *difference*. The evil of his birth had tainted every experience he'd ever had. He stood and glared at the preacher, who continued to rave with his face raised to the heavens and his eyes closed.

Jelani gave up, swallowed his temper and walked on.

The message came again — this time not from the preacher's words, but by some magic that sent the thought spearing into his mind. The taunt took him back to his childhood, when his schoolmates would tease him about his pale skin. The preacher too had referred to the sinister joining of a black man with a white woman. Jelani felt the blood rush to his face, and the bile rise from his stomach.

He spun around and marched to the steps of the decrepit building and glared up at the old preacher, who at first ignored him then, looking down to find him standing before him, smiled.

'Does the Lord send you here to pray wit' me, boy?' he asked kindly.

The unexpected gentleness of his voice threw Jelani completely off-balance. He couldn't maintain his anger in the face of such benign serenity. He must have been mistaken: the man's speech had, after all, been barely decipherable. But he wanted a *fight*.

The preacher held his smile.

Jelani hesitated a moment, then hurried away, confused and embarrassed.

A block away, he sat on a kerbside bench and wondered if he was ever going to outgrow the shame of his mixed parentage.

The answer came to him as clearly as the preacher's message had. It wasn't the idea of one black parent and one white that tormented him: it was not knowing who they were that was at the core of his pain.

He got up from the bench seat and felt that a load had been lifted from his shoulders. He had at last found a way to clear his head of all the childhood fears that still dominated the question of who he was.

He walked back to the preacher and threw a dollar into his bowl.

He was no closer to finding the answers he needed, but at least he now had the right question.

CHAPTER 49

Fiona rang Emerald to discuss their plans to go dancing at the Hammersmith Palais de Danse on Saturday night.

'Why don't I pick you up? Mummy has let me have our chauffeur for the occasion,' said Fiona.

'Great. What time?'

'I'll say seven-thirty. That way we can practise a few steps at Clarice's before we go. Oh, and Miriam's coming too.'

'That's brilliant. I'll bring "The Bumble Boogie" and "Twelfth Street Rag" — they're my new ones I mentioned yesterday.'

'Why don't you stay the night with us at Clarice's?' Fiona asked. 'It could be fun.'

'I did mention it to Mother: she flatly refused. I think she's still recovering from the ordeal of letting me go to Henley.'

'Pity. But speaking of Henley … Do you remember that funny-looking chap with the fair hair that we met with Laurence's friends?'

'Oh … do you mean Raph?'

Raph and his passionate speeches had surfaced from Emerald's memory at odd times over the weeks since Henley. She could no longer hear her stepfather's blistering attacks on *Clement-bloody-Attlee* and the *welfare-bloody-state* without Raph coming to mind.

Fiona's mention of him made her regret she'd not made an effort to contact him before leaving Henley. She wondered if it was his extremism that interested her, for he was certainly not the type of man she'd normally find attractive. With no way to make contact, she had decided to simply put him from her mind.

'Yes, Raph. Well, I heard from Laurence that he's gone to New York,' Fiona said.

'Oh, how nice for him.'

'To stay with his brother,' Fiona continued, relishing the gossip. 'Apparently, he's very well established on Wall Street.'

'Raph?'

'No, his brother, of course. Wasn't Raph interested in art, or photography, or something like that?' Fiona asked, probing.

'I'm sure I have no idea,' Emerald said.

* * *

'I think I'd rather study photography than watercolours,' Emerald said to her mother later.

'Photography?' Dana asked. 'Whatever for? It's a very plebeian hobby, don't you think?'

'Not at all. I went to a groovy photographic exhibition a couple of months ago.'

Her mother winced. 'Must you use those frightful expressions?'

'And I don't think I'll bother with the Red Cross any more.'

Dana sighed. 'Do you think you'll ever know what you want, Emerald?'

Emerald thought about the question for a moment.

'Yes, actually, I already do,' she said. 'I'd like to learn to be a photographer so I can become a photojournalist.'

'A photojournalist? What in heaven's name is a photojournalist?'

'It's the latest thing. I read about it in *Harper's Bazaar* last month. Some of these photojournalists are quite famous, recording history with their cameras.'

'It sounds very American to me, dear.'

'It is. That is, I think it is. At least that's where the best photojournalists work. Which brings me to another idea I had.'

Her mother raised an eyebrow. 'Yes?'

'I should like to go to New York to study properly.'

Instead of scoffing as Emerald had expected, her mother looked at her rather oddly then, to her surprise, gave a slight nod of acknowledgement. It wasn't the outright agreement Emerald might have hoped for, but the nod meant she would consider it and, if satisfied it was a good idea, discuss it with Papa.

Having only just thought of the idea herself, Emerald was suddenly immensely excited by the prospect.

* * *

Emerald again checked her dress, spinning in front of the mirror to see the printed taffeta bounce on the layers of tulle. A floaty lilac chiffon stole draped across her shoulders, picking out the lily of the valley pattern on her dress, and a strand of her mother's Mikimoto pearls demurely set off her décolletage. She was ready for the dance.

It was already seven-thirty — the agreed time. She couldn't wait to tell Fiona and the girls about her plans to go to New York to study photography. It was only a matter of time, and the sooner the better. She had no idea how she'd locate Raph, but she would find a way. Fiona's brother was obviously in touch.

She still hadn't made up her mind about her earrings and decided to ask her mother's opinion. She made her way down the stairs while struggling to get the clip onto her earlobe. When she looked up, Dana was down in the hall, staring up at her.

'Mother, what is it?'

'Nothing, darling. Just marvelling at how you've grown. And changed. When did you say Fiona will arrive?'

'Actually, she's supposed to be here already.'

The doorbell sounded.

'Oh, that must be her,' Emerald said. 'I'll get it.'

She swung the door open to find Fiona standing in the entryway in obvious distress. She wasn't even dressed for the Palais de Danse.

'Fiona! What is it? Is something wrong?'

'The night's been cancelled.'

'What?' Emerald said. 'Whatever for?'

'Emerald?' Her mother's voice trilled from behind her in the hall. 'Emerald, what are you thinking? Leaving the poor girl on the doorstep.' She joined Emerald at the door. 'Fiona, do come in. Oh … are you unwell, dear?'

Fiona sniffed into her lacy handkerchief and stepped past them into the hall.

'No, I'm all right,' she said. 'Really.'

Dana led them into the drawing room, where Fiona sat daintily on the edge of a large Georgian chair, her handkerchief crushed in her fist.

Emerald's instinct told her that Fiona's news should be saved till they were alone, but in the face of her obvious distress, and feeling powerless to intervene, she allowed her mother to take charge.

There was a long moment in which no one spoke.

'What is it, dear?' Dana offered by way of encouragement.

Fiona sniffed into her handkerchief; Emerald would later recall that she wore what romantic novelists might call a brave smile.

'I'm ... I'm going to have a baby,' she said.

* * *

Dana lay sleepless that night, mulling over the issues surrounding Fiona's pregnancy. She had wrapped the poor girl in her arms when she heard her news, knowing more than anyone how she would be feeling. Dana did and said all she could to reassure her and to advise that the future was not so bad as she might be imagining. She did her best to prepare the girl for the reproachful, even heartless advice her family might give her. She might be accused of bringing shame on them. In her presence they would discuss her as if she wasn't there. They might discuss various solutions. Some would insist the boy face his responsibilities and marry her. Others would say it was best to keep the matter quiet. Fiona could take a long holiday and have the baby offered up for adoption. Perhaps she would be told to have an abortion. Having long regretted her choice to seek an abortion when she was in a similar situation, Dana gently implied that it would be natural for Fiona to feel secret relief if this decision were made for her. Of course, she needn't do any such thing, if she was prepared for the sacrifices — and rewards — that continuing her pregnancy would entail.

She and Emerald had bundled Fiona back into her car with offers of moral support when the time came to tell her parents the truth. The girl had looked far less tragic by then, but Dana felt dreadfully sorry for her nevertheless.

What kept Dana awake now though was that Emerald's friends were not nearly as sheltered as she had been led to believe. Fiona was her daughter's closest companion. If she wasn't safe, then neither was Emerald.

She knew that Oswald loved Emerald very much, but he was a very conservative person and demanded decorum from members of his family. If Emerald disgraced him, she would never achieve the heights that Dana hoped she would. The Middlebridge empire would pass to others.

She made her decision. She was not prepared to bet her daughter's future on the chance that she might behave differently from Fiona. Her only option was to take Emerald away from her friends. With Emerald's new interest in photography, it was likely that Oswald would agree to her going to New York to pursue it. And there would be no need for him to know Dana's reasons.

CHAPTER 50

September 1951 — Emerald in New York! ran the headlines in her head. She couldn't believe she was there: it all seemed like a script straight out of Hollywood.

The Statue of Liberty, Times Square, the Met. She'd been in a whirl since arriving, leaving her mother exhausted by her increasingly frantic pace.

'Emerald, no,' Dana said. 'I've had enough. You said the Empire State Building would be the last stop today.'

'But *Mother-r-r*, there's this smashing photographic exhibition I simply must see.'

'Tomorrow.'

'And I still haven't signed on for my workshop in photojournalism.'

'Photojournalism! I still really don't know what that is. Anyway, I'm sure it can wait until tomorrow.'

Emerald flushed. 'Applications close today.'

Dana sighed. 'Oh, Emerald. My feet are killing me.'

'You said you wanted to visit NYU — well, that's where I enrol, and the exhibition is in the same neighbourhood.'

'No, I'm sorry. I need to rest before the opera. If you must go, you may go yourself. I'm going back to the hotel.'

Emerald tried to look disappointed.

'You have taxi fare,' Dana added. 'Just give the driver the name of the hotel, the Algonquin, and —'

'*Mother!*'

'Yes, Emerald. You're almost twenty. But this is New York City.'

'Is it *really*?'

'Don't be brazen.'

Emerald kissed her mother. 'Thank you, Mummy,' she said, and spun on her heel, pleased to be on her own at last. They'd been in New York for a week and Emerald had scarcely had a moment to herself.

'And don't be too late,' her mother called after her.

Emerald skipped down the stairs of the subway and proudly found her way to New York University without the need to ask for assistance.

By the time she'd completed her application for the course, it was too late to do justice to the exhibition in Washington Square, but as she was leaving, she found a small exhibition described as *a retrospective* in an adjoining room in the university.

It was an example of some early photography by Ira Ketterman — an alumnus and past benefactor of the university. The pictures were taken in Africa; and Emerald, her interest in Africa recently piqued, was drawn to investigate.

Even a beginner like Emerald could appreciate the photographer's keen eye. His antelopes and zebras had real movement as they crossed the grasslands in clouds of swirling dust, and his birds appeared snap-frozen in flight. In his photos of African dancers, she could almost hear again the flute and drums of the African musicians at the pub in Henley. And Ira Ketterman had an empathetic eye for people's emotions. His monochrome study of a handsome young black native was done with such tenderness it almost brought tears to her eyes. He had caught both the young man's wistful innocence and his obvious fascination with the science he was witnessing.

She was suddenly aware of the lateness of the hour, and hurried back to the hotel, but the old photographs remained foremost in her mind during the long evening at the opera.

* * *

It was clear that her mother was not the least interested in photography, so a few days later, Emerald again tackled the streets of New York alone.

Washington Square Park was crowded with exhibits tied or clipped to makeshift boards.

Most of the photographers were students at NYU; they were pleased to talk — especially to a foreigner — about their work. What remained of the day slipped away, and she'd seen only half of the exhibits. She hurried along the lines to catch a glimpse of what remained as the students started packing up their work.

A young man with a shock of fair hair was bent over a box, packing his work. Emerald stopped. He had lost his moustache, but it was definitely Raph.

He was absorbed in his task and didn't notice her standing, waiting for him to see her. Her heart thumped. What if he didn't recognise her? What if he did, and wasn't interested? Her face still flushed when she recalled throwing herself at him and being rejected.

Raph stood and flicked his hair — now longer that she remembered it — from his face. He glanced at her, held her eyes for an instant, and then resumed rummaging in the box.

Emerald wanted to just die, or to shrivel up, or to flee, but her mortification rooted her to the spot. Then she noticed his small smile and a moment later he stood.

'Miss Emerald Eyes,' he said, grinning now. 'My, my. What are you doing in New York?'

'I ... I'm here with my ... that is, I'm visiting. I mean, I'm here for the season.'

She could have bitten her tongue for mention of the social season.

'Oh ... the season,' he said raising his eyebrows emphatically. But he smiled again. To her relief he passed up the chance to tease her. 'It's good to see you,' he said instead.

He moved towards her and lightly touched her arm. Then he kissed her cheek.

She was disappointed, but wasn't sure what else she could have expected.

'It's good to see you too, Raph. How do you like New York?'

He shrugged. 'Same old capitalist shit as home in England. Worse, in some ways.' He appeared reflective, then shrugged again. 'But what about you? When did you arrive? What are you doing?'

'Oh, I've been here a week or so. All a little boring, don't you think? My mother insists on doing the rounds of the tourist attractions.' She rolled her eyes.

'Ah, I'm glad you have a chaperone. New York is full of evil temptations.'

She smiled with him. 'My mother is too busy touring the sights to worry about me. I'd rather get involved with the arts. Exhibitions like this one. But I missed seeing your work.'

He turned to the packed boxes. 'You did. All packed away.'

He looked at her and she had the almost irresistible urge to pat her hair into place or adjust the collar of her blouse.

'I have a buddy with a pick-up who'll be here soon to help me take this away. If you like, I can show you my work later.'

'I'd like that.'

He thought for a moment. 'Tell you what ... why don't you join me on Thursday? Most of us are attending a rally.' He indicated the students in the park. 'We could make our point to the powers that be, then I'll show you my work.'

'A rally?'

'Yeah. A protest against the new set of labour laws that this fucking government is about to inflict on their workers.'

Emerald knew he was putting her to some kind of test. She didn't flinch at his language, but a public protest against the government was another thing.

'Where is it?'

'We meet there at the arch at two, then we march all the way down Broadway to Times Square.'

He was grinning, daring her to accept. She wasn't going to let him win the bluff.

'So, what you're saying is ... wear comfortable shoes.'

'You'll come?'

'Sounds wonderful.'

'Until Thursday, then.' He kissed her on the cheek.

'I'll be there.'

* * *

The tiered lecture room was almost full. Emerald arrived just as the lecturer began to speak and found a seat near the top row.

'Photojournalism,' he began, 'is a new art form and is distinguished from other forms of photography by the following attributes.'

As he began to scrawl his notes on the blackboard, Emerald looked around her classmates. Most were quite young, no more than her age, with a few grey heads scattered among them. Everyone was taking notes. Emerald pulled a sheet of paper from her handbag and began to copy from the board.

Timeliness, objectivity and newsworthiness, she scribbled.

She learned that photojournalism was not as new as she had thought. It had been recognised as a separate section of photography for a hundred years, but it wasn't until printing processes improved and the enabling technologies of the 35mm camera and flash photography arrived that photojournalism became such a part of news reporting.

Emerald was pleased she'd not skimped on her equipment. She'd bought a Ferrania Condor with a coated 50mm lens and built-in flash synchronisation in London for almost twenty pounds. It was money well spent if she was to sell her work, which was her ambition. The final section of the lecture on commercial opportunities was therefore of particular interest to her. She noted the names of the big magazines willing to pay for journalistic photography.

In his inspirational concluding remarks the lecturer described the qualities of a good photojournalist: 'You must first and foremost be a reporter, able to sniff out a story and make an instant decision to snap the shot. This means you must always carry your equipment with you, though you may be out in bad weather, crushed in crowds or even exposed to physical danger. The true photojournalist is always on the lookout for a story.'

Emerald filed out of the lecture theatre with her classmates, filled with enthusiasm. She couldn't wait to test her ability to find a story and capture it on film. It occurred to her that she had a perfect opportunity in the student demonstration the following day. What better way to test her skills?

* * *

She arrived at the Washington Square Arch just after two o'clock to find a mass of young people surrounding it. There were maybe five hundred or a thousand people there, all of them animated and noisy, many carrying placards. She had no idea how she would find Raph. Then she heard him. He stood on the plinth beside George Washington, holding on to the marble elbow, telling the crowd that they mustn't be intimidated by the police presence.

'We have every right to march,' he bellowed.

A roar of approval went up.

'And we will!'

He climbed down, and the next speaker took his place, imploring the crowd to show solidarity by marching to Times Square.

She met Raph at the foot of the arch.

'Emerald,' he said, sweeping her into his arms and kissing her firmly on the lips. 'Isn't this great?'

Breathless, she spluttered that it was.

'We'll show these bastards that they can't stop the workers,' he added. 'What's that for?'

'I'm going to take some photographs,' she said, proudly brandishing her Ferrania Condor.

'What for?'

'If I get something good, I'll sell it.'

He looked confused.

'To a newspaper or magazine,' she added. 'I've decided to become a photojournalist.'

He burst out laughing.

'Are you kidding? To be a journalist of any kind you've got to have some experience of life. Real life, not a day at the Henley Regatta, or at Royal Ascot.'

'Well, that's what you say, mister big-time photographer.' She put on a brave face, but his derision hurt. 'Everyone has to make a start, and mine is today.'

He stopped laughing. Although she didn't feel she'd convinced him of her sincerity, she was pleased she'd spoken out.

The crowd surged towards Fifth Avenue.

'C'mon,' he said, and dragged her by the hand.

By strength of numbers, the students brushed aside the thin line of police facing the arch. They had clearly underestimated the size of the rally.

The happy throng marched down Fifth Avenue and at 23rd Street were joined by a few hundred more who had gathered in Madison Square. These were older men carrying banners of the various trades unions. They were singing stirring songs about workers united and red revolution. It seemed to Emerald that once the marchers had defied the police confrontation back at Washington Square and nobody was arrested, it vindicated their cause. A euphoric camaraderie was in the air. Emerald wanted to hug everyone, even the crusty old wharf labourers coming in from Madison Square. She smiled at the imagined expression on her mother's face if she could see her now. Then she remembered her camera and began to snap photos at random.

Someone in overalls thrust a pocket-sized bottle of whisky at Raph, who was shouting to the bemused pedestrians and making rude gestures to drivers who planted their hands on car horns to sound their disapproval of the disruption.

Raph befriended a young black man among the unionists, and was soon chatting excitedly with him, sharing the bottle. Emerald was on the other side of Raph, unable to hear much of the conversation as she snapped her pictures.

Raph turned to her. 'Emerald, meet Jelani. Jelani, this is Emerald.'

He had a handsome face and a pleasant smile. His accent was neither American nor British. She asked him where he came from.

'Kenya,' he said above the noise of the crowd. 'I am here on a study tour with the Longshoremen's Union.'

He passed her the whisky and, in the spirit of solidarity, Emerald took a swig. She almost choked. The fumes threatened to burst from her mouth in a fireball, but she held her breath until the burning sensation passed and she could risk speaking again.

She caught snippets of his story in the din. He was on a study tour. He had arrived a week earlier. He was a member of a union in Nairobi. He conveyed all his information in the slightly awed voice of the newcomer to New York. He reminded Emerald of herself. It was an odd feeling, but she felt that she and this left-wing, black African unionist had something in common.

As they came to the corner of Broadway and Seventh Avenue, a solid wall of blue uniforms awaited them, spreading from sidewalk to sidewalk, shoulder to shoulder.

The rally stalled, shifted and changed shape as the battle-hardened union leaders at its head sized up the opposition.

The officer in charge read the Riot Act and ordered the crowd to disburse.

'*The fuck we will!*' shouted someone behind Emerald, and the crowd, roaring their defiance, pressed forwards.

Later, Emerald remembered the mêlée that immediately followed the defiant call from the unionist: the flurry of batons and the placards raised as weapons; a mounted policeman — appearing from nowhere — forcing his frightened animal into the crowd; the horse, cutting a swathe through everyone, towering above her. A section of the crowd fell, or were pushed down, but she remained among the protesters and joined in the shouted oaths and swearing. During all of this, she couldn't remember taking photographs, but someone came from the other side of the police lines, shoved a business card into her hands and shouted that he might be interested in taking a look at what she had, and then was lost in the crowd.

Then she was running as fast as her shoes would allow, with Raph and Jelani beside her. They dodged and dashed down streets and alleys until they were all thoroughly spent and dropped to a doorstep, laughing.

Emerald, who was thrilled to have stood her ground despite her terror, now looked at the business card in her hand. It had the *New York Daily News* banner on it. That was one of the magazines her lecturer had mentioned! She was elated and simply wanted to hug and kiss her friends for sharing the most exciting time of her twenty years.

Raph handed her the whisky and she took a mouthful. Even it tasted better than it had before the confrontation. For the first time she actually felt grown up — though now the fading light reminded her of her mother's warning not to be late home.

When they'd recovered their breath, Raph took them to a hamburger café where he and Emerald laughed at Jelani's rapture in describing what he called the best *nyama choma* he'd ever eaten.

Raph made a great show of concealing the whisky under the table as he added a shot to their Cokes. Emerald held her handbag so that his hands were concealed and instead of feeling guilt over this rule-breaking, she was happy. The photographer was certainly the most thrilling person she'd ever met.

'OK. Let's go,' Raph said after they'd eaten.

'Where?'

'I know a place with great music.'

* * *

It was getting late, as Emerald and Jelani followed Raph down a half-flight of stairs under a flashing sign that said *Dooby's Downstairs*. Even before they opened the door she could feel rather than hear the drum beats.

The door swung open. The club was smoky and filled with a great deal of sound. On the small bandstand were a drummer, a saxophonist, two guitarists and a double bass. Most of the crowd were black, but one white couple were on the dance floor, making some great moves.

'It's African music,' Jelani said above the din.

'Rhythm and blues,' Raph added. 'Some people are calling it rock and roll.'

'It's fabulous,' Emerald said.

Raph took her hand and Emerald joined him on the dance floor.

The sound was like nothing she'd heard before, but she loved the primitive feel of it. Raph was a marvellous dancer, sending her easily into a spin and a slide recovery — drawing her back, close to his body. She found the music easy to dance to, listening to the constant back beat of the drums. Each time he pulled her to him, her heart raced.

When she'd mastered the basic steps, she dragged Jelani to the dance floor with them. Although not as accomplished as Raph, Jelani had a natural rhythm and his body seemed to fuse with the beat of the drums.

'Hey, I want my girl back,' Raph said as Jelani copied the close-in steps he'd seen Raph do.

Raph swept her away into the crush of dancing partners, and kissed her — right in the centre of the crowded dance floor. When she opened her eyes he was grinning at her.

Nobody took a shred of notice.

Emerald loved New York! And she thought she might love this wild, blond-headed communist even more.

CHAPTER 51

Jelani awoke next morning, Saturday, with the memories of the previous day still vivid in his mind. The whole day had been one long adventure. Firstly, there was the march with the Longshoremen, then meeting his new friends, Raph and Emerald, and finally dancing to the music in the nightclub. There'd been nothing in his life to compare with it.

It brought comparisons between New York and Nairobi into sharp focus and, as he lay in bed staring at the fly-specked hotel room ceiling, his thoughts went to Beth. He could tolerate being apart for a week while he worked in Nairobi and she in Lari, but somehow the vast distances that now separated them made the week since they'd seen one another appear so much longer. He missed her.

To lift his spirits he tried to imagine what he and Beth might be doing on a Saturday back in Nairobi. They would go to Jeevanjee Gardens for lunch as usual, then maybe they'd take a *matatu* to the markets at Dagoretti Corner. Or there was the Impala Club oval where they could spend an hour lying together on the grass, watching a soccer match.

He couldn't shake his mood and decided to get out of bed and write to her.

Dear Beth, he began, then tore the page from the pad to start again.

Dearest Beth,

How are you? I am fine. I am enjoying things here in New York. Everything is so big in America. The buildings are very tall. One place must be a hundred floors high. And there is a park here called Central Park, but it is not like our Central Park in Nairobi. No, this one is much much bigger. Even me, I haven't been able to see all of it yet. I have heard there are animals in this New York Central Park. They keep them in a zoo. Can you imagine?

Yesterday I joined the men from the union office, and we marched to Times Square.

He paused to consider how much he should tell her about his union activities. He wasn't sure if she approved of his work. He certainly didn't want to go into the details of his training with the International Longshoremen's Association, much of which covered methods of disrupting government business and organising strikes. Beth wouldn't understand why he needed to learn such things. Also, the longshoremen were accused of being communists by some, and Christians seemed to have a lot of problems with communism. He decided to leave out further reference to the longshoremen; and he also chose to omit the highlight of his day, which was his visit to the nightclub. Dancing with a white girl would be just too much for Beth to understand.

The march was very successful and I have made new friends. Everyone in New York is very friendly to me.

How are you going with your work at Lari?

It troubled him that she thought the Mau Mau were causing trouble for the people around Lari. It was obviously a misunderstanding — they were Kikuyus. He would talk to her some more when he returned home.

I miss you.

Love
Jelani

*   *   *

Emerald sat on the edge of her chair. Across the desk sat the *New York Daily News* reporter who had thrust his card into her hand at the rally, and in front of him was her folio of photographs taken on the day. He opened it and flicked through her prints.

'Nope,' he said of the first — her best, she thought.

'Really? What's wrong with it? I mean, look at the drama. The policeman standing over the fallen student, his baton raised.'

'Too dark. It won't print well.'

'Oh.'

He flicked to the next.

'Nope. Out of focus.'

He paused over the next shot for a while.

'Not bad. Pity you chopped his head off.'

Another.

'Nope.'

And another.

'Nope.'

He shrugged as he stuffed the stack back into the folio.

'Sorry I wasted your time, Miss Middlebridge. You've got nothing I can use here.'

'But I took some great shots! Drama. Action. All newsworthy.'

'I agree. But that's only part of it. The photos have to be useable.'

She took the folio from him, disheartened.

He sighed. 'Look, I'm sorry. Do you have anything else?'

'I've a few of my friends taken at the rally, but they're not what you're looking for.'

'Hey, who's the professional here? C'mon, let me see them.'

She took a smaller envelope of photographs from her briefcase. The reporter flicked through them, stopping at one showing Jelani standing on a park bench, whisky flask raised, and a line of mounted policemen in the background.

'Wait a minute, now. What do we have here?' He held the print at arm's length, studying it from different angles. 'This is more like it. You've captured the spirit of the march perfectly, here.'

'I have?'

'Look at this. A black guy marching with the unionists. A victory salute before the police mount an attack. And the quality's not half bad either.'

Emerald took another look at it. He was right. It was a good shot and, if you didn't know Jelani was just clowning around, it was quite dramatic.

'I'll buy this one from you,' he said.

Emerald was still smiling as she finished the paperwork the newspaper needed to use her print.

The reporter thanked her and led her to the door.

'That's a really good shot, but you'll have to improve your hit-rate if you're going to make a living in this business. One shot out of forty is pretty low. Where did you say you had your training?'

'London. Well … it wasn't really training. I did a couple of short courses on developing and stuff.'

'Developing and stuff. So no actual photography courses.'

'Well, I thought you can't learn that kind of thing. After all, it's art, isn't it?'

'So's architecture, but if an architect doesn't learn about beams and materials, his artistic buildings are likely to fall down. Tell you what you do. You go back to London, enrol in a real photography course, and then apply your art.'

She nodded, thanked him, and left the office.

Being independent and earning a living wasn't as simple as she'd thought.

*　*　*

Sam studied the memorandum of understanding that Joshua Samuels had put together for General Motors' lawyers. It had everything he wanted in it, including a very good price.

'And you say the Bradstreet and Gardiner guys will agree to this?'

'Guaranteed,' Samuels said. 'When I went to the GM head of department, he was pissed off. Those B&G guys got the livin' Jesus beaten out of them by GM. They'd given them a brief to deal fairly with you, but those two young guys thought they'd get cute. I reckon we've won a better settlement as a result. We owe those two turkeys a big thank you.'

'That wasn't my first thought,' Sam said. 'But I'm glad it's settled. What happens now?'

'Formalities. You need to go to Chicago to sign off. There's no need for you to be there personally, and I mentioned that to them, but they want to have some PR pictures taken. You shaking hands with the Vice President. You standing on the production line. It seems like GM want to show the world they are friendly to African countries. Are you able to postpone your departure for a day or so?'

Sam nodded. 'OK,' he said. 'Something's come up on another issue that I have to deal with, but it can wait until I get back from Chicago.'

He thanked Samuels and left the office.

He was glad the General Motors matter was resolved. The *New York Daily News* had carried a photo of Jelani Karura, the beneficiary of his study tour sponsorship, drunk and disorderly while engaged in a communist rally.

CHAPTER 52

Emerald knew she was skating on thin ice. Her mother had been furious with her after her late return from the nightclub, and it had taken a couple of days before things between them returned to normal. Now, as she applied her make-up using the bathroom mirror of their Algonquin suite, she could feel her mother's eyes on her from her seat in the next room. Emerald knew she could push her only so far, and then there'd be a backlash.

In Emerald's view, the trouble was that Dana had wanted her to come to New York to broaden her experiences yet wanted her tied to her apron strings every moment of the day.

They had agreed to compromise. Her mother would allow Emerald her freedom to come and go provided she kept Dana informed of her whereabouts and introduced her to her friends. How Emerald would arrange this, she was unsure; she and her mother had been busy attending balls, tea parties, musical events and art shows. She'd barely had any time for Raph and Jelani but had agreed she would arrange a suitable meeting.

However, she didn't want it to be a formal affair. She would not have her friends run the gauntlet of snobbish hotel staff and management, who insisted on knowing who was coming and going from the hotel. She would make arrangements for Dana to meet them on *neutral ground*.

Emerald gave her mirror image a final inspection, then joined her mother in the adjoining room.

'You look beautiful, dear,' Dana said as she prepared to leave.

'Thank you, Mummy.'

'Have a nice time, dear, and oh, I meant to tell you. I've organised a surprise. You know how you've wanted to see more of America? Well, I've arranged tickets for Niagara Falls.'

'Oh, that's wonderful,' Emerald said, resigned, even though it was clearly her mother's way of keeping her from becoming too involved with her new friends. 'When do we go?'

'In a couple of weeks. We go by train on what they call the *water level route*. I believe it's quite luxurious.'

'That's nice. See you later, Mummy.'

'Bye, darling.'

Despite the trip to Niagara, Emerald was pleased with the way things had transpired. She had gained some degree of freedom — and without telling a lie. She had allowed her mother to believe what she needed to: for example, that Emerald's new friends were female. And if Dana thought that Emerald was spending her time with a group of friends rather than just two, then all was well. Emerald knew her mother had no cause to worry: she knew what she was doing.

Once out of the hotel, Emerald walked smartly to the subway, passing the food stall vendors with their cheery smiles and tantalising aromas.

Today she'd paid special attention to her appearance

because that afternoon she would be alone with Raph for the first time.

She couldn't define the characteristic that attracted her to him, but there was no doubt he had something that made her heart jump when he looked at her, or touched her hand, or — a special thrill — took her into his arms and kissed her on the dance floor, having told Jelani she was *his girl*.

Raph shared an apartment on the Lower East Side with his brother, Kelvin, whom she'd never met. His brother allowed him to stay rent-free and use a spare bathroom as a darkroom. Emerald had not seen Raph's apartment or his photography although he'd promised to show her both since their first meeting in New York.

It would be a special day.

* * *

Emerald pushed the intercom button at the street entrance of the six-storey apartment block.

'Emerald?' came a voice after a short delay.

'Yes. It's me.'

'OK. Come up. Sixth floor.'

A buzzer sounded, followed by a click. Emerald pushed open the door and headed for the lifts.

Raph was leaning in the doorway of his apartment when the lift doors opened. He was casually dressed in cotton slacks and a T-shirt.

'Hello, Emerald Eyes. Come in.'

Emerald took off her hat and put it on the coffee table. The flat was quite large, with two doors off the hall — probably a bathroom and a study, and two more leading off the living room to the bedrooms. She could see the kitchen through a wide opening. A table took up part of the combined dining and lounge room, which was tastefully furnished — not at all what she expected from a person of Raph's haphazard disposition.

'It's a beautiful apartment, Raph.'

'Thanks to big brother Kelvin.'

'Where is he?'

'Hopefully earning enough money to pay the ridiculous rent on this place. Here, let me show you around.'

He took her on a brief tour of the kitchen, bathroom and living room. Although he dismissed her compliments on the furnishings and layout, he took modest ownership of some of the decorative pieces.

'That's an old oil lamp I picked up in Casablanca,' he said of a piece on the mantle. 'And the small weaving I got in Turkey.'

'Wow, Raph ... you've done so much. I'd love to travel the world like you. One of these days I'm going to Africa.'

'Really?'

'To Kenya, to be precise.'

She was ready to tell him about being born there, but he'd dismissed the subject.

He completed the inspection tour with a peep into a half-bathroom where he had all manner of contraptions, glass bottles and lights.

'The photo lab. A mess,' he said, closing the door.

'Well ... thank you for inviting me and showing me around. I've been dying to see your work.'

'Come on then, it's in the bedroom.'

The narrow bed was pushed against a wall leaving the remainder of the space to accommodate a long table and a frame containing large photographic prints.

'Here's the stuff I had on display in Washington

Square.' He spread a few of the prints on the table. They were good. Even with her inexpert eye, Emerald could appreciate the technical and artistic beauty of them.

'Oh, they're wonderful, Raph.'

He shrugged. 'Here's some earlier stuff.'

He opened a large envelope and spread out the prints. They were smaller, about the size of a foolscap page.

'Where was this one taken?' she asked, moving closer to the table and leaning over to study it.

He came in close behind her and peered over her right shoulder. She could feel the length of his body along her side.

'Oh, that's from Oxford. The Henley Regatta. You might recognise ...' he flipped through the prints '... this person.' It was a photograph of her, taken at the regatta, and obviously without her knowledge. She had attended with Peter, Michael and Fiona. It was the day after her introduction to champagne and her crude proposition to Raph, which he had gallantly ignored.

So Raph had been at the regatta but, seeing her there with her boyfriend, kept his distance, biding his time until he found her sufficiently apart from her friends to snap the shot of her standing alone. It was a very flattering picture, capturing her smile perfectly.

She was delighted that he'd secretly photographed her, and even more pleased that he'd kept it all this time.

He remained close behind her and now casually put his left hand on her waist. Her skin tingled under his touch.

'You looked beautiful that day,' he said, whispering into her ear.

As she straightened, she turned into him. He held his position and she was in his arms, kissing him. She felt a rush of excitement, like she'd peeped over the railing of a very tall building. His lips were parted and he touched the tip of his tongue to hers. She felt like she'd fallen off a cliff.

Raph pressed her against the table. He crushed her lips with his and held her so close she could scarcely breathe. She felt him fumble with the buttons on her bodice and then his hand slipped inside her brassiere. His short, sharp breaths matched her own.

Her breasts were alive to his touch. She had underestimated the effect someone else's touch would have on her. She was afraid, as she would be at any dangerous or unfamiliar emotion. It was like a walk in darkness, not knowing what lay ahead, but she was determined to enjoy the sensation until it ended.

She let him undress her, which he did with difficulty, barely able to take his lips from her for a moment. In the end she had to assist him, and then watched, fascinated, as he struggled with his trousers, nearly falling while trying to dislodge a shoe.

He drew her to the bed.

* * *

'Christ, Emerald! Why didn't you tell me you were a virgin?'

'Well ... I didn't know.'

'You didn't *know*?'

'I mean, I didn't know that I should have told you. I thought you'd know I was.'

His chest dropped, letting a slight sigh escape with his breath. 'I'm sorry; I would have been more gentle.'

He sounded repentant, but she couldn't recall him being rough. There'd been only a moment, when the short stabbing pain made her suck in a cry of discomfort.

And after that, she had felt more like a spectator than a participant.

She'd heard girls talk about *doing it*. Some said it wasn't what they'd expected, but Emerald always thought it would be exciting and romantic. With Raph, it hadn't been either. What was the missing ingredient? Technique? She imagined that Raph was experienced in such things. Perhaps if she had more skills herself?

Or was it love that made the difference? Because as they lay there in the deepening shadows of early evening, she had no idea whether she was in love with Raph. How did people know? She thought she had more in common with Jelani, the rather self-conscious young man from a different culture.

'When I go to Kenya, I think I'll look up Jelani,' she said, more to herself than to Raph.

'What are you talking about?'

'I was just thinking out loud that it'd be nice to have someone to show us around.'

'Hey, girl. You're in my bed. Naked. Right? So where do you get off thinking about other guys?'

His outburst took her by surprise and she needed a moment to respond.

'What do you mean *other guys*?' she asked. 'I just mentioned Jelani because we were talking about Kenya and —'

'Don't think I haven't noticed how you two chatter like a pair of magpies when you're together.'

'Raph!'

'And at the nightclub. I could hardly prise you apart.'

She said nothing to this, but in his petulance he'd answered her question — she was not in love with Raph.

And it came as something of a relief.

CHAPTER 53

Emerald couldn't decide what she wanted to do about her friendship with Raph. He had an exciting if dominating personality; he was amusing when he wanted to be; and he could be a lot of fun, such as when they fled the police on the day of the protest march, but he had an unpleasant side to his nature that she'd only just started to see. She wondered if she was attracted more to the idea of Raph rather than to Raph himself.

When she could get away from her mother in the afternoons, she would go to him, full of excitement and expectations, but as soon as they'd made love, he became remote. She wanted to hold him afterwards, to feel his body close to hers. And she wanted him to hold her, but he became restless and irritable. He was uninterested in her thoughts and feelings and plans. Recently, he'd been making more of those snide remarks about her friendship with Jelani; and their petty arguments were becoming increasingly nasty. She wanted to put a little distance between them while she untangled her thoughts. In spite of that, when he rang her at the Algonquin, she again agreed to have lunch with him.

They met in the restaurant near NYU they'd chosen as their regular meeting place.

'Where've you been, dressed like that?'

'What do you mean?'

'That blouse. Leaves nothing to the imagination. Every guy in town can see your tits.'

'I thought you'd like it,' she said, looking down at the blouse.

'It's not what I like to see my girl wearing when she's out on her own.'

'I've only been to my photojournalist class.'

'And that's another thing. What a fucking waste of time that is.'

'It is not!'

'In that whole roll of film at the march — no, two rolls of film — you only had one lousy photo that was worth anything. Why bother?'

'I bother because one day I'm going to earn my living at it.'

'Don't make me laugh. You have no need to make a living. All you have to do is put out your hand and take whatever Mummy and Daddy give you.'

Emerald was about to retaliate again, but held back. She didn't like the way the conversation was going — or the way he seemed to think he could now take control of her life.

'Why are you acting so mean?' she asked.

'Am I? Well, life's like that. A struggle. Rich against poor. Workers against bosses. Privileged against the underprivileged. But you, little Miss Moneybucks, wouldn't know. And probably wouldn't care.'

Emerald had heard enough. She pushed her chair back and stood, blinking the tears of humiliation and anger away.

'You have no right to speak to me that way, Raph,' she said. 'I'm sorry I can't live up to your socialist ideals. You make me feel like a traitor to the human race because my family has money. Perhaps we shouldn't see each other until I'm able to overcome the sin of coming from a privileged background.'

* * *

Jelani sat with Emerald in the rotunda by the lake in Central Park. It was late afternoon, and they had the popular picnicking spot to themselves.

'It made me happy when you called,' he said. 'How did you know where I'm staying?'

'I went to the Longshoremen's offices,' she said. 'I couldn't think of any other way to contact you.' She smiled. 'If my mother knew I'd gone there she'd have a fit.'

'Why?'

'She doesn't approve of unions. Actually, it's my stepfather who doesn't approve and she just goes along with him. Anyway, someone else was looking for you too. The man in your office said a black man wanted to speak with you.'

'Really? Maybe it was Randolph.'

'No, Randolph was the one I spoke to.'

Jelani puzzled over this. He hardly knew anyone in New York. And Randolph was the only black man who knew him.

'Well, I'm glad you called. Raph's coming too.'

'Oh?'

'After we spoke, I called him, and he said he'd love to come.'

Emerald said nothing.

'I didn't think you'd mind,' Jelani said, seeing her uneasiness.

'Yes, of course it's OK. It's just that I didn't know.'

Her response was not as he expected and made Jelani think again about his conversation with Raph. The Englishman had actually said: 'Then I'd better be there.' Jelani thought it was his unfamiliarity with the English idiom, but the conversation became a little strained after that.

'Tell me about Kenya,' she asked him, interrupting his thoughts.

'Why? It is only a small country, so far away,' he said.

'I'm interested. I was born in Kenya. I think it was somewhere near the capital … what's its name?'

'Nairobi. Then you are close to my homeland. I grew up near Embu, not far from Nairobi.'

He told her of his childhood, and it emerged that they'd been born in the same year.

'Eleventh of January, 1932,' she said.

'I don't know the month,' Jelani said, a little embarrassed at his ignorance. 'The Kikuyu don't take much notice of birthdays.'

'I'd love to go there someday. Tell me about where you lived.'

'Ah, now you are asking me something,' Jelani began, smiling. 'It is such a small village. Nobody knows we are there.'

'Tell me anyway.'

'Well … my home is called Kobogi. It's in the big forest, high in the hills …'

He could see the little village with its huts of mud and daub and thatched roofs. Drying racks for the hides. The kids and lambs bleating in their staked enclosure. Children running about, laughing. The wood smoke from cooking fires. Dry dung and damp earth.

'You can see the Aberdare Ranges from the village,' he continued, 'and on a clear day, if you climb the ridge to the north, you can see Kirinyaga. Emma, I tell you, it is so beautiful.'

'Kirinyaga?'

'It means mountain of brightness. The Kikuyu people believe that God lives there. The white people call it Mt Kenya, but oh, it is so beautiful. You must see it if you come to my country.'

'I will, if you take me there.'

He laughed, not sure if she was joking.

'My mother had a maize garden near the stream. And we had many goats. When I was a boy I had to tend them during the day and lock them in the pens at night in case of leopards.'

Then he remembered Kobogi didn't exist any more. His whole extended family now lived on Cook's farm except for those, like Jelani, who'd left to find work in the cities.

'What does your name, Jelani, mean?' she asked.

'It means *mighty* in Swahili.' He smiled self-consciously. 'Maybe everyone thought I was going to grow tall.'

He remembered the fat Ugandan clerk at the administration office and his joke about his first given name, Zesiro — first born of twins. It had never left his mind that he might somewhere have a twin, possibly someone as light-skinned as he.

'But you *are* tall. And very handsome, of course.'

He laughed to cover his embarrassment. Emerald was always teasing him about his appearance.

'Do you have a girlfriend in Kenya?'

'I do.'

'Tell me about her.'

'We met when I was about thirteen or fourteen,' Jelani said. 'Beth was a little younger. Then something happened and she went away.'

'Oh, how sad. What happened?'

Jelani wondered how Emerald, or any white girl for that matter, could ever understand the Kikuyu culture. She would think all Kikuyu were savages if he told her about the old chief's desire to have his Beth as a wife. Sitting in a park in New York made the whole matter of his culture too exotic — too strange for that day and that place. Such stories could only be understood in their homeland.

'It was nothing. Her family ... moved away, that's all. But we're together again now.'

'Wonderful. Have you had a letter from her?'

'No. I don't think it would reach me before I leave.'

'Are you in love?'

He thought about it. He had no doubt that his feelings for Beth were different from those he had for any other girl. 'I'm not sure,' he said. 'How can you know?'

Emerald shrugged. 'If you're not sure I suppose it's not real love. Aren't you supposed to feel something really special about that person when you're in love?'

Jelani shrugged. 'Maybe. Yes, I think so.'

'When you see her, does your heart jump?'

He nodded. 'Yes ... I think it does. Like a gazelle.'

'And when she smiles at you, does it make you feel special?'

'... Yes.'

His thoughts carried him into Beth's arms. And even when I just touch her hand, I want to make love to her, he thought. His heart thumped inside his chest and at that moment he wanted to be home in Kenya with her. 'I miss her very much,' he said.

'That's another sign,' Emerald added. 'It certainly *sounds* like you're in love.'

He hesitated before asking, 'Do you love Raph?'

'Hmm ... I'm not sure.'

Jelani smiled. Emerald had failed her own test. He liked her, but Raph could be difficult at times. Jelani admired Raph's commitment to the union movement, but he didn't like the way he talked to Emerald. He was very demanding of her, and Jelani sensed she didn't like it, although she said nothing. He would have liked to ask her more about her feelings for Raph because in Jelani's view, he was not good for her.

They sipped their drinks in silence.

'When was the last time you went back home to see your family?' she asked.

'I've not been back for so many years, I've almost forgotten them.'

'Don't you miss them?'

He thought again about his family. Every time he'd done so in recent years he resolved to go back to visit them, but then he found reasons or excuses to defer it again. Cook's farm was not Kobogi, which would have made it easier for him, but that, he realised now, was yet another excuse.

'I do miss them,' he said. 'And being here in this great big city makes me miss them more.'

She reached across the table, and put her hand on his arm. 'Oh, Jelani, when you go back to Kenya, you must visit your home again.'

The warmth of her hand on his arm made the skin beneath glow.

'Well ... isn't this a cosy little scene?' It was Raph, who was now standing at the rotunda steps. 'Making a move

542

on my girl, are you, Jelani?' He was smiling, but the smile hadn't quite reached his eyes.

Jelani could see a flash of annoyance in Emerald's expression, and he had his answer about her feelings for Raph.

* * *

'Raph, don't be silly,' Emerald said, withdrawing her hand from Jelani's arm. 'We're just talking.'

'Oh, yeah ... talking about what?' Raph said.

'Well, if you must know, I told Jelani I was going to visit Kenya one day, and he was telling me about it.'

'Kenya? Huh! Another example of Mother England's fucking imperialism.'

'There's no need for that kind of language.'

'Oh, really? Listen to Lady Emerald Northcote-fucking-Middlebridge.'

'Raph,' Jelani said softly. 'You heard Emerald. Please be quiet. She doesn't like to hear you talk that way.'

'She didn't seem to mind it the other day in my bed — did you, sweetheart?'

Emerald coloured; she snatched her hat from the table. Tears of anger welled in her eyes. She blinked them back, determined to be strong. She'd had enough of his crudity and his domineering attitude.

'I'm going,' she said.

'Not until I'm finished,' Raph said, grabbing her by the arm as she swept past him.

'Raph! *Let go*. You're hurting me.'

'Leave her alone,' Jelani said, this time with a hint of threat in his voice.

'This is none of your business, nigger,' he snarled.

Jelani was on his feet in an instant, spinning Raph about and simultaneously landing a roundhouse punch to his jaw.

Raph, stunned, hurled himself at Jelani, who sprang aside, swinging a wild punch that missed Raph by a foot as he went by.

Jelani's slim build gave him the edge in speed and agility over Raph, who was slightly heavier. They sparred; Jelani dropped into a crouch, circling. Raph swung a kick at his legs. Jelani caught his ankle and spun him, throwing him to the ground and then leaping onto his back. He slipped an arm around Raph's neck and tightened his grip. Even Emerald could see that in a few seconds, Raph would be either unconscious or dead, depending on how long and how tight Jelani kept the hold.

'*No!*' Emerald screamed. 'Jelani, stop. You'll kill him!'

He hesitated a moment and then let Raph go.

Raph coughed and choked, spluttering obscenities and threats.

'Come on, Jelani,' she said, dragging him by the arm. 'Let's go.'

She almost ran, dragging Jelani behind her by the hand. He followed reluctantly. His chest rose and fell with deep breaths, as if he was trying to get his rage under control. She'd never seen him in such a state. The young man — normally so shy and quiet — had become a frightening sight. A potential killer.

When they were some distance away from the incident, she drew him to a quiet bench seat away from the path.

'Are you hurt?' she asked.

He looked at his scraped knuckles. 'No,' he said.

'Thank you for defending me. You won't have to worry about Raph any more. That's the last I'll see of him.'

He nodded.

'Mother and I are leaving for Niagara Falls the day after tomorrow, and she's decided that we should leave New York immediately we come back.'

He nodded again. It was hard to read his emotions.

'So, I may not see you after tomorrow ...'

Again he remained silent, studying his clenched fist.

'Unless you can come to see me off at Grand Central. Would you do that for me ... Please?'

'I will be there.'

She kissed him on the cheek. 'Thank you, Jelani. And no matter what, we'll stay friends, won't we?'

He nodded.

'And one more thing.'

This time he met her eyes. 'Yes?'

'I want you to meet my mother.'

'Your ... mother?' His smile faltered.

'Yes. Tomorrow. I promised her I'd introduce my friends and now I have to convince her we have to go to Kenya, so I can see the place I was born. And you, of course. It's OK: we'll just have tea at the Algonquin.'

'You mean that big hotel in the middle of the city?'

'Yes. You'll love it.'

CHAPTER 54

Dana strolled down West 4th Street with plenty of time to spare. They were leaving for Niagara the next day, so she was pleased that her last-minute shopping excursion had been successful. She had an hour or so to kill before meeting Emerald for tea with her friend.

A small banner slung outside an entrance to NYU caught her eye. It advertised a retrospective exhibition of African photographs. She decided to take a look.

Most of the photos were large black and white prints, and the photographer — a man by the name of Ketterman — had been remarkably successful in capturing the essence of Africa as Dana recalled it. As she studied the photos of landscapes and wildlife, she realised most of the collection came from Kenya and, in a flash of recognition that took her breath away, she recognised Sam in the portrait of a young warrior.

Dana's immediate thought was that she had projected Sam's likeness onto this image of a stranger — a Kikuyu man, in full traditional dress — because of a subconscious connection between him and the essence of Kenya that was portrayed in the photographs. But no, it was unquestionably Sam Wangira as a young man.

She leaned closer, raising her hand towards the print, feeling an urge to touch it; to touch *him*. Her fingers hovered near his torso; she remembered the silky hardness of his body. She sensed his maleness and she could smell the scent of wood fire, dry grass and sweat, when he came to her after a long trip from Abyssinia with his horses.

There were others of him. Sam in a uniform — perhaps as a safari porter. Another in a bush shirt, staring into the lens with a look of intense concentration. Something had enthralled him in that moment as the photographer snapped the shot. Her eyes roamed around the gallery. There was a significant portion of the body of work devoted to Sam. Dana went from print to print.

She again contemplated the life she and Sam might have had if she'd sent for him or merely told him she was expecting a child, for she felt sure he would have come to her. Her decision to give up one child to ensure security for the other could be seen, she knew, as brave or selfish.

The passing of twenty years had done nothing to ease her mind. She had oscillated between the two over those years, but she had no doubt that if she and Sam had chosen a life together they would have been shunned by both white and black societies. It was an impossible situation.

No one in her life had affected her like Sam. Merely thinking about him made her old desires, so long dead, stir in their crypts. But it was a thing of the past, and she was surprised that it still had such intensity.

She looked at her little diamante wristwatch. Time had vanished. She would be late for her afternoon tea with Emerald and her friend.

She glanced one more time at Sam the young warrior, and reluctantly headed to the exit.

Emerald had delayed honouring the promise she'd made to her mother about introducing her friends, hoping that the passage of time and their departure for England would make the introductions unnecessary. Now that she had the ambition to visit Kenya, she had a reason of her own to introduce Jelani. Without the derisive Raph, and his caustic cynicism about the wealthy, it would be much easier.

She had made arrangements with Jelani to meet for tea in the Algonquin lobby but the morning was quite fine after two days of showers, so Emerald decided to wait for him outside the hotel.

He arrived on time, wearing a suit. She was pleased she'd worn her hat and gloves, but the suit surprised her. She didn't know he owned such a garment.

She gave him a hug. 'Jelani, you look so handsome. What a nice suit.'

He seemed pleased by the compliment, and looked down at his navy-blue suit, white shirt and blue tie with some pride.

'Thank you,' he said. 'The man said it was almost new. The previous owner only wore it to church on Sundays.'

Emerald smiled. 'Well, it fits you quite well.'

She hadn't dared to ask Jelani to dress conservatively, but now everything would be perfect. Her mother couldn't help but be impressed by his old-fashioned respect.

She led him into the lobby bar with its moulded ceilings, wood panelled walls and large padded chairs. Jelani was obviously impressed by the architecture and ambience. His eyes wandered around the interior as she chose a table.

They took their seats on opposite sides of a glass-topped coffee table. Jelani sat on the edge of his chair and looked uncomfortable.

Almost immediately a waiter appeared at Emerald's side. That's service! she thought, but the waiter was grim-faced.

'I'm sorry, madam, but I am unable to serve you.'

'What do you mean you can't serve us? I'm a guest in the Algonquin.'

'I am aware of that, madam. But madam should also be aware of our service policy.'

'Whatever are you talking about?' She was becoming flustered now.

His eyes didn't leave hers, but he inclined his head in Jelani's direction. 'We are unable to serve the ... dark person, madam.'

Emerald stared at him for a moment, uncomprehendingly. Then she looked at Jelani, sitting opposite, with an expression of utter embarrassment.

'But he's African,' she offered, lamely.

'I'm sorry, madam. It's the hotel's rules.'

'Oh,' she said. She could think of nothing else to say. All her recently found confidence and sophistication abandoned her. She was a mumbling, stumbling child again, being admonished for a misdemeanour. She summoned all her dwindling courage and stood, almost meeting the diminutive waiter eye to eye.

'Well,' she said in a huff. 'I shall speak to my mother, I mean, the *manager* about this ... this ... outrage!'

* * *

Jelani now had no heart for a meeting with Emerald's mother. It had been difficult enough to come at all, but with the white waiter looking at him as if he were an unwanted dog, he just wanted to flee. In Kenya, he railed at patronising white settlers and the paternalistic white administration. In America it had been worse. On the streets of New York, whites looked at him as if he carried a bad odour.

Emerald had tears in her eyes and he felt sorry for her.

'I didn't realise there could be such monstrous restrictions in a place like New York,' she said. 'I'm so sorry, Jelani. I ... I'm going to do something about it, so it can never happen again.'

But her mortification made no difference to Jelani. He'd had similar snubs in the past and shrugged off his feelings of unworthiness by reminding himself he was a proud Kikuyu warrior, and a member of the feared Mau Mau. He would not let these white men make him feel shame.

He smiled. 'Don't worry, Emerald. I'm not upset. He said it was the hotel's rules.'

'Still ... It's not good enough.'

'Come on. If it makes you feel better, I could still meet your mother.'

She took his arm and squeezed it.

During the walk from the elevators to the door of her suite, Jelani had second thoughts. Being with a white girl in Kenya was unthinkable and he knew that Americans held similar views about friendships between blacks and whites. Before he could devise an excuse, they were at the door and Emerald swung ahead, dragging him in by the hand.

Jelani stood in the middle of the sumptuously furnished room, its chandelier dripping with twinkling stars of cut glass, never more aware of the stark differences between his world and Emerald's.

Dana heard Emerald's voice from the door. With a touch of annoyance she quickly checked her appearance in her bathroom mirror. Emerald was supposed to wait for her in the lobby bar. She straightened her dress, touched a hand to her hair, and then walked into the sitting room.

Her first sight was of Emerald, visibly upset. But it was her friend who most astonished Dana, and took her mind from her daughter's distress. He was black. And a Kikuyu. At that moment she couldn't explain how she knew, but of that fact she had no doubt.

Emerald introduced him. Dana spluttered a welcome, recovered her decorum, and invited him to take a seat while Emerald began a breathless explanation of the embarrassing confrontation in the lobby bar. She went on to say that Jelani was from Kenya and that he was in the USA for only a short period.

Dana tried to concentrate, but she couldn't take her mind off the Kenyan — Jelani. And she couldn't stop taking furtive glances at him. He was a handsome young man, light-skinned for an African, with intelligent eyes and an engaging if somewhat reserved smile.

Hearing Emerald's rendition of the incident in the lobby bar made her annoyed with the waiter and the hotel's policy, but as she gathered her thoughts, she became more annoyed with Emerald for not telling her that her friend was black. If Dana had known, she could have warned Emerald of the likely outcome. It was her daughter's irritating habit of trying to shock her that had led to the embarrassing situation in the first place.

She put her aggravation with Emerald to one side. 'Would you like tea? I have coffee, but it's the hotel's — that appalling *instant* variety, I'm afraid.'

He said he'd like tea and she went to the alcove where she'd had the hotel staff place a tea trolley and urn. It was an opportunity for her to take stock of her thoughts because the young man's appearance had taken her off guard. She realised she knew nothing about him and that as a responsible parent she should. How had they met? Why was he, a Kenyan, in America? What was the extent of their friendship?

She made the tea and, as she placed the cups and accoutrements on the tray she realised that she had completely forgotten the visitor's name. A further embarrassment for the poor young man. The morning was deteriorating rapidly for Dana.

When she returned with the laden tea tray, she said, 'I'm sorry, it's completely unforgiveable of me, but in all the confusion, I've missed your name.'

She heard his answer, but instead of laying the tea tray on the table, she remained standing, staring at him. It was Sam's image that came to her mind. It was the reason, she now understood, why she knew Jelani was a Kikuyu. But the resemblance was strong — almost too strong to be explained by tribal similarities.

'Mother? Are you all right?'

'What? Yes, of course,' she said. 'Jelani, would you care for milk or sugar?'

She'd been unnerved, but now realised the unsettling thought that Jelani was the image of Sam was because of the photographic collection she'd seen at NYU only a couple of hours before.

She dismissed her thought as sentimental nonsense, and poured the tea.

*   *   *

Jelani was relieved to leave the Algonquin. His face again burned with embarrassment as he recalled the incident with the waiter, and he avoided looking into the lobby bar as he passed. There couldn't have been a worse precursor to his meeting with Emerald's mother.

He knew it would be stressful. He was never comfortable in the presence of whites, and Emerald's mother had an aura of importance about her from the outset. It was obvious that she was a strong woman, attractive and with olive skin and short brown hair tinted with honey-coloured strands. And those green eyes — almost as green as Emerald's — seemed to be fixed upon him from the moment he stepped into the hotel suite. She was obviously suspicious about his friendship with her daughter.

Now he wondered how he'd ended up in such a friendship. He'd felt an attraction towards Emerald since their first meeting, but it was not like the feelings he had for Beth. Beth excited him; and through this period of separation from her, he felt increasingly sure he loved her and wanted to be with her forever. Emerald had a different but also special quality. They seemed to share the same feelings about many things. She was close to his heart rather than to his body.

Thoughts of Beth made him yearn for home. New York was exciting and new and he'd learned a lot while he'd been with the Longshoremen, but he'd had enough.

He'd promised to see Emerald off to Niagara Falls the following morning. He would then go to the Longshoremen's offices and tell them he wanted to go home.

With his resolution now in place, he picked up the pace of his step. He felt better already and his mind turned to Beth and Kenya — to his love and his home.

CHAPTER 55

As Jelani approached in the taxi, the imposing structure of Grand Central Station, with its rampant stone horses and classical carved figures, stood out from the surrounding lesser buildings like a colossus.

He paid the fare and entered the grand hall, which was awash with people scurrying over the large flagstones. His task was to find Emerald among that swirling mass of humanity, but his eyes were drawn up the high stone walls to the sunlight falling through the beautiful arched windows in long slanting shafts. He stopped to admire it.

'Oh! *Pole sana*,' Jelani said as he bumped into someone.

'*Sawa*,' the man replied, also in Swahili, then, in surprise, 'Karura!'

It was Sam Wangira.

'I need to talk to you,' he added before Jelani could recover from his surprise.

'What about?'

'I've been looking for you to talk about your scholarship,' Wangira said.

Jelani paused. 'I haven't time,' he said. 'I'm here to meet a friend.'

'I saw your picture in the paper. You were in that march down town.'

'What is that to you?'

'It's against the rules of the scholarship. No political associations. It's in the forms you signed.'

'It wasn't political: it was a union march.'

'Organised by the Communist Party of America,' Wangira said. 'I haven't sent you over here to be brainwashed.'

'Your white friends in the government sent me, not you. You're the one who is brainwashed — you're just a pawn in their game.'

'And you're an ungrateful fool.'

Jelani stiffened at this. He took a deep breath and looked away, tightening then releasing his balled fists. He caught sight of Emerald, standing in a column of sunlight with her camera pointed at the gilded clock above the information booth.

He turned back to Wangira. 'I don't have time for you,' he said. 'But it's you who is the fool. And a Kikuyu who will stand by and let the British take everything from us is a traitor.'

Jelani turned from Wangira and headed in Emerald's direction.

* * *

Sam watched Jelani weave a path across the crowded concourse. He shook his head. What a shame, he thought. He's smart, but he'll be eaten up by the likes of Chege Muthuri and his pack of thugs.

Jelani went to a dark-haired and very attractive white girl carrying a camera. The pair made tentative contact. She gave him a brief kiss on the cheek as friends might. They looked like relatively new friends rather than lovers.

Well, well, he thought. A budding romance between the fair-skinned, white-hating Mau Mau and a green-eyed white beauty.

Sam edged closer to them — close enough to see her more clearly. She was certainly a beauty, with stunning green eyes that shone as she animatedly spoke unheard words amid the rumble of background noise. She pointed to various parts of the building. Then she pointed to a corner of the concourse, and took his hand. He held back, smiling, resisting her pleas.

He couldn't quite place it, but there was something fascinating about her — something familiar, although he felt sure he'd never seen her before. It drew him even closer to them. He studied her movements; and when she inclined her head the gesture transported him twenty years into his past. It hadn't been her appearance — although now that he looked at her more closely he could see a certain resemblance — but it was her mannerisms that reminded him of Dana. The way she propped a hand on her hip and inclined her head to the opposite side as she tried to convince the young man; it was Dana, all those years ago.

Her point of view apparently prevailed and she led Jelani away towards the far corner of the concourse.

He smiled, remembering that getting her own way was another of Dana's compelling personality traits.

* * *

'Jelani! You're here,' Emerald said, giving him a peck on the cheek. 'Thank you for coming. And look, isn't this a beautiful building?'

'It is. See how high those windows are.'

'I've been busy with my camera. I tried a three-second time exposure from the end of the concourse. You know ... to give the impression of the movement in here.'

Jelani had no idea what she was talking about, but nodded.

'And I've taken shots from all around the outside. Mother's exhausted and went to sit.' She pointed to the far end of the concourse. 'See? There she is.'

Jelani peered in the direction she was pointing, but could see nothing except people dashing in all directions.

'We have a little time before the train leaves. Would you like a Coke?'

'That's a good idea.'

'Well, I have to tell Mother first. Come with me.'

'Me? Maybe I'll go to the *duka*, I mean the café. I'll buy the drinks.'

'No, I'll lose you. Just come. It'll only take a minute.'

Jelani was trapped again. Again he had to confront Emerald's mother and again he felt uncomfortable about being under her intense scrutiny.

* * *

Dana watched Emerald move around the cavernous interior of Grand Central Station, snapping pictures. She was pleased that she'd found an interest in photography, and her ambition to be a photojournalist — whatever that really might mean — was touching. But her enthusiasm had its disadvantages. She was exhausting, dragging Dana all over the place, waving her camera at every conceivable architectural aspect, nook and cranny of the building.

Emerald was standing in a pool of light falling through the high glassed space between the stone columns. Dana was proud of her daughter and, without any false vanity, could see her likeness in her. It was as if the gods had sucked up some of Dana's essence and breathed it into her beautiful daughter.

She then saw Jelani arrive and Emerald kiss him. Dana was startled. She craned her neck to keep track on them as the crowd passed by, obstructing her view.

There was a period when she couldn't see them at all, then suddenly, just as she stood to get a better view, they were coming towards her. She resumed her seat and tried to compose herself.

Emerald arrived, dragging Jelani behind her. 'Mother,' she said. 'Jelani's here. We're going to get a Coke.'

Jelani greeted her and, holding his extended right forearm with his left hand, offered the handshake that Africans employed when greeting those they respect.

Dana was touched, and took his hand, smiling. 'Hello, Jelani,' she said.

'Hello, Mrs Middlebridge,' he replied.

As he leaned towards her his pendant fell out from his open-necked shirt and dangled on its leather thong in front of her eyes. It was a fang — a lion's fang, she thought — in a silver clasp.

Dana stared at it for a long moment, still gripping Jelani's hand.

'Mother? What is it?'

'What? Oh ... nothing, dear,' she said, releasing Jelani's hand.

'We won't be long,' Emerald said, and whisked Jelani off into the crowd.

Dana watched them go. She knew that fangs, claws and the tusks of small animals such as warthogs were common items of jewellery in Africa. However, Jelani's was an unusual piece in that it was set in a silver clasp: it was very similar to the one she'd placed around her infant son's neck when she sent him away shortly after he was born. To think Jelani's pendant had been hers was a preposterous notion, but she had to be sure.

She stood to follow the young pair strolling across the paving stones. Emerald was swinging her hips, chatting to Jelani with her hand tucked under his arm. She could remember being her daughter's age and the body language was telling. Here was a young woman heading — no, rushing — into a romance.

Dana took a step in their direction, but decided to resume her seat. They'd be back, and she would then have some questions to ask.

* * *

Jelani finished his Coke and watched as Emerald slowly sipped hers.

'We'll stay in touch, won't we, Jelani?' she said.

'We will … yes.'

'I haven't asked Mother about visiting Kenya, but I plan to. It's so important to me, but I don't want to ask her yet. She seems a little out of sorts. Will you meet me there?'

'Of course.'

'And introduce me to your beautiful Beth?'

He smiled at her memory. 'You will love her, just as I do.'

'I know I will.'

She made a slurping sound with the drinking straw.

'Oops!' She giggled. 'We'd better go,' she said, lifting her handbag and slipping her arm through his.

Jelani felt apprehensive as he walked with her back to where her mother waited. He didn't like making farewells. It was not in his nature, nor those of most of his countrymen, to make a public display of emotion and he hoped that he could show Emerald how much he'd miss her without too much embarrassment. He would rather have parted the previous day at the hotel.

Dana was waiting for them and stood when they reached her.

'We must hurry, darling,' she said to Emerald.

'I suppose so,' she said reluctantly. Turning to her friend, she said, 'We'll write, won't we, Jelani?'

'We will … yes.'

'And we'll discuss that other matter, won't we?'

'Yes.'

'What other matter, dear?' her mother asked.

'Oh, it's nothing, Mother. I'll tell you later.'

Dana appeared unhappy, then, businesslike, said, 'I'm sorry, Jelani, we must go. It's been very nice meeting you.'

'It has also been very nice for me, Mrs Middlebridge,' he replied.

'There is one thing I must ask you before I go,' she said. 'I noticed you have a very interesting pendant. May I enquire where you bought it?'

Jelani's hand went to his throat. The offending pendant was there as it always had been, but now he regretted wearing it. He couldn't reveal the details of his personal story, but he also couldn't lie to Emerald's mother. 'It … was a gift when I was a child.' He fingered it nervously.

'It's beautiful. May I take a closer look?'

Jelani held the pendant out for her perusal. Dana took an age to inspect it.

'A gift, you say. From whom?'

'*Mother*,' Emerald said, moving to Jelani and placing a protective hand on his arm.

'Oh, I know dear, I'm being very nosy. It's just that I'm interested in this type of thing. And I'm sure Jelani won't mind sharing his story with us. Do you, Jelani?'

Jelani tried to smile, but his heart thumped against his ribs. 'I can tell you. But it's a very strange story.'

* * *

Dana grew more and more anxious as Jelani revealed the story of his pendant in excruciatingly small steps. Each word tightened the grip on her heart; each detail focused a scorching searchlight on the part of her life she had hidden for twenty years.

He was born in 1932, before the long rains.

January or February.

He never knew his real parents.

He was adopted.

He was brought to his parent's village by a stranger — a friend of his real mother.

Dana found her voice. 'Do you know the names of your real parents?'

'No.'

'Do you know anything at all about them?'

At this, Jelani dropped his gaze to the floor, but before he answered, he met her eyes again. 'I was told my mother was black and my father was white.'

It's not him after all!

'I'm sorry, Jelani,' she said. 'You must think me very rude asking all these questions, but as I'm sure Emerald has told you, I lived in Kenya for some years, and I have a fondness for it.'

Jelani nodded and a reticent smile crept back to his lips.

'And I'm sure you were loved by your new parents,' she said in conclusion.

'She was a Ugandan woman,' Jelani added, unbidden.

Dana felt the blood drain from her face.

'Ah,' Emerald said. 'So you're Ugandan, not Kenyan.'

'No, she brought me from the coast. From Lamu.'

Dana stepped back; she took the arm of the bench seat to lower herself onto it. Her heart raced and she felt weak.

Emerald quickly took the seat beside her. 'Mother, what is it?' she asked. 'Are you feeling unwell?'

Dana couldn't answer. She stared up at Jelani.

At last!

The question that had lurked at the back of her mind for all those years was answered. *He lives.*

How could she be so blind? Those features. There could be no doubt about his real father. It was Sam's strong jaw and keen eyes that she'd noticed when she first met him. Tribal similarity, indeed. Now she knew the truth: it was Sam's eyes that looked down at her with kindness and concern.

'You don't look well, Mrs Middlebridge,' he said, standing beside Emerald.

'She doesn't,' her daughter said.

'My, my!' Dana said. 'Is it warm in here? I feel a little ... well, a little faint, yes. But ...'

She looked again at Jelani. She knew she was embarrassing him, but she couldn't take her eyes away. Jelani was her son. Of that she was certain. And now Lamu, and Amina, and Cahill, and the pain — the unbelievable pain of separation — flooded back. Two babies and a kind of Solomon's choice. Should she keep both infants and damn her life — their lives — or should she sacrifice raising her son herself so that each baby could have a chance at a life she could never offer either of them on her own?

She had kissed the soft down on his head the day she handed her baby son to Amina, to be given to an unknown woman in the distant Kenyan highlands. A knife had pierced her heart. She prayed that Sam never found out what she'd done to their son.

She raised a hand towards him. To touch him. But she couldn't. Of all the ironies with which fate could punish her, this was the ultimate. Having found her son after so long, she still couldn't claim him.

The details of her life in Kenya had to remain a secret. Oswald was an extremely conservative man. If he ever found out his wife had become pregnant to two men within days of each other, it would shock him to the core and end their marriage. If so, it would also end Emerald's chance to inherit his company. More importantly, if she declared herself to her son, it would mean revealing to Emerald the lie she had lived for twenty years. And although doing so could reinstate her son in her life, it might mean losing her daughter.

Jelani had his hand resting on Emerald's shoulder. It could be a simple show of support for a friend in a difficult situation, or it could be a sign of intimacy. If so, there was an even worse calamity approaching. If she'd read the signs correctly, Emerald and Jelani were falling in love. The prospect galvanised her.

She stood and took a deep breath. She had no choice. She must reveal to Emerald and Jelani the truth of their birth. It would mean telling her daughter, who had no reason to suspect her mother was anything but a staid and upstanding member of London's society, that she had concealed a hideous secret. How Emerald would receive that information was unknowable, but she had to tell her.

'Emerald,' she said. 'We need to ... talk.'

'Now? We'll be on the train together for hours. I'd like to talk with Jelani until then.'

'We're not leaving. We're going to talk.' She turned to Jelani. 'And Jelani, I want to talk to you too. But not here. We're all going back to the Algonquin. We'll go up to our suite, and ... talk.'

* * *

Utter silence prevailed as her mother, sitting in the large armchair in the corner of the room, told her story. Emerald felt she'd left her body and floated to the curlicued plaster ceiling rose, hovering there among the chandelier's pieces, a witness to the bizarre events unfolding below. It was simply inconceivable that she and Jelani were twins. Her eyes met his and she saw the same shocked disbelief in them.

Emerald's first thought was that her mother was playing a cruel joke, but she immediately rejected it. Nobody, least of all her mother, could be so malicious.

Her next thought was: How is such a thing possible? Although she'd asked the question she was almost too afraid to hear the answer.

She flushed as her mother replied using a number of medical terms, most of which required their own elaboration. But her explanation, delivered in a soft toneless voice, was not credible. In fact, it was surely quite *in*credible. Emerald would not dispute the physiology of it. Stranger things happened in science. She'd heard of a camera that could develop its pictures right before your eyes. But the very idea that her mother — her very proper, prudish, punctilious mother — could have been impregnated by two different men, was absolutely astonishing.

When Emerald regained her concentration, seated not five paces from her mother, she could see how Dana's face had lost its tension and the knot of frown lines on her brow had melted. Her eyes were mostly lowered, but when she briefly raised them to gauge if a point she'd made had been understood, they were full of tears. Her usually tight lips had softened, and almost trembled as she described the other man — the black man she'd had an affair with. She loosened her grip on her hands; and one went to her hair where it found a loose strand. She absent-mindedly twirled it around her fingers like a schoolgirl lost in her studies.

The woman sitting opposite Emerald, talking wistfully of the mistakes of her younger years, was not the mother she knew. She'd become tentative and vulnerable; she was flawed and human in every respect.

After overcoming her shock, Emerald's heart went out to her. She wanted to reverse the roles, to comfort her mother and to tell her everything would be well.

She then began to wonder what could have motivated her to reveal such humiliating secrets. Certainly, her disclosure would mean Dana could start to build a relationship with the son she'd abandoned as a baby. Any mother would find it difficult to pass up such an opportunity. But her mother could have confessed all immediately she recognised Jelani's pendant. When Dana mentioned her regrets that she and Jelani had not had the opportunity to grow up together, as brother and sister, Emerald got her answer. Her mother thought they were lovers, or at risk of being so!

Emerald could scarcely contain her smug smile at the revelation. She knew her mother better than she realised. It was typical that she would be so sure of herself; so intent on reading Emerald's emotions that she couldn't see beyond the most obvious truths. Emerald liked Jelani, very much, but she had no romantic inclinations towards him. She was also quite sure that Jelani was of a similar mind.

* * *

Jelani's first reaction was to doubt that he correctly understood what Dana had said. He shot a glance towards Emerald, and when her eyes met his, he knew he had heard correctly.

His second thought was that Dana had mistaken him for another person, one who also had a lion fang pendant. They were, after all, not uncommon. She had jumped to her conclusion as to his identity merely because he was light-skinned.

He shook his head as she talked, trying to gently dissuade her of her unbelievable notion. He'd heard that many older English women were prone to a condition that caused them to become fixed on an idea that defied logic. In Kenya, the whites said it was the African sun. But the Africans joked that the women simply had too little to keep them occupied.

He kept shaking his head until Dana correctly described his birthmark — the one on his ankle. He then had to face the terrible fact that she had identified him and that she — a member of the English tribe and the sworn enemies of his people — was indeed his mother.

He found it difficult to concentrate after this until she'd finally reached the end of her long spiel. He exchanged glances with Emerald, who appeared as shocked as he, though at least her father and mother had been married. Presumably they were, or had been, in love. But what of Dana and his father? Perhaps he had been conceived in a brief burst of passion, the unwanted consequence of a moment of wanton lust long since regretted. And Emerald's parents were of the same tribe. Jelani's father was unknown, and might never be found.

Beth came suddenly to mind. She would find this bizarre situation very difficult to understand. If his mother could act in such an uncivilised manner, would she be concerned that he might also exhibit similar tendencies? And what effect would his bad blood have on the children they planned to have together?

'Do you know where Jelani's father is now?' Emerald asked.

'No.' Turning to Jelani, she added, 'I'm terribly sorry, Jelani. Can you ever forgive me? He doesn't know about you; and I've lost touch with him. I have no idea where he is or what he's doing now.'

'Is he a Kikuyu?' he asked, straining his voice to surmount his emotions.

'Yes, he is.'

It felt strange to dislike this man — his father — a man he'd never met and knew little about. What he did know was enough. He couldn't respect a man who could tie the grass with another man's wife. He couldn't believe how, at a time when the whites were already moving the

Kikuyu from their traditional land, he could lower himself to lie with the enemy.

He took a deep breath and slowly let it escape. He'd had enough of New York before he learned of this horrible truth. Now he felt exhausted, weighed down by the facts of his life. He needed time to think. Part of him wanted to find his father, but he was afraid that, in spite of his behaviour in the past, he might find him a person he could admire.

'What's his name?'

It was Emerald. He'd noticed that she often thought and acted an instant before him.

'It's a fairly common name, I'm afraid,' Dana said.

'What is it?' he asked after a moment's hesitation.

'It's Wangira. Sam Wangira.'

Jelani stared at her. Whatever sympathy he'd felt for her dissipated. In its place was contempt. She had not only abandoned him as a baby, she'd begotten him through a man he knew and already greatly disliked.

'Do you know him, Jelani?' Emerald asked.

'... No.'

'Perhaps you could find him. Will you look for him?'

'No.'

CHAPTER 56

1952

Jelani rolled onto his back, panting in the stifling heat of his hut. He turned his head to Beth. Her body glowed in the faint light escaping the blanket he'd hung at the window. Her eyes were closed and her small rounded breasts rose and fell rhythmically.

It still amazed him how Beth was able to be two different beings: the modest Christian assistant to Deacon James of the African Inland Mission; and the hot-blooded woman who could transport him to the heights of passion.

It had taken time for them to become lovers. Beth's Christian principles intruded every time an opportunity arose until, three months before this, he asked her to marry him. Beth agreed, and the transformation was immediate and breathtaking. Whenever she was able to come down to Nairobi they would spend most of their time together in bed. In the dim light of morning, the heat of the afternoon or at night, they made love. Jelani was in heaven.

He made his long-awaited return to Cook's farm and won his parents' blessing for the marriage. The next steps had been complicated. In traditional Kikuyu culture, each family would appoint a representative to haggle over the details of the marriage and, importantly, the bride price. Much beer and goat meat would be consumed during protracted negotiations until agreement was reached. The wedding day could then be fixed. This was not the case with Jelani and Beth.

Beth's Wambui family had foresworn traditional customs. They insisted the marriage be in the Christian tradition; and they would therefore pay no bride price.

The Karuras' negotiator thought it a scam to avoid handing over a few goats, and stonewalled for weeks.

Jelani pleaded with his parents to reach a compromise. Beth did the same with hers.

Only the day before, Jelani had received word that both families were finally in agreement. There would be a modest dowry paid so long as the ceremony was performed by Deacon James in the mission's church. At Lari.

He had just two duties remaining. Firstly, he had to reveal to Beth the story of his family.

'Beth, are you awake?'

'Hmm?'

'I have something to tell you.'

'Uh-huh.'

'My mother is coming to our wedding.'

'Of course she is, Jelani.'

He sighed. 'No … I mean my *real* mother.'

Beth raised herself onto her elbow and turned towards him with a stunned expression. 'I don't understand.'

His explanation, rambling and at times emotional, took him nearly an hour. Beth listened in silence, only occasionally asking a question for clarification.

'How do you feel about it?' she asked when he'd finished.

'I feel terrible. It was bad enough to suspect I had a white father, but having a white mother and a black father is somehow much worse. And it's very strange having a white sister.'

'How do you feel about her?'

'I like Emerald. She was so nice to me.'

'And your mother?'

He thought about it for a long moment. He wasn't sure how he felt now. At first he'd hated the idea. 'But that's not so important,' he said. 'What I need to know is how do *you* feel about it?'

'I'm ... sad. Very sad.'

'Yes, I can see it, but we mustn't let it spoil everything for us. Beth, please, I can't change who my parents are. I'm the same *me* I was when we fell in love. It needn't stop us going ahead with our wedding.'

'Jelani, hush,' she said, putting a finger to his lips. 'I'm sad for you. Not for us. Your story hasn't changed anything for me. I'm just glad you could tell me. It can't have been easy. Nothing's changed between us. I love you. You love me.'

He took her hand in his and kissed it.

It had been a difficult story to tell, but easier than revealing his second secret — his support for the Mau Mau cause. It occurred to him that it shouldn't be hard to reveal something he truly believed in. He'd had some trouble understanding recent reports about Mau Mau tactics, and many people were questioning some of their activities, but in a few days he would join Dedan Kimathi on a retribution raid that would restore the Mau Mau's reputation as a champion of the black Africans.

* * *

It was shortly after midnight. The light of the new moon lay in dappled pools on the forest floor. Behind the column of ten men, the Aberdare Ranges rose like a black colossus against the star-studded sky. All was silent except for the familiar calls of night birds and the occasional manic screeching of a tree hyrax.

Jelani walked immediately behind Dedan Kimathi, careful to place his feet only in his leader's footprints. A false step, a stumble, or the snap of a twig could alert a Home Guard patrol.

The Home Guard had proudly proclaimed they'd rid Ndiara — the farm lands at the foot of the Aberdares — of the Mau Mau. It was one of the reasons Kimathi chose that area for his raid. The people needed to see that the Home Guard were not the force they claimed to be. The more important reason they were there was to wreak havoc on white settler, Ben Wiggerink.

Wiggerink callously exploited his squatter-labourers. He beat them, cheated them of their wages, and deprived them of their fair share of the crops they helped him raise. But the complaint that aroused Jelani's ire most, and which allayed any reluctance he might have had to extract retribution from the settler, was his treatment of his female workers. Wiggerink was a womaniser and one not averse to using his position of power to bully the women into his bed. The situation was all too reminiscent of Chief Muraimu's lustful claims on Beth.

Kimathi gathered his men together where the road to Ndiara town swept along the edge of the forest. They had two farms to cross before Wiggerink's. One of the Mau Mau's spies — a cook on a neighbouring property — was there to meet them. He carried a burlap sack from which he took five crudely made torches. The strong odour of paraffin confirmed their purpose.

'What news do you have for us?' Kimathi asked the man.

'The house is in darkness,' he said.

'And the Home Guard?'

'To the north of the town.'

'Good. Then we proceed.' Turning to his men, he added, '*Ithaka na wiyathi.*' Land and freedom.

Their guide led them quickly and silently through the night until they reached a darkened farmhouse in a field of ripening maize. The house had a high thatched roof sitting above a squat, rectangular farmhouse with a small veranda leading to the front door.

Kimathi studied the farmhouse and its outhouses for many minutes before he issued his orders.

The men lit their paraffin-soaked torches, and slipped silently into the night. Moments later the maize crop was ablaze and flames rose from the outhouses.

Kimathi handed a torch to Jelani.

'Go!' he ordered, pointing to the house.

Jelani ran through wafting clouds of smoke, barely able to see.

He heard a shout from the house and saw the settler on the veranda, wearing long white flannel pyjamas. He held a shotgun to his shoulder. A moment later there was a flash from the barrel and a loud report. A roar of pain came from the direction of the outhouses.

Jelani ran down the side of the house and smashed a window with the butt of his torch. A scream came from within as he prepared to toss the burning staff inside. He hesitated a moment, and out the corner of his eye saw the man with the gun at the corner of the building. Jelani dashed away. The shotgun boomed, and a large chunk of timber exploded from the wall beside his head.

He flung the torch onto the thatch and bolted.

The settler swore as he reloaded.

Jelani's shadow ran ahead of him, intensifying as the flames from the tinder-dry roof turned the night into day.

* * *

Dana sat at the window with the letter in her lap, watching the rain. Her thoughts were not on the puddles forming among the rose bushes, but far away. She was in the saddle, Dancer beneath her, and the rolling hills of the Aberdare Ranges climbing above her into the ice-blue sky. A lone rider comes into view over the distant ridge, driving a herd of magnificent Abyssinian horses. She nudges Dancer, who leaps into a gallop. Moments later, their horses standing side by side, she leans over to him, and they kiss.

The letter had taken her back through the years. Jelani had written it in schoolboy English, advising her of his impending marriage and formally inviting his *English family* to attend.

'To Kenya!' Emerald had said when Dana showed her Jelani's invitation. 'Oh, Mother, we simply have to go. Think of it — an African wedding!'

There was no doubt they'd have to go, and for more than one reason. Since returning from New York nearly a year ago, she'd often thought about it. Her time with Jelani in New York had been short: too short. There would never be enough time for a mother to mend the damage inflicted by abandoning her son at birth, and she sensed Jelani's reserve. They'd had three days together before the union could organise his flight. He had been very polite and tried to show how pleased he was to learn of his family, but his mood was sombre and always fell short of any sign of affection. Dana knew how strange it must be for him and her objective was to help him understand the circumstances of his birth and, if possible, to forgive her and build a bond from there. There had been insufficient time for that in New York. Maybe with more time, and in Kenya — his home — she might have more success.

In spite of her decision to attend the wedding and see her son again, she'd already begun to feel apprehensive about being so close to Sam. If Jelani had changed his mind and found his father, what could she say to him to explain her behaviour? Perhaps he would despise her for keeping his son from him for all these years. It would be an understandable sentiment, but to have him feel that way about her, after having once been so close, would be extremely painful.

* * *

It was October: the dark clouds warning of the imminent arrival of the short rains scuttled across the Nairobi sky, alternatively plunging the assembled mourners and surrounding tombstones into deep shady hollows and, just minutes later, bathing them in brilliant sunlight.

The assembly was to honour Chief Waruhiu, a Christian and a strong supporter of British law and order, who had denounced the Mau Mau at a public meeting at Kiambu in August. Six weeks later, his Hudson was stopped at a roadblock and three gunmen, posing as police officers, shot him dead in the back seat.

Jelani stood with Chege Muthuri, representing the Trades Union Council. Jomo Kenyatta stood with them, signalling the new solidarity between the militant pro-independence union movement and Kenyatta's Kenya African Union.

The new governor, Sir Evelyn Baring — a handsome man, resplendent in his navy-blue British military uniform, white gloves and belt, shoulder epaulets and high-crowned helmet decked out in ostrich feathers — presided. His address was intended as much for the British and local press representatives, who had attended in numbers, as it was for the mourners and representatives of all the major community, political and industry groups. Nobody dared not attend as it was feared it would mark them as sympathisers of the movement that had so blatantly and brutally murdered the elderly Kikuyu chief.

On the other side of the open grave, among other members of the Legislative Council, stood Sam Wangira. It was the first time Jelani had seen him since learning he was his father — a fact he'd refused to make known to him. Wangira so diametrically opposed Jelani's point of view on almost everything that he couldn't identify with him. Wangira was a member of the oppressive government. His claim that he represented the views of all Kenyans, but particularly all black Kenyans, was hollow. Jelani knew if that were true he would be standing beside the freedom fighters dying in the jungles in defence of their rights.

Jelani had to admit Wangira was, however, an impressive sight in his fine suit, white shirt and tie. No wonder the whites gave him grudging respect.

Baring enumerated Waruhiu's many fine qualities, including his outspoken criticism of the Mau Mau and undeniable loyalty to the government, then he turned to the matter of what he intended to do about the escalating violence. The press corps scribbled notes and cameras flashed.

'Since I have only recently arrived, I have exercised patience while I take counsel from my predecessor and other advisers. It would never do to react intemperately to atrocities such as the murder of Chief Waruhiu, no matter how one may personally feel.' The Governor's brow furrowed. 'But the British government will not stand idly by while its citizens are threatened, beaten and murdered by ruthless and criminal gangs. There are those who have suggested that the Kikuyu have foregone all advances and reverted to godless savagery. Well, I can't accept that. I know that there are as many loyal subjects among the Kikuyu as there are among all the tribes of Kenya. And I say to those loyal natives: continue to resist the bullying tactics of the few. The Kenyan government, and the British people, will not abandon you.'

A round of thin applause followed his speech, and the Anglican archbishop of Nairobi concluded the service.

The Governor accepted the good wishes of various people as they drifted off to awaiting government and official cars. Jelani and Muthuri stood by as Kenyatta wished the Governor good luck.

Immediately behind Kenyatta was Sam Wangira, who shook the Governor's hand.

'Mr Wangira,' Baring said. 'I received your proposal and I'm giving it some thought.'

'Thank you, Governor. I believe I can be of some service.'

'I don't doubt it,' Baring responded. 'Leave it with me for a day or two, will you?'

Wangira nodded. 'Certainly, Your Excellency.'

Baring moved away with his entourage of officials and, with Muthuri and Jelani at his side, Kenyatta stepped in front of Wangira, blocking his path.

'How does it feel,' Kenyatta said, 'to be a running dog of the oppressors?' He spoke in Kikuyu so the white journalists would not understand.

Sam narrowed his eyes, looking first to Muthuri and then Jelani.

'No need for you to use your communist rhetoric on me, Kenyatta,' Wangira replied defiantly. 'I'm a Kikuyu, and a loyal Kenyan.'

'You have a strange way of showing it, my friend. In fact, you've been rather strange ever since you were a child. Strange ideas. Strange way of life.'

'There are many ways to express loyalty,' Wangira said. 'I don't feel the need to murder innocent people to prove my point.'

'Nor do I, but others do. And it certainly makes the British press aware of our cause.'

'Didn't you learn anything while overseas on your junkets?' Wangira said. 'Don't you realise that the Mau Mau are doing damage to our fight for independence?'

Kenyatta scoffed. 'Since when has independence been your cause? You're a supporter of the foreign invaders.'

'I'm a supporter of Kenya for the Kenyans: white and black. And I was fighting that fight while you were trolling through Moscow's bars cadging vodka.'

'How would you propose we go about winning our freedom if not by fighting for it?'

'Not by dehumanising people, as the Mau Mau are doing. Peaceful protests and constant pressure will win it for us. Just as Gandhi did it.'

'You're a dreamer, Wangira,' Kenyatta said. 'The British will never give up.'

'They will. They have no choice,' Wangira said. 'The Atlantic Charter is our ticket. It was signed by the Allies even before the war ended. The Americans agreed to help the Europeans in the war, provided they agreed to give up their colonies after the peace.'

'If that's the case, why are the Europeans holding on so tightly?'

'Libya is already independent. Egypt is about to follow. There's talk about the Sudan and other Arab countries following within a year or so,' Wangira said.

'Commendable. But what about Kenya? Why are the British still here?'

'This fellow Baring has been sent here for two purposes: to finish the Mau Mau and to bring in self-government. But he can't do the second until he completes the first. Can't you see? As long as the Mau Mau continue to hold out, the British won't grant us independence. Look, Kenyatta, you can use your influence with the Mau Mau to stop the bloodshed. And you must if we are to get what we all want.'

Kenyatta's laugh boomed in the silence of the cemetery.

'Now I know you're mad, Wangira. First point: I deny having any influence with the Mau Mau. Second point, and more importantly, you're just a puppet in this whole sham of a government. Worse than that, you actually believe your own propaganda.' He turned, adding as they departed, 'You make me sick!'

Jelani looked back at Wangira, who stood with his hands thrust deep into his pockets, and a look of exasperation on his face.

The whole conversation had been illuminating for Jelani: he hadn't realised that Sam Wangira had many similar thoughts. He was hopelessly optimistic of course, and had a different view on how to reach the goal, but his goal — independence — was essentially the same as Jelani's own.

* * *

A fuzzy sliver of moon languished behind a film of smoke haze. Over the last few days many Kikuyu huts had been torched to set an example to those who had refused to take the Mau Mau oath. As a consequence, the oathing ceremony that night in the Mathare slums was attended by a large number of new recruits. Jelani was invited as a witness.

It was the first ceremony he'd attended for some time; he was surprised by the changes that had been made. The arch of rushes framed by arrowroot and sugar canes remained, as well as the bowls of traditional food, but the space that night was adorned with figures made from bundled grass and others crudely carved from green timber taken from the forest. At the centre of the clearing among the rough sheet-metal and packing-case huts was a section of a tree trunk with its limbs entwined in a tight embrace, very suggestive of copulating lovers.

One unfortunate goat was lashed into a cradle in the clearing but just outside the cast of the firelight were the remains of another, its viscera and blood already poured into earthenware pots. Its skin was cut into a single long strip to bind the initiates together as had been the case with earlier initiation meetings he'd attended.

The ceremony began, leading to the original oath, but this time the celebrant added another. The assembled men held a ball of earth to their abdomens and recited: 'I swear by my blood that I will fight to protect the sovereignty of our holy soil that the white man has taken from us. I will strangle, shoot or stab him. I will trick him and do him harm whenever I am able. I will kill his wife and defile his daughters. I swear I will never break this solemn oath and if I do may I die and all of my family die a painful death.'

The assistants doused the kerosene lanterns, leaving only the light of the fire to show what happened next.

The first of the men drank from his bowl of blood, goat excrement and bile, then approached the female goat that was bound to the cradle and, to Jelani's utter horror, proceeded to masturbate until he had obtained an erection. He then inserted his penis into the goat's vagina. Each man did the same in turn, reciting the words: 'I will kill anyone opposing this movement,' as he went about his obscene task.

Jelani stood in stunned disbelief and was only vaguely aware of what followed. He left the clearing like a man who had seen the devil. Soon he was beyond the firelight and into the surrounding darkness. He leaned into an open drain and retched.

A touch on his arm made him jump.

'Come with me.'

It was Chege Muthuri.

Jelani was mortified that he'd been discovered in a moment of weakness, but Chege seemed to have other things on his mind. He led Jelani to a small bar on the edge of the fetid alleys of the slums.

Chege ordered two bottles of Tusker in a disorienting echo of their earlier meetings. Jelani took a mouthful of the beer. 'The ceremony tonight ...' he said, pausing to choose his words.

'Yes, there were many there. And why not? Who has the power to resist taking the oath when the Mau Mau tap him on the shoulder? Have you seen it, Jelani? I mean the horrible death that comes to those who resist them. Wives and family too.'

'But what has happened to it?' Jelani asked. 'Why must the oathing ceremony include that ... that disgusting act?'

'That's what I must talk to you about. So much has happened recently. It started when you were in America. There's been a change of leadership. The young ones in the movement want to step up the battle. Kimathi and his type. They seem to think that the more vicious they are, the better they can control everyone. Each one is striving to outdo the others in perversity. The movement's now under the influence of these mad young ones. Each new leader introduces even more disgusting things.'

'But why?'

'I agreed with the strategy initially ... binding recruits closely to the movement. But these things go way beyond that.'

'Why are you telling me this?' Jelani asked, the full import of Chege's disclosure now dawning on him. They were breaking Mau Mau rules by talking about the oathing ceremony at all, let alone critically.

'Because I can't believe in it any more. I must get out. And you must too. The movement has lost its way. I now believe there'll be a civil war, Kikuyu against Kikuyu. And not only that, the war will end any chance we have for independence.'

Muthuri reached under his jacket and pulled out a cloth bag and put it on the table.

'I want you to take this,' he said. 'Get rid of it for me.'

Jelani felt the outline of the handgun through the bag. He slipped it quickly into his pocket.

'Why have you needed this?'

'It's not important. Just get rid of it. Tonight. Take it out past the national park. Throw it in the river.'

'You know how dangerous it is for us to talk like this,' Jelani said. 'How long have you been thinking this way?'

'I spent some time with Sam Wangira working on the scholarships. He's always been a man I could respect. Ever since he set up his small bank for the farmers.'

'What do you mean?'

'Wangira came back from America years ago with money. I don't know how he got it, but he started a bank, making small loans to people in the bush. My father was one of them. Wangira loaned us enough money to tide us over a bad spell. It was a pity he lost everything in the Depression.'

'He loaned his own money to our people?'

'He did. And lost it. But he must have found more so he could set up the scholarship program.'

'I thought it was government money.'

'No, it was Wangira's. Didn't you know? I suppose not: he's not one to sing his own praises.'

Jelani realised he didn't know Sam Wangira at all. It made him wonder what else he had assumed, incorrectly, about his father.

* * *

Sam sat across the wide mahogany desk from Governor Baring, watching him tap his elegant, steepled fingers together in thought. The sleeves of his steel-grey suit coat rested at precisely the correct length above the exposed inch of his white shirt cuffs.

'We can certainly use the kind of intelligence you are offering, Mr Wangira,' the Governor said. 'Our troops have an impossible task, scouring the forests for the Mau Mau. It's like trying to find a needle in a haystack. Or more correctly, many needles in a haystack: Kimathi, Kaggia, Mathenge and all the others. I don't mind admitting that when I accepted this commission I had no idea of the scale of the conflict. The Aberdares alone cover nine hundred square miles! And then there are the foothills of Mt Kenya too. As far as we know there are more than twelve thousand terrorists scattered throughout that area, in as many as fifty groups.' He shook his head. 'It's impossible to cut off all supply lines and starve them out. We have to find a way to focus our resources.' He was thoughtful again. 'You say you enjoy the confidence of the ordinary Kikuyu out in the bush,' the Governor said. 'Exactly why is that?'

'I am well known among them. Many years ago I set up a modest loans fund for farmers, small landholders and graziers. Mainly Kikuyu. These days I suppose you might call it a rural bank, but a small one.'

'What happened to it?'

Sam shifted in his seat. 'It went bust in the Depression.'

'I see. And you believe you still have the goodwill of that community?'

'I'm sure of it. If they didn't trust me, I wouldn't be able to get the information I have already received.' He paused. 'And if I couldn't trust them, I'd be dead within a week.'

Baring studied him for a moment.

'Mmm ... yes,' he said, then dropped his eyes to the proposal Sam had prepared for him. 'You've asked for quite a budget.'

'If love of the crown isn't enough to motivate people to risk their lives, it will have to be greed.'

'And you suggest you should be a member of the Colony Emergency Committee.'

Sam knew it would be the most difficult point for the Governor to accept. The committee was headed by General Sir George Erskine, whom Prime Minister Churchill had given full command over the colonial, auxiliary, police and security forces. Other members of the committee were the nominal heads of each of those forces. Baring himself attended most meetings.

'It's essential,' Sam said. 'Otherwise I shall have to withdraw my offer.'

Sam watched Baring closely. His features remained unchanged, but he stiffened ever so slightly.

Sam continued: 'As a civilian, but more importantly, a member of the Legislative Council, I feel no obligation to become involved in the conflict. Nor can you order me to do so. I am offering my services voluntarily as a means of ending this war as quickly as possible. As you yourself have noted, Governor, the haystack is enormous. I can gather information on the movement of the Mau Mau from a dozen different sources scattered all over the Aberdares and Mt Kenya. But I won't risk my life in some academic exercise. If my information is to be useful, it must be coordinated with Erskine's proposed operations. The only way I can achieve that is to be part of that committee.'

Baring smiled thinly. 'Don't misunderstand me, Mr Wangira. Courtesy dictates that I discuss with General Erskine any new members of the committee. I'm sure there won't be a problem.'

He stood, indicating the meeting was over. They shook hands when the Governor came around from behind his desk. He placed a hand on Sam's shoulder as he escorted him through the outer office to the door.

'It's a very decent thing you're doing here, Mr Wangira ... Sam,' he said, giving Sam's shoulder a brotherly pat. 'If we had more patriotic Kikuyu chaps like you, loyal to Britain and the Queen, we'd have these Mau Mau animals, these so-called freedom fighters, on the gallows by now.'

Sam turned to him. They were now alone on the wide veranda, surrounded by expansive lawns and manicured shrubbery.

'You're right, Sir Evelyn, I am a patriot. But a Kenyan patriot. I am completely supportive of the Mau Mau's objectives of land rights and self-government. Our only point of disagreement is the right means by which to achieve them.'

He walked down the steps of Government House, leaving Baring on the veranda, tight-lipped and fuming.

CHAPTER 57

A knock on the door of his cabin woke Jelani shortly after midnight. The previous evening had been long and demanding with the meeting of union members running late into the night. He was groggy with sleep; he lay there for a moment unsure if he'd heard the sound or dreamed it. The knock came again and he was instantly awake.

A member of the Home Guard, a Luo by the look of him, stood at the door.

'Yes?' Jelani said. 'What is it?'

The reservist pulled a notebook from his pocket and flicked open a page.

'Are you Karura?'

'Yes. What is this about?'

'The sergeant said I'm to bring you to Fort Hall Road.'

'What for?'

'Sergeant Boothby just said to tell you to come and then shut up.'

Jelani mumbled that he should wait while he put on some clothes.

In the car, Jelani nervously wrung his hands. He desperately wanted to know why he'd been collected in the middle of the night and what was happening on Fort Hall Road at that time of the morning. The Home Guard was a paramilitary force consisting of black Africans, led by white officers, some of whom had criminal convictions. Many of them were callous thugs, pleased to be paid to inflict misery on their fellow humans. They used torture to extract a confession from anyone they suspected was a member of the Mau Mau and brutally beat people who stood in their way or complained to the authorities about their tactics.

'What's this about?' Jelani asked again.

'The sergeant said to just bring you, and that's what I'm doing.'

Jelani's first concern when the man appeared at the door was Beth, but she was in Lari, where she should be quite safe.

If it was about his association with the Mau Mau, then he was in serious trouble. Torture and incarceration in one of the notorious concentration camps outside Nairobi was likely.

Maybe it was about the union. Some leaders of the movement, Chege Muthuri in particular, had begun to warn their members to resist pressures from the Mau Mau and to support their unions instead. It was the main item on the agenda of the meeting at the Ainsworth Bridge earlier that night — Chege had made his strongest condemnation of the Mau Mau yet.

The guardsman drove past the meeting place at the bridge over the Nairobi River and continued along Fort Hall Road to the end of the tarmac where a number of vehicles were parked with their headlights trained onto a featureless mass on the side of the road.

The driver took Jelani by the arm and led him to a burly Home Guard sergeant.

'Who are you?' he asked.

'He's Karura, sergeant.'

'Did I ask you, *kafir*?' he snarled.

'I'm Jelani Karura.'

'Good. Come over here.'

'What do you want of me?'

'Just do what you're bloody well told, and come over here.'

He took Jelani to the focus of the headlights. The lump was a body covered by a gory sheet. The sergeant pulled back the sheet and asked Jelani if he could recognise the man.

Jelani was blinded by the headlights. He shielded his eyes and peered at the mangled mess on the roadside. He felt sick to the stomach. The body appeared to have been run over by a truck. He turned quickly away.

'How could anyone recognise that? Why do you think I can help you?'

'You're a union man, ain't you?'

'Yes, but —'

'Well, this is one of your mob. The car is registered to the Transport and Allied Workers' Union, and he's wearing a Trades Union Council badge on his shirt.'

Jelani strained his eyes against the glare. There was a mass of torn flesh and bone where the face should be, but he recognised the watch. It was Chege Muthuri.

'My God ...' he said. 'It's my boss, Chege Muthuri.'

'Muthuri,' the sergeant said. 'Are you sure?'

'Yes, I'm sure. W-was it an accident?'

'Hah!' the sergeant said. 'Not unless you call a twelve-gauge to the face an accident.'

'Who would do this?'

'That's what we want to know, but I can guess. Have your blokes been stirring trouble with the Mau Mau?'

Jelani remembered his conversation with Muthuri in the *duka* a few weeks earlier, and his boss's speech the

590

night before. Fort Hall Road was on Muthuri's way home. Whoever did this was at the meeting and followed him until they reached this quiet part of the road. He felt sick. And angry.

How could Kimathi turn so quickly against Muthuri? Were they also suspicious about Jelani in view of his close association with his boss? They could be watching him speaking to the police right now. They might have spies among the Home Guard. He looked around. Dozens of men moved about in the darkness. Any one of them might be listening to his conversation.

'Do you have anything that might help us find the person or persons responsible for this?' the sergeant asked.

'No.'

The sergeant shook his head. 'I thought as much.'

He closed his book and slipped into his pocket.

Jelani wasn't sure what to do. He waited until the sergeant turned back, surprised to see him there.

He gave him a firm push in the chest.

'Go on,' he snarled. 'Get out of here. You're all the same ... too shit-frightened to talk.'

* * *

The dimly lit *duka* at the end of the tarmac on the outskirts of Naivasha was quiet when Sam entered. It was the night before the civil servants' payday, and only a handful of men, each as shabbily dressed as Sam in his patched farmer's overalls and felt hat, sat sipping their cheap, illegal grog.

He spotted Collins Mutisa — his most important source of information west of the Aberdares. Mutisa was a double agent, feeding information to Sam for cash, and to the Mau Mau for security. As a Kisii, he was a fringe dweller, never entirely accepted by the predominantly Kikuyu Mau Mau. He trod a very dangerous line, syphoning favours from each side. He was grateful to Sam because his loan had saved him from ruin in 1927, though he ultimately lost his farm when the local chief cheated him out of his title. Thanks to the income he received from Sam, he was able to rent a small house in Naivasha for his family, and to ease the pain of his memories with *changa'a*.

Sam joined Mutisa, who was impatiently tapping his fingers on the rough timber of their usual table.

'*Jumbo.*'

'*Habari.*'

Sam needed Mutisa, but didn't like him or approve of what he did. He was impatient to hear whatever the spy had found in recent weeks, and be gone.

'Have you heard anything?' he asked Mutisa.

'Oh-oh, *bwana*,' Mutisa said with an ingratiating smile. 'Are we not friends? Ah? And is it not true that friendship needs warming before comes business?'

Sam was irritated, but called for two drinks, and they sat in silence awaiting them.

When the drinks arrived and Mutisa had taken a thirsty swig, Sam again asked his question.

'Kimathi and his gang have moved camp,' Mutisa said.

'Do you have any details this time?' Sam asked.

'I do. They are camped a day's march west from Barako, on the swampy land to the north of Mt Kinangop.'

Mutisa had never been able to get exact details before, and it was timely. General Erskine now had at his disposal nine Lincoln heavy bombers on loan from the Royal Air Force. The existing Harvard light bombers had been chosen because they were slow enough to fly low over the mountainous terrain without overshooting their targets. They carried only eighteen-pound bombs that did little more than scare Mau Mau and animals alike. The Mau Mau soon learned to stand at the base of the largest trees to avoid injury. Because of their low flight paths, a few Harvards had been lost when strong downdrafts caught them, meaning the Mau Mau could spread the rumour that they had brought one down with their primitive rifles.

The Lincolns carried one-thousand-pound bombs, enough to blast the largest trees out of the ground, but dropping them from a greater height required better coordinates. Sam would pass this new information on to Erskine as soon as he returned to Nairobi.

'Anything else?' Sam asked.

'Lari. It is becoming a hot place.'

'What do you hear?'

Mutisa took a swallow from his glass and coughed. 'I hear there are many men from the mountain gathering there.' His voice was rough from the raw alcohol. 'They are waiting for something and then they will make a big problem in Lari.'

'What are they waiting for?'

'I don't know. They keep very quiet about this. I don't think the Mau Mau soldiers know about it. If they do they are afraid to talk, but when it happens Lari will be in big trouble.'

'They have chosen Lari because of Chief Luka,' Sam said.

Mutisa nodded, and took another drink from his glass, emptying it.

The village of Lari, perched on fertile farming land above the Great Rift Valley, was a mixed community of loyalist Kikuyu under Chief Luka and landless squatters sympathetic to the Mau Mau cause. The white government had compulsorily acquired the community's original land in Kiambu in 1940 for use by white farmers. Many Kikuyu refused to leave their farms, resisting the acquisition by force, but they were eventually beaten and gaoled for several years. Meanwhile, Chief Luka and his loyalist followers, who had cooperated with the administration, received first choice of the land at Lari that was offered in compensation. By the time the antagonistic farmers were released all the land had been allocated and a simmering animosity had continued between the two groups ever since. Occasionally, the resentment burst into attacks and counter-attacks until the police imposed a return to the uneasy peace.

'Do you know when it will happen, this big trouble?'

He shook his head. 'No. Nobody will speak of it.'

Mutisa lifted his glass and pointedly studied it.

'I'll see you again a month from now,' Sam said, pushing his untouched glass towards Mutisa. He then pulled some money from his pocket, tossed the notes on the table and left the *duka* through the back entrance.

* * *

At the next meeting of the Colony Emergency Committee, Sam reported the Lari situation to General Erskine, who thought Chief Luka's one hundred and fifty well-armed members of the Home Guard would be more than adequate to dissuade the Mau Mau from attempting anything serious.

'We've never seen any sign that the Mau Mau can muster more than a score of men,' he told Sam.

'I have a number of reports from people who are afraid there is a major build-up of Mau Mau forces in the Lari area.'

'Alarmists. Excitable people who imagine a Mau Mau under every banana leaf.'

Sam knew Erskine well enough to know he would resist any advice Sam offered. He'd been difficult to deal with since Baring cajoled him into letting Sam join the Colony Emergency Committee.

'General,' Sam said. 'I deal with all sections of the Kikuyu, not just those who support your views. On both sides of the fence I hear about groups of strangers coming in from the bush, camping for a day and then moving on. They make none of the usual courteous approaches. It's as if they are sizing up the situation. Many people are living in fear of a blood bath.'

Sam also knew that going behind the General's back would further alienate him, but he was so sure there was imminent danger, he could not afford to take chances. 'I've spoken to Governor Baring about it,' he added.

The General studied him for moment, straightened his shoulders, and sniffed.

'I'll talk to General Hinde,' he said in a measured tone. 'He may be able to send a company of the KAR up there.'

* * *

The white community of Kenya waited breathlessly for the predicted massive uprising from the Mau Mau, but it didn't come. In October 1952, Governor Baring had gazetted a State of Emergency, banning the Mau Mau. Although Kenyatta had made a speech in Kiambu condemning the Mau Mau, police arrested him, and the military purged the city, arresting nearly two hundred men. Even Sam thought this was extreme. The outcome of this trial was foregone, as it was well known within government circles that the trial judge had recently been awarded an unusually large pension.

By the early months of 1953, many began to suspect that the Mau Mau threat was an exaggeration and the uprising would remain a series of minor skirmishes and cruel attacks on farm animals — all of which would soon be mopped up by the strong British military presence and the local Home Guard.

In March, Sam heard that the newly arrived contingent of the King's African Rifles was preparing to decamp from Lari. He rushed to Nairobi. In a heated exchange with Erskine, he asked if the General wanted to have the massacre of defenceless farmers on his conscience.

'I'm fighting a war on a hundred different fronts, Wangira. I can't afford to tie up a company of men waiting for an attack from a dozen or so bushies that never eventuates.'

Sam took a deep breath. He knew of Erskine's record in the Second World War, and his intelligence work in Egypt and India, but he also knew it could obscure his understanding of the Mau Mau's unconventional tactics, which were more like those used during the First World War by General von Lettow-Vorbeck in Tanganyika. The experts were starting to refer to it as guerrilla warfare.

'Since talking to you last, I now believe there are significantly more Mau Mau and their supporters involved.'

'Even if there were a couple of hundred, the Home Guard and the KAR can handle it.'

'Make that thousands.'

'What?'

'There may be over two thousand men surrounding Lari right now, General. You must order the company back there.'

Erskine stiffened; and Sam cursed his choice or words as he saw the General's blood rise.

'Listen to me, Wangira,' he growled. 'I've tolerated your interference to appease Baring, but if you think I'm going to run my campaign on some ... some ... piece of jungle scuttlebutt, you're howling *fucking* mad!'

Sam stood, silent, before the fuming Erskine, angry at himself for handling the testy general so clumsily. He'd lost his chance to influence him and, as a result — if the rumours were true — hundreds of innocent people in the Lari area were at dire risk. He could only hope that he'd been misinformed, for there was now nothing anyone could do to prevent a massacre.

*   *   *

Jelani left a union meeting early to see Beth before she left Nairobi that morning. He'd lately been troubled that he hadn't yet told her of his association with the Mau Mau. He'd promised himself he'd do so before their wedding, but there was now a complication. Recent events, including his fear that Chege Muthuri had been murdered by the Mau Mau, meant telling her was harder than ever — but he knew that time was running out. Today he would have to start the explanation and, if the initial discussion went as well as he'd hoped, he'd tell her of his involvement and his doubts, and hope she'd understand.

'The bus is late,' Beth said, after greeting him with a kiss. 'Maybe you should just leave me here. You're meeting your family in an hour.'

'No, I need some time to talk to you.'

'Of course. Oh, I do wish I could be there when they arrive, but I have to see Deacon James about the arrangements for the wedding.'

'It's all right,' he said. 'My ... mother will understand.'

'Now, let's sit and talk,' she said, leading him to the bus shelter, where they sat as she waited for him to begin.

The silence lengthened until it became pronounced.

'I'm going to miss you,' he said at last.

'Oh, that's sweet. But you're coming to speak to Deacon James tomorrow, remember? Today's the twenty-sixth. We get married in exactly a month.'

'Yes.'

'And Chief Luka.'

'Chief Luka?'

'Yes. Didn't I tell you? He wants to talk to you.'

'Probably to lecture me.'

'What do you mean?'

'Everybody's heard his speeches. Babbling on the radio about loyalty and the evils of the Mau Mau.'

'Well, they *are* evil, aren't they?'

'No! I mean ... there's a lot of talk about attacks on innocent people. But how innocent are they? Some white farmers beat their workers. They use them like slaves. And they treat the women very badly. Well ... so I've heard.'

'What do you hear?' she asked.

'The Movement, that is, the Freedom Struggle Association, is trying to win our land back. Kikuyu land.'

'Freedom Struggle Association?' she said. 'They're the *Mau Mau*, and they're attacking innocent people. Even Chief Luka. Deacon James says he's had death threats from them. We have to keep the King's African Rifles in Lari to protect him, and us.'

'Those Lari people have been fighting for years. You can't blame the Mau Mau for that.'

'Are you defending murderers?'

He stopped short. All his carefully constructed arguments seemed to have leaked out of his head; and the doubts that had lately arisen came flooding back. Were the Mau Mau simply murderous thugs? There was no proof they'd killed Chege, but how could anything be proven in such a case?

'Can't you see we have to do something to get our land back?' he answered lamely. 'What if we want to farm our own land when we're married? My family have lost all their land — land we've had for as long as anyone can remember. And your family are the same. Until we Africans have our independence it can't change. We will never get justice until we chase the British away.'

Beth frowned, trying to choose the words. 'We may not have justice, but it's ... it's just how things are these days. Isn't it?'

She searched his eyes, hoping, he suspected, that he had the answers. But he didn't. What once had been an article of faith — that the Mau Mau were on the side of justice — was now hopelessly compromised.

A blast from the arriving Lari bus cleared people from the kerbside.

'There's my bus,' Beth said. 'I don't know what's come over you, Jelani. Yes, of course we need somewhere to live. And if you want some land when we're married, I'm sure Chief Luka will look after us.'

She stood and headed towards her bus.

'I don't want Chief Luka to look after us,' he said, following her. 'I want what is ours. We must be able to stand on our own feet.'

She turned back to him from the step.

'Your right to have your initiation. Justice. Freedom Struggle,' she said with a sigh. 'You've always fought for one cause or another, haven't you?'

He watched her move down the aisle to find a seat at the window.

She rubbed the grime from the glass and looked down at him, smiling.

I love you, she mouthed.

CHAPTER 58

Dana stepped from the taxi and ran her eyes over the Norfolk Hotel. Everything had changed. The big gum trees that towered over the oblong turret were gone, and a macadam surface and cobblestone gutters had replaced the dusty, unmade street. A rather grand gabled edifice now ran from the stone arch above the entry steps to the edge of Government Road.

A doorman appeared, giving Dana and Emerald a snappy salute.

'*Karibuni*,' he said, greeting them, then helped the cab driver unload their suitcases from the trunk.

In the foyer they were met by a distinguished-looking man with wavy grey hair, safari jacket and a paisley cravat.

'Good afternoon, and welcome to the Norfolk,' he said. 'I'm Brian Durrows, the hotel manager.'

Dana did the introductions and Durrows invited them to the veranda bar for a cold drink while their baggage was delivered to their rooms.

'Thank you, Mr Durrows,' Dana said, as they took a table fronting the street. 'It's nice to see that some things don't change. The Norfolk's service has always been excellent.'

'You've been here before, Mrs Middlebridge?'

'I have. Many years ago. Emerald and I are here for a wedding.'

'Marvellous. Would I know the happy couple?'

Dana smiled. 'I don't think so. They're … from out of town, but I'm not sure exactly where.'

'Oh, I do hope they're safe. I've heard there's a lot of Mau Mau activity in the regions — especially up around Lari. In fact, we have quite a few families from Kikuyuland staying with us because of the security problems. You're the only overseas visitors we've had in months. Terrible for business.'

'There's quite a bit of talk about it in the English press too,' she said. 'But I assume it's all newspaper talk.'

'Not at all. The government's taking it very seriously. General Erskine's called in two battalions of fusiliers. He has ten thousand troops in all. And a squadron of Lincoln bombers.'

'Surely not!'

'Indeed, madam. Families are being murdered in their beds by servants who have been with them for decades. Nannies strangling the babies in their care. I tell you, there's not a settler who'll employ a Kikuyu these days. People are demanding that every Kikuyu in Nairobi be rounded up and put in detention. Murderous beggars! I'd like to see them whipped and gaoled — the lot of them.'

Dana could see Emerald bristle, but she was quicker to respond.

'Mr Durrows —' she began, fixing him with an icy stare.

'*Jelani!*' Emerald cried as her brother approached from the street. She rushed to him and they embraced. Dana joined them and all three hugged. Jelani was bewildered by all the attention, but smiled in spite of his embarrassment.

Dana turned back to the hotel manager, who stood, open-mouthed.

'Oh, Mr Durrows,' she said with a smile. 'May I introduce you to my son? This is Jelani Karura.'

* * *

In the Lord Delamere Room that night, Dana noticed their table received a number of curious glances. If Jelani — wearing the same navy-blue suit and clean white shirt as he'd worn in New York when they met — noticed the looks, he didn't show it, but listened attentively as Emerald chatted.

'It's an Arts degree I started during the year, but I've taken electives in photography and journalism,' she said. 'In fact, you could say I'm here on assignment. My tutor gave me time off provided I submit a folio of material collected while I'm here in Kenya. So it's up to you.'

'Me? What do you mean?' he asked.

'It's your job to show me around.'

'Nairobi is a very boring city,' he countered.

'No, not the city, silly. The animals. The people. The landscape.'

'Oh.'

'Don't bully your poor brother,' Dana said. 'He's probably busy making arrangements for his wedding day.'

'Are you?' she asked.

'I'm supposed to go to Lari tomorrow to see Deacon James.'

'Lari?' Dana said. 'The hotel manager mentioned Lari as a trouble spot.'

'Everywhere is a hot spot to some people. There are plenty of soldiers and Home Guards around the place. There's nothing to worry about.'

'I knew it!' Emerald said. 'That old stuffed shirt is talking through his hat. Jelani, I'm coming with you. It's a great chance to start my folio.'

Jelani looked at Dana, pleading for help with his eyes.

Dana shrugged. She knew it was impossible to beat Emerald once she had her mind set on something.

* * *

During dinner at the Norfolk, Jelani struggled to overcome his unease about Lari. He'd also heard stories about a gathering of the Mau Mau and had tried to get word to Dedan Kimathi through his network of contacts in the hope that Kimathi would dispel the rumours, but he'd heard nothing. He decided to follow it up in the morning when he went to Lari to meet Deacon James.

After dinner, Dana and Jelani had coffee on the veranda, but Emerald excused herself to retrieve the gifts she'd brought Jelani from London. Dana took the opportunity to ask the question Jelani knew she'd been yearning to ask all evening, but wanted to do so in private.

'Have you found your father?' she asked.

'I have seen him,' he said.

'And what did he think of you? Was he happy to find you after all this time?'

'He doesn't know me. I mean, he doesn't know I'm his son.'

'But you've seen him.'

'I knew him even before I knew he was my father.'

'Oh ... I see. Then ... why didn't you tell him about yourself?'

How could he answer? In the beginning he couldn't tell him because he disliked him. Now he couldn't tell him because he didn't want his father to think badly of him because of his membership of the Mau Mau.

'I'm ... not sure how.'

'But you must. It's wrong to let him go on not knowing he has a beautiful son in the world. Jelani, you simply must tell him.'

Jelani was annoyed by Dana's attitude. She'd been in the country for less than a day and assumed she knew everything about his life.

'If it is so wrong, why did you not tell him yourself?' Immediately he'd said it, he regretted it.

Dana's face fell and she dropped her eyes. 'I didn't tell him, because I was afraid,' she said. She raised her eyes to him and reached across the table to take his hand in hers. 'I was weak and afraid, Jelani. And now I'm ashamed of what I did, not only to your father, but to you. I felt I had to choose between two paths; and I abandoned you. Can you ever forgive me? You deserved as much as I've been able to give Emerald. And I'm so, so sorry.'

Tears rolled down her cheeks and Jelani felt bad for what he'd said. He wanted to reach out to her. His hand travelled halfway across the table, but fell short of touching her shoulder. The dining room was too public for such things. Instead, he placed his hand on hers.

'Dana ... Mother ... I don't feel I've been abandoned. And I had a good childhood with my ... my parents.'

She looked at him and smiled gratefully.

'You want me to tell my father,' he continued. 'And one day I will, but I know he will also have questions —

questions that only you can answer. So, maybe *you* should be the one to tell him.'

She stared at him, patted his hand and nodded. 'You're right,' she said.

* * *

Beth arrived late into Lari and went to the missionaries' small communal hut for supper. She found Deacon James and Chief Luka seated at a table taking tea. She joined them, hoping to discuss plans for her wedding day, but they were deep in conversation about recent events in Lari and the surrounding countryside.

They greeted her, then resumed their discussion.

'Do you remember the incident in the village down by the Morani stream?' Deacon James said, looking sideways at Beth. 'The young man who had his ... his private parts removed?'

'Yes.'

'Well, I spoke to his wife today.'

'Terrible, terrible,' the chief muttered, shaking his head.

Beth had heard the story as soon as she had returned to Lari. A young farmer was caught by a Mau Mau gang and castrated for refusing to take the oath. His wife found him before he bled to death.

'I called in all the people from his village,' the chief said. 'I thought they'd be safer here. But that was before the Home Guard left.'

'The Home Guard have gone?' Beth asked.

'Today. General Erskine said they're needed elsewhere.'

'But what about the Mau Mau?'

The elderly chief shrugged. 'We will have to rely on our own people to defend Lari.'

'Is that possible?'

He patted her hand and smiled. 'In my day it was the Maasai. Oh, you should have seen them. Oh-oh-oh ... But I will call the men together in the morning and make some arrangements. All will be well.'

Beth felt uneasy. The talk was that dozens of thugs had come from the forest in recent days.

'Oh, I'm too weary,' Chief Luka said. 'And my wives are waiting for me to join them to eat.'

Deacon James rose too.

Beth said she'd like to confirm the plans for the wedding day with him, but he said it was late and they could discuss it in the morning when Jelani arrived. He bid her good night.

Beth sipped her tea alone, thinking of the conversation she'd had with Jelani at the bus station. She admired his ability to see the better side of people and situations. But if he were to leave the security of the city and hear stories such as that of the young man in the nearby village, or see the fear in the eyes of the people in the bush, he might have different views of the Mau Mau.

She walked through the warm night towards her hut. There was hardly a stir; and the sound of the breeze that nightly rose from the hot floor of the Rift Valley to ruffle the highest branches of the podocarpus trees was absent too.

Even the dogs were at peace.

An old woman, shrouding her head in a colourful *kanga*, scurried among the huts. She was the only person Beth had seen since leaving the mission. People were fearful and remained indoors at night.

The distant shrill whistle of a night bird carried pure and clear in the still air. It found an answering call from across the forested hills above Lari.

At the door of her hut she paused. The Rift Valley breeze stirred into life. She was pleased. It would freshen the air and cool the night.

Above her, the tree canopy remained unchanged, yet the whisper, which was at a distance, was quite pronounced.

She pulled the door closed behind her and, in bed, succumbed to the effects of the tiring bus trip from Nairobi to the upland forests.

* * *

On the evening of the twenty-sixth of March 1953 — the same day that Erskine removed his company of the King's African Rifles from Lari — a skittish breeze sent a flurry of dust devils along the quiet streets of Naivasha towards the police barracks. The town was home to a permanent contingent of the Kenyan Police Force and sundry members of the military. As well as the barracks, the police had several substantial administrative buildings surrounded by a patchy barbed-wire fence.

A sentry sat in the guard tower overlooking the compound, his rifle propped against one of the tower's posts and his head resting uncomfortably against another. It was approaching nine o'clock, two hours into his shift, and he was already bored and sleepy. None of the police took the watch seriously. They all knew the Mau Mau had kept to the fringes of the forest, never daring to poke their heads out to risk confronting the Kenyan Police. And Naivasha would be almost the last place they would dare attack.

A clattering sound interrupted his musing, followed by a dog's furious barking. He yawned and, rising from his chair, peered into the shadows at the edge of the flood-lit perimeter. He couldn't quite see the dog, but knew it could not be more than twenty paces into the darkness, beyond his vision. It was making a terrible din and he was about to yell at it to shut up, when it suddenly stopped.

He raised his hand to shield his gaze from the light in the tower above him, which had intruded into his peripheral vision. At that moment there was a savage blow to the side of his neck. It knocked his head sideways into the guardhouse post.

He cursed, but the words came bubbling from his throat. When his hand came from the place where he'd felt the blow, it was black with blood. He tried to scream in horror, but again the sound was drowned before it could pass his lips. Now the shadows under the lights were alive with movement. He took a step towards his weapon, but his legs turned into rubber and he couldn't raise his arm to reach the rifle. He fell to the floor.

Shouts, screams of pain and shots shattered the night.

*　*　*

Eighty Mau Mau soldiers, many wearing the new badge proclaiming the battle cry *Blood and Fire*, drove boldly from the Naivasha police station armoury with rifles, sub-machine guns, and a truckload of ammunition. With them were one hundred and seventy-three Mau Mau prisoners they'd released from the detention centre.

They escaped up the Nairobi road in stolen vehicles and high spirits, long before the four platoons of

Lancashire Fusiliers billeted elsewhere in the town could reach the police station. Their destination, less than thirty miles away on the escarpment overlooking the Great Rift Valley, was the village of Lari, where they would meet the three thousand Mau Mau fighters who surrounded it.

*　*　*

Beth awoke from a deep sleep: something very strange was happening.

The night breeze was a roar — a howling rage.

She pulled on her shift and pushed open her door. There were flickering lights in the branches. People were everywhere — running and screaming.

Three men appeared from the darkness.

They were Kikuyu, but screamed terrible insults at her. *Traitor. Whore.*

They swarmed onto her, and pushed her back into her hut.

She fought them.

They tore her shift away.

CHAPTER 59

Jelani waited outside the Norfolk in the dim light of dawn with the engine of the union's Ford still running. He'd warned Emerald they had an early start, and she'd promised to be on time. She arrived a few minutes late, a camera bag slung over her shoulder, full of apologies.

He drove quickly through the quiet streets of Westlands. It was Friday, but they were early enough to avoid the traffic.

On the highway they chatted about the day ahead. Emerald said she wanted to shoot plenty of portraits of Lari people going about their daily chores.

'You will see many people, many things,' he said. 'Old women feeding the chickens, the boys tending the goats. If we're not too late, we'll see the women milking the home cow for the *totos*' breakfast.'

A police car hurtled by on the narrow road, siren blaring.

'*Ai-ya*,' Jelani said. 'He's in a hurry.'

A few minutes later, a military vehicle marked with a red cross overtook them in Uplands, bouncing over the speed bumps.

A tinge of apprehension entered Jelani's mind.

A few miles before Lari the road was crowded with vehicles. People were gathered into tight huddles and there were no children in their colourful school uniforms making their way along the roads.

When they turned the last bend before Lari, and they could see the smoke curling above the trees, Jelani felt the cold hand of fear clutch at his heart.

* * *

Emerald had to run to keep up with Jelani, who hurried among the remains of burned huts. She'd already seen several covered bodies lying on the ground amid smouldering ruins. Many old women were wailing and tearing at their face and hair. Mothers hugged little ones to them, rocking and weeping. Farm animals lay disembowelled in black pools of blood; some still twitched in their death throes in the dusty earth. The sickening stench of death was everywhere.

Jelani stopped to exchange urgent words with one old man, then hurried on. A milking cow, disembowelled and crippled, lay in a pool of entrails as it panted its life away. A man stood alone, staring at the still smouldering ruins of his house. They passed a mother weeping over the mutilated body of the child in her arms. Emerald fought back a wave of nausea.

The sheer savagery surrounding her was enough to stir a primeval fear within her — a feeling of being far away from the world she knew and trusted — and she was also aware she was the only white face in the village, and therefore a prime target should the Mau Mau return.

She pulled her camera out and started to snap shots. Somehow the view through the camera lens tempered the savagery surrounding her. She kept an eye on Jelani as he hurried on ahead, but became consumed by the images in the viewfinder. When she next looked for him, he was gone.

She ran in the direction he'd been heading and caught a glimpse of him as he dashed through the charred remains of a what might have been a school and church.

'Jelani!' she yelled into the eerie silence. 'Jelani!'

He was gone, and there was no one about. She feared that whatever tragedy that had fallen on the village might return. She fought back her rising panic, and ran on, more fearful now that she was alone.

She saw him then, crouching inside the doorway of a hut that was largely intact.

She ran to it.

The door of the hut was broken open and she quickly peered into the dim interior. There was nothing spared in what must have been a mammoth struggle. Then she realised Jelani was cradling the naked body of a young woman to his chest. His head was pressed into her shoulder and she couldn't see his face, but his body shuddered in the painful convulsions of utter misery.

When Emerald saw the condition of the corpse she quickly turned aside and vomited.

* * *

Jelani could see what had happened: the door broken from its hinges by the forceful entry of one or more men, the heavy bedside lamp broken as Beth tried to defend herself, the chair smashed in the confusion of bodies, the torn and discarded cotton shift, the bruised and bloody and finally mutilated body, left where they'd used her.

The Mau Mau's gruesome tactics were plain to see. Beth's once beautiful body had been sliced open from vulva to throat, exposing her organs between the puckered edges of raw flesh. Her face, so often composed in a gentle smile, was now frozen for all time in an expression of absolute horror.

Savagery was the weapon they used to cower innocent people into terrified submission. Now he understood why the oathing ceremony had become so bestial: it was meant to dehumanise a man to the point where nothing — not the vilest act or most wicked sin — was too evil. The Mau Mau's indoctrination could entice the beast from the darkest depths of even the most decent man's soul. And here was the proof, if ever he needed it, of how vile that beast could be.

He felt Emerald's touch on his shoulder, drawing him away with her words and her insistent hand.

'Jelani,' she said. 'There's nothing we can do here. Leave it to the police. Let's go.'

'No, I can't,' he sobbed. 'I have to ... I have to ... do something.'

But he could think of nothing he *could* do. What was there now but an empty gulf where life and love had so recently been?

'I have to tell Beth's family,' he said, clutching at the one thing that came to mind.

'Not now. You can't do that while you're in this state.'

'But ...' His eyes were drawn back to Beth's broken body, and the agonising stab of sadness pierced him again. He clutched at his gut.

'Come on, Jelani. Come away from this,' Emerald whispered.

Like a sleepwalker he obeyed, pausing to first remove his bloodied shirt and drape it ineffectively over Beth's body.

He turned towards Emerald and saw her distress in her misted green eyes. He buried his face in her shoulder and wept.

* * *

Sam received a call from a contact at police headquarters and immediately drove to Lari.

The stink of burned flesh hung in the smoke haze when he climbed out of the car. He thought he was prepared for the worst, but anyone would have been shocked at the savagery that had fallen on the village the previous night. The bloody hand of the Mau Mau was everywhere to be seen. Police and medics moved among the devastation, removing bodies and triaging the injured.

Sam felt sick in the stomach. The extent of death and destruction was well beyond all previous Mau Mau atrocities. These had consisted of mainly isolated attacks — no more than small skirmishes using primitive weapons. Here was evidence of a large, well-equipped, and coordinated force. This was obviously intended to show the loyalist Kikuyu what was in store for them should they continue to defy the Mau Mau — and to prove to the white population, and the administration, their ability to strike at will.

Sam had considered Erskine's plans to deploy heavy bombers to attack the Mau Mau's jungle strongholds as unnecessary and heavy-handed. He now had to reconsider. Surrounding him was evidence that the rebels were not only cruel and ruthless, they were a formidable and determined force.

The first deployment of the Lincoln bombers was scheduled for the twenty-ninth of March — in just two days' time. It was fortuitous: it would send a quick reply to the Mau Mau that the administration was also serious about winning.

As he wandered through what remained of the village, trying to find his bearings amid the desolation, he noticed the young union organiser, Jelani Karura. He appeared distraught and was in an animated conversation with a young white woman. She was so strangely out of place in that bleak scene, with her soiled white slacks and floral cotton top, it drew him towards them.

'Is everything all right here?' he asked.

Jelani turned to him. 'Yes,' he said. 'Thank you.'

He displayed none of his usual aggression; in fact Jelani was devoid of any expression at all. Sam looked at the young white woman with him, who nodded towards a circle of ruined huts.

'It was Jelani's fiancée,' she said. 'A young woman by the name of Beth … She's been … We found her … I can't —'

'It's all right; I understand. I'm sorry, Karura,' Sam said.

Jelani nodded an acknowledgement, and then added, 'Look, there are things to be done. I wonder if you could take Emerald back to Nairobi when you go.'

'No. I want to go with you,' she responded.

'Emerald, I told you: I have to go alone. It's important for me to do this right. I have to tell Beth's family about this. Alone.' Jelani turned to Sam again. 'You understand. Will you take her back for me?'

'If the young lady doesn't mind, I'd be happy to help.'

Emerald's silence indicated her reluctant agreement.

'Thanks,' Jelani said, and headed towards his car.

After a couple of paces he turned back to Sam. 'And one more thing,' he said. 'Will you take her back to her mother in the Norfolk? I mean, go with her in person.'

'Jelani!' she cried.

He waved away her complaint. 'I promised to look after her,' he said. 'And if you could speak to her mother for me ... I'd appreciate it.'

'Don't worry,' Sam said. 'I'll see to it.'

* * *

Jelani watched them go, relieved to be alone. He looked around the village, seeing the wider destruction for the first time. He'd been so frantic to find Beth that he'd seen nothing else until now.

The ambulances were full and the medics were loading bodies into utility vehicles and flat-bed trucks. A number of volunteers were assisting the police to bring the bodies in from the outlying parts of the village. Each pair of bearers led a solemn procession of family and friends, silent except for their sobs.

It hurt Jelani to think of his Beth being touched by strangers, so he took a bag and walked back to her hut. He could hardly bear to look at her brutalised body again as he laid her out and slipped the calico material over her legs and torso, up to her neck. He looked at her unmarked face one last time, trying to imagine her as she had been in life. Through his tears he could see her laughing with him, teasing him, loving him.

He sat with her, feeling strangely comforted by the silence of the village that had, until the terrible events of the night, resonated with voices and laughter. He whispered to her, reminding her of their plans: perhaps they'd have a small farm where they could keep goats and grow maize; they would fill their house with children.

The voices of the medics intruded. They had concluded their grim tasks in the centre of the village and had now worked their way to the huts at the edge of Lari.

Jelani closed the bag above Beth's head and pulled the cord tight.

As he carried Beth back to the medical units he shrugged aside the volunteers, feeling oddly angered by their offers of assistance.

He tried to compose the words he would say to her parents, but he couldn't think. The images of her rape and murder intruded like vicious demons intent on wounding him again and again. When he'd first found Beth's body he was so distraught that he felt his grief would never be expended, but now, as he laid her gently in the back of a postal delivery van beside other similar bags, it was transforming into a deep hatred of the Mau Mau. He hushed the voice in his head that said he was choosing hatred because it hurt less — and because he had done nothing to stop the rebels, or save his beautiful Beth from agony and terror.

The driver slammed the doors shut and climbed behind the wheel. After another moment he drove off and Jelani watched the van disappear down the winding road leading out of Lari.

Jelani had no heart to visit Beth's family.

All remnants of his grief were now gone. Even his aching pain had receded, leaving in its place a cold, murderous rage.

Kimathi.

CHAPTER 60

As soon as Sam Wangira's car was out of sight of Lari, Emerald started to shiver. She bit her lip to keep her teeth from chattering; and sat on her hands to stop them shaking. Tears welled in her eyes as the horror she'd witnessed in the village came flooding back to her.

Nothing in her life had prepared her for such an experience, and she knew it would remain with her for a long time, perhaps forever.

She tried to take her mind to a better place, a safer place, where savage men didn't maim animals, grind children's skulls into mash and rape and murder innocent young women. She thought of the previous night's dinner in the elegant Lord Delamere Room at the Norfolk Hotel. She and her mother had dressed for the occasion. Her mother wore a pretty printed suit of pinks and greens with an A-line skirt, short-sleeved jacket with large pearl buttons, canvas summer shoes and matching handbag. She'd completed her finery with a wonderful wide-brimmed straw hat and cotton gloves.

Emerald had felt very sophisticated in her London fashions. She wore a full skirt of the finest organdie silk in a soft peach colour with a white velvet sash. It was very much reminiscent of Dior's New Look, with the bodice hugging her wasp-like waist. Instead of a hat, which she thought might be too hot for the evening indoors, she wore a large white velvet bow, stiffened by wire, rakishly set at an angle. It matched her white gloves, shoes and small handbag.

Jelani had been nervous in his second-hand blue suit, but he was as friendly as she recalled him being in New York. They chatted about the wedding and other diversions they'd indulge over the following month. It had all sounded so wonderful. Now she couldn't believe such a normal evening could precede the obscenity she'd just witnessed. She was twenty-one years old, but until yesterday she'd felt little more than a child. Now, with the horror of Lari fresh in her mind, she felt she'd taken another frightening step towards knowing the realities of life in Africa.

When her mother had revealed her secret, it changed their relationship. They became much closer. Now Emerald looked upon her mother as a woman — flawed and human. She understood why she'd been so strict and controlling. Dana wanted the best for her and she had spared nothing — including Jelani — to make it so. Well, she didn't need to worry about Emerald wasting her hard-won opportunities on regattas and Oxford boys any more.

Which raised the question of Jelani. Emerald had felt guilty since learning that she was the lucky twin. Now Jelani's loss of Beth compounded his misery and disadvantage.

Dana had asked Emerald to keep the fact that Jelani was her brother a secret from her stepfather. She was mature enough to understand why. Dana also said that she wanted to bring Jelani closer to them and, although they might nearly always live a world apart, to strenghten the bond between the three of them. Emerald agreed to do everything she could to make him feel loved, and a part of their lives.

In Lari, Emerald had felt genuinely vulnerable for the first time in her life. Africa was a very different place to her home in England, but as the car bumped along the road to Nairobi, she gradually began to relax, somehow feeling quite secure in Sam Wangira's care. In spite of witnessing the same atrocities she had, he appeared calm and in control of his world. Emerald's, though, was changing faster than ever.

*   *   *

A solemn silence persisted during the first half of the drive to Nairobi. Sam made a number of attempts to get Emerald talking about what she'd seen at Lari, but failed. He then tried a different tack, asking her about Jelani. She slowly began to engage with him, telling him how patient and kind Jelani was, and how Beth and Jelani had planned to marry in the next few weeks.

'I never had the chance to meet Beth,' she said. 'But by the way Jelani talked about her, he was obviously very much in love.'

It was another revelation to Sam.

'Telling Beth's family is going to be difficult for him,' he said. 'Where do they live?'

'I think it's a place called Kimathi,' she said. 'I'm not sure. But Jelani just kept repeating the word *Kimathi* over and over. He was too upset to speak.'

Sam knew otherwise. The murderous attack on Lari was *the trouble* that his informant, Collins Mutisa, had predicted, although at the time he didn't know it would be led by Kimathi. But Jelani obviously knew he was responsible and had some impetuous idea to avenge his fiancée's death.

On Sam's latest information, Kimathi was somewhere outside Nakuru with a strong band of bodyguards. Sam had been reasonably sure Jelani Karura was a Mau Mau sympathiser, but now he didn't know. In the last hour, his view of Jelani had changed. He felt sympathy for his loss, and hoped he would not be foolish enough to try to find Kimathi, who was reportedly not simply committed to the Mau Mau cause, but insane.

As he drove through the winding forest road to Nairobi, he continued to encourage Emerald to talk. She told him about her interests in photography and the course she was taking in London. She wanted to be a photojournalist — a term Sam had not heard before.

Sam recalled Ira's passion for photography and how he, as a young man scarcely ever out of the village, had been fascinated by it.

At the Norfolk, Sam followed Emerald through the lobby and into the garden. They passed the aviary where golden weaverbirds darted and squabbled, then continued down the frangipani-scented path to the door of a garden suite where Emerald stopped and offered her hand.

'Thank you,' she said.

'Not at all. Perhaps I should stay to help you tell your mother about this.'

She smiled. A little more colour had come to her cheeks. 'That won't be necessary.'

'It's been a terrible morning for you.'

She nodded. 'For everyone.'

He said goodbye, and as he joined the path towards the hotel lobby, he heard the cabin door open and a woman's voice greeting Emerald.

His feet were leaden, and when he reached the aviary where the weavers darted about, squabbling and twittering, he lowered himself to a bench seat. In spite of the birds' noisy chatter, the tranquility of the garden gave him a respite from the discomforting memories of Lari. It pained him to see his fellow Africans inflicting such savagery upon one another instead of using those energies to win independence from the whites. He'd seen the bloody results of tribal warfare during his days in Abyssinia, but the brutality inflicted by the Mau Mau against their brother Kikuyus had shocked him. It must have been traumatic for the young white girl too, who had shown remarkable courage after witnessing the consequences.

He recalled promising Jelani Karura to see her to her door and to assure her mother that she'd come to no harm. Perhaps he was concerned that she know he'd been careful to arrange the girl's safe return. Sam decided to introduce himself before leaving, and to see that Emerald was still coping after her trauma.

He returned to the cabin door and knocked, turning to study the garden as he waited. Hibiscus hedges broke the neatly trimmed lawn into squares, in the centre of which were frangipani islands.

At the sound of the door opening, he turned back.

'Sam!' she said.

'Dana, how ...?' Sam looked from Dana to Emerald, who stood behind her. He suddenly remembered the resemblance he'd noticed at Grand Central.

Dana opened her mouth, but seemed unable to speak.

Emerald found her voice. 'How do you two know each other?'

Sam and Dana exchanged glances. Dana was the first to speak. 'It's quite a story, which I'll explain later. Right now, I want to speak to Sam. Why don't you go to your room, darling? I'll come by when it's time for dinner.'

* * *

'Come in, Sam,' Dana said, stepping aside to let him pass once Emerald had left. She closed the door behind him and took a deep breath as he ran his eyes around the suite. He still looked good in a suit — he was tall and his wide shoulders tapered to narrow hips.

He turned back to her and smiled. 'Dana. I can't believe it's you.'

'It's been a long time, Sam.' She indicated the sofa. 'Please, make yourself comfortable.'

He sat at one end, she sat at the other, leaning back on the pillow and crossing her legs. She thought she probably appeared more at ease than she felt. She was forearmed by the knowledge that Sam was somewhere in Kenya and there was always a chance they'd meet — she just didn't know when. On the other hand, the normally unflappable Sam had no knowledge she was there and, as a consequence, seemed quite shaken.

She guessed that Jelani had somehow contrived to get him there. It was just as well. She would have found it difficult to summon the resolve to approach him. But she hadn't prepared herself for what must be said; and she knew if she postponed telling him for too long, she would lose what little courage she had.

'Sam, I'm glad you're here, I —'

'I'm glad too, Dana. I've often thought about you, wondering where you are; how your life has turned out. You look good, by the way.'

'Thank you.' She smiled. 'So do you.'

'And that beautiful young woman is your daughter,' he said. 'My God. She has your eyes.'

'And several of my bad habits, I'm afraid.'

'I saw her in New York about a year ago. At Grand Central. She was with young Jelani Karura at the time. I'm curious, how do know —'

'You were in New York at the same time as us?'

'You were there too? We are plagued by coincidence, you and I.'

'Hmm ... I suspect this meeting isn't as much of a coincidence as you might think.'

He raised an eyebrow. She remembered the expression and the memory made her heart ache. She wondered if he still used the toe of one shoe to prise off the other rather than untie the laces.

'How do you know Jelani?'

It was an opening. She took a deep breath.

'Sam, I have a terrible ... admission to make.' She had trouble meeting his gaze. 'And I must ask that you say nothing until I've told it all.' She looked at him again. 'Can you agree?'

He nodded.

'It's been so long ... so long. I can't believe that we — who were once so very close — are now sitting here like second cousins.' She reached a hand to him. 'You seem so distant, Sam. Will you hold my hand?'

He smiled, and slid closer to take her hand in his.

'That's better.' She tried to compose her thoughts. There was no easy way. 'I have something to tell you.

When I do, you will wonder why I kept it a secret, and then you will want to know why I waited so long to tell you. Let me answer the second question first. I am a coward, Sam. Try as I might, I've been unable to find the courage to do the decent thing. I've wanted to write to you for twenty years, but I was frightened. You see, I didn't want you to think badly of me.

'I often think about my time in Kenya. I'm not proud of some of the things I did here, but I have never regretted knowing you. We were so good together, Sam. I never met anyone else who — Maybe we're only allocated so much passion to spend during one lifetime and when it's gone, it's gone. I'm not sure if that's true, but I do feel that our time together spoiled me for others. You were enough for one lifetime. I never felt the same about anyone else.

'So I didn't want to spoil that wonderful connection we had. I deferred telling you year after year, hoping that it might become easier. It hasn't. And now, leaving it for so long, I've made it worse than ever.

'And now to the reason I kept this a secret from you. I have two children — a boy and a girl. My daughter's father is my ex-husband, Edward, who you'll no doubt remember. It's more complicated than that, but that will do for the present.'

She paused, and cupped her other hand over his.

'I've thought about how I would put all this in a letter, but as I've already said, it was too difficult. But the thing is — what I've wanted to tell you for all these years — is that you are the father of my son.'

She felt his hand tighten in hers, and when she lifted her eyes from his hand to his face she could see his mind was in a turmoil. Disbelief. Shock. Was there anger?

'It was easier to avoid confessing until I met him last year.' She could see from his expression that he hadn't yet guessed his son's identity. 'You've met him, Sam. He has your features: he's handsome and tall.'

The spark of awareness grew in his eyes.

'Forgive me, Sam. He already knows you're his father.'

'Karura?'

She nodded, and gripped his hand tighter, trying to prevent his earlier good feelings for her from sliding away. She didn't want to lose him again. Not with anger and resentment.

But he slowly slipped his hand from hers and, with great dignity, stood.

'I need to leave now.'

'Sam —'

'No. I have to go.'

* * *

Over the next hour, back in his flat, Sam alternately sat on the bed or paced the confined space of his room. At first he raged in silent fury. Dana's duplicity, her selfishness, her betrayal, infuriated him. How dare she keep such a secret for so long? Only when it suited her had she revealed the earth-shattering news to him. She'd cheated him of his son for all that time.

Coming, as it did, so soon after witnessing the viciousness of Lari, when his spirit had sunk so low, it was devastating.

Slowly the intensity and focus of his emotions changed from anger to sadness. He'd built and lost businesses; he'd found and abandoned relationships. What he didn't know, and would never know, was how his life might have been if he'd known about his son.

The question left a numbing vacuum at his core — a sense of enormous loss. A parallel universe had been in existence for twenty years. Now knowing he had a son, the man he thought he was vanished. He was not a businessman, a politician, a loner. He was a father.

Suffused throughout this surge of emotions was Dana — a vision from his wild and intemperate past. As she'd talked, unfolding her secret, he had trouble concentrating on it. Memories intruded: vivid recollections of their impetuous love-making. He saw himself tearing her underwear away, pushing her to the wall of his flat in Muthaiga, and sinking into her as he smothered her with his mouth.

She'd changed little: a few lines and creases where once there were none, but she was still the vibrant and sexy woman from his past.

He slumped onto the bed, trying to imagine how Dana could be so cruel. He recalled her explanation about why she kept her secret. He could almost forgive her, given the difficulties having a mixed-race child would have created. And he thought how much having her as his wife would have enormously complicated his life too.

Anger returned like a charging lion, demanding attention, roaring so loudly inside his head it erased all other thought. He stood and paced and pounded his fist into his palm until he felt suffocated.

At the open window he rested his hands on the sill. He was exhausted by the surge of emotion. A deep breath of the cool midnight air calmed him and, as he became more peaceful, his thoughts went to his son. He recalled his disillusionment after his good first impressions of him: not a bravely independent and conscientious worker but a Mau Mau sympathiser, perhaps even a full-fledged member of that brutal and misguided movement. He couldn't imagine how any child of his blood could be part of such an evil cult.

He took another cleansing breath of air. The boy had always been impetuous; and there was no doubting his commitment to an independent Kenya. There were likely plenty of young men in The Movement who had joined with good — if warlike — intentions. Kikuyu men were warriors after all.

Dana said Jelani knew Sam was his father. Why hadn't he declared himself? He might have been able to help him.

The problem stemmed from Dana not telling him about the boy. If she had, he could have found him, and steered him down the right path. Then he recalled that in those early years he'd been less than a model father, trading in smuggled gold and horseflesh. But if he knew he had a son, it all would have been different. They might have worked together, maybe built a farm.

He spent a restless night, with dreams where he and Jelani merged. Jelani was like an echo from a distant time; a different life. Even a distant land. A place where his genes and Jelani's were formed. He felt his son's love for Beth and the agony when he found her raped and murdered. He could feel his blood rise with Jelani's as he swore to avenge her.

He awoke with a start, remembering what Emerald had said about Jelani: he'd stormed out of Lari intending to find Dedan Kimathi — the person responsible for his fiancée's death. But Kimathi was a murderous tyrant, surrounded by psychopaths. His son probably knew where he was hiding and would be walking to his death.

He had to stop him, but he had no idea where Kimathi was hiding.

He only knew one man who might know, but Jomo Kenyatta was in gaol — a victim of Governor Baring's State of Emergency — and under maximum security. Even if he could get permission to see him, Sam could think of no way to convince Kenyatta to give him the information he needed to save his son.

* * *

It took Sam two phone calls to find where Jomo Kenyatta was imprisoned. It was more difficult to arrange a special visitor's pass as he was in solitary confinement, awaiting transfer to Lokitaung — a bleak outpost in the barren wilderness on Kenya's northern border.

In spite of the complications, Sam had his visitor's pass shortly after noon, and by three he was in the secure meeting area at the lock-up.

Kenyatta came from his cell, escorted by a policeman. He paused when he saw Sam sitting on the opposite side of the wide wooden table.

'Wangira? What are you doing here?'

'I need some information from you, Kenyatta.'

'Well, well. The famous Sam Wangira, member of the white man's Legislative Council, is asking help from a convicted Mau Mau sympathiser.'

'I'm not here as a member of the Legislative Council. This is a personal matter. Between Kikuyu brothers.'

'I see,' he said, nodding. 'Brothers, are we?'

'I need to know where I can find Dedan Kimathi.'

Kenyatta's chest-heaving laughter filled the small room. 'You're not the only one! When I've asked to see my lawyer, they tell me it's not possible. And yet here you are, Sam Wangira, a Legco man, here to tell me jokes.'

'I'm not joking. It's a matter of life and death. I must know.'

'Your life, my death. Are you not aware that I have an appeal pending? And you ask me to admit to knowing the whereabouts of the most wanted man in Kenya? Don't make me laugh, Wangira.'

Kenyatta stood to go.

Sam had nothing to offer — no way of buying the favour he needed. He and Kenyatta had been rivals all their lives and it appeared they would remain so. Kenyatta had no reason to help him.

Sam stood.

'I'm a father, *damn you*, Kenyatta! Just like you.'

Kenyatta stared back to him. 'What is that to me?'

'And I've only just learned of my son,' Sam said, his voice falling away. 'I don't want to lose him so soon.'

Kenyatta shook his head, and headed towards the door.

Sam wanted to leap the table and hold him by the throat until he told him what he needed to know. An old memory flashed into his mind. 'You once predicted you'd be a leader one day,' Sam said. 'Well, congratulations, that much seems to be coming true. But you also said you owed me something for that time when I found you in the dry stream, surrounded by hyenas. Does Jomo Kenyatta keep the promises made by Johnstone Kamau?'

Kenyatta stopped. His shoulders dropped. He looked back at Sam, and studied him for a long moment. Finally, he nodded. 'He does.'

'There's no need for this to go any further,' Sam whispered, as Kenyatta resumed his seat.

Kenyatta's smile was grim. 'If it does, your congratulations are premature.' He was silent for a long time. Sam could almost see his second thoughts.

'I give you my word,' he said, his heart pounding.

'Kimathi's in the Barako camp,' Kenyatta said. 'He's the commander.'

'What happened to General Kago?'

If Kenyatta was surprised by Sam's knowledge of the Mau Mau hierarchy, he didn't show it.

'When all the Central Committee were arrested, the young ones — the illiterate hot heads in the forest — took over. I tell you, it's the end of them. And good riddance. I will make my way without them.'

'Barako! Did you say Barako?'

'Yes, why?'

'The Lincolns!' Sam muttered as he leaped to his feet, toppling his chair.

'What's wrong with you, Wangira?'

'What day is it? Is it the twenty-ninth?'

'It's the twenty-eighth. Are you mad?'

Sam banged on the door.

'*Guard!*' he called. '*Guard! Get me out of here!*'

CHAPTER 61

Jelani avoided the small village of Barako. He wanted no one to see him heading towards Mt Kinangop. His presence in such an isolated spot could only mean that he was going to the Mau Mau camp and, in Barako, The Movement had many supporters. Kimathi had introduced him to a few as he led him to the Mt Kinangop camp when General Kago was its commander.

He walked north through the almost trackless dense bush that clung to the lower ridges of Mt Kinangop until, in late afternoon, he entered one of the occasional clearings found throughout the Aberdares. It had been created by a large herd of browsing elephant. The trees within an area of some three or four acres had been torn down or stripped bare. As a boy he'd seen similar sites where, for reasons only known to the elephants, they found the area satisfactory in every regard and regularly returned to feast until the land was denuded. Such pockets of grassland had a beneficial effect on other grazers, and he disturbed a large number of impala and other antelope as he entered it.

It was growing dark and he was still an hour from Kimathi's camp. He decided to wait until morning. He didn't want to blunder into one of Kimathi's lookouts in the dark — he needed the element of surprise if he was to be successful.

He spread the canvas sheeting he'd brought from the car under a tree at the edge of the clearing and pulled the revolver from its sheath. It had been in the boot of the union's Ford since Chege Muthuri quit the movement. Jelani had forgotten about it until coldly planning this assault.

He checked the chambers. He'd never used a firearm in his life. Under the Emergency, even the possession of such a weapon invoked a mandatory death sentence.

His courage wavered. To attempt to murder the leader of the Mau Mau in his own camp was suicide. Then he thought about Beth; and the anger that immediately arose made breathing a difficult task. But it gave him strength.

*   *   *

It was dark and treacherous on the Naivasha–Nairobi road. Sam threw the car into the corners and thrashed it along the straight stretches, arriving at the small bar that Collins Mutisa frequented just before eight. He was relieved to find his man sitting alone with a jar of spirits in front of him.

Sam pulled out the chair opposite and leaned across the table to him.

'Mutisa,' he said in a whisper. 'I have to find the Barako camp.'

Mutisa blinked like an owl caught in the light. '*Habari, bwana,*' he slurred. '*Habari yako?*'

'Listen, I have to get to Barako urgently.'

'Well ... *bwana*, that is very very difficult.'

'Damn it, Mutisa, sober up. I need you.'

He looked bewildered. 'Sorry, *bwana*, just a few drinks, and ...' His voice trailed off into a mumble.

Sam reached across the table and took him by the scruff of his collar, shaking him so much that his head snapped back.

Mutisa's eyes bulged.

It was useless; Sam gave up. He consoled himself with the thought that it was probably foolish to try to find his way in the forest at night. He'd have a few hours in the morning before the sun melted the fog, and the Lincoln bombers took off on their secret mission to bomb the Mau Mau's Mt Kinangop camp, using coordinates that Sam himself had provided to General Erskine.

He pulled a couple of bench seats together. He would sleep for a couple of hours before trying again to get some sense from Mutisa.

* * *

Jelani slept poorly and awoke before dawn. His canvas sheet had done little to fend off the chill mountain air. He was stiff with cold and fatigue. When the clearing brightened with first light, he climbed out of his canvas cocoon, stretched, and vigorously rubbed his arms to warm them.

His hands shook with the cold as he checked the pistol, working the safety catch on and off and spinning the chamber. Then he replaced it in its sheath and tucked it into his belt.

The clearing skirted the lion's head landmark. On the other side was the path to the camp. He couldn't recall how much further it was from there, but he thought it probably another mile or so. He remembered a swampy lake fringed with rushes that would afford him the cover he needed to make his final approach. Before that, the path rose with the ridge; he'd be able to reconnoitre there and refine his plan.

The bush was coming alive with sounds. Every snap or scuttle in the undergrowth made his heart leap. A gentle breeze came up, shaking the dew from the high branches. It fell in heavy drops like the sound of approaching footsteps.

A hadada ibis gave its long mournful cry: *Haw haw haw!*

Following it was the shrill keening call of a fish eagle. He looked up. The clouds had cleared and the eagle hovered against a pale blue sky.

The lake! It must be close, which meant he was nearer to the camp than he thought.

He caught a movement out the corner of his eye. A man with matted hair, in a ragged shirt, trousers torn off at the knees and bare feet, stepped from the foliage.

He pointed the barrel of his ancient rifle at Jelani.

* * *

The Aberdare Ranges brooded in the long shadows of morning. Sam thrust his aching body through the bamboo forest where the thick poles resisted his every step. The dew on the scimitar leaves drenched him and the blades cut him and itched him, but he pressed on up the steep rise until he reached the crest.

The continuing cloud cover gave him hope. He had no way of knowing the exact time the bombers would come, but if the clouds didn't lift, the bombing run would be aborted. Of course, the Lincoln bombers were only part of the problem. His son was in even greater danger should he end up in the hands of the Mau Mau.

Before him stretched the endless foothills, climbing layer on layer into the hazy blue where the jungle disappeared into the clouds. On the rise directly ahead, was the lion's head rock. It was just as Collins Mutisa had described it when Sam left him at the track out of Barako village. Mutisa was suffering badly from the *changa'a* of the previous night, and Sam knew he'd be more hindrance than help, so he left him there to make his way home.

He arrived in a clearing and rested on a fallen tree while his heart pounded in his ears and his vision clouded with tears of exhaustion. He was fifty-four, and felt it.

Somewhere in the distance, a bull elephant grumbled in annoyance, then silence returned briefly before he heard rustling in the bush.

He froze. A small herd of male impala came into the clearing, pawing the ground in the heat of the rut and jousting with lowered antlers. They did mock battle for a few minutes before they caught his scent and bounded away.

He considered what to do when he reached Kimathi's camp. He now thought it unlikely that he would catch Jelani before he got there. He therefore needed to anticipate Jelani's next move. What was in his head? Why had he come here? What did he plan to do? He guessed Jelani would do what Sam would have done at his age and under similar circumstances: he would try to kill Kimathi — the man responsible for the death of his loved one. But he knew Jelani was smart enough to know he must watch and wait for an opportunity. In that case, Sam might have time to find him before he put himself at risk. His next task would be to convince his headstrong son to abandon his mission. That would be more difficult, but it was a problem for another time.

He dragged himself to his feet, and followed the edge of the clearing towards lion's head rock. Just off to the side, under a tree, he noticed a canvas sheet. He kneeled to examine it and found it was clean, and appeared to have been very recently discarded. Had it been Jelani's?

He turned to the clearing to find it awash with sunlight. Above him, the cloud had lifted, and the sun flared brightly in a pale blue sky.

* * *

Jelani headed down the track with the rifle of his taciturn captor close to his back.

The Mau Mau camp was a shambles. There was no shame in living in huts made entirely of bush materials, nor of cooking on simple open fires that could be doused should enemy aircraft be heard, but the camp was dirty and unsanitary. There was nothing of the noble warrior in any of the men's demeanours. They watched him pass with greedy eyes: *What did he have that could be useful to them?*

Jelani and his guard were joined by two others and they led him to a hut, slightly larger than the others, but equally shoddily made. Kimathi sat outside it with a long-bladed knife, slicing strips of bark from a small sapling. He was now heavily bearded and his hair, which had been braided into Rastafarian rat-tails, had grown out, and hung in long matted coils. He had a rolled newspaper cigarette hanging from his mouth.

Jelani stood flanked by his escorts for some time without comment from Kimathi. He seemed preoccupied by his whittling. Finally, he looked up through the curling smoke with bleary red-rimmed eyes.

'So ... you've come,' he said, as if he'd been expecting no one else.

He took a long draw on the cigarette and exhaled a lung-full of smoke into the air above him. The acrid scent of cannabis struck Jelani's nostrils.

'Hello, Dedan,' he said.

'You may address me as Field Marshal Kimathi.'

Jelani guessed he would have to choose his words carefully. This was not the young man he had helped escape from custody and who had sat with him in the Ngong Forest discussing philosophy and freedom.

'I'm sorry. Of course. Field Marshal Kimathi.'

'A long time, my friend,' Kimathi said. 'You are looking very prosperous. Life in Nairobi must be good, ah?'

One of his guards placed Jelani's holstered revolver on the ground beside Kimathi.

'Oh-ho! What is this, my friend? Have you brought me a gift? No? Or were you planning a hunting expedition?'

He looked at Jelani, but he made no response.

'Green eyes. That's it. I always wondered about that little bit of green in your eyes. And your fair skin.' He took the revolver from its sheath, and twirled it around like a Hollywood cowboy. He pointed it at Jelani. 'Bang!' he said, grinning. Then he pointed it at his own head. 'Bang!'

He flicked off the safety and pointed the pistol in the air and let off a couple of quick volleys.

Two of the guards fell to the ground.

Kimathi roared with laughter. 'Look at them!' he said, pointing to the men now climbing to their feet, abashed. 'Cowards. And they are meant to protect me. *Hah!*'

He narrowed his eyes at Jelani. 'And look at you, my friend,' he added with venom. 'You are a spy.' He spat on the ground beside him. 'And I sentence you to death.'

*　*　*

Sam heard two quick reports of a firearm. The sound echoed around the valley. He strained to hear anything more, but the low belly rumble of a distant elephant was all he heard.

He hurried on, trying to imagine what might have prompted the shots. His gut was in a knot; he pictured his son confronted by armed Mau Mau thugs, struggling with them, attempting to flee. Falling. Bleeding.

A gasp of exasperation and anxiety escaped him. He was panting, straining every fibre of his body to get to the camp while he could still help him.

The rumble came again on the wind. This time it was more of a roar. But it was not an elephant as he had imagined.

'Oh, *no!*' he groaned.

Like soaring vultures high in the heavens, the Lincoln bombers appeared.

He dashed on, missing the turn in the track, plummeting into the thick understorey, bounding, falling, rolling, rising and running again. He sobbed with the effort and he knew he would be too late. The deep droning of the heavy engines were above him, but he kept going.

The first thousand-pound bomb struck the hillside a half-mile ahead of him. The ground shook. Moments later another fell. And another. The ground heaved with every ear-shattering explosion.

From immediately ahead came a trumpeting shriek. Moments later, the forest was torn apart as a herd of stampeding elephants crashed from the undergrowth, shattering saplings and small trees in their path.

Sam dived for the cover of a large tree and cringed at its base until the herd had thundered past.

Scrambling to his feet, he returned to the track.

A high-pitched whistle hurt his ears and, an instant later, the earth erupted in a fireball ahead of him. He was thrown backwards by the concussion. He was oblivious to the shower of splintered plant debris, rock and dirt that fell on him.

* * *

When the first bomb came whistling from the sky, Jelani remained standing as Kimathi and his guards dived to the ground. It struck an enormous tree a hundred yards away, splitting the massive trunk into kindling. A succession of bombs caused chaos and men dashed about in all directions.

After his initial shock, Jelani regained his senses and darted for the bush. Amid all the surrounding noise he didn't hear the pistol shots, but Kimathi's bullet zinged close to his ear. He ran on in a crouch and rolled into the concealment of the forest.

Behind him were screams and explosions. The whole jungle seemed alight with star bursts. Trees shattered. Rocks bounced around him like basketballs as he ran.

He was about a mile away when, as abruptly as it had started, the bombardment ceased.

As he continued his dash through the forest, the ringing in his ears slowly abated and the sounds of the bush returned. He stopped when he came upon a forest hog snorting and snuffling in the newly turned earth of a bomb crater. It looked at him with baleful red eyes before it grunted and turned away. Jelani waited until its bristly ridged back disappeared into the undergrowth.

Jelani looked to the sun to gain his bearings, then continued down the mountain at a brisk walk.

* * *

Sam climbed from the abyss of unconsciousness into a realm of searing light and a deafening ringing in his ears. He was on his back, looking at the sky through tree branches that had been stripped of their canopy of leaves. His head pounded and his body was numb and heavy.

He looked around him. It took him a moment to regain his bearings. He was in the forest. Near Mt Kinangop. The Mau Mau camp.

Jelani.

He lifted his head, but the remainder of his body refused to respond. He looked down to his feet. His leg looked very strange.

* * *

Bomb craters pock-marked the forest around Jelani as he hurried down the track. He thought it unlikely that Kimathi would bother rallying his troops to pursue him, but, unarmed and revealed, he knew he was best to leave retribution to the administration's heavy weaponry.

He picked his way through the remains of a huge podocarpus tree that blocked the track. It had been shattered by a bomb, and the ragged stump, four feet thick, stood defiant and alone at the centre of a space denuded of all vegetation. The deep crater had exposed even the roots of the once mighty monolith.

He saw a man lying off to the side of the track. Most of his clothes had been torn from him and he lay unmoving, an arm shielding his face.

A splintered section of tree trunk had smashed and partially removed his leg below the knee, severing an artery. Blood continued to weakly pump from the mutilated stump. There were no other wounds, except one ear that oozed blood.

Jelani looked around, then kneeled by the body, and reached to take the man's pulse. The figure lifted his arm from his face.

'Sam!'

He opened his eyes.

'Jelani,' he whispered. 'Thank God. I was coming to get you, before … before …'

'It's all right,' Jelani said, but knew it wasn't. He was amazed to find his father still alive. He stared at his leg. He knew little of medical matters, but it was obvious his father would not make it out of the forest.

'It's not good,' Sam said.

For a moment, Jelani thought he should lie. Wasn't there something about making a dying man comfortable in his last moments? But looking into Sam's eyes he could see that attempting to deceive him would be useless. And in the case of someone as smart as his father, demeaning.

'No,' Jelani conceded. 'It's not good.'

'I can't hear you,' Sam said, 'but I'd say you agree with me.' He smiled and added, 'For once.'

Jelani reached for his hand and held it. He was surprised to feel the strength in his father's grip.

'There's so much to say,' Sam said. 'So much time to make up, and yet ... there's no time.'

'Sam,' Jelani said. 'Father.'

'Shh,' Sam said, gripping his hand tightly again. 'I can't hear you, remember?' He closed his eyes and struggled to take a breath before continuing.

'I didn't know about you. I didn't know I had a son. Tell Dana, your mother ... tell her it's all right. Tell her I understand. I only wish she could have told me. It might have been different. I could have ... I could have ...'

His hand went limp in Jelani's grip.

There had been too much death in a short space of time, and it took Jelani a few moments to accept that his father was gone.

He didn't weep. Sam had been too remote; too far removed from his life until recent times. Even then, he'd emerged as a figure more easily identified with his enemies than with his friends and family. He couldn't weep for his father, but he could weep for a man who'd lost his life while trying to save another.

And he could weep for the other lives lost in the savage war to win precious Kikuyu land. The war — which he could now see was a long way from over — was between white and black; between the colonial government and the Mau Mau, with idealists bent on compromise trapped and immobilised in the middle. It was a war that would have no winners.

Jelani decided that he, and all the combatants, would simply have to find a path to peace that as many Kenyans as possible could accept.

EPILOGUE

13 DECEMBER 1963

Nyayo Stadium was buzzing with excitement. In the section of the grandstand decorated with national flags and red, green and black bunting, was the podium that awaited Jomo Kenyatta, the recently elected Prime Minister of Kenya.

The Duke of Edinburgh chatted with the Governor and in the tiered seats at the back of the stand were members of the Kenyan government, seated in strict order of seniority.

Jelani had reserved Dana's seat among the special guests immediately she agreed to come to the independence celebrations. She was grateful for it. Her health had not been good since her heart attack; and standing among the crowd, even in the cool of the Nairobi night, would have challenged her. But she would not have missed seeing Jelani take his place, seated about midway among the government seats of this, the world's newest independent nation.

The muted monotone of crowd sounds rumbling around the packed stadium suddenly changed. It was as if the night had become charged with static electricity. A camera flashed at the foot of the stairs to the podium, followed by a dozen others — one of them undoubtedly Emerald's.

A collective sigh escaped the twenty thousand throats before everyone was on their feet, roaring as Jomo Kenyatta mounted the steps to the podium.

It had been ten years since their last reunion. On that occasion no one had been joyful. And although it took something as monumental as Kenya's independence to draw the three of them together it gave Dana enormous joy to witness her two children reunited.

She seldom saw Emerald since she'd taken up her position as the *New York Times*' senior photojournalist. At the tender age of thirty-one, she was considered among the best in her field. The appointment vindicated her decision to forgo the position of chairperson of the Middlebridge industrial empire. Dana had supported her in that decision, much to Oswald's chagrin. When he died a year later, Emerald inherited half his fortune anyway, and had the luxury of pursuing her career without the need for it to support her.

The last time Dana had come to Kenya was two years after Sam's death, when she'd helped Jelani set up the trust that would continue Sam's scholarships for young Kenyans. The government had buried Sam a hero who died while trying to verify the position of the Mau Mau's main camp. Governor Baring called him a true patriot. At least he got that part right.

Before that trip she had not been as close to her son as either of them were to Emerald, but during that time, as they worked together to create a legacy for his father, she knew that Jelani came to feel real love for her. He'd made two visits to London since then, one as part of the Kenyan delegation to negotiate the terms for independence, and they had used those visits to build a friendship she felt very lucky to have.

After Oswald died, Dana moved to a small house in Mayfair, where she lived a quiet, some said lonely, life. But she was content. She'd had a memorable youth and those memories kept her well entertained even now. They had been tumultuous days with Edward and the Zephyr club and her dear horses — and, of course, Sam. She had loved every minute with him. They'd been among the happiest moments of her life. To be in Kenya again, a country barely healed from a period of brutality, greed and fear, surrounded by tentative hope for the future — and her two beautiful, shining children — was more excitement than she had imagined she would experience again.

Kenyatta held aloft his signature colobus monkey-fur fly whisk and waited until the stadium was silent.

Then he began: 'This is one of the happiest moments of my life ...'

AUTHOR'S NOTE

This book is a work of fiction. Many of its events are historically accurate, but all characters are fictitious except for the British officials, some of the Mau Mau leaders and Jomo Kenyatta.

I have taken poetic licence in attributing words and actions to all historical characters in the interests of creating an entertaining story.

In this novel I have given to the character of Jomo Kenyatta certain attitudes towards the Mau Mau. Many of his public utterances condemned the Mau Mau, but historians disagree on his real involvement. The viewpoint I ascribe to him in this book is a product of my imagination and is not intended to imply my views on his role.

ACKNOWLEDGEMENTS

Echoes from a Distant Land owes its creation to a balcony suite aboard P&O's *Pacific Sun*, a bottle of champagne, and the very lovely Ms Wendy Fairweather — although not in that order of importance. This is to thank Wendy for her assistance in developing the outline of this story.

Writing a novel is like walking a long and lonely road where we authors sometimes wonder why we started the journey at all. Wendy's creativity, enthusiasm, and her constant encouragement during the writing of this book made that journey far more enjoyable than it might have been and the story, in my opinion at least, considerably enriched.

I would also like to acknowledge the following people and to thank them for their valuable and expert assistance during the writing of *Echoes from a Distant Land*:

Ms Charlotte Smith, author and the curator of the Darnell Collection (www.darnellcollection.com), for her expert assistance in matters of period dress.

Ms Wangari Maathai for her recollections of a Kikuyu childhood in her memoir, *Unbowed*.

Mr Ian Johnson, formerly an employee of East African Airways, for his assistance with aircraft types and schedules.

Mr Garry Keown for his enthusiastic and expert support on firearms of the period.

Finally, I'd like to thank my agent and friend, Selwa Anthony, whose support, advice and encouragement are always selflessly given; my editors Nicola O'Shea, Anna Valdinger, Kate Burnitt and Kate O'Donnell; and my friend James Hudson, whose opinions and advice on writing popular fiction I greatly respect.